EMILIA ROSSI

To all the disabled hotties who know they would absolutely bring a Mafia Don to his knees.

AUTHOR'S NOTE
READ THIS FOR CONTENT WARNING

The main character in this book, Sofiya, has hypermobile Ehlers-Danlos syndrome, which is a rare genetic connective tissue disorder. EDS is a complex and often misunderstood syndrome. While hypermobile EDS (hEDS) is the most commonly diagnosed, there are thirteen different types of EDS, and symptoms can be wide ranging. I have done my best to present one version of hEDS, Sofiya's version, with care and accuracy. But hers is just one experience and may differ significantly from others with hEDS. With most chronic illnesses and disabilities, the body can be unpredictable and present different challenges from day to day. My hope is that anyone with chronic illness and disability will feel seen in this story, even when Sofiya's journey may differ from your own.

This book contains adult content, including explicit sex scenes and elements like spanking, bondage, cock warming, and light degradation. All physical intimacy between the main couple is completely consensual.

This book contains content that some readers may find disturbing, including violence, gore, kidnapping, descriptions of torture, conversations about sex trafficking, threats of sexual assault, emotional and physical abuse by parents, a description of an upsetting sexual experience in the past, *perceived* other woman drama, and a very brief mention of an incident of past animal cruelty (not on page).

This story has chronic illness and disability representation. The Mafia world in this book is steeped in ableism, much like our world. The characters use harmful ableist language, including the use of an ableist slur, and they hold ableist beliefs. There is also internalized ableism, which is when disabled individuals absorb the ableist beliefs and judgements of the broader culture, often causing them to have negative feelings about themselves and their disabilities.

Other general content includes pregnancy.

This book ends in a happily ever after!

PROLOGUE

MATTEO

The first gunshot rends the air, and the clock starts ticking.
One.
Two.
Three.

Just one bullet, followed by a scream. It echoes through my mind, the horrific soundtrack to my nightmare. Was it a killing shot?

Or did I still have time?
Four.
Five.
Six.

Even in the midst of this memory, all these years later, I can feel the echoes of that bullet vibrating in my very bones.

The knowledge that I am to blame brings more pain than any physical injury ever could.
Seven.
Eight.
Nine.

I see their blood every night in my dreams. It's my punishment for not seeing it in real life. It's all too easy to imagine it dripping onto the floor. I've spilled enough blood since then to know what it must have looked like, how the metallic tinge of iron would have filled the air.

Ten.

Eleven.

Twelve.

Each second brings death a little closer, and there I stand, frozen. Then, Sienna's small hand fills mine, and the decision is made.

I pull her with me toward the hidden door at the back of the house.

Thirteen.

Fourteen.

Fifteen.

The second gunshot splits the air.

WE BARELY MADE it out alive, but the seconds between those two gunshots haunt me. Did I still have time to save one of them? I would never know because I abandoned my parents, our home, my rightful inheritance.

It took two years for me to win it back. Two years of enduring the slow and painful death of Matteo Rossi, son and brother, to rise again as Matteo Rossi, Don of the Italian Mafia, head of the Five Families in New York City.

1

MATTEO

A lcohol burned a line down my throat as I took another sip of
my drink.

This had been a shit day on top of a shit week on top of a shit
month.

Another one of our warehouses upstate had been hit. The dead
man in the basement twenty floors down had finally confirmed what
I long suspected—the Albanians were trying to encroach on my
territory.

My hand clenched around my glass.

I'd spent the past thirteen years as head of the Five Families,
extending our reach to the north and west of the state. Many had
tried to infiltrate my territory—most of them with a desire to bring
the skin trade to New York City. The Albanians had been pushing at
our borders for the past five years, but their attacks had escalated
with the death of their last boss. His idiot son, Arben, had gotten it
in his head that he could challenge me.

My office door opened, and in walked my second-in-command,
my brother in all but blood—Romeo. He sat down across from me,
throwing a folder on my desk.

I eyed it, taking another drink. "Is that what I think it is?"

"Yes." Romeo's usual easygoing expression was absent. Nothing was amusing tonight after losing two of our men in the warehouse fire.

I scrubbed my hand across my face and forced myself to flip the folder open. I stared at the picture inside.

"At least she's pretty," he said.

Pretty was an understatement. Piercing blue eyes stared at me, framed by golden blonde curls. Full red lips. Dark brows. Small, straight nose. Pink cheeks. Sofiya Ivanova was the most stunning woman I'd ever set my eyes on. There was a strange stirring in my chest the longer I looked at her.

I pulled my gaze away. "How old is she?"

"Just celebrated her twenty-first birthday."

"Fuck." I set down my glass. "She's practically a child."

"You don't have much of a choice, fratello. If we want the Russians on our side, we need this alliance with Rustik."

Rustik Ivanov was head of the Bratva in Chicago. Tension had been growing between us until war seemed imminent. Then he'd reached out with the offer of a truce. He wanted access to our eastern trade routes to run guns and drugs, and in return, the Russians would support us against the Albanians.

"You really think we should do this?" I asked.

Romeo hesitated and I arched my brow. He wasn't one to withhold his opinion.

"I think we're too isolated here," he finally said. "Russians to the west, the Irish to the east, and now the Albanians. We have a stronghold here in the city, but we need allies. This could be a start."

"I just don't know why it has to start with me getting married," I said, my eyes returning to Sofiya's picture. The capos had been whispering for years about their still-single Don. I needed heirs to secure my empire, but a wife and children would make me vulnerable.

Romeo leaned back in his chair, eyeing me closely. "I know it's the anniversary. Sienna tried to find you earlier today."

I looked out the window. "Don't start." I didn't need his reproach, his judgement for what a coward I was, hiding away. I gestured to the file. "What do we know about her?"

A muscle in Romeo's jaw ticked, but he didn't push it. "Not

much. Rustik is protective of his two daughters. They completed school at home and are rarely seen. The next page is what he sent over about her."

I moved the picture to reveal a mostly blank page. It listed Sofiya's age, height, and hobbies—cooking, baking, and reading.

"I'm sure you could insist on meeting her before the wedding."

I shut the folder to stop myself from getting distracted by Sofiya's picture.

"It doesn't matter," I said. "It's not like we'll be real husband and wife."

"Oh?"

"We'll live together, but we won't be more than roommates." I'd had my fair share of women throughout the years, but one night was all they got from me. I'd decided long ago that I would never let a woman make me weak.

Romeo raised an eyebrow. "What about heirs?"

I waved my hand. "We have years to figure something out. What's important now is stopping the Albanians." The growing tension with the Bratva had demanded too much of our manpower, distracting us from Arben's threat.

Romeo leaned back in the leather office chair, watching me closely. A slow smile spread across his face as he crossed his arms.

"What?" I asked, scowling.

"Just interested to see how this goes. The unshakeable Matteo Rossi living with his pretty little *roommate*."

My irritation grew the longer he smiled. "Fuck off. This is a business decision, nothing more."

"Whatever you say." He got up. "I'll let them know we can set the date."

"Small wedding," I said. "Let's get this done quickly."

Romeo nodded and then reached for the file.

"Leave it," I barked.

He just hummed as he left my office.

2

SOFIYA

Mila snuggled closer to me like she had so many times growing up. She'd spent more nights in my bed than out of it. Our house was always cold—both in temperature and emotion—so we soaked up all the warmth we could get.

"Are you really going to marry him?" she whispered, sounding younger than her nineteen years.

My throat and chest were tight. My father had just delivered the news. His exact words were, "When you marry Matteo Rossi and cement this alliance with the Italians, you'll finally be useful to me." My mama had stood silently beside him.

"I guess so," I whispered back.

"Do you know anything about him?"

"He's head of the New York Mafia."

Mila snorted as she smacked my arm. "Sofiya, be serious."

"But that's all I know," I protested. My lip jutted out in a pout as I rubbed my arm.

"That didn't even hurt," she said, rolling her eyes as she grabbed our shared secret phone. "I'm going to look him up."

I opened my mouth to tell her not to, but then stopped myself. Why shouldn't I find out everything I could about this man I was supposed to spend the rest of my life with?

Mila typed on the phone and then gasped. "He's so hot."

I grabbed the phone, biting my lip as I looked at the picture underneath an article headline that read, "NYC's Hottest Billionaire Leaves New Year's Eve Party Early." It was a candid of Matteo outside a hotel. He was scowling in his perfectly tailored black tux, which stretched across his broad shoulders. His dark hair fell messily in his face, and there was a firm set to his square jaw.

I felt a tiny flutter in my stomach. "I guess he's... fine."

"Oh, he *is* fine," Mila said, grinning widely. She'd always been boy-crazy. I couldn't count the number of times I'd covered for her as she snuck out the window to hook up with her boyfriend of the month, whereas I'd gone to one single party last year and never wanted to repeat the experience. I shuddered as I pushed aside the memory and focused again on the picture.

"How old is he?" I asked. He was obviously older than me, since he was already the head of the Mafia. The man in the picture wasn't quite silver fox level, but he had a maturity to him that I might have found just a little bit sexy.

Mila took the phone, her frown deepening when her searches yielded no new information. After thirty minutes, we finally had to give up. It was impossible to find personal information about Matteo Rossi.

Mila set down the phone with a huff. She turned so she was lying on her side, facing me. "At least we know your fiancé is hot."

"I wonder if he's nice," I murmured. God, I felt so stupid even saying the words out loud. I'd never seen a kind husband or happy marriage in the Bratva, but I clung to the hope that Matteo wasn't as awful as my father. Maybe things were different with the Italians. Maybe they treated their women better.

Mila's face fell, her forehead creased with worry. "He better be." Her voice was fierce.

As the older sister, I had always been protective of Mila, stepping in to take care of her when our parents ignored us and the nannies went home. But as my health issues grew more severe over the years, she had been the one protecting me.

"What about Dimi?" Mila asked. Our half-brother, Dimitri,

lived a life shrouded in secrecy. Our father constantly sent him away to do his dirty work abroad, unable to stand his son's presence for long. Dimi reminded him too much of his first wife. A woman, if the rumors were to be believed, he had actually loved.

I squeezed her hand. "I'm sure he knows. Maybe he'll come for the wedding." But my words lacked conviction. The wedding was two days from now. Dimi didn't have a stable phone number, so we always had to wait until he reached out to us.

"Do you think Matteo knows about my—" I gestured my hand at my body.

Mila's lips parted. "The Pakhan had to tell him, right? Matteo probably got tons of information on you before he agreed." We'd stopped calling our father "papa" years ago. All he was to us, to anyone in his life, was the Pakhan.

I took a deep breath, relief filling my chest. "Yeah, of course." A tiny thread of hopefulness joined my anxiety. Matteo must be a decent man if he was choosing to marry me as I was. Although... maybe an alliance with the Bratva was too good of an opportunity to pass up, even if that meant accepting a bride like me.

"I'm going to miss you," Mila murmured.

I blinked to keep my tears from falling. Years of my father screaming at me to toughen up had done nothing to stop me from being deeply sensitive.

"Maybe he'll let you visit," I said.

"Yeah, maybe."

Tears fell down my face as I pulled my little sister into my arms.

3

MATTEO

Romeo and I sat in the back of the car on the drive from the airport to the church. Two SUVs filled with my men flanked us on the road. Sienna had been enraged that I wouldn't allow her to attend my wedding, but I didn't trust the Russians enough to risk my sister's safety.

I glanced at my watch. I had a meeting back in the city this evening to inspect a new shipment of weapons with Domenico, my enforcer, so this ceremony needed to be succinct.

"You might want to practice your smile," Romeo said.

I met his gaze with a scowl.

"No, no, the opposite of that."

"Fuck off. Why do I need to smile?"

"To make a good impression on your bride."

Romeo just chuckled at my responding glare. Fucker. He was the only one, besides my sister, who interacted with me without even an edge of fear.

"I won't hesitate to shoot you," I said, looking out the window. He just snorted.

I didn't need to put this woman at ease. She would live in my apartment and join me for events when we needed to keep up the appearance of a strong marriage. I wasn't cruel—she would have access to money and whatever else she needed—but that was it. I refused to disrupt my life for her. Refused to do anything that would make it easy for her to gain an advantage over me.

We pulled up to the church on the north side of the city. Traditionally, Family weddings happened near my apartment in Manhattan, but Rustik said if the wedding was to be Catholic at our insistence, it would take place in Chicago at his. It was an inconvenience for me, and I was already dreading the two-hour plane ride back with my new wife.

Rustik Ivanov might've been my new ally, but I still despised him. He had shed plenty of Italian blood through the years, and we'd retaliated in kind. This alliance would take some getting used to.

Angelo, our driver and one of my most trusted soldiers, signaled that our men were in position. I exited the armored SUV and buttoned my jacket. I'd worn my standard black suit for the wedding. Business attire for a business event. My Glock pressed comfortably against my back.

I checked my watch again as we entered the church. Two minutes until the ceremony.

"Cutting it close," Romeo muttered.

"No need to linger," I responded.

An elderly woman working at the church ushered us to the front, where the priest waited. Half my men filed into the empty pews on the groom's side while the others were stationed around the perimeter. The pews to my right were sparsely filled with the bride's guests. I was surprised at how few people there were after Rustik's insistence on having the wedding in his city. The Pakhan was seated in the front pew and tipped his head at me. I didn't return the gesture. I had expected him to walk his daughter down the aisle, but maybe the Russians did it differently.

Rustik's wife sat next to him. The woman was thin and there was a blankness in her eyes, although her dress made me blink twice. *Loud* was the only word to describe it—bright orange with ruffles around the neck. Beside her was a pretty girl with dark brown hair—Sofiya's sister, I assumed. She met my gaze and held it unflinchingly.

Interesting.

The music started and the back doors of the church opened. The sun shone through the stained glass window, creating a halo of light around a young woman *sitting in a wheelchair.*

I kept my face blank, refusing to look at Rustik, who had clearly withheld this information about his daughter. What else was the bastard hiding? Did he think I would have rejected the marriage proposal if I'd known? I felt Romeo's presence beside me, and I could almost hear him saying, "Maybe this is why you should have met her beforehand."

Sofiya wheeled herself down the aisle, her lace veil trailing behind her and a tight expression on her face. She'd been beautiful in her picture, but in person, she was breathtaking. Her hair was like gold as it framed her delicate features, and I couldn't stop my eyes from flitting down to her full lips. When her blue eyes met mine, I felt a weird jolt of electricity so strong it almost broke through my blank mask.

Sofiya's dress ballooned around her lap, making it hard for her to maneuver her wheelchair. A strange, uncomfortable feeling formed in my chest at seeing her struggle down the aisle alone. I told myself it was because she was a Mafia queen now and needed to look strong in front of my men.

Sofiya finally made her way to the front of the aisle, and I made room for her beside me. She gave me a shy glance before looking at the priest, and I had the strange urge to demand she put her eyes back on me.

The priest had been told to keep the ceremony as short as possible, so it wasn't long before we were at the vows. He cleared his throat, giving me an anxious look before looking at his paper. "Matteo Rossi and Sofiya Ivanova, have you come here to enter into marriage without coercion, freely and wholeheartedly?"

"I have," I said.

"I have," Sofiya said. Her voice was gentle and sweet, and I felt a strange twinge in my chest.

"Are you prepared, as you follow the path of marriage, to love and honor each other for as long as you both shall live?" the priest continued.

"I am," I said, and Sofiya echoed my response.

"And are you prepared to accept children lovingly from God and to bring them up according to the law of Christ and his Church?"

When I ascended as Don thirteen years ago, I'd known producing heirs was part of my responsibility. But the prospect of children had never felt so real as it did now, with my pretty little bride beside me.

Sofiya and I responded affirmatively.

The vows were next. When the priest asked Sofiya if she vowed to "love, honor, and obey" me, her jaw clenched tight. Her eyes flitted to her father and then up at me. I could see the rebellion play out, her eyes so expressive I could practically hear her thoughts.

The priest cleared his throat, and she gave an annoyed huff before saying, "I do."

Fuck, that was... *cute*.

It was almost enough to make me smile.

4

SOFIYA

"I *do.*" That was it. No going back now.

It was time to exchange rings. I briefly panicked since I hadn't been given a ring for Matteo, but he produced bands for both of us. I gave him a grateful smile, and something in his jaw ticked. My smile fell and a sick feeling twisted my stomach. Did my husband hate me already?

The priest blessed the rings and then Matteo slipped the plain gold band onto my finger. A brief flash of disappointment went through me before I stuffed it down. I'd spent hours as a child circling my favorite rings in the jewelry catalogs I fished out of the trash after my mama was done with them. I'd dreamed of an art deco-style ring with a large diamond in the middle and smaller stones surrounding it. But nothing about this wedding was like the one I'd imagined when I was younger. Not the dress, which my mother had chosen, even though it would make moving around in my wheelchair a nightmare. Not the guest list, which mainly consisted of old, powerful Bratva men. And not the groom.

To be fair, I couldn't have picked a more attractive husband even if I'd had a choice. The pictures Mila and I found hadn't done him justice. Matteo was devastatingly handsome. His dark hair was casually messy, contrasting with his otherwise stern, put-together demeanor. His suit—not a tux—was impeccably tailored and showed off his tall, muscular body. But I'd always imagined getting married to someone who loved me. Or at least *liked* me. I swallowed the lump in my throat as I slipped the plain gold band on his finger, his rough fingertips brushing against my skin.

I signed the marriage certificate with a hand that was steadier than I felt. I braved another glance up at my new husband, but he was staring straight ahead with the same flat expression he'd worn since I entered the church. I'd never been able to control my face, to the immense disappointment of my father. According to him, I was too easy to read, too vulnerable, too pathetic. I didn't know if I should be impressed or terrified by Matteo's ability to cover his emotions.

"I now pronounce you man and wife. You may kiss your bride," the priest said, closing out the ceremony.

I froze.

Oh no oh no oh no.

Matteo would have to bend down to kiss me, but doing that would be degrading to a Mafia Don. His expression remained unchanging as he leaned down, took my chin between his thumb and forefinger, and pressed his lips to mine. The kiss was soft, barely a brush, but his touch was electric and left me wanting more. All too quickly, it was over. My husband nodded to the priest before finally meeting my eyes, jerking his chin at the exit. "Time to go."

I swallowed hard. It wasn't like we had a reception planned. My father would never want to show off his defective daughter in such a public way. He'd only invited his inner circle, men who were aware of my disability, to the ceremony. But I still thought I'd have more time to say goodbye. I nodded and turned my chair to go back down the aisle. I stopped by my family's pew and reached my hand out to Mila, who squeezed past my stony-faced parents to join me. Matteo strode ahead until he realized I wasn't beside him. He stopped and turned towards me. I bit my lip, not wanting to make him angry, but I couldn't leave without saying goodbye to my sister.

"I guess we're leaving right now," I said, grasping her hand.

She nodded, her chin wobbling. I squeezed her hand harder to keep my tears from coming. She leaned down and wrapped her arms around me.

"Don't let him push you around, Sofiya. You're too sweet for your own good," she whispered.

"Okay," I whispered back. I'd always been good at standing up for Mila, but I'd never been able to do it for myself. I guessed it was time to learn.

I met Matteo's gaze over Mila's shoulder. He looked down at his watch, and I took that as my sign that my time had run out.

"I love you." I squeezed my sister hard before reluctantly letting go.

I glanced at my mom, but she stared straight ahead. Being married to my father had slowly made her fade away until she was an overmedicated shell. I took a deep breath and moved down the aisle towards my new husband and new life.

My arms ached, each push of the wheelchair straining my wrists and shoulders. Luckily, the front of the church had a ramp, so I made my way around it to the street, where three black BMWs waited.

"This is ours," Matteo said, gesturing to the middle vehicle. His eyes flickered down to my chair.

Mila and I had spent hours watching videos of how to transfer from my wheelchair to the car, and then we'd snuck out late at night to practice in the garage. Of course Matteo would use massive SUVs, just like my father. It made the transfer all the more challenging since I would have to pull myself up into the seat with my massive dress, but I wasn't about to show any weakness in front of these men, who had formed a circle around Matteo and me.

This was so freaking embarrassing.

One of the soldiers stepped in front of me. My eyes widened as I took him in. He was probably the biggest guy I'd ever seen—at least 6'6", maybe taller, and ridiculously muscular. My heart jolted anxiously until I took in his slightly boyish face, gentle smile, and man bun. "Hi, Mrs. Rossi, I'm Angelo. I can help you get in if you tell me what to do."

For a second, I didn't know who he was talking to, but of course, *I* was Mrs. Rossi now. That would take some getting used to.

"I can do it if you open the door for me." He nodded and did what I asked.

I rolled up to the car at an angle and put on my brakes. I wished I could ask everyone to turn their backs because I was feeling especially weak today and already knew it would be a struggle. I moved to the edge of my chair and then transferred to the car's running board. Now I just needed to pull myself up to the seat. I grabbed the handle above the window and used it to leverage myself up, clenching my teeth against the pain in my shoulders.

"Impressive, bella," Angelo said, helping me pull the skirt of my dress into the car. "I'll put your chair in the back."

I gave him a little smile, and Matteo made a sound almost like a growl. His jaw was clenched and his eyes seemed to blaze with anger before he slammed the door shut behind me.

I closed my eyes, refusing to allow myself to cry. After growing up in such a cold house, I'd dreamed of marrying and starting a family. Now I wondered if signing my name on that paper had sealed my fate of living in another loveless home.

5

MATTEO

I pulled out my phone the second I was in the car, mindlessly scrolling through messages to distract myself from my new wife beside me. I had no idea what had come over me when she smiled at Angelo. All I knew was that I hated it. I'd assigned him to be Sofiya's guard, but now I was second-guessing my choice.

She'd done a good job getting in the car herself, but my fingers had itched with the urge to pick her up. I clenched my fist. I couldn't let her get in my head. I wouldn't let her be a distraction. My loyalty was to the Mafia, my men, and Sienna. That was it.

"I have a work call I need to take on the plane," I said, cutting through the silence as I continued staring at my phone.

"Oh, okay," Sofiya said, her voice soft.

I couldn't stop myself from glancing over. Her hands twisted in the white skirt of her dress. She looked so young, so fucking *innocent*. She wasn't what I would expect from someone raised in the Bratva. Romeo's words about Rustik sheltering his daughters came back to me. Did she know anything about my world?

"So make sure not to disturb me," I added, jaw clenched.

Sofiya swallowed, her eyes wide as she nodded before quickly looking away.

I felt a strange twinging in my chest.

Every muscle in my body was tense for the rest of the inter-
minable ride to the airport. The moment we came to a stop outside
my private jet, I was out the door, needing to create as much distance
between Sofiya and me as possible.

I buttoned my suit jacket and turned towards the plane, eyeing
the metal stairs leading up to the door. As Angelo lifted Sofiya's
wheelchair from the back of the car, it hit me—how did people in
wheelchairs get on planes? I'd never given it a moment's thought
until now.

I signaled Enzo, one of my top guards. "Check with the airline
staff to see how to get her on the plane," I commanded, voice low.

I ran my hand through my hair as Romeo joined me. "What are
you thinking?" he asked.

"Rustik kept some secrets."

"Would it have changed your decision?"

I knew what he was asking—would I have rejected this match if
I had known she was in a wheelchair? As Don, I knew that any sign
of weakness would be exploited. Having a wife already made me
vulnerable—my enemies would certainly try to use her to get to me
—but having one who was so visibly *defective*? I grimaced. The
word felt wrong in my mind as Sofiya rounded the car, stopping
when she was beside me. She tilted her face to meet my gaze, her
plump red lips mesmerizing me. Wheelchair or not, she was
perfection.

We stared at each other in silence, a slight blush darkening on her
cheeks as the seconds ticked by.

Enzo re-joined us. "Boss," he said, glancing at Sofiya. "The crew
said there is a wheelchair ramp, but because we didn't notify them, it
could be up to an hour before it's available."

"That's unacceptable. Tell them to get it here faster."

Enzo grimaced. "I tried, Boss."

I closed my eyes, breathing through the rage. This was why I
didn't like to leave New York. Everyone in the city knew who I was
and who they were dealing with, which wasn't always the case
elsewhere.

"How do you usually get on planes?" I asked Sofiya.

She looked startled. "I've never been on a plane. But I guess I could, um, scoot up the stairs."

I glared at her, utterly confused at what her life had been. How had she never traveled before?

"I don't have time for this. I'll carry you up the stairs and then we can fucking get out of here."

Sofiya fidgeted with the skirt of her dress again. "Oh, well, it's not super safe to be carried..." She trailed off as she took in my expression.

"I'm not going to drop you," I gritted out. "Come on."

I strode to the plane stairs, not looking behind to see if she was following. She would if she knew what was good for her.

Romeo kept pace with me. We reached the bottom of the steps and turned. Sofiya was making her way towards me, every push of the wheelchair slow and awkward. Angelo walked beside her, leaning down slightly to speak. She laughed at whatever he said, and my jaw clenched.

"You still married her." There was something in Romeo's expression—a *knowing* in his smile—that put me on edge.

"What was I supposed to do? You were the one who said we needed this alliance."

"We do." Romeo shrugged.

We watched Sofiya and Angelo approach in silence. Did he have to walk so close to her? And what the fuck could possibly be so funny to make Sofiya smile so much?

"I can carry her onto the plane," Romeo said.

I whirled to face him, something hot burning inside me.

He laughed, clasping my shoulder before heading up the stairs. "I'll check with the pilot to make sure we're set for takeoff."

"Finally," I said when Sofiya stopped in front of me. I eyed her, trying to figure out the best way to lift her. "Put your arm around my neck." I managed to get one arm around her back and the other underneath her legs. Angelo had to help when the many layers of her dress got in the way, but then she was in my arms with a little squeak.

Her dress made holding her a bit cumbersome, but something about the feel of her loosened the knot of tension in my chest. She clutched tightly at my neck and shoulder as I headed up the steps. The warmth of her skin pressed against mine, and the wind brushed her hair across my face.

"Not quite the traditional way to carry the bride over a threshold," Sofiya quipped as we entered the plane.

I placed her in a seat and fixed her with a stern expression. "This marriage is an alliance between our families. Nothing more. You are not my *bride*. I expect you to behave in a manner befitting your position, but do not expect a real marriage from me. Understand?"

Hurt flashed across Sofiya's face, her expressive eyes giving away everything she was feeling. Doubt filled me again about how she could possibly survive this life. The criminal underworld would chew her up and spit her out.

"Okay," she said softly. "Are we... I mean... Will we live together?"

I cleared my throat and adjusted my cufflinks. "Of course. We will present a strong marriage to the outside world. In private, we will have separate lives." I forced myself to turn away and took a seat across the aisle from her.

Romeo sprawled in the seat beside me, still wearing a sly smile that set me on edge, and Angelo sat down next to Sofiya, crowding her against the window.

"Are you nervous?" I overheard him say.

"A little," Sofiya responded. "It's safe, right?" She covered her cheeks with her hands. "Sorry, that's a stupid question."

"It's perfectly safe, bella. The flight's just over two hours, so not very long."

I huffed and pulled my phone back out, randomly scrolling through my messages. "Is everything prepared for this meeting?" I asked Romeo.

"This incredibly non-urgent meeting with an arms supplier that I could go to without you, or that we could reschedule? Yeah, I think we're all set," he said dryly.

I scowled. "Now is not the time to sit back and relax. The Albanians are pushing in. We need to be on alert."

"Whatever you say," Romeo said, sitting back in his seat and closing his eyes.

I resisted the urge to shoot him. He was being way too fucking smug, and I wasn't even sure about what. But I didn't like it.

The flight attendant returned to inform us we were ready to take off. Her red dress was low-cut, showing off her large tits, and the indecent skirt left her long, tan legs on display. I'd fucked her in the bedroom at the back of the plane last month, and the hungry way she was looking at me told me she wanted a repeat experience. But now I couldn't remember what I'd found attractive about her.

The plane started moving, and I had to force my eyes to remain on my phone instead of letting them drift to my new wife.

"Pull all her medical records, anything you can find about her," I said quietly to Romeo. "I want to know everything about her and this fucking family. Rustik may have proposed this alliance, but giving us this daughter was a slight. He wants the upper hand and I won't fucking let him get it."

He nodded, pulling out his phone. For as much as Romeo annoyed me, there was no one I trusted more.

As the plane lifted off the ground, Sofiya let out a little gasp. I couldn't stop myself from looking over at her. She gripped the armrests as she stared out the window, her lips parted. The evening sunlight hit the window, bouncing off her golden hair and making her look like an angel.

If she was an angel, I was the devil. And we would never belong together.

Once we were in the air, I headed to the back to make some work calls.

6

SOFIYA

Mila and I spent countless hours dreaming of everything we wanted to do in the outside world—the destinations we wanted to travel to and what we wanted to do when we got there. We'd called it our Dream List, and I could already check off my first item: flying on a plane.

Of course, I'd never expected to be on a private plane with wide, soft seats and a flight attendant bringing snacks and champagne. I gave her a quick smile as I took a package of warm chocolate chip cookies. She was gorgeous, her dress highlighting her curves, and I felt a flash of jealousy, especially when I saw how her gaze lingered on Matteo.

I tried to focus on how exciting it was to be above the clouds, to see the sunset paint the sky in oranges and pinks as we hurtled towards our destination, but there was a hard lump in my throat. My new husband had made clear I would never complete several items on my list—being loved, creating a happy home for children.

It had been childish to even put them on there. What woman in my world ever got happiness? We learned to live without it. The unlucky ones ended up like my mother—empty shells, destroyed by cruel husbands. The fortunate ones with absent husbands spent their days looking after kids, shopping, and complaining to friends.

Matteo was brusque and serious, but there weren't signs yet that he was cruel. He hadn't commented on my wheelchair, hadn't called me a "waste of space" like my father had when he saw me using it this morning. Matteo had even carried me up to the plane, his touch gentle, instead of forcing me to scoot up the stairs on my butt.

I wished I could have met my husband on a better health day, but I'd woken up this morning, like I had too many mornings lately, with my knees and hips ready to give out at any moment. Would Matteo have been interested in a real marriage with me if I were prettier or skinnier or less damaged?

"What do you think of flying?" Angelo asked, breaking me out of my melancholic thoughts.

I turned to the guard with a smile. "It's amazing."

"You've never traveled before?"

"I've never left Chicago." The truth was, I'd barely even left the east wing of my house. When Mila and I were younger, before my condition worsened, we would sometimes attend parties or go on outings with our nanny. But that seemed like a lifetime ago.

"New York is a great city. I think you'll like it there," he said.

"Have you lived there your whole life?"

"Yeah. Born and raised. I grew up poor and sort of fell into all of this"—he waved his hand at our luxurious surroundings—"when I was younger. The Boss has been good to me."

I met his gaze, looking at him intently to see if he was telling the truth. Mila always said I was too trusting, but I would rather believe that people were fundamentally good than spend my life expecting them to lie or hurt me. Maybe I'd been born into the wrong world.

"Can you tell me more about him?" I whispered.

Matteo had headed to the back of the plane a while ago, but Romeo was across the aisle from us, and more guards were sitting on the couches—yes, freaking *couches*, which couldn't possibly be normal—and I didn't want them to overhear.

Angelo gave me a kind smile. "You might have guessed that he's not very expressive. But he's a fair Don. He rewards people who are loyal to him."

The unsaid words hung in the air—what happened to those who weren't loyal.

"Does he have a family?" I asked.

"He has a sister. She lives in the same building as him. But I think that's it. You know his parents were murdered?"

I furrowed my brow and shook my head. I hadn't known that. I knew essentially nothing about my husband except that he looked good in a suit.

"By his uncle," Angelo said, voice low. "It took the Boss two years to overthrow the traitor and reclaim New York."

"When was that? How long has he been Don?"

"That was thirteen years ago."

My eyes widened. "How old is he?"

Romeo chuckled from across the aisle, and I realized I'd spoken too loudly. I blushed and curled in on myself. My father couldn't stand when I asked questions.

"Don't worry," Romeo said with a wink. "The Boss ran away, so now he has to face the consequences."

I raised my brows, shocked at the way he was talking about his Don. If anyone spoke about the Pakhan like that—even his right-hand man—they would be punished.

"Matteo is thirty-eight," Romeo continued. "Old fucker."

Angelo snorted. "And how old are you?"

Romeo flipped him off. "Thirty-seven," he answered begrudgingly, and I couldn't help but laugh. Romeo just winked at me again.

I couldn't believe how young Matteo had been when he became Don, and I felt a burst of sympathy for my new husband. No wonder he was so serious. He'd been responsible for all of New York for so long. I bit my lip, thinking about the seventeen years between us. The age gap didn't bother me, but it was probably another reason Matteo wasn't interested in me. I was young and naïve... why would he want to spend any time around me?

"Tell us about yourself, Sofiya," Romeo said.

I shrugged. "Not much to tell. I'm not very exciting."

"On the contrary, I expect you're about to bring no end of excitement into our lives," he said, leaning back in his seat.

I gave the gregarious second-in-command a hesitant smile. "I like baking and reading. Boring, like I said."

"Are you any good at baking?" Angelo asked, rubbing his stomach.

"I'm not sure." I shrugged. "My sister and our bodyguard seemed to like my creations enough." My parents never stepped foot in the kitchen so it had been a safe place for Mila and me to spend our time, surrounded by sympathetic staff. But my health had stolen even that from me as it became harder for me to go up and down the stairs. Would my new home have stairs?

"I don't actually know what traditional Russian desserts are," Romeo said.

"I do make some Russian baked goods, like piroshki, which are little hand pies, and blini, which are like crepes. But I mostly learned from watching American and British baking shows, so I make a lot of cookies and cupcakes and things like that," I said.

"Any Italian desserts?" Angelo asked, an interested spark in his eyes. "Tiramisu is my favorite."

"I've never made it, but I'd love to try," I responded. I kept a notepad with all my favorite recipes, along with a list of ones I still wanted to make. My list had grown long this past year as I'd spent months on end stuck in bed.

"My favorite is cannoli," Romeo said. "And I'm much more important than this guy, so you should definitely make my dessert first."

Angelo snorted and crossed his arms. Warmth settled in my stomach at their playful banter. Maybe I wouldn't have a loving husband, but there was already more kindness in these small interactions than I'd ever gotten at home. Mila and I had done our best to create our own world in our wing of the house, and our guard, Nikolai, had gone along with our antics. But with the rare exception of when Dimitri visited, we had been an island in the midst of cold, harsh men.

"I'll have to make both," I said. "What's Matteo's favorite?"

Romeo frowned. "You know, I'm not sure I've ever seen him eat a dessert."

Just then, the man himself appeared. I hadn't heard him coming, and I jumped a little.

"Ahh, perfect timing, Matteo," Romeo said. "What's your favorite dessert?"

Matteo's icy expression fixed on me as if he knew I was the reason for the question. He quickly looked away, dismissing me, and my heart broke a little.

"I need you in the back," he said, jerking his head. Romeo gave an exaggerated sigh before getting up and following the Don.

Angelo must have caught my crestfallen expression because he patted my hand. "The Boss has been dealing with a lot in his territory. It's keeping him very busy."

I nodded, turning back to the window. Night had fallen and the blinking lights over the wings of the plane joined the stars in illuminating the sky. My father didn't believe that women should know anything about Bratva business, and I guessed it would be the same in my new home.

We had another hour or so of the flight and I decided I would let myself wallow in self-pity until we landed. Then I would be ready to face my new life and make the best of it.

7

MATTEO

The gentle ding of the elevator sounded before the doors slid open. I gestured for Sofiya to get on first, followed by Romeo and me. The doors closed, leaving Angelo waiting for the next one with Sofiya's two suitcases and the large box she'd brought. I'd managed to stay away from her the entire plane ride, but now I was trapped in this tiny space. Unable to escape her.

The elevator ascended from the underground garage to the twenty-second floor, where my penthouse apartment waited. I'd bought this historic building on the west side of Central Park after becoming Don. Sienna and I couldn't stand being in the home we'd grown up in, the walls groaning with memories of our parents, the floors stained with their blood.

The lower floors of the building included housing for Sienna and my inner circle, along with offices for my legitimate and illegitimate businesses. The building surrounded a large courtyard and garden. Sienna ate lunch out there when the weather was nice. It was one of the few spots outside she could be without a convoy of guards. But only I had access to the rooftop. Some nights, I would sit out there alone with a drink, the faint sounds of the city reaching me from the street below. In those moments, I felt like the king of this city.

The elevator door opened, revealing the large entryway and front door. Sofiya looked exhausted as we exited the elevator.

"There's fingerprint access to get in," I told her. "Romeo, Angelo, Enzo, my sister, and I are the only ones with access."

She nodded as she chewed on her lower lip. I wanted to snap at her to cut it out. What did she have to look so nervous about? *I* was the one whose home was about to be invaded.

By the time I added her fingerprint to the lock, begrudgingly giving her access to my private space, the elevator doors had opened again to reveal Angelo and the suitcases. He smiled at Sofiya. "I'm the head of your security team and will be your personal bodyguard. I'm sure the Boss will tell you how to get in touch with me, but I'll be stationed outside the apartment during the day if you need anything, and I'll drive you if you need to go anywhere."

"Thank you," she said.

"It was nice meeting you, Sofiya," Romeo said. "I'll say good-night now. Let you two get acquainted." He cocked an eyebrow at me before getting back on the elevator with a chuckle. He lived a couple of floors below, and I had the urge to demand he stay. What was I supposed to do alone with this girl?

Angelo placed Sofiya's two suitcases inside the apartment before giving me a nod and heading back out to the entryway. I gestured for Sofiya to enter and followed after her, the door shutting with a *thud* behind us.

The apartment was plenty big, but it had never felt as small as it did in this moment. Sofiya might be a tiny slip of a girl, but her presence filled the space. "It's really pretty," she said, glancing up at me.

I just grunted. Sienna had thrown herself into designing all the apartments in the building. I'd stayed out of it besides vetoing a few of her wilder ideas.

I picked up Sofiya's suitcases, wondering where the rest of her things were. I had expected her possessions to take up several cars, but maybe her parents were planning to send everything later.

I jerked my chin to the left side of the apartment, where a hallway branched off from the living room. "Your bedroom is that way." The furthest one from my bedroom.

Sofiya maneuvered her wheelchair through the living room and followed me down the hall. I opened the guest room door and placed her suitcases by the bed. No one had ever stayed in this room before —it wasn't like I had guests—but I'd asked Gianna to make sure it was ready for my new wife.

Sofiya took in the room, looking like she was about to say something.

"I'll get the rest," I grunted, leaving before she could.

Something rattled in the cardboard box as I carried it through the apartment, and I was tempted to look inside. But I was determined to show as little interest as possible in my new wife, so I kept my mouth shut and placed it by the foot of the bed.

"Thank you," she said.

"Gianna Pesci is my housekeeper and cook. She and her daughter come a couple times a week to take care of things, but they're gone for the next month for a wedding." Gianna's son was getting married, so she was taking rare time off. I always told her she should take more, but she insisted I couldn't survive without her, which was probably true. I had to admit I was relieved she wasn't here now, though. She was an opinionated woman and completely unafraid of insulting me. I didn't need her commentary to complicate this situation.

"Do you have any other staff?" Sofiya asked.

"Not who come into the apartment."

She nodded, looking so fucking small in her wheelchair.

"I have a meeting to get to," I said gruffly.

"Oh." She bit her lush lip again. "You're leaving?"

I clenched my jaw at the sadness in her expression. Why couldn't she hide what she was feeling? "I told you this wasn't going to be a real marriage," I snapped.

She blinked slowly before giving a small nod. "Of course. Sorry."

A thousand irritated retorts were on the tip of my tongue, but I swallowed them, turned on my heel, and headed out of the apartment. There was a strange, unsettled feeling in my chest as I walked past Angelo and got back on the elevator. I rubbed it absentmind-

edly as the elevator doors opened to the lower floor that housed my
office.

8

MATTEO

I t took me three attempts to tie my tie this morning. And it was definitely not because my thoughts were consumed by my new bride.

She was way too young.

And way too fucking beautiful.

After my meeting with the arms dealer, I'd stayed in my office, drinking alone until three in the morning. When I'd returned to my apartment, the door to the guest room was shut and the lights were out. Even in the stillness, I swore I could feel her presence.

I might be a bastard for leaving her alone right after we arrived, but she wasn't anything to me, really. Just a stranger. A roommate.

But that didn't explain the urgency I felt to get out of my room and find her.

Looking in the mirror at my still-crooked tie, I rolled my eyes as I ran my hand through my hair. I was *Matteo* fucking *Rossi*. Head of the Mafia. A twenty-one-year-old girl wasn't going to disrupt my life.

I strode out of my bedroom while adjusting my cufflinks but came to an abrupt stop when I saw Sofiya standing at the kitchen island.

Fucking *standing*.

Was this some kind of a joke? My brain whirled as I tried to understand why she had lied about being in a wheelchair. Was it to get some kind of advantage over me? Was it her idea or her family's?

The morning light streamed through the window, making her hair shine as she tucked a strand behind her ear. She was writing something down on a piece of paper, completely oblivious to me. That didn't sit well with me, either. Why wasn't she more aware of her surroundings?

I walked into the kitchen, my anger driving every step.

"What the fuck do you think you're playing at?" I growled.

Sofiya gasped with a jolt, her eyes flying to mine. "Oh! Sorry, I didn't see you." Her round cheeks grew pink as I stared at her, unblinking. "Umm, good morning?" Her words came out as a question.

No, I refused to be swayed by her innocent act.

"You didn't answer my question," I seethed.

She chewed her lip, her cheeks growing redder. "I didn't catch it. Sorry."

Why was she playing dumb? I rounded the kitchen island and that was when I saw it. The walker in front of her. How she was leaning all her weight on the counter.

Shit.

My insistence that I didn't need to know anything about my bride before our marriage seemed idiotic now. I had to check with Romeo to see if he'd gotten her medical records yet.

"Is something wrong?" Sofiya asked. She had to tilt her head up to meet my gaze.

"You're in the way," I snapped, my anger at her quickly transforming into embarrassed irritation towards myself. "You might live here now, but that doesn't mean it's your home to do with as you please."

Her lips parted and she quickly looked around the massive penthouse apartment, as if trying to figure out whose way she was in.

"Do you... should I..." Her voice was a whisper as she stumbled over her words.

"Spit it out." I didn't want to have to look at her big, sad, blue eyes anymore.

"You want me to stay in my room?" she finally got out.

"Yes, fine," I said, needing this conversation to be over.

She averted her gaze and gave me a little nod before moving her hands to her walker. It was on the tip of my tongue to ask her about her disability, but that would mean staying in her presence. And every second I spent with my little wife, the more I got drawn in. I had made the mistake of trusting people in the past, and it had cost me everything. I wouldn't do it again.

Sofiya walked slowly back to her room, leaning heavily on the walker. I caught a hint of her scent as she walked past me—something sweet and floral. I looked down at the paper she'd been writing on. At the top of the page, it said "Sofiya's Famous Cinnamon Rolls," and it looked like she had been checking off the ingredients she needed.

Something stirred in my chest. A sharp pain that felt almost like... regret. I adjusted my sleeves and pushed the feeling away. I needed to get to the office. I found myself hoping that the Albanians would cause some shit today. Getting my hands dirty would get my mind off my wife.

I left the apartment, jerking my head at Angelo. "Make sure she doesn't leave."

He nodded, keeping his position by the door.

9

SOFIYA

I closed the bedroom door behind me, leaning heavily on my rollator to keep my balance. My hips were aching, and a weariness that had nothing to do with my disorder was settling into my bones. I didn't know how long I could live like this. Mila was always the brave one, the one who fought back. Without her by my side, I felt myself wilting.

I curled up on the bed, haphazardly throwing a blanket over my body. My eyes burned with unshed tears until I finally gave into them, letting them drip down my cheeks. It wasn't like there was anyone here to judge me for crying. I wondered if my new husband would scream at me if he saw my tears, like my father always had. I didn't understand why I had to be born with such a freaking tender heart. I wished I could be cold and unfeeling... like Matteo.

I wrapped my arms around my pillow and let my eyes drift shut. Maybe my dreams would carry me to a better life.

—————

THE LIGHT in the room shifted as the sun set, turning gold, then pink, then blue. I hadn't moved from my spot on the bed all day and didn't have the energy to turn on a lamp.

I should have asked more questions this morning. Was I allowed to leave my room to get food? Matteo hadn't specified, which, in my experience, meant *no*. Would he hit me if I disobeyed? My stomach lurched at the thought.

A few months ago, I had dared go downstairs after my father told me to stay in my room. I'd gotten my period but didn't have any supplies, and Mila was out. My father caught me searching through my mother's bathroom vanity and backhanded me across the face. I'd crumpled to the floor, hitting my hip hard enough to leave a nasty bruise. I'd had to crawl back to my room, holding back my screams of pain, as my father berated me for not obeying him. Something in me had broken that day as I lay in bed, blood soaking through the towel I'd stuffed in my underwear.

Based on what I'd seen and my conversations with his men, Matteo didn't seem violent, but even I could hear how naïve that sounded. He was the Don. He had surely murdered and tortured people. Just because he was attractive didn't mean anything. Monsters hid behind pretty faces.

Darkness enveloped the room and I stared unseeingly out the window. Hunger gnawed at my stomach, but I was too scared to venture out into the kitchen. I hadn't heard anyone moving around the apartment all day, but I was sure Matteo had cameras. Was this all a test to see how obedient I was?

There wasn't a clock in the room so I didn't know what time it was when I finally broke down and rolled out of bed. I went to the bathroom and then snagged my purse, knowing Mila had slipped a chocolate bar in there the morning of the wedding. Was that only yesterday? It felt like a lifetime ago.

The sugar hit my lips, but I could barely taste it. I ate mechanically, folded the wrapper, and put it back in my bag. Numbness washed over me, pulling me under.

I had no more tears to cry. This was my life—to be hated and forgotten—and I just had to accept it.

10

MATTEO

"I hear you're avoiding your new wife," Romeo said. He gave me a shit-eating grin as he collapsed into the leather chair across from my desk.

I knew I should have gotten that chair removed. I didn't want anyone to be comfortable in my office. Now my number two was reclined back in the chair with his feet *on my fucking desk*.

"I'm not avoiding her." I rubbed my jaw. I'd developed a tic with how hard I'd clenched it the past few days.

Romeo cocked a brow. "Sure. That's why you slept at the Star last night."

"It was more convenient," I said. The Star was one of the luxury hotels I owned downtown.

Romeo hummed as he crossed his arms. "Pretty little thing must be getting lonely. Maybe I should go over and keep her company."

I was out of my seat before I realized what I was doing, my hand moving towards the gun I kept hidden under my jacket.

Romeo laughed as he raised his hands in surrender. "Fuck, Matteo. Feeling a little possessive?"

My breaths were heavy, and I felt an inexplicable need to see Sofiya. The thought of any man being around her made me murderous, and I couldn't understand why.

"We'll talk about the drug run later," I gritted out, grabbing my phone and keys and storming out of the office.

"Say hello to your bride for me," Romeo called out after me.

———

"REPORT," I commanded Angelo. He was stationed outside the apartment where I'd left him yesterday morning. Enzo was assigned to the night shift. They would have switched off a few hours ago.

Angelo shifted uncomfortably, putting me on high alert.

"She's been in her room," he said.

"So?" I barked. Angelo was hiding something, and it was pissing me off.

"I mean, she hasn't left her room, Boss. This whole time."

Angelo and Enzo were the only ones besides Romeo and me with access to the video feeds inside the apartment. While I had cameras in all the common spaces, I drew the line at having them inside the bedrooms.

"Since yesterday morning?"

Angelo nodded.

"Why the fuck didn't you tell me?" I snarled. That strange feeling in my chest kicked up again. I resisted the temptation to rub it. What the fuck was she doing in there?

"You said you didn't want to be disturbed, Boss. Unless she tried to leave."

My fist clenched with the urge to punch him. Angelo had quickly risen through my ranks. I'd chosen him for my inner circle after he'd saved my life in an ambush. He was one of the best shots in the entire Family and had proven himself loyal. But right now? I wanted to kill him. He swallowed hard, but didn't avert his gaze.

I would deal with him later. Right now, I had to deal with my wife.

I jerked my head, signaling him to open the door, and swept into the apartment. I glanced over at the kitchen as if Sofiya would be there, sweetly smiling as she tucked her hair behind her ear or pulled cinnamon rolls out of the oven. I would never admit it to anyone, but they were one of my favorite foods.

But the apartment was quiet.

I went to her room and knocked on the door. When there wasn't an immediate answer, I strode in to find my wife curled up under the covers, facing away from me. That weird twinge in my chest started again. Maybe I needed to see the doctor to make sure I wasn't having a heart attack.

"What are you doing?" I asked, my voice sounding loud and harsh in the silent room.

Sofiya jolted, and I realized she'd been sleeping.

"Matteo?" She scrambled to sit against the headboard. She kept her eyes averted, tension lining her shoulders. Her oversized black sweatshirt made her look pale, eyes shadowed by dark circles.

"What are you doing?" I asked again, this time trying to control my voice.

"I was sleeping. Sorry," she added in a whisper. Her hands twisted in the covers.

"Why are you sorry?" I took a few steps towards the bed.

"You seem angry."

I had been angry, but it was hard to hold on to the emotion when staring down at this frail girl.

I let out a loud sigh, unsure where to take this conversation. "I heard you've been in this room since yesterday."

She nodded but didn't offer an explanation for her absurd behavior.

"Have you eaten?"

She bit her lip, eyes briefly meeting mine before she looked away again. I clenched my jaw to stop myself from demanding she keep her eyes on me.

"I had a candy bar in my bag," she mumbled.

"You ate a candy bar?" She'd holed up in her room all day and night with a single candy bar?

To my horror, her bottom lip started trembling and her eyes filled with tears. "I'm sorry. I don't know what to do or what the rules are. I can do better. Just tell me what to do."

I stood frozen as Sofiya curled in on herself, her shoulders shaking. Nothing in my training had prepared me for this.

"Stop crying," I snapped.

Sofiya made a tiny hiccuping sound and pursed her lips together to silence her sobs.

I ran my hand down my face. Should I call someone? My sister would know what to do. But calling someone else right now would be to admit I'd been defeated by this girl.

Clenching my jaw to keep myself from lashing out, I sat down on the edge of the bed and put my hand on her shoulder. She stiffened, and my mood soured even further. I removed my hand.

"Will you tell me what I did wrong?" she asked softly.

I furrowed my brow. "Nothing. But you need to eat. Come on."

I stood as she put her legs over the side of the mattress. She reached for her walker with shaky hands, fingers white as she clenched the handles. My scowl deepened as she tried to stand and fell back to the bed.

"What's wrong?" For once, I wished I knew how to speak... *gently* or some shit like that.

"Sorry, I'm just a little shaky." She bit her lip and took a deep breath, as if bracing for something. "Could you get my wheelchair?"

Her wheelchair was in the corner of the room. It would be easy for me to get it for her, but for some reason, I found myself leaning down and picking her up. Her front was plastered to my chest, and her arms flew around my neck, her legs cradling my hips. I knew now she could move them, but I clearly needed to understand her medical issue. For now, that could wait. One of my arms supported her waist and the other moved under her ass.

"I can really just use my chair," she said. Her breath ghosted against my neck, causing me to tighten my hold. When was the last time I'd been this close to someone? I had fucked women while touching less of their bodies.

"Am I hurting you?" I asked, voice low.

"No."

"Okay, then." I walked out of the room, taking her straight to the kitchen. I hesitated before setting her down on the island. The thought of letting her go seemed unacceptable.

I braced my arms on either side of her. "Can you sit here?"

Sofiya's eyes were wide, but she had stopped crying so I called that a win. She nodded.

"You're not going to fall off?"

The tiniest smile tugged at the corner of her lips. "I'm not going to fall off."

I just grunted and opened the fridge. The cold air wafted against me as I stared unseeingly at the shelves. I'd spent my entire childhood learning to keep a tight fist of control over myself and others. This had only intensified when I took over as Don, and it had been years since I truly felt out of control. But here, in my own fucking kitchen with a tiny girl sitting on the counter behind me, something began to unravel inside me.

"Um, do you need help?" The sweet voice behind me held an edge of laughter, and I realized I'd been staring at the inside of the fridge in stony silence for longer than appropriate.

"No."

Yes. I couldn't remember the last time I cooked something. Why wasn't there any prepared food here?

I shut the door. "I will order something. What do you want?"

"I'm not picky."

I fixed my gaze on her. "You will tell me what you want."

"Pizza?" she almost squeaked.

"Assimilating to your new Italian life?" I asked, texting Angelo to get us pies from my cousin's place.

"I like pizza." She tucked a curl of her hair behind her ear, and I followed the movement. "And I could cook sometime..." She trailed off, a stricken expression on her face as she looked away.

I thought of the cinnamon roll recipe from yesterday morning. Maybe she liked to cook, although I wasn't sure why that would make her look so upset.

"Why haven't you eaten anything?" I asked, crossing my arms.

"I didn't know if I was allowed to," she whispered.

"Why wouldn't you be allowed to?"

"You said I should stay in my room, so I just wasn't sure..."

My brain whirred as I tried to understand what she was saying. When had I told her she couldn't leave the room? The only conversation we'd had was yesterday morning...

Shit.

Fuck.

I put my phone down on the counter and stood in front of Sofiya.

"Look at me." There, my voice sounded soft enough. To my confusion, she didn't do what I said. When was the last time someone had defied me?

I gripped her chin with my thumb and forefinger and tilted her face up. Her skin was so fucking soft.

"I didn't mean that you couldn't leave your room."

"Oh."

"This is your house now. You can use whatever room you want. And if you want to cook or make cinnamon rolls, you can."

Sofiya blinked, looking tired and confused. The urge to *comfort* her overcame me. I dropped my hands and stepped back to prevent myself from doing something ridiculous.

"Sofiya," I said, a touch of exasperation in my voice, "you're married to the Don of the Italian Mafia now. That makes you queen. You can't just let people push you around."

"You want me to fight against you?" She cocked her head, and an edge of sass entered her voice. Instead of irritating me, my lip twitched as though tempted to smile. I controlled my expression just in time.

"No." Then I decided to push her a bit to see what response I would get. "You should *obey* me."

Irritation flashed over her face, and this time, I couldn't stop my amused expression. I found I didn't mind a bit of fire in my new bride. I brought my hand to my face to hide my smile, but the slight widening of her eyes told me she caught it.

I cleared my throat. "You can ask me questions, Sofiya. This might not be a real marriage, but I'm not your jailer." If we were going to convince the Family this was a real marriage, she couldn't be afraid of me.

She bit her lip and averted her gaze before nodding. An awkward silence fell over us, and I glanced at my phone, willing the pizza to arrive to save me. Sofiya fidgeted, her legs bouncing against the kitchen island. I stared at them.

"What's wrong with your legs?"

She froze at my harsh tone. "Oh, um, I have something called hypermobile Ehlers-Danlos." She dug her fingers into her thighs. I had to physically stop myself from replacing her hands with my own.

"What is that?"

"It's a connective tissue disorder, so my joints aren't super stable. My hips and knees are the worst. They can dislocate or do something called subluxing, which is like a partial dislocation. I started using the rollator a couple of years ago, but recently it hasn't been enough, and I've had to use a wheelchair."

Her voice had quieted until it was almost a whisper, her cheeks turning bright red. In our world, image was power, so it wasn't surprising that she carried shame. But I found I didn't care much that this made her vulnerable. Did it really matter when I was here to protect her?

"Is it dangerous?" I got out through gritted teeth.

"I don't think so?" It came out as a question.

"How do you not know?"

My stomach swooped when Sofiya flinched at my harsh tone.

"I've never had consistent access to medical care, so I've just had to piece things together."

I clenched my jaw, nodding for her to continue.

"I started having issues when I was little. I rolled my ankles all the time and my legs were always banged up from where I'd tripped and fallen. I had horrible growing pains, headaches, and other random symptoms. As I got older, things got worse and I had a series of bad dislocations. I finally convinced my parents I wasn't making it up. They took me to see several doctors before one finally diagnosed me, but I never saw him again after that."

Fuck. I wouldn't have been surprised if Rustik had the doctor killed just for knowing about such a weakness in his family. Sofiya and I had both grown up in top organized crime families, but it was clear our childhoods couldn't have been more different. My father had been strict with me, rarely showing affection as he prepared me to be the next Don, but I had never doubted his love. I had never doubted that everything he did was for our family's benefit. Whereas Rustik obviously didn't give a damn about his daughter.

"What's the treatment?"

"I don't think there really is any. I mean, pain medication and heating pads can help, and I think some people do physical therapy. And, of course, the mobility aids. But there's no cure or anything."

A knock at the door prevented me from responding. I pulled up the hallway camera on my phone and saw Romeo with our pizza. I opened the door just wide enough to grab it from him.

"What, you're not going to invite me inside?" he asked with an infuriating smile.

I ignored his question. "Did you get her medical records?"

His expression sobered. "I've been meaning to update you on that. Franco can't find anything."

Franco was my top hacker and had never failed to get me the information I needed. "What do you mean?"

"If she had medical records, someone destroyed them. And I mean *destroyed*. You know Franco could have found them if they were just hidden."

This had Rustik all over it. Bastard.

I gave Romeo a curt nod before shutting the door in his face.

I set the pizza down on the kitchen island and grabbed two plates. At least I knew where those were.

"We'll schedule a doctor's appointment to see what they say." I was sure there was a treatment for her disease if only she saw the right person.

"Thank you. That's... that's really nice."

My chest grew tight, and I busied myself by grabbing a few slices of pizza. "Eat your lunch. I have work to do." I started towards the door but stopped when Sofiya called my name.

"Would you be able to get my wheelchair?" she asked.

I scrubbed my hand down my face, my irritation at myself growing. First, I'd made her think she was trapped in her room, and now
I'd stranded her *on the counter*. Some fucking husband I was. This
was why I couldn't allow myself to get close to people. It left me
unfocused, scattered.

I got her wheelchair, pushing it to the kitchen island. Then I
lifted her off the counter and helped her get in.

"Do you need anything else?"

She shook her head. "You have to go?"

"Yes."

She nodded slowly. "I hope you have a good afternoon."

Her sweet words followed me as I strode to the door and
slammed it shut behind me.

Angelo gave me a nod as I got in the elevator to my office. I had
work to do, an empire to oversee, and I couldn't let anyone get in the
way of that.

11

MATTEO

I was in the middle of my squat reps when the gym door crept open. Sofiya rolled into the room, looking nervous. I hadn't seen her since I stormed out yesterday—she'd been in her room by the time I returned late in the night. This morning, she was wearing tight black leggings and a top so small it was closer to a bra. My heart rate sped up even as I set down my weights.

"Is it okay if I'm in here?" she asked. Her eyes crept down my bare chest before snapping back to my face, and I felt the inexplicable urge to lift something heavy.

I raised my chin in assent, and she gave me a little smile before going over to the dumbbell rack. I picked up my own fifty-pound weights as I watched her grab the never-before-used five-pound dumbbells. I kept an eye on her as I continued with my reps, the burning in my muscles forgotten as I tried to figure out what Sofiya was doing. She grasped the weights clumsily and started doing shoulder presses. I gritted my teeth at her shit form. She was going to hurt herself.

I dropped my weights again and stormed over. "What are you doing?"

Her lips parted as she tilted her head up to look at me. "Umm, lifting weights?" She looked so fucking adorable it made me irritated.

I crossed my arms. "You're doing a terrible job."

She blinked before averting her gaze. "I just want to strengthen my shoulders so I can push my chair easier."

I let my eyes wander down her arms, taking in the expanse of smooth skin, before forcing myself to look at the wheelchair she was using. I hadn't paid much attention to it before, too focused on the beautiful woman in it, but it was black and clunky. It looked too big and heavy for her.

"Is that the best wheelchair for you?" I blurted out before I could stop myself.

She froze and one of the dumbbells slipped from her hand, hitting the floor with a *thud*. I grabbed the other one before she dropped it and sat down on the weight bench so I wasn't looming over her.

"Sofiya?" I arched my brow.

She twisted her hands together before glancing at me. "Well... I just... I did something really bad."

My chest constricted. Was she going to admit to lying to me? Spying on me? The sound of two gunshots echoed through my mind.

"Tell me," I demanded through clenched teeth.

She looked back down at her hands, her shoulders hunched. "About six months ago, walking started to get really hard for me. I was still using my rollator, but my legs were weak, and I was getting these dizzy spells when I stood up. I was in a lot of pain, and I kept falling and dislocating my knee. My father refused to allow me to get a wheelchair. He said I just needed to be stronger and try harder."

My hands flexed.

"My sister and I were trying to figure out how to get one for me, but they're really expensive, and we didn't know what to do."

"What do you mean, they're expensive?"

Sofiya gave me a confused expression. "They cost a lot of money?"

"Your father is head of the Bratva. He has almost unlimited money."

"Mila and I don't, though," she said, smiling sadly.

"He didn't give you an allowance?"

She shook her head. Motherfucking bastard.

I ran my hand through my hair. "So how did you get this?" I gestured at her chair.

Sofiya buried her face in her hands. "Please don't judge me. I know I'm a horrible person, but we were getting desperate. I hadn't been able to leave my bed for weeks and Mila was panicking, so she convinced our bodyguard to help her break into a medical supply store and steal this."

I waited for her to say more, but she remained silent.

"And?"

"And what?" Sofiya responded, her voice rising. "This is a *stolen* wheelchair. It's not custom or anything, so it's not like someone was waiting for it, but it's still horrible." Her eyes snapped to mine and she reached out to touch my hand. "It's not Mila's fault. I made her do it." Her voice carried an edge of panic, as if she thought I was about to whip out my phone to report a crime.

My lips twitched. My innocent little wife.

"Let me get this straight. You're telling me you had to steal a wheelchair that clearly doesn't fit you because your father wouldn't give you money for one, and you thought I'd be most upset about the theft?"

"Stealing is wrong," Sofiya said seriously.

I gripped her chin. "You were a Bratva princess, and now you're a Mafia queen. You're surrounded by much worse criminals than wheelchair thieves."

Sofiya gave me a reluctant smile. "That's what Mila said."

"Are things better since you got it?"

"Yeah, it's been better," she said softly.

"What did your father do when he saw it?"

"Oh... he didn't know about it until the morning of the wedding."

I cocked an eyebrow.

She shrugged. "Mila and I pretty much stayed in the east wing of the second floor. We rarely saw our parents." She cleared her throat.

"He wasn't happy when he saw it, though. That's why he refused to walk me down the aisle."

A muscle ticked in my jaw.

I was a cold man. It was who I'd been created to be, who I *had* to be. But it was hard not to feel *something* when staring into Sofiya's big blue eyes.

"You need to engage your core and keep your elbows in when doing shoulder presses."

She blinked at the abrupt change in topic.

I picked up the two dumbbells and handed them to Sofiya before pushing off the bench and standing behind her. I caught her reflection in the floor-to-ceiling mirror covering the back wall of the gym. She was all light—bright hair, bright eyes—to my darkness. My eyes trailed down her body. From this position, I could enjoy all her curves—the spread of her thighs, the soft roll of her stomach, the way her hard nipples pressed against her top. My fingers itched to move, to touch, to figure out *why* she had such an effect on me.

She sat up straight, clenching the weights in her hands, and lifted them above her head.

"Keep your elbows soft," I said, tracing my fingers up her arms. She inhaled sharply and the sound went straight to my cock.

Fuck. I had to stop. This was dangerous. Purposeless. The whole reason I'd agreed to this marriage was for the alliance. The arrangement was supposed to be simple, straightforward. I *never* mixed business with pleasure.

I cleared my throat. "I have work to do."

Sofiya's quiet "thank you" followed me out of the gym.

Her sweet scent haunted me into the shower.

The image of her tits in that tiny top played in front of my eyes as I stroked my cock.

I came embarrassingly fast.

I needed to get laid, or I was in serious danger of making a move on my wife.

12

SOFIYA

M y cheeks were wet with tears when I woke, and nausea churned in my stomach. I took a deep breath and wiped my face. The room was completely dark—no sunlight streamed through the crack in the curtains—telling me it was the middle of the night.

I'd gone to bed early, unable to stand the oppressive loneliness of the apartment any longer. Matteo had escaped after our time together in the gym, and I hadn't seen him for the rest of the day.

I hadn't seen anyone.

I'd puttered around the apartment. Watched some TV. Tried and failed to find an interesting book to read in Matteo's library. Even my favorite romance—a well-worn book written in the eighties with a dramatic clinch cover—couldn't keep my attention. Mila and I had found a stack of romance books in the attic a couple of years back in a box belonging to our baba—our maternal grandmother. I'd left most of them with Mila, but I couldn't resist bringing this one with me. I'd tried reading some of my favorite scenes, but my attention kept wandering. Reading about love just made me feel empty right now.

By 8:30 p.m., I'd been so bored out of my mind I'd taken a long bath and then gone to sleep.

Until my nightmare woke me.

I pushed myself up to a seated position, cringing at the way my pajamas clung to my sweaty skin. There was no way I could fall back asleep now.

I was used to nightmares. I'd had them since I was a child, although they didn't happen as often when Mila slept in my bed. I'd never admitted that to my sister because I didn't want her to feel guilty if she chose to sleep in her own room. She shouldn't have to take care of me. But she'd found her way to my bed most nights. Maybe we both needed each other.

Here, in the vast, silent apartment, it seemed like my nightmares were my only consistent visitor.

I pushed myself to my feet, leaving my rollator and wheelchair behind as I slipped out of my room. Soreness was sinking into my muscles after my morning workout, but I didn't want to use a mobility aid and risk making noise.

I stood in the middle of the living room, unsure of what to do. I didn't want to be in this apartment anymore. I needed space to *breathe*.

I headed to the window leading out to the fire escape and slid it open. A rush of chilly air hit me and I grabbed a blanket off the couch before returning. I eased my way out of the window, praying all my joints stayed in place, and then my butt landed on the cold metal.

I grinned.

The fire escape landing looked over the city. Lights twinkled below me, cars still filling the streets. It made me feel less alone to know I wasn't the only one awake right now. Something about sitting on a fire escape seemed so freaking *cool*. If I had a phone, I would take a picture and send it to Mila.

After a while, curiosity got the best of me. We were on the top floor of the apartment, but metal fire escape stairs extended above me to the roof. A sense of adventure and maybe recklessness seized me. What was up there?

My knees creaked as I stood, but I ignored them. I would climb the stairs, consequences be damned. My body would just have to suck it up.

I walked slowly, careful not to trip on the blanket wrapped around me like a cloak. My smile widened when I reached the top. I *could* get on the roof. My wrists twinged as I pulled myself over a small ledge, scraping my palms against the rough concrete.

And then I was there. Standing tall above the city.

I'd expected something bare and industrial, maybe random pipes and utility equipment, but as I squinted into the darkness, I found something much more luxurious.

A few lights along the perimeter illuminated a large seating area to my left. A free-standing pergola covered a set of outdoor furniture that formed a circle around a metal firepit. To my right, there was a large, slightly raised slab. I couldn't see it clearly in the dark, but I bet it was a helicopter landing pad. I recognized it from the medical shows Mila and I used to watch.

I headed towards the seating area, letting out a small squeak of excitement when I saw string lights wrapped around the pergola. I felt around until I found the outlet and plugged them in. The glowing light made the space feel cozy and highlighted a set of wooden planters lining this side of the roof. When I peered inside them, I didn't find any plants, just dirt. It was probably too early in the year for gardening, anyway, with the city only just now yielding to spring. I dragged my fingers through the dirt. Maybe I could plant some things. Herbs for baking and cooking. Flowers for the dining room table.

When I could no longer ignore the pain in my knees, I flopped down on one of the couches. I didn't dare try to start a fire—I'd probably burn the entire building down—but as I snuggled deeper underneath my fleece blanket, I imagined being up here with Matteo with a fire going. We could make s'mores—it was one of the items on my Dream List.

I sighed, my eyes falling shut. Here, surrounded by the tall New York City buildings, the faint sounds of the street below, my list felt incredibly childish. *I* felt incredibly childish. Even though I'd grown up in the Pakhan's home, I was so freaking sheltered. Women didn't have agency in the Bratva, and my disability had made them treat me even more like a child.

Or a prisoner.

Mila's words came back to me—*you're too sweet for your own good.* I needed to grow a backbone. Be stronger. I hadn't left this apartment yet, but I knew I would, eventually. Matteo wanted a *queen,* whatever that meant. He'd definitely picked the wrong bride if he wanted someone powerful by his side. I'd spent the past few years practicing being invisible and making myself small. It made me less of a target.

But maybe it also made me less of a person.

Like I'd slowly stripped myself of all humanity.

I only ever let myself be genuine with Mila and Dimi. Those were the only moments I felt *real,* felt *strong.*

When I teased Mila about her million TV crushes.

Taking care of her when she came back drunk after sneaking out to some party.

Forcing our bodyguard, Nikolai, to watch girly rom-coms with us.

Going out to the gun range with Dimi. Feeling powerful with a weapon in my hands as I hit the target.

These days, my primary emotion was fear, but I wanted to feel *more.* This new life with Matteo, this sham marriage, wasn't what I would have chosen, but I needed to make the best of it. And that required taking inspiration from Mila's bravery.

I was lost in thought when the sound of someone clearing their voice cut through the quiet. I jolted on the couch and let out a little shriek before I saw Matteo standing before me.

"Oh, hi," I choked out. I wanted to smack myself for sounding so squeaky and breathy. *Way to be strong, Sofiya.*

The string lights illuminated Matteo's hard jaw and the way his dark, long-sleeved tee stretched across his broad chest. His sweatpants sat low on his hips, and I quickly brought my eyes back to his.

He wasn't saying anything. He just stood there, his piercing gaze fixed on me.

I fought against the urge to apologize for being up here. He had told me I was allowed to explore the apartment. He hadn't said the roof was off-limits. If he wanted to be alone, he could leave. The petty part of me said *I was here first.*

"How did you get up here?" he asked.

"I levitated." The words were out of my mouth before I could stop them. I held my breath as I waited for his response to my sarcasm, but his face remained blank. I tried to match his expression, staring him down without blinking, but I quickly caved. "I took the stairs."

"Hmm," was his only response before he sat down across from me.

My chest was bursting with relief and excitement. I was starved for company, and he was choosing to be here with *me.*

"No walker, then?"

I cocked my head. "It would be a bit hard to use on the stairs."

Matteo nodded, gazing out at the city, ice clinking in his drink in his hand. He looked deep in thought, but the silence wasn't uncomfortable. I wrapped my blanket tighter around myself and watched as he rubbed his thumb across his lips. Something sparked low in my stomach.

I didn't look away.

"Why are you up so late?" he finally asked, sipping his drink.

I chewed my lip, wondering what to tell him. "A nightmare," I finally admitted.

"Something we have in common."

I blinked, shocked that he had revealed something personal about himself. The way his fingers clenched around his drink told me he was just as surprised as I was.

"I'm sorry you have nightmares," I said, my voice almost a whisper.

He took another sip of his drink. "What are yours about?"

My mind flitted to my most recent dream. They were always the same—me, helpless and unable to move while the people I loved were harmed. I'd watched Dimi get shot, Mila sliced to pieces more times than my heart could take. No matter what I did to save them, I could never move. I was always stuck, trapped inside a frozen body that couldn't even crawl to them.

Tonight's nightmare had been the same, except this time, it was Matteo in front of me. A masked figure had dragged a knife across his bare chest as I screamed. I'd woken with his name on my lips.

"The people I care about getting hurt," I finally said. "What about you?"

I was sure he wouldn't answer, but after a few long moments, his words came, so soft I almost couldn't believe I hadn't imagined them. "The same."

We held each other's gaze and something shifted in the air between us.

The darkness wrapped around us like a blanket, cloaking us in a secret cocoon. This moment between us had an air of un-realness, as if the rays of the rising sun would wash it all away. But I wouldn't forget it—his intent gaze, the electricity between us. I would treasure this memory as the first time I didn't feel alone in my new life.

We would never be lovers. He had made that clear. But maybe we could be friends.

I shivered, and it broke the spell between us.

Matteo cleared his throat. "It's cold. You should go inside."

What would it be like for him to join me on the couch, to wrap his arms around me and warm me with his body? To feel the press of his lips against mine, but this time without an audience?

A pang of sadness squeezed my heart at the thought of what I'd never have. "We should probably both try to get some sleep."

He stood, glancing back over his shoulder at the fire escape. "I'll carry you down."

"I can manage it." I didn't know what I wanted more—to assert my ability to handle a flight of stairs or to be pressed tight against my husband's chest again.

I pushed to my feet. An icy breeze whipped across the rooftop and chills wracked my body.

"I won't have you injure yourself," Matteo said.

"I won't." I tightened my hold on the blanket and walked to the stairs. My knees ached, but I kept going.

I would show him I was capable.

I would show myself.

He didn't rush me, didn't comment on how slowly I moved. When we got to the window, he pushed it open for me. His hand brushed against my back as I clumsily crawled inside. Matteo followed, somehow looking graceful as he went through the window.

I caught a hint of his scent—leather and rain—and I fought the urge to press my face into his chest. I must be more tired than I thought.

My blanket slipped, and Matteo moved it back up my shoulder. His touch lingered, and then he inhaled sharply and turned away, heading back to his room.

13

MATTEO

I sat down on my bed, my head in my hands. I'd followed my wife up to the roof, and then I'd run away like a coward *at the sight of her bare shoulder.*

Fuck, I was such an idiot.

A phone notification from my alarm system had pulled me from my fitful sleep, showing that the window to the fire escape had been opened.

Prowling through the dark apartment to the roof had been the perfect distraction from the unceasing thoughts in my mind— thoughts of Arben and the Albanians, the health of our investments, the new soldiers entering our ranks...

But nothing could distract me from thoughts of my wife.

I stood up with a groan. I couldn't be here anymore—in this apartment, near Sofiya. I got dressed and headed downstairs to my office.

I STARED at the latest report Franco sent. He'd managed to break into the email server of Arben's underboss. The issue was that they were all encoded, and Franco hadn't been able to crack the code yet.

It struck me as odd. The Albanians had never been particularly sophisticated. Either Arben was smarter than I thought, or the Albanians were getting help from somewhere. No one had announced an alliance, but I was growing increasingly confident that they'd made one.

I tapped my pen against one of the empty coffee cups littering the side of my desk. I'd been in my office since three o'clock this morning, throwing myself into work to distract myself from thoughts of Sofiya. Had she gotten back to sleep? How often did she have nightmares? Did she have everything she needed?

I wanted to strike, attack, do something *physical*, not stare at my computer, trying to decode fucking emails until my eyes swam. Everyone coveted my position, dreamed of being the most powerful man in New York City, but none of them realized how much tedious paperwork was involved.

My head jerked up as my door flew open. Sienna burst into my office in a flash of color and flopped down in the chair opposite my desk.

I massaged my temples. I really needed to remove that chair.

"Why are you keeping your wife from me?" she whined.

"Sienna, I'm working."

"Yes, I know. You're *always* working. It's seven o'clock in the morning and here you are, wearing a suit."

The same unsettled feeling I always had around Sienna clenched my chest. My mom's struggle with infertility meant my sister and I were twelve years apart. Sienna was only eleven when our parents were murdered. Overnight, my role had transformed from older brother to parent. We had lived in hiding for two years while I worked to rebuild my empire and overthrow my uncle. I'd locked my heart away behind impenetrable barriers to become Don. Along the way, I'd lost the ability to be a brother.

Sienna was a constant reminder of my failures—my failure to save our parents, my inability to love her the way she needed.

"What do you want, Sienna?" I asked, exhaustion drenching my voice.

"I just want to meet her. We live in the same building. It'd be nice to, I don't know, be friends."

"She's not here to be your friend."

A flash of hurt crossed my sister's face, and that uncomfortable feeling in my chest intensified. When I'd agreed to this marriage, it seemed so cut-and-dried. I would stand in a ceremony, sign a piece of paper, and secure a Russian alliance. I'd forgotten that I would be marrying an actual person—a living, breathing human being I was now responsible for. I didn't like the idea of Sienna and Sofiya being friends—it was a blending of two worlds I wanted to keep separate. But it wasn't realistic to keep them apart forever. I had to accept that Sofiya was a permanent fixture in my life.

"Sorry," I muttered. "I'm still getting used to this all."

Sienna leaned forward in the chair. "What's she like? Is she nice? Is she pretty?"

"I don't know her." I wasn't about to admit that I found my wife rather... captivating.

Sienna frowned. "Come on, tell me something."

I tapped the pen against my desk again. "There's something wrong with her legs."

Her brow furrowed. "What do you mean?"

"She has this disease—Ehlers-Danlos? She uses a wheelchair or walker to get around."

"Oh." Sienna cocked her head. "Is that a problem?"

"It could make her more vulnerable. Make *us* more vulnerable."

She let out a long sigh. "There aren't enemies around every corner, Matteo."

"That's because I shield you from them," I snapped.

Sienna's face hardened, her jaw clenched as she got up and headed to the door.

"Day after tomorrow," I said through gritted teeth.

"What?" She glanced at me over her shoulder.

"Come over the day after tomorrow. You can meet her."

The smallest smile tugged at her lips, and I hoped I was forgiven.

"You deserve to be happy, you know," she said softly.

I swallowed hard, unable to look at Sienna as she slipped out of my office. Leaving me alone.

14

SOFIYA

I was sore and tired as I puttered around the kitchen. I used my rollator to keep balance, but it was hard to put any weight on my arms with how much they were hurting after yesterday's workout. I hoped the exercises would pay off in the long run, because right now, the pain was just making me irritable. I'd taken my pain meds, but I knew the pain would probably last all day... all week if I was unlucky.

Nothing I tried to alleviate my symptoms ever seemed to help. Mila had gone on a "wellness" kick a while back, convinced she could fix me if we only did the right things. We drank green coffee bean extract and meditated and did yoga. The last time I tried yoga, my knee had subluxed and I'd fallen over on top of Mila. We'd laughed so hard I'd actually peed myself, which had just made us laugh harder.

Our enforced isolation in the Pakhan's mansion the past few years had been agonizing, but there were also things about it I missed. It had been Mila and me against the world for so long, and now I was on my own.

I ate a banana from the fruit bowl while trying to figure out what to do with my day. The kitchen was fully stocked. I grinned as I decided to do some baking and cooking. Only to pass the time, of course. *Not* to secretly impress my husband with the one skill I had. I would just need to choose recipes that didn't require much upper body strength.

A knock at the door pulled my head from the pantry. I chewed my lip. Was I supposed to answer? I was still on edge in this beautiful, huge apartment, just waiting to do something wrong and get yelled at.

The person at the door knocked again. I grabbed my rollator and made my way slowly to the entrance. I peered through the peephole to see my bodyguard standing there.

"Good morning, Mrs. Rossi," Angelo said, a wide smile on his face as I opened the door.

"Good morning. And please just call me Sofiya."

"I'm not sure the Boss would like that."

I cocked my head. "But you're my bodyguard, right? So I don't know... don't I get a say?"

Angelo chuckled. His laugh was warm and deep and instantly put me at ease. "The Boss has his work cut out with you, doesn't he?" He winked at me. "Alright, *Sofiya*. As you wish." He gave a little bow with a flourish, making me snort.

"Do you want to come in?"

"No, thank you, bella. I just needed to give you this." He held out a brand new, top of the line cell phone.

My eyes widened. "Really? For me?"

"Of course. The numbers you need are already programmed in. There's me and Enzo—he has the night shift guarding the apartment. Also Romeo, the Boss's second-in-command, and Domenico, his enforcer. If you're ever in an emergency and can't get in touch with me or the Boss, you can call any of them."

The phone felt smooth and cool in my hands. "Am I allowed to call other people? Like my sister?"

"Of course."

"And... can I go on the internet and stuff?" Mila and I'd had a phone the past couple of months an old model that Nikolai had smuggled in. I'd left it with Mila and had hoped I'd find a way to contact her, but I never expected to just be *given* a phone.

His brow furrowed. "You're not a prisoner here, Sofiya." His voice was low, and he bent down so our eyes were level. "You're married to the Don. That gives you power, status. Do you understand?" He took in my bewildered expression and sighed. "I see you don't, yet, but you will. You'll get used to your position and I'm confident you'll play your role beautifully."

"Thank you," I whispered. It was one of the nicer things anyone had said to me, not that there was much competition. Although it was another cold reminder that I was just here to play a *role*.

"Do you need anything else?" Angelo asked.

I shook my head. "No, this is great, thank you. I'm going to do some baking."

His eyes were bright. "Ahh, tiramisu?"

A smile tugged at my lips. "I haven't decided yet." It was exciting to have free rein over the kitchen, a phone to look up recipes, and people who wanted to taste what I made.

"Well, I look forward to finding out," he said with a wink.

I returned to the kitchen and took a few minutes to set up my phone. Maybe I could buy a case for it. I'd seen some cute ones online.

Once it was all set up, I dialed Mila's number. We kept the phone on silent to prevent anyone finding it and punishing us, so I squeezed my eyes shut, praying she would answer.

"Hello?" Mila sounded slightly out of breath. Hearing her voice made tears spring to my eyes.

"Mila," I choked out.

"Oh my God, Sofiya! I've been waiting and hoping you would call. Are you okay? I miss you so much."

"I miss you, too," I said with a sniff. I pulled a paper towel from under the sink and wiped my tears.

"What's wrong?" Her voice was fierce and I could picture her expression, how that little line between her eyebrows appeared when she was stressed.

"I'm just happy to hear your voice. I'm totally fine, promise. I have a new phone, so we can talk whenever we want."

"Fuck, I've been driving Nikolai crazy worrying about you.

How's your husband? Is he treating you okay? Did you, you know...
do it?"

My cheeks heated. "Matteo is... I don't know, confusing?" I said,
sidestepping her question. "Not like I have much experience with
men, but he's really hard to read. I don't think he likes me very
much." I pulled out a bag of chocolate chips from the pantry. All my
father's staff raved about my chocolate chip cookies, so it felt like a
safe thing to start with. And there was a stand mixer in the kitchen,
which meant I wouldn't strain my wrist mixing the dough.

There was a beat of silence before Mila responded. "What makes
you say that? Has he hurt you?"

"No, not at all. But he said he just wants us to live as roommates.
He's gone most of the time and we have separate rooms." I wasn't
about to tell her about my idiotic misunderstanding—how I'd
cowered in my bedroom for a full day out of fear of punishment. It
was pathetic.

I also wasn't about to share how Matteo's hands had lingered on
my skin in the gym... or our middle-of-the-night roof conversation.

I could practically hear Mila's chaotic thoughts. "Do *you* want to
just be roommates?"

I pulled eggs and butter from the fridge. "I don't really have a
choice. Maybe this isn't the life I would have chosen, but it's not bad.
Matteo has been... nice." I cringed, pressing my face into my hands.

"Nice? The head of the Mafia is *nice*?"

"Okay, that's a bad word to describe him. But he hasn't said
anything cruel." I glanced at the kitchen island, remembering how
Matteo had been worried I would topple over if he let go of me as I
sat on the countertop. For a second, I'd even imagined some sort of
spark between us.

"What aren't you telling me?" Mila asked, suspicious.

"Nothing," I said too quickly. "There's nothing to tell."

"Uh huh... So, what are you doing now?"

I sighed with relief that she wasn't pushing it. "I thought I would
make some cookies. And then maybe something Italian for dinner."

"Dinner and dessert. It sounds like you're trying to impress your
husband."

I stayed silent as my cheeks burned.

"Sofiya!" Mila gasped. "You *are*. I knew it." The excitement was palpable in her voice and reminded me she was only nineteen. "I bet he's more than *nice* to you. He's too freaking hot to be your roommate."

I huffed. "He's not interested in me that way."

"You can't possibly think that I'd believe that."

"Well, I don't know what to tell you. He's been very clear." Except for when he wasn't. Like when he carried me, or looked angry hearing how my father had treated me, or sat with me on the roof.

Before Mila could say anything else and add to the confusion I was already feeling, I changed the subject. "Have you heard from Dimi?"

Mila sighed, seeing straight through my deflection, but she answered anyway. "No."

"Do you think he's okay?"

"He knows how to take care of himself," she said, but our shared anxiety was heavy on the phone. Dimi was the only member of our family who actually loved Mila and me, and I missed him.

"Do you think he's still abroad?" I asked.

"I assume so. Maybe I could ask the Pakhan—"

"No," I cut in. "Don't do that. He won't tell you anyway." Panic cut through me so viscerally I had to sit down on my rollator. I breathed through my dizziness. Our father had never hit Mila, and she didn't know he'd ever hit me. But now that I was out of the house, I was terrified he would turn his anger on her.

"Okay," Mila huffed. "I won't."

"Just... just be sure to stay out of his way, okay? And if Dimi calls, will you give him my new number and tell him to call me?"

"Of course."

Mila updated me on her life. Our father was allowing her to leave the house more often now that I wasn't there. Guilt filled me that she had been trapped in that house because of me, because of the shame my body caused my family in public.

"How's your pain been?" she asked.

"It's fine," I lied. I measured out the flour and baking soda.

"Sofiya." Mila's voice was scolding.

"Okay, it's been kind of bad. But my knees are stronger than on my wedding day. I'm using my rollator around the apartment."

"You need to get the Don to take you to the doctor. I'm sure there's better medication or something that will help you. I don't trust any of the Pakhan's doctors."

"Don't worry about me, Mila. I'm the oldest. It's *my* responsibility to protect *you*."

Mila made an irritated sound in the back of her throat. "I'll *always* worry about you because I love you, Sofiya. I wish... I wish you could let other people love you. You're so convinced you have to do everything for everyone, but the people who really love you don't need you to do or be anything for us."

Tears pricked at my eyes. "I'm not sure that's a long list of people."

"I would find that annoying if I didn't know you actually believed it. You're the most beautiful person I've ever seen. You're kind, talented, and you have this energy that draws everyone into your orbit. I think that's one of the reasons *he* hid you away. You outshine us all."

I let out a laugh. "What are you talking about? Our dear father has only ever felt contempt towards me."

"Maybe," Mila conceded. "But I think there's more to his hatred."

I rested my cheek on the cool marble counter as the two of us sat in silence.

"I miss you," I finally said.

"Miss you, too." Mila's voice was tight, like she was crying, and it made a tear streak down my cheek. My sister hardly ever cried. She used to say I had enough tears for both of us.

"You sound lighter," she whispered.

I wiped away my tears. "I feel lighter. There's a whole world outside of the east wing."

"You can start crossing things off the list."

I grinned. "Already crossed off the first thing. We flew back to New York on a *private jet*. It was so cool."

We continued talking and dreaming about our list until Mila said she had to go. The Pakhan was making her attend some lunch with the Bratva wives. I was afraid he was already thinking of marrying her off. Nothing made me feel as helpless as not being able to protect Mila from every bad thing.

"You better text and call me all the time, Sofiya. I want updates."

"I promise. You too, okay?"

"Yeah." I heard a knock on the door at her end. "Shit, Nikolai is here and I haven't gotten dressed yet. I'll have to send you a picture of the dress mom is making me wear. It's hideous."

Our mother had the worst fashion sense of anyone I'd ever met. We couldn't figure out if her outlandish outfits were some sort of statement, a small rebellion against the Pakhan, or if she legitimately thought they looked good.

"Love you. Stay safe," I said.

"Love you, too."

The quiet in the kitchen weighed on me after hanging up. I found a music app and chose a random pop playlist. Upbeat notes started playing through the speaker. Mila and I had always been careful not to make a lot of noise. It was safer to be quiet and fly under the radar. Even though the song was playing softly, it still sent a thrill of fear and excitement through me to be making noise, taking up space.

The oven timer went off, and I pulled out the first batch of cookies and sprinkled sea salt on top of them. I put the next batch in and then pulled up a browser on my phone to search for Italian recipes. I was determined to make dinner a success.

15

MATTEO

Giuseppe caught my eye the moment I entered the Star lobby. He was slightly out of breath when he met me at the private elevator. The short, stocky Star manager wore a blue and white pinstripe suit today. Absurd attire for a Made Man, as was his cheerful smile.

"Good evening, Boss."

I gave him a curt nod.

"Your usual, or something new?"

"Surprise me." I tapped my fingers against my leg, impatient as I waited for the fucking elevator. It finally dinged.

"Very good. I'll send her up right away," Giuseppe said. "And, might I say, congratulations on your new bride."

I clenched my jaw, but the doors closed, saving me from responding.

I adjusted my sleeves. I wasn't doing anything wrong. I had every right to be here, to do what I wanted. But the strange, tight feeling in my stomach didn't go away as I entered my private penthouse suite.

I poured myself a glass of whiskey and looked out at my city. The city I'd bled and killed for. Nothing could be more important than the Family. I might have thought something different when I was young, but that Matteo had been killed alongside my parents.

I turned around as the door opened and a woman entered. She was tall, her black dress highlighting her long legs, and *blonde*. I took another drink. Giuseppe usually sent up dark-haired Italian women. Was this a coincidence, or was he trying to find someone reminiscent of my wife?

Except this woman was nothing like Sofiya. Her lips were painted red, her expression confident and sultry as she approached me.

"They told me you were handsome," she said, stopping so close in front of me her large tits brushed against my chest. "But *handsome* doesn't cut it." She trailed her fingers down my jaw.

My wedding band weighed heavily on my finger.

My father had been loyal to my mamma. He always said, "The Family's life revolves around the Don. The Don's life must revolve around his wife." It was no secret he'd allowed mamma to have an opinion on Family matters. She'd even convinced him to ban the skin trade in our territory, an unpopular decision that lost a few of the capos a significant amount of money. My father had also come down hard on husbands who abused their wives. His actions stirred dissension in the ranks from men who felt they had the right to do whatever they liked in their own homes. My uncle capitalized on that dissension to gain power.

My father's devotion to my mamma had destroyed them.

Almost destroyed Sienna and me.

But now, faced with the opportunity to cheat on my wife, I found I couldn't do it. My cock was soft, my skin crawling with discomfort. My father was the man I'd admired most in the world—steady, strong, and loving in his own way. It was a hard thing for a Made Man to raise his heir because he could never fully be a father—he would always be Don to his firstborn child. But my papà had been a husband first, above all else.

My hand reached out and seized the woman's wrist, pulling her off me. "Get out." My voice was harsh, but I didn't care. Her touch felt like poison.

Her eyes widened. "Sir?"

I released her wrist, and she stumbled back a few steps. "Get. Out," I repeated.

She turned on her heel and rushed out of the room.

My hands shook as I downed the last of the liquor. What the fuck was wrong with me? Why did I have some misplaced sense of loyalty to a woman I didn't even know just because I had signed a sheet of paper?

"Fuck!"

I threw the empty glass against the wall, bits of glass and liquid shattering against the floor. I needed something to distract me, to make me feel in control again, and I wouldn't find it in this room.

I picked up my phone and dialed.

"Romeo, meet me outside the Star. We're going hunting."

————

It was dark as Romeo turned the car off the road, concealing it behind a copse of trees.

He cut the engine, and the night's silence surrounded us.

"This is one of the more stupid ideas you've had recently," he said.

I pulled another gun from under the seat and checked that it was loaded. "Stay here, then." The cool night air cleared my head as I got out of the car. This was what I needed. Focus. Control.

Romeo followed me, muttering curses as he cocked his gun. "You know, some men buy sports cars when they're having mid-life crises. Or a private jet. They don't go ambushing Albanian safe houses for the thrill of it."

"I already own a private jet." I set off towards the small house ahead, a lone light in the window the only thing illuminating the way.

"Oh, he's practicing his comedy routine now," Romeo huffed.

"If anyone else spoke to me like that, I would have killed them by now."

"Yes, but if I were anyone else, I'd be tucked away in bed with a sexy woman on my cock. Not here on some suicide mission."

I rolled my eyes. "It's only a suicide mission if you fuck things up."

We kept to the shadows as we approached the house, but there was no one outside and no visible alarms. Franco's intel suggested this previously abandoned house was being used by the Albanians— probably low-level soldiers. They were unimportant, unlikely to have any helpful intel. Arben might be an idiot, but even he wasn't stupid enough to tell foot soldiers his plans. That didn't matter, though. I wasn't here for intel.

I shot the door's lock and burst inside, Romeo covering my back.

Three men sat in a dingy living room—two in just their under- wear and the third in a dirty t-shirt. They shouted, reaching for the weapons they had carelessly set to the side, but I was too fast. I shot the first in the hand, the second in the knee, and the third in the shoulder. Screams of pain filled the air.

"Why the fuck did I even need to be here if you were going to get all of them yourself?" Romeo grumbled.

"Go clear the rest of the house if you need something to do. You three, on the ground."

The Albanians collapsed to the floor, their cries filling the air. I quickly removed their weapons. They were obviously young and unskilled. Of no real value to me.

I would still enjoy toying with them.

"Matteo." Romeo's voice carried from one of the back rooms. "Ci sono due ragazze qui."

Shit.

Romeo returned to the living room, fury in his eyes. "Fucking scum." He spat at the soldiers and trained his gun on them. His eyes flashed to mine. "Back room to the left."

I braced myself for what I would find as I pushed the door open, revealing two girls huddled together in the corner. They looked young—seventeen? Eighteen? Their clothes were torn, and long, dirty hair fell in their faces. Metal cuffs were attached to their too- thin ankles.

A dirty mattress was the only thing in the room.

Only a lifetime of practice hiding my emotions allowed me to keep my face blank as white-hot rage churned in my stomach. My uncle had revived the skin trade for the brief time he was in power, but I had put a stop to it when I ascended as Don. This was a direct affront to my authority.

I crouched down, hoping it made me less intimidating. The girls' blank stares met mine.

"What are your names?"

They said nothing.

"I'm going to get you to safety," I murmured. "How did you get here?"

The girls looked at each other as if silently communicating before turning back to me. One said something in a hoarse whisper, but she wasn't speaking English.

"What was that?"

The girl repeated her words, her voice growing stronger. It sounded like she was speaking an Eastern European language—Russian, possibly? For a second I considered calling Sofiya to see if she understood them, but I dismissed the idea. I needed to keep her separate from my life, my work. She might seem sweet and innocent, but I couldn't trust her.

"I'll be back," I said, even though they couldn't understand me, and returned to the living room.

"Well, this gives us some clarity on why the scum is trying to take control of my city," I said to Romeo.

"You think it's more than the two girls?"

"Yes." I'd suspected Arben was dealing in the skin trade in Boston, but I'd stayed out of it—that was Irish territory. But now he was not only trying to take control of my city, he was preparing to bring in the skin trade.

My eyes flicked to the three pathetic men huddling together on the ground in front of us. "Congratulations, you three just became much more useful to me." I took a step closer, savoring their whimpers of pain as their injuries pooled blood on the gray carpet.

"Who are you?" the man I'd shot in the knee spat out.

I crouched down in front of him. "I'm the one you'll beg for death before the end."

His face contorted with rage before he lashed out with a shout. A glint of steel came towards me. I jumped out of the way but wasn't fast enough to fully avoid his knife slashing a shallow gash in my side. I barely felt it as blood dripped down my skin.

In one swift movement, I kicked the man's injured knee, flipped him over on his stomach, and pinned him to the floor by putting the knife through his hand. I brushed off my jacket as I stood and looked at the two other soldiers. "Are either of you feeling brave? Now's your chance to attack."

Their eyes were wide as they shook their heads, stealing covert glances at their wailing companion.

"Good choice. Where is the handcuff key?"

One soldier gestured at the man I'd stabbed. I reached into his pocket and fished out the key, making sure to grind his knee against the floor as I did.

I turned to Romeo. "Call Domenico and Stefano to take out the trash."

I returned to the back room, crouching down again as I approached the girls. The younger of the two had tears streaking down her cheeks, but both remained silent.

I held out the key and pointed at the cuffs. "I'm going to remove these." They seemed to understand what I meant, staying still as I unlocked them. I let out a loud curse when I saw the bloody red marks left by the metal, causing them both to jump.

I reached deep inside myself to the soft voice I used to use with Sienna when she was younger, when I would wake in the middle of the night to find her curled up on the floor by my bed after having a bad dream. Before my heart had turned cold.

"I'm not going to hurt you." I reached a hand out to them, but they cowered away. "That's okay. I won't touch you. Can you walk?"

I slowly stood and took a few steps to the door, gesturing at the girls to follow me. Their movements were stiff as they got up. They clutched each other's hands and hobbled to the door.

"They're on their way," Romeo said when the three of us entered the living room. He'd hogtied the Albanian soldiers on the ground and bound their bullet wounds to prevent them from bleeding out. I wanted them alive for a good, long time. "Where do you want to bring the girls?"

I ran my hand through my hair and gestured for the two girls to sit down at the lopsided kitchen table. I got them water and found packages of crackers in one of the cupboards.

"I'll ask Aria if they can stay in a clinic room until we figure shit out."

Aria was my cousin on my mother's side. She'd been allowed to attend medical school, rare for Family daughters even now, and she ran our private clinic.

The girls gulped the water, their eyes fixed on their three captors. I leaned against the kitchen countertop, wondering what Sofiya was doing. I felt the strange urge to check on her, but it was late. She was probably in bed, and Enzo was stationed at the apartment, anyway.

Romeo pulled out his phone and nodded at me. "They're here."

I gestured for the girls to follow. Romeo went out the front first, signaling when all was clear. Stefano and Domenico passed us on the way to the car, and I lifted my chin at them. I would meet them in the basement after we got the girls to the clinic.

The Albanians could wait. They would wish I'd stayed away by the end.

16

SOFIYA

I'd struggled to sleep all night, which was why I was certain my husband never came home. I'd waited for him with dinner. I was used to eating around seven but knew Italians ate late, so I'd stayed hopeful. Once it neared eleven p.m., I gave up and ate while sitting on the kitchen floor, blasting music as loud as my phone would play it.

If I was living essentially alone, I might as well break all the etiquette rules that had been drilled into me.

Pain in my hips had kept me tossing and turning, desperate to find a tolerable position. That, in combination with my loneliness and lack of sleep, had put me in a bad mood. I'd gotten out of bed in the early morning hours, needing something to distract myself. I used the fancy Italian espresso machine to make myself a latte and then explored the rest of the apartment, doing my best to navigate with my bulky wheelchair.

The apartment had an air of neglect, like no one really lived here, but it was beautiful—the perfect combination of historic architecture and modern touches. Large windows let the light of the rising sun stream in, and it bounced off the white walls and dark wood moulding. It was nothing like the cold opulence of the Pakhan's house that was meant to intimidate everyone who entered with its extravagance and wealth. There were four bedrooms—I hadn't dared enter Matteo's, but the rest were decorated simply and tastefully— five bathrooms, a formal dining room, living room, and the gym, but my favorite room by far was the library.

That's where I decided to curl up—on the large leather couch in the library with my second cup of coffee as I watched the sunrise. Floor-to-ceiling shelves were filled with books—beautiful, old tomes that looked gorgeous but made for terrible reading. Actually, there didn't seem to be anything actually remotely readable in the whole house. Figured. I guessed the Don didn't find much time for leisure. Well, except for his nights. Seemed like he found *plenty* of time for extracurriculars then. Images of Matteo with other women had flitted in and out of my dreams until I was on the verge of screaming.

I leaned my head back on the couch with a groan. It didn't do any good to dwell on life's disappointments.

I was trying to get the energy to get up and make breakfast when there was a knock at the front door. At first I wasn't sure I'd heard correctly, but there it was again. For a moment, my heart lurched when I thought Matteo was back, but then I realized he wouldn't have knocked.

I got in my chair, breathing in sharply at the pain shooting through my joints, and rolled out of the library. "Come in!" I called out once I got to the living room.

The door slowly opened, revealing a smiling Angelo. "Morning, bella. I was worried I might have woken you."

I pasted on a smile. I was happy to see him, but I couldn't quite stop my heart from aching at my husband's absence.

"I've been up for a while." I grimaced when I realized I was still in my pajamas—hot pink silk pajamas with flamingos on them, cour- tesy of my mother.

"Those are cute," Angelo said.

I shook my head and rolled into the kitchen. "Can I get you something? Coffee? I was trying to decide what to make for breakfast."

"I wouldn't say no to some coffee. What did you end up making last night?"

"Chocolate chip cookies and mushroom risotto." Angelo's face lit up, and I eyed him with amusement. "There are leftovers if you want some?"

"I would love some." He rubbed his hands together.

I laughed. "At eight in the morning? Rather odd breakfast." The risotto had been delicious, but eating alone just wasn't the same.

I started maneuvering over to the fridge, but Angelo quickly stopped me. "Let me get it," he said, eyeing my wheelchair with concern.

"I can move around the kitchen, Angelo."

"But why do that when I'm here, Mrs. Rossi?"

I wrinkled my nose. I wasn't sure how long it would take to get used to being called *Mrs.*

I grabbed a granola bar as Angelo pulled out a container of leftover risotto from the fridge.

"So, are you just here to raid the fridge?"

Angelo grinned at my prickly tone as he popped the container in the microwave. "Nah, that's just a bonus. I'm here to collect you. The Boss scheduled an appointment for you."

"Oh," I said, sitting up straighter. "Is he coming back?"

Angelo's expression fell slightly, and he busied himself with the leftovers. "No, he's busy."

A lump formed in my throat, and I felt beyond stupid. Why should I be upset that my husband stayed out all night, obviously in the company of more interesting women? He had made it clear we were nothing to each other. I just thought he might wait at least a week after our wedding to take a mistress.

I'd allowed myself to be too hopeful, to believe in romantic fairytales.

I swallowed hard before speaking and was pleased at how steady my voice sounded. "What kind of appointment?"

"A wheelchair assessment to be fitted for a custom chair."

My lips parted, and all I could do was blink as Angelo took the risotto out of the microwave and took an appreciative bite.

"This is really good," he said. "I don't even like mushrooms."

"Thank you. But what do you mean, a wheelchair appointment? I already have a wheelchair."

"Boss said it's no good," Angelo said with a shrug. "He was very insistent that you deserve the best."

My eyes were unfocused as I tried to make sense of my enigma of a husband—cold, harsh, and absent at one moment, and seemingly caring in the next.

"He's a confusing man," I finally said.

"Not half as confusing as women," Angelo said.

I rolled my eyes, scooting forward so I could snag the container of cookies out of his hand. "Sexists don't get cookies."

"No, bella, please don't be like that." His lip jutted out in a pout. It was such a ridiculous expression on this huge, muscular man that I couldn't stop myself from laughing.

He snagged the box out of my hand and shoved a cookie in his mouth before I could say anything.

"You're ridiculous," I said. "I have to go get ready. Don't eat all the cookies."

———

I FIDGETED with the car radio, turning it to a pop station. Mila and I had spent hours passing the time listening to the radio when we were little, before we smuggled a TV into our wing of the house.

"So, Angelo, tell me more about yourself."

We were stuck in Manhattan morning traffic.

"Uhh, what do you want to know?"

"I don't know. Anything. What do you like to do in your free time?"

The light changed and we inched forward again.

"Don't have many hobbies... I do attend a weekly poker night, if that counts."

"Oh, that's cool. I've never played. Mila and I had a deck of cards, but we didn't know any games, so we just made stuff up. Are you any good?"

A smile tugged at Angelo's lips. "I'm decent."

"Can you teach me? Maybe I can come to poker night if I get good."

He shot me an incredulous look. "A woman at poker night?" But at my scowl, he cleared his throat and quickly added, "It's about time."

I crossed my arms.

"Don't take the cookies away from me," he pleaded.

"Maybe I'll forgive you if you teach me how to play." I knew Angelo was only here with me because that's what the Boss commanded, but I was desperate for a friend. "Oh!" I said. "Do you have a gun range you use to practice?"

Angelo took a right turn and parallel parked on a busy street in Midtown. "Why?"

"I thought maybe we could go sometime. I need to keep my skills sharp."

My bodyguard snorted. "Your skills?"

"What, you don't believe me? My brother taught me to shoot when I was younger."

Dimitri had taught both Mila and me, determined that we needed to know how to protect ourselves. Every time he visited, we all snuck out together to the range to practice shooting. Mila had been hopeless, but Dimi said I was a natural. The last time he visited, six months ago, we'd practiced shooting from my chair.

"Not sure the Boss will go for that," Angelo said before getting out of the car. I waited for him to get my chair out of the back. I grimaced as I got out, my hips aching. I needed to use a heating pad once we got back.

Angelo pulled open a large glass door with the sign *Mobility Center* on it, and I rolled into a massive space lined with all sorts of wheelchairs.

"You must be Mrs. Rossi." A middle-aged woman with pretty eyes and a brown ponytail came out from behind the reception desk to greet us. "I'm Sandra. I'm the physical therapist doing your eval today." She shook my hand and then Angelo's before introducing us to two male staff members working with her—Ted and DiMarco.

"We'll do a variety of assessments today to make sure we have everything we need to get you your custom chair, which is a good thing because I can already see that one is not right for you," Sandra said with a calculating expression. "The assessment will include asking you a lot of questions about your mobility and what your goals are, and we'll do some physical evaluations as well. Any questions before we begin?"

I shook my head, still a little dazed that this was happening. It was disorienting to be around people who wanted me to be comfortable in a wheelchair after having to hide the severity of my disability for so long.

And the fact that my husband had set up the appointment made it all the sweeter.

17

MATTEO

I rested my forehead against the shower wall as water ran down my body. Sofiya and Angelo had already left for her appointment by the time I returned. Probably a good thing since my clothes had been drenched in blood.

I watched the last of it wash away down the drain.

One of the Albanian soldiers had died while being transported back to the basement, and the other two had known nothing useful. Their screams still rang in my ears. At least I'd made them suffer for what they'd done to those girls, but we weren't any closer to finding out if the Albanians had more women and where they might be.

I got dressed and headed to the kitchen. I needed to get something to eat and then go to the office to start figuring this shit out. The sooner Arben was destroyed, the better.

A box of cookies rested on the counter and I snagged one. I took a big bite and stopped in my tracks. It was the best fucking cookie I'd ever had. I usually stayed away from desserts—it didn't seem right for the Mafia Don to eat sweets—but I needed to figure out where these were from.

I made myself a coffee and then grabbed another cookie to take with me to the office.

I MANAGED to stay in my office for forty-three minutes.

Forty-three minutes of agony, my skin itching knowing that Sofiya wasn't upstairs. There was no reason for me to feel this way, no reason for me to feel the need to know she was safe and waiting for me.

Sienna told me I couldn't trap my wife in the apartment.

I didn't want to trap her. I just needed her to be within reach at all times.

I slipped into the wheelchair store unnoticed by all except Angelo, who lifted his chin at me as I moved behind a tall display.

I didn't want Sofiya to know I was here. *I* wasn't even sure why I was here. The only reason I'd even set up this appointment was because as the Don's wife, Sofiya needed the best. And I would always give her the best.

I ignored the satisfaction I felt at the thought of providing for her.

Three employees were running Sofiya through a series of muscle tests, using machines to evaluate her strength. Even when she struggled, she kept a smile on her face and joked with the staff. After a while, they moved her into a wheelchair. Sofiya focused intently on what the man in front of her was saying while a woman adjusted the height of the back of the chair. I bristled at how close the man was but forced myself to stay back as Sofiya wheeled back and forth. This wheelchair looked much lighter and better fitting than her stolen one. The back and bottom were cushioned, and my wife's smile was fucking radiant as she spun around. My chest ached as I watched her.

"Is that seat comfortable? Is it putting too much pressure anywhere?" the woman asked.

Sofiya wiggled a bit. "No, it feels really good."

"Excellent. As you probably know, with Ehlers-Danlos, you typically have thinner, softer skin that's easier to bruise and tear. We want to make sure you have a cushioned seat and backrest to keep you comfortable and avoid any pressure wounds."

"How does it feel on your shoulders?" the male employee asked.

"There's still a strain when I'm pushing, but it's not as bad as the other one," Sofiya answered.

"This one is significantly lighter than your old one, so it should be much better for daily use," the woman said.

Sofiya bit her lip. "How often should I use it?"

"Oh, well, you can use it whenever you need to," the woman responded.

"But... I don't know, maybe I'm relying on it too much? Like I'll get too dependent on it if I use it all the time instead of my rollator."

I bristled at the anxiety in her voice and braced myself for how the staff would answer. If they said anything to upset her...

"No, not at all," the woman reassured her. "You probably have times where your symptoms flare more and then subside for a while. Has that been your experience?"

Sofiya nodded.

"You can always use your rollator when you need to, but I would encourage you to use your chair most of the time. Not only can it help when you're in pain or experiencing dislocations, but it can also prevent them. You very well may be able to walk around if you push yourself, but you'll pay for it afterward."

Sofiya's shoulders softened as if a weight had been lifted. I hadn't realized she was concerned about this, but I should have after hearing how her father treated her when he found out about the wheelchair.

But she lived with me now, not him.

"There's also physical therapy you can do to strengthen your muscles and help stabilize your joints," the man said as he pulled some sort of device out of a box. "It will help keep you strong."

"What's that?" Sofiya asked.

"You said one of your goals is to go outside more often. This is a motorized power assist. It attaches to the back axle of your chair. It powers your chair and helps you go off-road, up hills, and just save your arms and shoulders."

Sofiya's eyes lit up. "How fast can it go?"

Angelo snorted. "You planning on doing some racing?"

Sofiya blushed. "Maybe. It could be fun."

The more I watched her, the more I wanted to be close to her. For the first time in years, I felt the urge to take time off from work. I imagined spending the day with Sofiya, going outside with her how she wanted. But I had responsibilities. I needed to find an interpreter for the girls to see what information they had, and check in with Franco, who was monitoring the Albanians' movements.

But for some reason, my feet weren't moving to the door.

"Alright, we are all set, Sofiya," the woman said. "We will give your husband a call once your chair is ready."

"Thanks so much for everything. It was really nice to meet you all." She gave them a wave as she followed Angelo towards the entrance. I met them at the door, getting some enjoyment at how Sofiya's eyes widened at seeing me.

"Matteo," she breathed. "What are you doing here?"

"I need you to come help me with something." I'd made up my mind. Sofiya would come with me to the clinic to see if she could get information from the two girls. If Sofiya could translate, everything would be much more efficient.

She raised her eyebrows. "Oh, okay."

I scanned the street as we left the store, more on edge than usual.

"Thank you for setting up this appointment." Sofiya's voice was soft and sweet.

I cleared my throat. "Were you satisfied with the result?"

"Yeah, the new chair should be amazing." She bit her lip. "I forgot to ask how long it will take to come in, though."

"It will be ready in a week," I said.

"Wait, a week? I thought it took forever to get a custom wheel-chair made."

Angelo snorted. "You don't get it yet, do you? You're married to the Don. Normal rules don't apply."

A pretty blush spread across her cheeks, and I felt like puffing up my chest.

I tossed Angelo my keys. "Follow us to the clinic."

"Yes, Boss."

Sofiya took my offered arm to get into the armored BMW, and it filled me with a sense of satisfaction.

Almost as much satisfaction as seeing her in my passenger seat when I rounded the car, her cheeks pink and lips smiling like she was happy to be with me.

18

SOFIYA

"Did you say we're going to a clinic?" I asked a silent Matteo as he wove in and out of traffic. The radio was off and I wasn't brave enough to turn it on.

"Yes."

I didn't know whether to laugh or scream at his short response.

"Are you being charged by the word? Because I was under the impression you'd be able to afford some sort of unlimited speaking plan."

Matteo glanced at me, brow furrowed. "What?"

"That probably cost you another ten cents," I muttered.

I didn't know why I was being so bratty, why I cared so much about talking to this man, about him *liking* me. I could blame it on the pain—the wheelchair assessment had pushed my already hurting body—but if I was honest, it was the thought of spending the rest of my life in a cold, loveless marriage that was too much to bear.

Matteo cleared his throat. "Last night, Romeo and I went to an Albanian safe house. We found two young women there, and we suspect they've been trafficked. But they don't speak English. It sounded like they were speaking Russian, so I was wondering if you could see if you understand them."

I stared at him, lips parted. Not only had he spoken *multiple* sentences in a row, he was letting me get involved in Mafia business. But the part I was most fixated on was the fact that last night, he was at a safe house, not with a mistress. The ugly, jealous monster that had been festering inside of me pumped its fist in victory.

"That paragraph probably cost me a dollar fifty," Matteo said.

"Oh. My. God." Did he just make a joke? I stared at my husband in befuddled awe, which only grew as his expression transformed into a smirk. It was *almost* a real smile.

"We're here," he said, pulling into an underground garage.

"Are we close to the apartment?"

He nodded. "Just around the block. The clinic used to be in my building until Dr. Amato insisted on a larger space."

"Are the girls injured? Is that why you brought them here?"

"Stay there," Matteo said, getting out of the car and rounding to my side. He opened the passenger door and leaned in toward me. His large frame caged me in, imposing but somehow comforting.

"They had some injuries, yes, but mainly, we needed a safe place for them."

I stared up at him, this cold, hard Don who showed more kindness than I'd ever expected of a Made Man. My eyes traced over his strong, square jaw, his lips that looked impossibly soft, the little scar under his eye I'd never noticed. We seemed to both be taking the other in, and then our eyes met. Were we leaning in closer to each other? A little spark fluttered in my stomach, and I looked back at his lips. Would he kiss me? Our kiss at the ceremony had been too brief, and I wanted another.

Matteo straightened abruptly. "I'll get your chair."

My heart sank and I squeezed my eyes shut for a second before opening them again. I was being stupid.

I eased my way out of the car, forcing myself to breathe slowly as pain shot through me. Everything hurt. I wished I could lie down with a heating pad and my meds and sleep until the pain went away, but there were more important things to do right now.

And it's not like the pain ever fully went away, anyway.

I sat down heavily, wishing I had my new cushioned chair already. And then a wave of resentment hit me all at once. Resentment that I needed a wheelchair at all. Why couldn't I just be normal?

I went to push, but Matteo beat me to it, grabbing the wheelchair handles and propelling me forward.

"Oh, umm, wait," I said, twisting around. "Can you not do that?"

"Do what?"

"Push my chair. I don't really like people touching it." I braced myself for his anger, or at least his frustration, but he just released the handles.

"But you're tired," he said.

I cocked my head. "How do you know that?"

He crossed his arms. "I know everything." He sounded so grumpy I couldn't stop myself from smiling.

"Right..."

"So, if you're tired, why can't I push you?"

I didn't have much experience with anyone touching my chair when I was in it, but then, most of my wheelchair experience was puttering around Mila and mine's little private island in the Pakhan's mansion. I'd never had to push myself for any distance like I had the past few days, and my shoulders were paying for it.

I chewed my lip. As frustrated as I was about having a wheelchair, it was an extension of my body. Having someone else control my movements made me anxious, although it wasn't like Matteo couldn't overpower me in half a second anyway, if he wanted to.

"I guess it would be okay. If you *ask* first." I must have had a death wish, but I did get some enjoyment at seeing Matteo's eye twitch. Even if it was the last thing I ever saw.

He huffed and ran his hand through his hair. "And here I thought you were so meek and quiet. A Don doesn't ask permission, Sofiya."

I turned my chair to face him. "I didn't realize there was a handbook for Dons. Is there a copy in your library?"

Just then, a car parked up beside us and Angelo got out. I met his gaze. "Did you know Dons have a handbook?"

He grinned. "What's that?"

"Sofiya's decided to be a nuisance," Matteo said, but there was no bite in his voice.

"As she should be," Angelo said. His expression immediately sobered when Matteo glared at him.

I rolled my eyes. "Oh come on, he's not *that* scary."

Matteo just gave me an exasperated look. "I will warn you before I touch your chair. That's the best I can do." Then he turned to my bodyguard. "You're not to push her in the wheelchair without asking her permission."

Angelo looked down at me and nodded seriously. A warm fuzziness filled my chest.

"Let's fucking get going. I'm going to push you now."

I snorted but sat back as my husband moved me to the elevator. Having him at my back was strangely comforting.

The elevator took us up two floors and opened onto a large lobby. I had expected it to be white and sterile with fluorescent lights, but instead, there were warm wood floors and soft, glowing lamps.

A beautiful woman who looked to be in her forties with dark brown hair, olive skin, and a stern expression walked quickly to meet us. "About time, Boss," she said, crossing her arms. Then she looked down at me. "I'm Dr. Aria Amato, and you must be Sofiya. You are far too lovely to be stuck with this one."

"I thought you were in a hurry," Matteo huffed.

I raised my eyebrows, looking between the two of them with a grin. "You two sound like siblings."

"I've known him all my life. Haven't been able to get rid of him yet," Dr. Amato said, but a smile teased at her mouth.

"I buy you a whole fucking clinic and then have to listen to this?"

"That's right," she responded. Her eyes were warm when she looked at me. "I appreciate you coming, Sofiya. I'm not entirely sure the girls speak Russian. I've tried to use a translation app, but they've been pretty unresponsive. That could be due to the trauma, though. I've gathered their names are Anastasia and Kateryna. I examined them when they arrived. They had some cuts and bruises, but the worst was the sexual trauma."

My heart lurched and I blinked quickly to keep from crying. I felt so inadequate. What could I do to help these girls? But this wasn't about me or my sadness. They deserved someone to listen to them, so I would do whatever I could.

"They're obviously scared and untrusting," she continued. "So I really hope you can understand them and that they'll speak to you. If they have a home to go back to, we'll get them there. If not, we'll get them somewhere safe."

"And get information about who took them and what they saw," Matteo added gruffly.

Dr. Amato shot him a disapproving look before turning back to me. "I'll go see if they're alright with seeing you."

I waited outside the door while Dr. Amato went in.

Matteo moved close to my side. "You alright to do this?" he asked.

I looked up at him with a frown. "Yes, I'm fine. Are you okay?"

He scoffed. "I'm always okay."

I just hummed. He seemed tense, but I had no idea why.

Dr. Amato came out of the room. "I think they understood enough to agree for you to talk with them. Why don't we give it a try?"

I gave her a smile as she opened the door for me. The room had a large window and two beds, but both girls were huddled together on one of them. They looked to be close to mine and Mila's ages, and just like the two of us, one was blonde and the other had brown hair. Their eyes were wide and haunted as they took me in.

"Hello, my name is Sofiya," I said softly in Russian. "Can you understand me?"

The girls held each other closer but said nothing.

"I'm sure it doesn't feel that way, but I promise you're safe here. I will make sure of it." It wasn't really in my power to make that promise, but I trusted Dr. Amato.

I awkwardly looked around the room, unsure of what to do. I moved over to a small bookcase and picked up a romance book I recognized.

"This is a really good one," I said, feeling stupid as I held it up to them. "I don't know if there's a Russian translation, but I can look into it if you want. That is, if you like reading romance. My sister and I got pretty hooked on it." I put the book back on the shelf. "Or maybe Russian isn't the right language?"

"We understand you," the brown-haired girl whispered. She cleared her throat and then repeated it, her voice stronger this time.

My heart sped up. "It's so nice to meet you," I said. "Are you sisters?"

They both nodded. "I'm Katya and this is Stasya," the brown-haired girl said. Her sister curled into her side, resting her head on her shoulder. My chest clenched as I thought of Mila and me doing the same.

"Did someone hurt you?" Stasya asked, speaking for the first time.

I cocked my head to the side. "What do you mean?"

She gestured to my wheelchair.

"Oh no. I was born with..." I trailed off, realizing I didn't know how to translate Ehlers-Danlos. "Well, a medical condition that makes it hard for me to walk sometimes."

She nodded, her shoulders relaxing slightly at my answer. "Do you know the men who brought us here?" she asked.

I nodded. "One of them is my husband, Matteo." Saying *husband* out loud made it feel more real.

"He gave us candy because I said I liked chocolate," she said softly. She pulled out a large paper bag from behind her and tipped it to show me—it was absolutely bulging with candy bars. "Do you want one?"

I was about to refuse, but then my stomach growled. Breakfast felt like ages ago. "I'd love one, thank you." I wheeled forward so I could grab my favorite chocolate caramel bar.

I hummed as I took a bite. "How old are you two?"

"I'm nineteen," Katya said. "Stasya is seventeen."

I swallowed hard and pinched my thigh to keep from crying. "Could you tell me what happened to you?" When the two of them stayed silent, I added, "Please, I only want to help."

Katya stroked her sister's hair. I was sure they would refuse to talk to me. I was a stranger. They had no reason to trust me. But then Katya started speaking.

"There was a man back home." She blinked quickly, and Stasya clenched her hand tight. "He said he could get us jobs in America. Our parents died a few years ago, and we didn't have a lot of opportunities in our town. So we said yes. He brought us to Boston."

I cocked my head. Her Russian sounded accented. "You're not from Russia, are you?"

Katya shook her head. "Ukraine."

I smiled and switched languages. "My grandmother on my mother's side was Ukrainian." My baba had lived with us when I was little. She'd died before I turned six, but I only had happy memories of her.

The girls relaxed at hearing their native language, and I even got a little smile from Stasya.

"What happened when you got to Boston?" I asked.

"We were put in a cramped apartment with three other women, and all our documents were taken. We worked cleaning homes at night. I'm not sure how long we were there... a few weeks? A month? And then one night, as we were getting ready to leave for our cleaning job, a group of masked men came into the apartment. They put us in the back of a van. We spent a few days going to different warehouses and homes until... until three men took us to a house."

I couldn't stop my tears from coming as she told me what they'd endured in that house for two days before Matteo found them.

All three of us were crying now, but the tears felt right. How else could we express the suffering they'd been through?

"I'm sorry. I'm so, so sorry." My words weren't enough, but then, nothing would ever be enough.

The three of us sat in silence for a while. "Do you want to go back to Ukraine?" I finally asked. "Or we could try to find you another place to stay?"

"There's nothing back there for us," Stasya whispered. "But there's nothing here for us either."

I leaned forward and grasped each of their hands. "We'll find a place where you belong, I promise. In the meantime, you can stay here. And I'll come visit."

We lapsed into silence again. Katya offered me another candy bar and I took it. We ate quietly, all lost in our own thoughts. The girls looked exhausted, so after a few minutes, I put the empty candy wrappers in my pocket, said my goodbyes, and slipped out into the hall. Matteo, Angelo, and Dr. Amato were all waiting. To my horror, a sob slipped through my lips.

Dr. Amato put a hand on my shoulder. "Let's go to my office and talk." Once we were situated in her large office, she handed me a box of tissues and I told them what I'd learned.

"They didn't see who took them from the apartment in Boston?" Matteo asked.

I shook my head. "They just said masked men. They didn't see anyone's faces until they were in the house where you found them. And those men..." I broke off with a sob. "Sorry, sorry," I mumbled, wiping my tears.

"You've done a wonderful job, Sofiya," Dr. Amato said kindly. "And we'll find a safe place for them. Don't worry."

I sniffled and gave her a shaky smile. I stole a glance at Matteo, wondering if he was angry I was crying. But his expression was unreadable.

"We need to find who took them," Matteo said.

"I know what you're thinking," Dr. Amato responded. "But don't jump to conclusions yet."

I didn't know what she meant, but he just grunted.

She turned her gaze to me. "Matteo said it's been a long time since you've seen a doctor for your EDS. Why don't you come in tomorrow? I can examine you and you can talk with the girls again if you want."

"Tomorrow won't work," Matteo said. "Sienna's insisted on coming over."

"Day after, then. I'll be sure to have plenty of embarrassing stories prepared," she said with a wink.

"No fucking respect," Matteo muttered.

Angelo held out a small trash can for me to throw my used tissues into. I kept a few clean ones for the tears that might still come. I felt so fragile. Seeing Katya and Stasya clinging to each other made my heart ache for Mila. I'd texted her throughout the day, but she hadn't answered.

"Come on, let's go home," Matteo said, his voice uncharacteristically gentle. "And I will push you."

I was too tired to argue. I sat tensely in my chair as we returned to the car, every bone and muscle in my body screaming in pain, and my heart along with it.

"What did Dr. Amato mean when she said she knew what you were thinking?" I asked once we were back in the apartment.

Matteo's jaw clenched and he stared out the living room window. "The Irish are in Boston."

I didn't know much about the Irish Mob. Occasionally they would be mentioned at some Bratva dinner party, but not often.

"You think they're involved with sex trafficking?"

Matteo sighed and scrubbed his hand down his face. "I don't know. Their boss, Ronan Finnegan, and I have always had a sort of unspoken agreement. But if he's teaming up with the Albanians..." He trailed off. "I need to get to the office. You should get some rest."

"Okay," I murmured.

He headed to the door, but turned back before leaving. "You did well today, Sofiya. Thank you."

A smile tugged at my lips as he shut the door behind him. I let out a deep breath, and the pervasive knot in my stomach loosened.

19

MATTEO

Sienna burst into the apartment in a vibrant swirl of energy.
"Where is she? You can't hide her away anymore!"

I rubbed my hand down my face. It was only eight in the morning and I was exhausted.

"Haven't seen her this morning," I said with a shrug.

"What do you mean you haven't seen her? Did she go somewhere?"

"What? No."

"Then, didn't you wake up next to her?"

Shit.

If we were going to convince people this was a real marriage, I needed to be more careful. But this was Sienna, and she was sure to find out eventually. I took a sip of my coffee. It was black and bitter and made me crave something sweet.

"Matteo," she hissed, voice full of reproach. "What's going on?"

"This marriage is about the alliance. You know that."

"But..." Sienna was, for once, at a loss for words. "You are being nice to her, right?"

"What's that supposed to mean?" I snapped.

A noise down the hall stopped her from responding. Sofiya entered the kitchen using her walker.

"Oh my gosh, it's so good to meet you, Sofiya," Sienna gushed. "My brother has been keeping you all to himself."

Sofiya blinked and furrowed her brow as she looked between my sister and me, as if trying to understand how we could possibly be related. Sienna and I shared the same dark hair, dark eyes, and olive skin, but the resemblance stopped there. Sienna was friendly and extroverted and everything else I wasn't.

Sofiya's voice went soft as she tucked a piece of hair behind her ear. "It's nice to meet you."

"Here, come sit down. Do you want coffee?" Sienna asked.

"That'd be great, thanks." Sofiya sat down on one of the kitchen stools, but her movements were stiff, jerky. There were dark shadows under her eyes. Was she in pain?

Sienna poured her a large cup of coffee. "Cream? Sugar?"

"Both, please."

"I'm so mad I missed the wedding," Sienna huffed. "Matteo didn't think it was safe for me to go. Tell me all about it! Wait, I have to see your ring."

She reached out and grasped Sofiya's hand, but her smile faded as she took in the plain gold band. Her disapproving gaze landed on me. "Where's the engagement ring?"

"We weren't engaged," I said, finishing the last of my coffee. It was true, but as Sofiya gently removed her hand from my sister's grasp, her smile falling, an uncomfortable tightness settled in my chest. I glanced down at my plain gold band. I hadn't given the rings a moment of thought. Romeo was the one who'd reminded me I needed to get them in the first place.

"I like it," Sofiya said softly.

Sienna scowled at me again before turning towards my wife. "I came over to see if you wanted to go shopping."

"I have work to do," I said gruffly.

Sienna just rolled her eyes. "I wasn't inviting *you*, brother. As if you've ever gone shopping in your life. I want to go with my new sister-in-law."

Sofiya blushed and looked at me as if asking permission. I had the sudden urge to run my thumb along her lower lip, to feel the softness of her pink skin. I broke eye contact and gripped the countertop.

"You will take guards and be back by lunch," I said, turning away from the two women.

"We'll be back by dinner," Sienna called after me. My jaw clenched, but I kept walking, tearing the front door open.

Angelo stood at attention in the hall.

"They're going shopping," I growled. "Anything happens to them, it's on you."

"Yes, Boss."

I huffed as I headed to the office, unsure why I was so unsettled.

20

SOFIYA

My eyes were wide as Matteo stormed out of the apartment. Had I done something to upset him? After how we left things yesterday, I'd been hopeful about things going forward. But now, the uncomfortable feeling in my stomach was back. Whenever my father got mad, it always meant worse things later.

"These Mafia men are so dramatic," Sienna said, spinning back towards me. "And they say women are the emotional ones." She was smiling, completely unconcerned with her brother's behavior.

"It seemed like he didn't want us to go?" I asked hesitantly.

"As if Matteo's going to stop us." She winked and handed me the cup of coffee. "We should start by getting something for breakfast. There's a cute bakery next to my favorite shops."

"That sounds lovely."

I desperately wanted Sienna to like me. My loneliness surrounded me like a thick blanket. I'd cried all night, thinking about what Katya and Stasya had gone through, and missing Mila. I'd tried to call her, but her phone was off.

"Excellent," Sienna said, clapping her hands. "We're going to have the best day."

Her excitement was infectious. I smiled and took a sip of my coffee. "Just give me a minute to grab my stuff."

I moved off the kitchen stool, my legs screaming in pain. I crept back to my room and sat down heavily on my unmade bed. I hadn't had the energy to make it this morning. I eyed my wheelchair. I should take it today. My knee was subluxing, my joints were aching, and I felt lightheaded. But it would be such an inconvenience to Sienna to lug it around.

And I was embarrassed.

I couldn't hide the wheelchair from Matteo and his men, but I didn't want to be out in public with it.

I mustered up the energy to get up from the bed. I grabbed my purse, phone, medication, and the thirty dollars Mila had given me before the wedding. I'd refused to take it, but she had slipped it into my purse when I wasn't looking.

It had been years since I went shopping. Once I started using mobility aids, the Pakhan forbade me from leaving the house. He said it was because his enemies would target me, but I knew it was really an effort to hide his dark shame—the head of the Bratva with a disabled daughter. Matteo didn't seem to have the same reservations about me being seen in public, although maybe that was why he'd been angry at the idea of Sienna and me going out. I clenched my jaw as a wave of overwhelming emotion washed over me. The urge to make myself small, to hide away, was strong. I had to be stronger.

I put my things in my bag. Thirty dollars wouldn't go far, but I was just excited to get to leave the apartment and get to know Sienna. And if I could buy a new shirt or phone case or something, that would be a bonus.

Sienna smiled when I returned to the kitchen. "All set?"

"Yep." I clung to my rollator, resting as much of my weight on it as I could without aggravating my wrists.

"Before we go, is there anything specific you need? Or that would be helpful to you?"

My chest grew tight at her concern, and especially the way she asked, as if it were no big deal. "Not really, but I appreciate it." The tension in my shoulders eased, and the smile on my face felt more real as I followed Sienna to the door.

"You would look so cute in this!"

I turned towards Sienna, who was holding up a sparkly silver dress. We were in the dressing room of an absurdly fancy department store on Fifth Ave. Angelo had directed three other guards to sweep the store before we entered, and within moments, the entire top floor had been cleared and personal shoppers were bustling around us, bringing armful after armful of clothing with price tags that made me want to throw up.

"Sofiya? What do you think?"

I blinked and forced a smile onto my face. I loved the dress. Somehow Sienna had nailed my style in seconds, although it was more revealing than anything I'd ever worn. I used to have a whole wardrobe of luxury clothing, but I hadn't had an excuse to dress up in years. It wasn't that I missed attending my father's Bratva cocktail parties, but being kept in the house was dehumanizing. Anyway, I'd gained too much weight to fit into any of my old clothes, so I hadn't even brought them with me. All I'd worn recently was leggings and sweatshirts.

"It's really pretty," I said, chewing my lip.

Sienna grabbed another handful of dresses from a nearby rack and brought them over to me. "Try them on."

My cheeks heated as I tried to figure out how to explain that I couldn't afford to buy a single sock in this store. Before I could find the words, the clothes were draped over my rollator and Sienna was holding the changing room door open for me. When the door shut behind me, I put my face in my hands.

Fuck.

I wanted Sienna to like me. I hadn't had anyone to talk to in ages besides Mila and Nikolai, and I was out of practice. Would she be embarrassed to be around me if she found out I didn't have any money?

I ran my finger along the sparkly dress material. It was light and gauzy, with a long skirt and high slit. Unable to resist the temptation,

I pulled off my clothes and managed to get the dress on, using the sofa in the dressing room to stand as I adjusted the dress. My breath caught as I saw my reflection. The soft light in the room bounced off the fabric, casting sparkles on the tall mirrors. The top of the dress accentuated my boobs and then flowed out over my hips, covering my new stomach rolls.

I'd never worn something so pretty.

I sat down on the seat of my rollator, but instead of feeling awkward and frumpy, a high slit parted to reveal my thigh, making me feel almost *sexy*. My EDS made my skin especially sensitive, but this dress fabric was silky soft and didn't cause irritation.

"Sofiya, are you dressed? Can I see?" Sienna's excited voice floated through the door. I unlatched it and moved out of the room.

Sienna's lips parted with a gasp. "Oh my God, you look like a literal angel. Fuck, I have a great eye. So that's a definite yes. You love it, right?"

I blushed. "I do, it's so pretty, but—"

Sienna looked around. "Let me see if we can get them to hem it. Unless you want to find heels with it?"

"I don't know that I could wear heels," I said.

"That's what I figured," she said with a smile.

Sienna pulled one of the store workers over, and I silently panicked as they talked about alterations. I couldn't let them alter a dress I wouldn't be able to afford in a million years.

"Alright, just go ahead and try on the next outfit and they'll take that dress for alterations," Sienna said, turning back to me. Her bright smile fell when she took in my panicked expression. "What's wrong?"

"I just..." I caught Angelo's eye over Sienna's shoulder. The bodyguard looked concerned.

"Let's come over here," Sienna said, gesturing to a seating area. We sat down and she took my hand. "What's going on?"

I took a deep breath. "Well, I really just wanted to come shopping to get to know you. I didn't really expect to get anything for myself."

Sienna's brow furrowed. "Why not?"

I shrugged, trying to feign a nonchalance I didn't feel. "I don't really need anything."

"Honey, let me tell you, you *need* this dress."

The corner of my lips tugged into a smile. I looked around to make sure no one else could hear. "I just... I can't afford it."

Sienna's face fell.

"It's totally fine," I rushed to say. "I'm happy to watch you try things on and get to know you."

"Sofiya, you're married to my brother." She spoke the words slowly.

I cocked my head, confused. I'd never had any sort of allowance from the Pakhan, and Matteo hadn't said anything different.

Sienna huffed. "Has he not given you a credit card?" At my silence, she swore. "For fuck's sake. Men are impossible." She pulled out her phone.

"What are you doing?" I asked quickly.

"Texting Matteo, the idiot."

"Wait, no, don't do that." Sienna must have heard the panic in my voice because she looked up from the phone, lips parted. "I don't want him to be mad."

Sienna slowly put down her phone. "Has something happened between the two of you?"

"What do you mean?"

Sienna glanced over at Angelo before leaning in and lowering her voice. "He hasn't hurt you or anything, right? Because if he has, I will kill him."

She looked so serious, so intense. Would she truly defend me against her brother? The head of the Family?

"No, he hasn't done anything like that."

Sienna relaxed, a soft smile teasing at her lips. "Good. He's not like that, Sofiya. He protects the ones close to him, I promise. But we can wait to address the credit card issue if it makes you nervous. I'll just pay for today." She already had her finger held up to ward off my protests. "No, I insist. I'll buy you things whether you want me to or not, so you might as well choose what you want."

Before I could say anything, Sienna waved one of the store assistants into the dressing room and instructed her to measure for the proper dress alterations.

21

SOFIYA

"Are you alright, principessa?" Angelo asked quietly as we made our way into the restaurant where we were eating lunch. It was a cute Italian cafe with ivy on the walls and fresh flowers on every table. Sienna said it was run by someone in the Family.

"I'm fine." My voice was hoarse, and I wished I could lie down. The car was already filled with bags—most of them containing clothes for me—and I was terrified of Matteo's reaction. Would he be angry Sienna had paid for them? There was a selection of stunning formal dresses, but also more casual clothing, including two bags of lingerie Sienna had insisted on. She refused my argument that there was no use in me having them, saying that I deserved to feel beautiful.

Angelo rested a gentle hand on my shoulder. "We're going home after this." He cocked an eyebrow as if daring me to argue, but I just gave him a small nod. I didn't want to disappoint Sienna by cutting our day short, but I also refused to embarrass her by collapsing inside a luxury clothing store.

I sat down across from her at a table in a quiet corner, my rollator off to the side. There was a large window beside us, and one of our guards was stationed outside it while Angelo stayed inside, close enough to protect us but far enough away to be out of earshot.

"I would say let's get menus, but the chef, Edoardo, will just bring us whatever he wants," Sienna said, smiling as she rolled her eyes. "It's always amazing, though."

"That sounds great."

Not a moment later, a smiling, silver-haired man wearing a chef's uniform appeared at our table, clapping his hand.

"Ahh, carina," he said to Sienna. "It's been too long." Then he turned to me and gave a little bow. "Mrs. Rossi, it is an honor to cook for the new wife of our Don." He took my hand and kissed it, and my cheeks heated as I greeted him. He reminded me of a kindly grandfather.

"Do you have any allergies?" he asked, and I shook my head. "Excellent. Prepare to have the best meal of your life." He gave my hand one more kiss and then bounded away.

"He's always like that," Sienna said with a laugh. "Always so happy and filled with energy."

"Definitely not what I would expect from a man in the Family," I said.

"Edoardo is unique like that." Sienna sighed. "I wish all Made Men were more like him."

"Bratva men, too."

A waiter came and placed focaccia and olive oil on the table, along with two orange cocktails.

"Aperol Spritz," Sienna said, lifting her glass in a toast. "To Made Women, far superior to Made Men."

I clinked my glass against hers and took a sip. The drink was fruity and sweet.

"Sienna, can I ask how old you are?" I hoped it wasn't a rude question, but she seemed so much younger than Matteo.

"I'm twenty-six," she said with a smile. "Not quite old enough yet to be embarrassed to answer that question."

I grinned. "That's a big gap."

Sienna took another sip of her drink. "My mom struggled to get pregnant, which is why there's twelve years between us."

"That's funny. My brother is twelve years older than me." At her confused expression, I added, "He's my half-brother. My father's first wife passed away. Dimitri lives abroad, so I don't see him much, but I love whenever I get to. It seems like you and Matteo are close."

Sienna fidgeted with her napkin and shrugged. "Not as close as we used to be when we were younger. He... he changed after our parents were murdered."

"I'm sorry they died," I said softly.

"Thanks," Sienna responded, smiling sadly. "I miss them a lot, and I miss the brother I had before."

My heart ached for her, and for what this life stole from all of us.

"What were they like?"

"Oh, they were amazing. They were both so excited to finally have another child that they spoiled me so much. My mamma was my favorite person. She was so bright and vibrant, always doing a project around the house and redecorating. My papà would pretend to be annoyed by it, but he couldn't refuse her anything. He was so gentle with me. He would sometimes even join me in my room and have tea parties with me. Can you imagine the Don sitting on the floor with a little pink teacup?" She sniffed and wiped her eyes with her napkin. I reached out and took her hand, giving it a squeeze.

"Papà was always softer with me than he was with Matteo. He said Matteo needed to be prepared to be Don. But we all loved each other. Papà loved my mom so much. It almost makes me glad they both died, because I couldn't imagine them living without the other." She took a sip of water and cleared her throat. "It made me certain I would never settle for less in marriage. I'm practically a spinster in Mafia years, but I can't settle. I made Matteo promise he would never force me to marry."

I wished I'd had the same life, the same certainty that love was waiting for me. "How did he change after they died?"

Sienna looked out the window and I worried that I had overstepped. Before I could apologize, she spoke. "He feels guilty, like he should have been able to save them. After they died, we went into hiding for two years while he planned the overthrow of our uncle. We were together, but it was like he wasn't there anymore. He thinks the only way to be a good Don is to cut himself off from his feelings."

I hated the pain they experienced and how lonely they had been in all of it. I couldn't imagine what it would be like to not have Mila to lean on.

"Anyway, that's enough depressing conversation." Sienna smiled brightly. "Tell me about your family."

"Oh…" I hesitated, not sure what to share. I wasn't sure anyone in the Bratva had a happy family. "There's not much to tell. Our family is pretty small—just my parents and Mila and Dimi. I was close to my grandma, my mom's mom, but she died when I was young." I took a bite of bread to buy myself some time. I finally settled on saying, "I'm not close to my parents," cringing internally at the understatement of the century. "But Mila and I are best friends."

"I love that. How old is she?"

"Nineteen."

"Aww, so young. She needs to come visit. There's far too much masculine energy in our building. We need more girls so we can over-power them."

I laughed at her disgruntled expression. "Overpower them?"

"With our feminine energy," she said with a wink.

"I would love for her to visit. I miss her a lot." Now it was time for me to get choked up. I took a long drink of my water.

"Well, that's one of the perks of owning a private jet. We'll have to get a visit planned soon."

I wasn't sure the Pakhan would let her come visit, but maybe the alliance with Matteo would make him more agreeable. If I could get Matteo to ask him.

The heaviness of our conversation dissipated as Sienna talked about the renovations she was doing in her apartment. She showed me pictures of her design ideas, asking my opinion and telling me I would have to come see it in person.

I tried to focus on the conversation, on this first chance to make a real friend, but my body was on the verge of collapse. I was relieved when lunch was over and Angelo said we had to return.

When we got back to the apartment building, Sienna invited me to her place, but I was holding back tears from the pain shooting through my joints. I made my excuses, waving at her when she got off on her floor, and headed to the penthouse.

22

SOFIYA

P ain woke me in the middle of the night. My ankles, knees, and hips screamed at me, and my head was splitting. I whimpered as I threw my arm across my face, cursing myself for using my rollator instead of my wheelchair while shopping. I had been stupid and vain, but Sienna was so perfect and beautiful. After spending the day with her, I couldn't imagine she'd judge me for using a wheelchair, but it was impossible to know that when I first met someone.

I was paying for my decision now.

I grabbed my phone, squinting against the bright screen light, and groaned when I saw it was two a.m. I needed my meds and heating pad, but that meant getting out of bed. I almost started crying when I realized I'd left my heating pad in a kitchen drawer. I'd been using it earlier this evening and, for some inexplicable reason, thought I should keep it out there.

I didn't know how many minutes passed before I got up the courage to sit up. I wiped away a few tears as the movement exacerbated the pain in my joints. My rollator was by the bed, but I'd left my wheelchair against the wall. Ever since being measured for my new chair, my old one felt even bulkier and more uncomfortable.

"God, you're so stupid," I said to myself.

Well, there was nothing to it. I reached out and grabbed the rollator, pushing up to a standing position. I couldn't stop myself from crying out, my vision going spotty from the pain. I took a halting step, another whimper slipping through my lips. My wheelchair was a few feet away, but it felt like a yawning chasm.

"Stop being a baby. Just keep walking."

Sweat dripped down my back at the exertion as I took another step. My knee felt like it was on the verge of dislocating, but before I could decide if I should try to sit on the floor and scoot to my chair, my ankle gave out and I crashed to the ground. My rollator flew forward, hitting the wheelchair with a metal clang so loud I could feel it reverberate through my bones.

I didn't have the energy to get up, so I curled up on the floor, tears streaking down my face. I was being a baby, but I'd always had Mila with me during bad flare-ups, and I missed her desperately.

My bedroom door crashed open and I cried out. I twisted my head to see who it was. The light from the hallway illuminated a large male figure. My heart pounded in fear until I realized it was Matteo.

He flipped on the overhead light, and I shut my eyes as the brightness sent a dagger through my head.

"What the fuck is happening?" he growled.

I should have apologized for waking him up, for making so much noise, but I knew if I opened my mouth, all that would come out was a sob. So I clenched my teeth and silently willed him to leave me.

"Shit. Did you fall?"

I cracked my eyes open to find Matteo crouched over me. He must have come home sometime after I went to bed because I hadn't seen him since this morning. His chest was bare and covered in tattoos, although my vision was too blurry to make out what they were. His pair of dark sweatpants hung low on his hips.

"Sofiya," he said, his voice stern, "did you fall down?"

My lower lip trembled, but I managed to whisper out a "yes."

"Okay, let's get you back in bed." Strong arms surrounded me as he lifted me off the floor and gently laid me on the mattress.

My face burned with embarrassment at him finding me like this. "I'm sorry," I croaked. God, this was not the way to get my husband to like me.

"What were you doing?"

"I was trying to get my heating pad and meds."

He brushed my hair from my face in a move that was surprisingly gentle. "Where are they?"

"Meds are in the bathroom and the heating pad is in the kitchen. The drawer by the fridge."

He nodded before glancing at the lamp by the bedside table. He turned it on and headed for the door, flipping the overhead light off as he went. My eyelids fluttered closed in relief at the softer light.

It wasn't long before he was back, supplies in hand. He stayed silent as he set a glass of water on the nightstand and plugged in the heating pad. I winced as I sat up, and Matteo quickly moved to help me, arranging a few pillows behind my back.

"Thank you," I said, my voice hoarse as I took the medication bag.

He just grunted.

I took my pain meds and a muscle relaxer before setting the bag down. "I should be fine now." I glanced up at my silent husband. "You can go back to bed. I'm sorry again for being a nuisance."

He crossed his arms across his muscular chest. He practically glowed in the warm light, and I felt the urge to trace my fingers down his skin. I quickly averted my eyes before I embarrassed myself further. Why did he have to be so freaking attractive?

"Why did you fall?"

I chewed my lip. "I was stupid and left my wheelchair too far away. My joints are hurting and my ankle just gave out while I was trying to get to it."

Matteo glanced at the few feet between my chair and the bed. "You're in pain?"

I must have imagined the strain in his voice. This didn't seem like the right time to tell him I was pretty much always in some level of pain, so I just nodded.

"What else helps?"

I blinked. "Oh, um, I don't know." At his stern expression, I huffed. "A hot bath with Epsom salts can sometimes help."

"Okay."

I raised an eyebrow. "Right. Okay. So anyway, sorry to disrupt your night. I'll see you tomorrow?"

Matteo pinned me with another unimpressed look before turning around and striding into the bathroom. My confusion built when I heard the water running. Was he really running me a bath?

He stormed back into the room, dropping an armful of bath products on the mattress in front of me.

"I don't know what Epsom salts are. Will any of these work?"

There were colorful bath bombs and oils in beautiful, expensive-looking containers.

"Are you sure I should use them?" I glanced up at my husband. "They look fancy."

Matteo rolled his eyes. "Choose one, Sofiya." He looked and sounded irritated, but I cocked my head as I observed him and wondered if there was a chance I was reading him wrong. He could have easily left me alone, but he was still here... as if he cared about me.

I picked up a small floral and gold container of bath salts. "This should work," I said, handing it to him.

He nodded and then, before I knew what was happening, I was back in his arms. I let out a squeak and clutched at his shoulders.

"As if I would drop you," he huffed, stepping into the bathroom.

"A little warning would be nice," I snapped back.

He just sat me down on top of the vanity, his arms caging me in on either side. "Can you sit here? Or will you fall?"

I scowled at him. "I'm not going to fall."

He smoothed his finger across my forehead. "Whatever you say."

My lips parted as he turned to the almost-full tub to put in the bath salts. I could have sworn I saw the corner of his lips twitch as if he was *teasing* me. I didn't understand my husband at all. He was so cold and closed-off, but in my short time here, he had already been kinder to me than most of the people in my life. Who, besides my sister, would ever care for me like this?

He turned off the tap and then spun around to face me. "Alright. Arms up."

"What?"

"Do you have a habit of getting in the bath clothed?"

"But you're in here," I said indignantly.

"Indeed, I am. Arms up, Sofiya." He stepped between my legs, his fingers teasing the bottom of the oversized shirt I was wearing.

I crossed my arms. "You can't see me naked."

He huffed, running his hand through his hair, which was falling messily in his face. There was the hint of a five o'clock shadow lining his jaw.

"You are my wife and I'm your husband. You're in pain, so I'm going to fix it."

"You said we were just roommates," I bit back. I would never have dared talk back to my father like this, and I wasn't sure why I was doing it now when Matteo was trying to take care of me. But the idea of him seeing me naked, at my most vulnerable, when I wasn't sure he even *liked* me, was too much to handle.

He just met my gaze with a stern, silent scowl. How was I supposed to understand any of this if he wouldn't use actual words?

A wave of overwhelm washed over me, and I couldn't stop myself from leaning forward and resting my head on his chest. I was so tired and my meds hadn't kicked in yet. "I'm so confused," I whispered.

Matteo's arms wrapped around me, and he pulled me closer.

"Come on, tesoro. I don't like seeing you in pain."

The tenderness in his voice made a lump rise in my throat. I lifted my arms above my head as tears streaked down my cheeks. He slowly pulled it off, keeping his eyes fixed on my face.

My cheeks burned, waiting for his judgement, but he just cupped my cheeks and wiped away my tears. My breasts pillowed against his chest as he maneuvered me enough to pull off my sleep shorts and underwear. And then I was sitting completely naked in front of my husband for the first time.

This was not a flattering position. My belly rolls were evident, my thighs were spread against the counter, and I hadn't shaved... anything. The last time I'd shaved was the morning of my wedding day. After his whole "roommate" talk, I didn't see the point of keeping it up. But now he was staring at me like... well, I wasn't sure.

His face was so freaking stoic all the time. Did he find me ugly? Attractive? Was he thinking all the nasty things my mama's friends said about my body when they came to visit? His jaw clenched as he took me in, and I wished more than anything I could hide.

I jumped when he gently ran his fingers across a bruise on my leg. "What's this from?"

"I don't know. I bruise easily."

He nodded and then stepped back, pulling off his sweatpants in one swift movement. Apparently he didn't wear underwear because now he was naked in front of me. My eyes were drawn to his cock—his *hard* cock—which looked impossibly big and intimidating. When I realized I was staring, I tore my gaze away, cheeks burning.

Matteo just leaned in to press a tender kiss to my forehead. "Consider this your warning." His voice was low and sultry. Before I could decipher his words, I was back in his arms and lowered into the bath. I moaned at how good the hot water felt on my aching joints.

"Move forward," he said.

"What?"

"Sit forward."

I scooted forward and Matteo slipped in behind me. I sat stiffly as his body cradled mine. This was more physical intimacy than anything I'd ever experienced. It was simultaneously everything I craved and feared.

His breath skated across the top of my head as he wrapped his arms around me, guiding me to rest back on his chest.

"What are we doing, Matteo?"

"I'm taking care of you."

I waited to see if he would say anything else, but my confusing husband stayed silent. I took a deep breath and allowed myself to relax back into him.

"Good girl," he murmured. "Is the water helping?"

My stomach lurched. *Good girl?* A spark of arousal shot through my stomach. I wasn't sure how I could be so turned on while also being in pain.

"Sofiya?" His lips skimmed the side of my face.

"Yes, it's helping. Thank you."

"Does it get bad like that often?"

I trailed my fingers through the water. "No, but I did more walking than usual earlier today."

"You didn't take your wheelchair?" There was censure in his voice.

I shrugged my shoulders.

"Why?"

"I didn't want to be a nuisance. Or embarrass Sienna."

Matteo made a noise deep in his throat. "You have to take care of yourself. Or I'll be forced to do it for you." He traced a finger across my shoulder. "But maybe I wouldn't mind that." He spoke the last words so softly I thought I must have misheard him. I tried to turn around to see his face, but he held me fast. "Just rest, tesoro."

It was the same thing he'd called me earlier. "What does that mean?"

He stayed silent until I was sure he would refuse to answer me. "Treasure," he finally said.

A smile teased at my lips. My medication was kicking in, making me sleepy and easing the sharpest of my joint pain. I let my eyes drift closed, feeling surprisingly safe in my husband's arms.

23

MATTEO

I was pretty sure I'd stepped into some sort of alternate dimension. That was the only explanation for how I was in the bathtub with my sleeping wife.

My sleeping, *naked* wife.

Pressed against my naked body.

I'd been sitting in the living room, staring out at the city with my scotch in hand, trying to escape my nightmares, when I heard the loud noise coming from Sofiya's room. I couldn't remember the last time I'd felt such sharp panic. I'd thrown down my glass, ignoring how it shattered against the floor as I sprinted to her. My heart had pounded as I threw her door open, visions of her covered in blood flashing before my eyes. But there hadn't been any blood. Just her, curled up on the floor. But I didn't relax, *couldn't* relax, when I saw the tears on her cheeks. Sofiya had told me she often experienced joint pain, but seeing her like that... It twisted something in my chest.

I hated being helpless. I couldn't protect her from her own body. But the feel of her skin against mine soothed me. I tipped my head back, resting it on the edge of the tub. I couldn't remember ever feeling this relaxed... at least not since my parents died.

Sofiya whimpered a bit in her sleep and I pulled her close, my hand skimming along her ribs. I'd done my best to not stare at her body—I shouldn't be fucking aroused when she was in pain—but I couldn't miss her perfect breasts, tipped with pretty pink nipples, and the blonde patch of curls tempting me to her pussy. My cock was like iron against her back.

I'd done my best to keep distance between us, but with each passing day—passing *minute*—Sofiya twisted me further and further around her finger.

The realization hit me like a ton of bricks: I wanted my wife.

It was physical attraction, nothing more, but maybe I should stop resisting. We were stuck with each other, and eventually I would need an heir. Would she be interested in having a physical relationship with me? I hadn't missed how her eyes trailed down my bare chest when she thought I wasn't looking.

For now, though, I was content to hold her in my arms.

After a while, the water cooled. I needed to get her into bed.

"Sofiya?" I squeezed her gently, trying to wake her. But she just made a disgruntled little noise and curled further into me.

I managed to get us both out of the tub, and she woke up enough to help me dry her off. Then she was back in my arms. I carried her back to bed and reluctantly covered her naked body with the blanket. I stared down at her, relieved to see her relaxed expression. I hoped she wasn't in pain anymore.

I should leave her and go to my own bed. She wasn't supposed to be anything to me. Just a player on the chessboard in this game Rustik and I were playing with the Albanians. But for some inexplicable reason, I didn't want to leave her.

My body moved of its own accord, lying down beside my wife. Maybe I would stay for just a few minutes to make sure she didn't wake up and need something. It would be very inconvenient if she woke me again with a loud crash. It was logical to stay.

I wasn't sure what logic made me pull her against my chest and wrap my arms around her, but when she let out a contented sigh, the knot that had been in my chest all night eased completely.

24

SOFIYA

I woke softly, as if floating on a cloud, from the best night's sleep of my life. I kept my eyes closed and snuggled deeper into my ridiculously comfortable bed. Then something behind me shifted— no, *someone*. Memories of last night flooded back. They were hazy, caught in a fog of sleepiness and pain, but the way Matteo held me in the bath was too perfect for even my dreams to manufacture.

His arms were still wrapped tight around me, his knee pressed between my legs. It was just the right position to take stress off my hips, like my very own body pillow.

I kept my breathing as quiet and steady as possible, unwilling to disturb him. Would he go back to keeping a cold distance, or was this the start of us connecting like a real husband and wife?

I felt it the moment he woke. He stiffened behind me and quickly rolled away. I closed my eyes, disappointment washing through me like a tidal wave.

"Morning," I said as I pushed myself to a seated position against the headboard. Matteo was already getting out of bed.

"Are you feeling better?" he asked, keeping his back to me.

"A lot better than last night, yeah. Thanks for helping me." I wanted to say more, wanted to say how much his care meant to me, but the words stuck in my throat. He was already at the door like he couldn't get away from me fast enough.

He opened the bedroom door and paused. "Use your wheelchair today." Then he left, shutting the door loudly behind him.

I got ready slowly, trying to be gentle on my body after my rough night. When I was finally dressed and made my way out to the kitchen—in my wheelchair—I spotted something on the counter. It was a black credit card with my name on it, and a note that said, "Use this. No limit."

I carefully folded the note and slipped it in my pocket alongside the credit card, a smile on my face.

25

SOFIYA

Angelo and I pulled into the apartment's underground garage. I was exhausted but encouraged after my appointment with Dr. Amato. I was finally getting the chance to learn about EDS. All the random puzzle pieces of symptoms I'd had all these years were coming together, and while it didn't fix anything, it made me feel less out of my mind.

I'd also hung out with Kat and Stasya. We'd watched a movie and I'd taught them some words in English. Their eyes were still haunted, and they were quiet and jumpy, but there were moments where it felt like we were just three girls having fun together. It made me feel like I had something to offer them... like I was useful in some way.

It was a good feeling.

Angelo rounded the car with my wheelchair and opened the door for me. As I was getting into it, another black SUV pulled up beside us. My heart started pounding as Matteo got out. His dark gaze was fixed on me as he buttoned his suit jacket and ran his thumb across his lower lip. Something fluttered in my stomach, and I wished he would sweep me into his arms and kiss me.

"Where have you been?" he asked, his voice hard as his eyes flitted to Angelo. I bit my lip. Was he upset with me?

"The clinic?" I said, hating the hint of nervousness that slipped into my voice.

Matteo swallowed. "How did it go?"

"Good."

He hesitated, almost like he wanted to push for more information, but then he turned to the man standing between him and Romeo. "This is Domenico. My enforcer."

Domenico was almost as tall as Matteo and muscular in the way I would expect from an enforcer. He stepped close to me and took my hand, leaning down to kiss it. His knuckles were covered in scars. "It's nice to meet you, Mrs. Rossi."

"Nice to meet you, too," I said, although the way he was looking at me gave me an uneasy feeling. I pulled my hand from his.

"Did you get any new intel from the girls at the clinic?" he asked.

"Oh, no, but I wasn't really trying to get, um, intel."

Domenico cracked his knuckles. "They might be hiding some information that would help us take down this sex trafficking ring. There's no limit to the depravity of these Albanians."

"I don't think they're hiding anything." I didn't like the insinuation. Stasya and Kat were victims in all of this.

Domenico's expression was full of condescension. "Perhaps."

Angelo moved to stand behind me, and I drew strength from his support.

"We have work to do," Matteo said, turning on his heel and heading to the elevator. Romeo gave me a wink before he and Domenico followed the Don.

"Fuck, I hate his pretentious ass," Angelo muttered once the elevator doors closed.

I turned to him and laughed. "Oh, yeah?"

"He's been trying to get us all to call him *Il Diavolo*." He rolled his eyes. "The Devil."

I grinned. "Mafia men are so dramatic with their little nicknames."

"Yeah, yeah. Let's get you upstairs. You hungry?"

"I could eat. Oh, Matteo gave me a credit card. I could order us something?" I chewed my lip. "Do you think he'll mind if I use it?"

Angelo snorted as we got on the elevator. "I think his bank account can survive takeout." He helped me download a food ordering app and we placed an order for burgers, fries, and milkshakes. I needed some comfort food.

I sent Mila a text checking in while Angelo went down to the lobby to grab our food. Her texts to me had been sporadic, so I didn't expect her to text back, but I still stared at the screen, willing a message to come through. I jolted when it actually started to ring. It was an unknown number, and I hesitated for a moment before picking up. Maybe Mila had gotten a new number?

"Hello?"

"Sofiya?"

"Dimi," I breathed out in relief, my brother's voice bringing tears to my eyes. I carried the weight of my worry for him every day. "Where have you been?"

There was a beat of silence before Dimitri answered. "You know I can't say. I called as soon as I could. Fuck, Sofiya. Matteo Rossi?"

"Yeah, I know. All part of the Pakhan's brilliant plan. Trade routes and all that."

"I don't know what he's playing at," he muttered. "Has Rossi hurt you?"

I hoped no one was listening in on this call. "No, he hasn't." I chewed my lip, unsure about my next question. "What do you know about him?" Somehow it felt like a betrayal of my husband to ask for information, but I needed all the help I could get to figure him out.

Dimi sighed, and I could imagine him pacing back and forth. He never could sit still. "I've never met him, and who knows how much of what they say about him is true. His uncle killed his parents and took over as Don. Rossi was only twenty-three when they were murdered, but was able to get enough men behind him that he killed his uncle and took back his city. His nickname is the Angel of Death."

I wanted to roll my eyes at yet another dramatic nickname. "Do you know anything about his personal life? I mean... do you think he'll be a good husband?"

There was a long silence. "I don't know that any of us make good husbands. But if he hurts you, I will end him, I promise you that."

I swallowed hard. "I miss you," I whispered.

Dimi sighed. "I miss you, too. Just... be careful, okay? I'm following some rumblings about sex trafficking. The skin trade isn't new, but this is focused on the Northeast. There's been some suggestions that the Italians are involved."

A cold chill spread through me. "No, that's not true. It's the Albanians."

"This is more than just the Albanians," Dimitri said. "But Rossi has traditionally been against the skin trade in New York, so you could be right. I need to look into Finnegan." He muttered that last sentence. "No matter what, you need to stay alert."

Angelo walked back in, two large paper bags in his hands.

"I will." My cheeks heated under my bodyguard's gaze, like I'd been caught doing something wrong. "Can I stay in touch with you on this number?"

"No," Dimi said. "But I'll reach out to you when I can. Stay safe." And then the line went dead.

"Who was that?" Angelo asked, putting the food down on the counter.

"My brother." There wasn't anything wrong with me talking to Dimi, but after hearing him be suspicious of my new family, I felt anxious about it, like I was hiding some secret.

Angelo pulled the food out of the bag, watching me closely. "Everything okay, principessa?"

I pasted a smile on my face. "Yeah, everything's fine. I just miss my siblings."

I wanted to ask Angelo about the trafficking, but something held me back. I'd never been allowed to ask questions about the family business, and I didn't want Matteo to turn any anger towards Dimitri. I refused to believe Matteo was participating in the skin trade—he had saved Kat and Stasya, was doing everything he could to figure out who was responsible—but there was obviously something big going on. The last thing I wanted was my new husband thinking I was trying to insert myself where I didn't belong.

"Everything's fine," I said, grabbing one of the bags from him. "Let's just eat."

Angelo tilted his head, eyes soft, but didn't press me, and I pushed the conversation out of my mind.

26

SOFIYA

I eyed the package of marijuana gummies on the coffee table in front of me. Angelo left a few hours ago, trading shifts with Enzo, who was at his post outside the front door. Night was falling, and I was in pain and bored.

Dr. Amato had given me the gummies, saying they could help with my pain, but I wasn't sure about taking them. What if I had some weird reaction?

I grabbed my phone and dialed Mila. She hadn't responded to my text so I had no expectation she would answer, so my heart leapt when I heard her voice on the other line. "Mila, where have you been? Are you okay?"

"Sorry," she said in a whisper. "I'm being watched closely so haven't been able to use the phone. I was just letting it charge before calling you."

My heart clenched at the fear in her voice. "What's going on?"

"I'm not sure," she said. "The Pakhan has been out most days, taking secret meetings. And he keeps sending me out to all these lunches and random functions with the Bratva wives. It feels like he's plotting something."

"He's always plotting." My jaw was clenched, my fingers tapping against the kitchen counter. "And mama?"

"Hiding in her room. Haven't seen her in days."

"Typical," I muttered. I guessed it was too much to ask for the woman who birthed us to take any interest in her daughter's wellbeing. "But are *you* okay? The Pakhan hasn't... hurt you, right?"

There was a beat of silence before Mila answered. "No, nothing like that. Why do you ask?"

Shit, had I given too much away? I didn't want Mila to know about our father's abuse towards me. Partly because I didn't want her to spend any more energy worrying about me than she already did, but also because I was ashamed. Deep down, it felt like there must be something wrong with me to have caused it. Even though it wasn't true, it still felt like a black mark on my soul.

"I've just been worried," I said.

"Well, I've been worried about *you*. Are you okay?"

"Yeah, things are... good?"

Mila let out an excited noise. "Oh my God, tell me everything," she whisper-shouted.

"I will, but first, Dimi just called."

"Oh, I'm glad. He got in touch with Nikolai and got your number, but I didn't get a chance to talk to him because I was at a stupid charity dinner. Is he okay?"

"Who knows," I huffed. "He told me nothing. But at least he's still alive." I wondered if I should tell Mila about the sex trafficking threat, but decided to wait. I didn't want to stress her out, and none of it should touch her out in Chicago.

"I think he likes being a man of mystery," Mila said. "Now tell me your updates."

"Well, I met Matteo's sister, Sienna. You would love her. She took me shopping for clothes."

"Ahh, send me pictures," she said. "You should see the dress mama picked out for me for yesterday's lunch."

"Neon orange?"

"Chartreuse."

"My second guess," I said dryly. And then the two of us started giggling. We'd learned long ago we had to just laugh at our mama's fashion sense.

"Okay, stop stalling and tell me about your hot husband."

My cheeks heated. I was used to telling Mila almost everything, but for some reason I didn't want to share how Matteo had taken care of me last night. There was something so sacred and tender about it.

"Matteo set up an appointment for me to get measured for a custom wheelchair. And I just got finished with a doctor's appointment for my EDS." There, that was completely true.

"Okaaay," Mila said. "I was hoping for a juicier update but Sofiya, that's amazing. He's taking care of you."

A smile tugged at my lips. "Yeah, he is."

"You deserve it," she said softly.

"Thanks. Is Nikolai treating you well?"

"He's being a perfect gentleman."

I covered my mouth to stop myself from laughing at how perturbed she sounded. Nikolai had been our guard for four years, and Mila had been crushing on him from day one. She denied it, but I thought the reason she snuck out to hook up with other guys was to make Nikolai jealous.

"Don't even start," Mila said. "What did the doctor say?"

"Mostly just stuff I know—use my mobility aids, wrap my joints, and rest. She refilled my prescriptions and... she also gave me weed gummies. She said it could help with my pain."

"No way," she gasped. "Have you tried it yet?"

"I'm nervous. What if something goes wrong?"

"What's going to go wrong? Do it! You deserve to live a little. You can cross it off the Dream List."

"Using drugs wasn't on my Dream List."

"Well it should be. It's on mine."

"Okay then, when you come visit, you can have one of my gummies."

"Do you think I will be able to visit?"

I swallowed hard. "I hope so. I really miss you."

"I miss you, too. Fuck, I have to go," her words were hurried. "Take the gummy, enjoy your high, and I'll talk to you soon. Love you."

"I love—"

The phone cut off. I stared at it, sadness rocking through me so intensely I felt sick to my stomach. I picked up one of the purple gummies and popped it in my mouth before I could second-guess myself. Maybe it would alleviate some of the physical and emotional pain I was feeling.

I changed into one of the high-end sweatpant sets Sienna had insisted on—definitely the coziest thing I'd ever worn—and flopped down on the couch. I flicked through the limited channel selection. Apparently Mafia Dons didn't have streaming subscriptions. Probably too busy being scary and murderous.

I flipped past the sports and news channels but stopped when I stumbled upon *The Godfather*. I laughed out loud. The movie was just starting. I'd never seen it, but what better way to get acclimated to my new life in the Italian Mafia?

About twenty minutes in, I started getting hungry. I grabbed my rollator and headed to the kitchen. Suddenly, every available food item sounded amazing. I peered through the pantry and my eyes landed on a bag of gourmet popcorn kernels, and inspiration struck. I grabbed the ingredients and started preparing caramel corn on the stovetop, snacking on a piece of cheese as I waited for it to be ready.

I giggled as I poured the popcorn into an extra-large bowl, balancing it on my rollator as I returned to the living room just in time to see a severed horse head on screen.

"Eww," I said, shoving caramel corn in my mouth. The room was spinning slightly, and I fell against the cushions. My body felt relaxed and heavy, and I ran my hand along a soft throw blanket on the back of the couch.

I didn't know how much time had passed when Matteo walked in the front door.

27

MATTEO

I hadn't planned to return to the apartment until Sofiya was asleep, but as each minute ticked by, I grew more and more restless.

I wasn't restless because of her. It had been a long day, that was all, and I wasn't going to let my wife keep me from my own fucking home. But nothing could have prepared me for the sight that greeted me when I entered.

Sofiya was lying down on the couch watching a movie in pale blue sweatpants, her hair tied up in a messy knot.

"Matteo!"

I frowned as I walked closer. "What is wrong with you?"

Sofiya stuck her lip out in a pout. "That was mean."

"Are you drunk?" I peered down at her. Her cheeks were flushed, pupils wide.

She shook her head before erupting in giggles as she fell back against the couch cushions. "I just took my new medicine."

What the fuck? I looked around the room until I found an opened package of edibles. "Pot?"

"Shh," she said, waving her arms. "I'm going to get in trouble."

I scrubbed my hand down my face. What was Dr. Amato thinking? "You certainly are trouble."

"Do you want to watch with me?" She pointed at the TV where *The Godfather* was playing. "Don't say no! I'll make you an offer you can't refuse," she said in a horrendous impression of Don Corleone.

"You're going to put a severed horse head in my bed?" I asked dryly.

"No, much better! I have caramel corn!" She held a large bowl of popcorn up to me, causing a handful of pieces to go flying onto the floor.

I quickly took the bowl before she spilled it all and placed it on the coffee table.

I should leave. Go to the gym. Or my room.

But somehow I found myself sitting down beside her.

"Have you seen this movie before?" Sofiya asked.

"Yes."

"Oh, of course. I bet you studied it growing up."

My scowl deepened. "Did not."

"Well, I certainly hope you're a better shot than these guys. They had to shoot that guy like a hundred times before he actually died."

"My shooting skills are fine."

"Oh, that reminds me!" She sat up with a gasp. "I asked Angelo if I could go to your shooting range. I want to keep my skills sharp. Wouldn't want to turn into one of these bozos." She waved at the TV.

"Bozo?" I raised my eyebrows. "However will they survive such an insult?"

"So can I go? Angelo said you would disapprove, but I don't see why. You could take me. It could be like a date."

The image of Sofiya holding a gun sent a weird, uncomfortable jolt through my chest. I should be the one to protect her.

I blinked at the thought that had unwittingly flashed through my mind.

"How much weed did you take?" I muttered. Fuck, she had probably never been high.

"You're *so* much hotter than Don Corleone and all his sons. None of them have hair as nice as yours." She leaned towards me and

I sat, frozen, as she ran her fingers through my hair. "Can I tell you a secret?" she whispered.

I was so stunned at her touch I could barely form words. "Yes, tesoro."

"I've been wanting to do that since I first saw you."

I ran my thumb across her cheek and then tucked a strand of hair behind her ear. "I think it's time for you to go to bed."

"But I haven't even seen if the Mafia guys win."

My lips twitched. "Don't worry, the Mafia guys win. Now, let's get you to bed. I'm sure you'll sleep well."

I got up from the couch, ready to move Sofiya's rollator closer to her, when she lifted her arms up to me. I raised an eyebrow.

"Carry me," she demanded.

"You're either really high or playing me," I grumbled. But I still leaned down and picked her up. She clung to me, running her nose along my skin.

"You should snuggle with me again," she said.

"No."

"Meanie."

"You have got to work on your insults."

I carried her into her room and laid her down on the bed.

She ran her hands down her blanket. "It's so soft."

"Yes, well, sleep this off. And I'll be talking to Dr. Amato about this."

"Dr. Amato is *sooo* nice."

"Simply delightful," I said dryly.

"Do you like her more than me? She's really pretty."

I huffed, running my hand through my hair. "Go to sleep, Sofiya."

"Wait, but do you?" she asked, lunging forward to grab my hand.

I sighed. "No, tesoro. I don't like her more than you. Now goodnight."

I forced myself out of her room, pushing down the tiny voice that told me I should have stayed.

28

SOFIYA

"How does it feel?" Angelo asked, crouching down so we were eye-level.

I bounced happily in my seat. The wheelchair people had just left after walking me through all the features of my new chair. "So good. It's so much better than my old one."

The front door opened and Romeo popped in. "I heard you had a special delivery today."

I grinned. "Yeah! Isn't it fancy? And I have the motorized assist, so I should be able to go really fast."

A mischievous look crossed his face. "How fast? We should test it out in the hallway."

"We don't have a hallway," I said, head cocked. Our elevator opened straight to the foyer with our front door.

"Mine and Sienna's floor does," Romeo said. "Let's go."

We headed to the elevator, pushing the button to take us two floors down.

"Where's Matteo?" I asked, trying to sound casual. He'd been gone when I woke this morning, which was probably a good thing since I'd lain in bed, hoping to be swallowed by a black hole after my behavior the night before. My memories of the evening were covered in a strange haze that made them feel unreal, but I was pretty sure they were, unfortunately, very real. I had *run my fingers through his hair.*

Romeo and Angelo exchanged a look. "He and Domenico had some work to do."

Well, that was mysterious. I was tempted to push for more information, but I'd long gotten used to being shut out of my father's business. Matteo had already let me in more than the Pakhan ever did, even if it was just because of my translation ability.

The elevator doors opened on a long hallway with three evenly spaced apartment doors.

"Who else lives on this floor?" I asked.

"The third unit is for Sienna's bodyguard. She keeps firing them, though, and it's driving Matteo crazy." Romeo looked very amused at the thought of Matteo's irritation.

Angelo grunted. "He should have known better than to assign Domenico to be her guard."

"Domenico?" I asked, eyebrows raised. "But he's an enforcer."

"Don't you mean *Il Diavolo*?" Romeo said with a sour expression. "Fucking ridiculous."

"Matteo thought Domenico could handle Sienna, but he underestimated his sister," Angelo said.

I grinned. I could totally picture Sienna running circles around all the Mafia men. "I don't blame her," I said. Something about Matteo's enforcer made me uncomfortable, even though he had been perfectly polite. I couldn't imagine having to spend my days with him, and was filled with relief that friendly Angelo was my guard. "Why does Matteo like him?"

Romeo rolled his eyes. "Domenico was one of the first to declare loyalty to the Don after his uncle's betrayal. He helped weed out traitors in the Family and supported Matteo in winning back his empire."

"Yeah, like a decade ago," Angelo muttered. "He's still an asshole."

I grinned at how grumpy he sounded.

"No argument there," Romeo said.

Romeo and Angelo kept bantering with each other as we made

our way to one end of the hallway, and I felt like I had friends for the first time. They probably didn't consider me a real friend since it was their job to watch me, but I didn't mind pretending.

"Alright," Romeo said, rubbing his hands together. "Let's see how fast this racecar can go."

I turned on the device and made some adjustments in the app. "Okay, now I should be able to go full speed." I took off down the hallway, keeping my right hand light on my wheel to steer. Being in a comfortable chair fitted just for me, and riding in it without straining my arms and shoulders, was pure freedom.

I laughed as I flew down the hall, reluctantly slowing down as I neared the end. I turned around to face the guys, throwing up my arms in victory. "That was so fast!"

Romeo snorted. "What was that, like four miles an hour? I could push a wheelchair faster than that. I think a turtle could outpace you."

I crossed my arms. "Only a really fast turtle."

Romeo rubbed his hands together. "I wonder if we could hack the unit so it can go faster."

Before I could get too excited about the process of racing in my wheelchair, Angelo shut us down. "The Boss will kill you."

"Worth it," Romeo said.

I returned to the other end of the hallway. "If you think you could beat me in a race, go get my old chair from upstairs."

"Oh, you're on," he said, laughing as he pressed his thumb against the elevator sensor to open the doors.

Sienna's apartment door opened and she poked her head out. Her hair was damp like she'd just gotten out of the shower and she was wearing sweatpants and a tank top, but somehow she still looked put together.

"I thought I heard something out here. What are you doing?"

"Romeo and I are going to have a wheelchair race."

Sienna grinned. "Oh, is that your new chair? So exciting! I definitely have to see this. Also, good timing because I was going to see if you wanted to order food. We could all eat together?"

"Sounds great."

While we waited for Romeo, Sienna took a turn in my chair, spinning in circles and going up and down the hall. "This is fun," she said, smiling widely as she returned it to me. Having her respond to my chair with such playfulness and excitement eased the heavy weight of the shame I'd carried around since I started using mobility aids.

Romeo returned with my old chair, and we raced up and down the hall, his shouted curses following me as I pulled ahead.

"What the fuck? This thing is terrible," he said, scowling. "I think I pulled something in my shoulder."

"Aww, big, strong Mafia man hurt himself," Sienna said. And then we both burst out laughing.

Eventually, we ordered food—sushi, which I'd never tried—and made our way into Sienna's apartment. Her home was similar to Matteo's, just smaller, and it felt cozier and more lived-in. There were collections of art on most of the walls, and all the furniture had bright pillows and blankets. I was sure Matteo didn't want me changing anything in his apartment, but maybe I could eventually ask Sienna to help me pick a few things to personalize my bedroom.

Angelo went down to the lobby to get the sushi delivery, and Romeo poured us glasses of sake. Angelo returned with an armload of bags, and I raised an eyebrow at the copious amount of trays they arranged on the dining room table.

"How are we going to eat this much?" I asked.

"You think it's enough? I feel like I should have ordered more," Sienna said.

I laughed, but then realized she was serious. The sushi did look good. Mila had always wanted to try some. I took a picture of the table to send to her later.

We sat down at the table and Romeo moved my wheelchair off to the side.

"To Sofiya's new wheelchair," Sienna said, holding up her glass of sake. We all toasted, and I took a sip. The drink was cool and crisp with an edge of sweetness, and I decided I liked it. I rarely drank, never having much access or interest in alcohol.

"Okay, start with this," Sienna said, using her chopsticks to put a colorful piece of sushi on my plate. "Put the ginger on top with some wasabi and then dip it in soy sauce."

"And then I just eat it in one bite?"

"Yep," Romeo said, popping his fourth piece into his mouth.

"Alright." I clumsily picked it up with my chopsticks and popped it in my mouth, chewing slowly.

"Well?" Sienna stared at me expectantly.

"That was good." My voice came out suspiciously high-pitched.

Angelo laughed. "You really are the worst liar."

"That's okay," Sienna said, putting two new pieces on my plate. "That's why we got a selection. This is spicy tuna and then this is a California roll. They're better for beginners."

I took several sips of sake to get rid of the taste of the first roll and braced myself before picking up the spicy tuna roll. The first one had truly been disgusting, and the second was just as bad. I wasn't a huge fan of seafood in general, and something about the texture of the sushi was really not for me.

I smiled at Sienna once I'd swallowed the two new pieces she'd given me, but based on her expression, it must have come out as a grimace.

"I'm sorry," I said, taking another long drink of sake. "It might not be for me."

"We're going to find one that you like," Sienna said, full of determination as she put another selection on my plate. Angelo and Romeo gave me sympathetic looks.

After consuming more sushi than I'd ever dreamed of or wanted, Sienna put one last piece on my plate, looking absolutely defeated.

"Okay, this is a vegetarian roll. It has cucumber and avocado. You *have* to like this one."

I dipped it in soy sauce and put the whole thing in my mouth, chewing slowly.

"Well?" Romeo asked.

I swallowed. "I don't think I like seaweed."

"Oh my gosh, you're hopeless," Sienna said.

I grinned. "Completely."

"Do you want me to order something else?" Angelo asked.

"Absolutely not," I said. "Sienna's practically force-fed me my bodyweight in sushi."

She sniffed. "I'm not sure how I can be friends with someone who has such an unrefined palate."

I stuck my lip out in a pout, and she rolled her eyes. "Okay, fine. We can be friends, but only if you make my favorite dessert."

"Hey, she has to make my tiramisu first," Angelo said.

"You'll get your tiramisu once you teach me how to play poker," I said.

"Poker?" Romeo asked.

"Angelo's invited me to his weekly poker night, and I'm determined to beat them all."

Romeo leaned back in his chair with a hearty laugh. "You invited her?"

"I've always said we need more women at poker night." Angelo winked at me as Romeo snorted. "But you're probably the worst liar I've ever met, so I'm not sure it's such a good idea."

"Have some faith, Angelo," I said, elbowing him in the arm.

My cheeks hurt from smiling so much. I couldn't remember having a better day than this one. The only thing missing was having Mila and Matteo here.

As if my thoughts had conjured him, the door opened and I broke out in a huge smile. "Matteo!" It was only when everyone turned to stare at me that I realized how exuberant I'd been. I cleared my throat and took another sip of sake. I could blame my outburst on the alcohol—I was deliciously warm and tipsy—but Angelo had been right that I was terrible at hiding my emotions. My parents had done their best to make me a good, obedient, robotic Bratva wife who expressed nothing. Sometimes I wished I would have at least internalized some of their lessons—it would leave me less exposed in the brutal world.

"Come sit down, fratello," Romeo said. "You might be able to find a couple pieces of sushi left that Sienna hasn't force-fed your wife yet."

"Move the fuck over," Matteo said to his second-in-command, who got out of the chair next to me with a good-natured huff.

I tried to keep my cool that Matteo wanted to sit next to *me*.

He nodded his head at my new wheelchair. "How do you like it?"

"I love it," I said, turning towards him. "Thank you so much for organizing it and getting it so quickly."

Matteo busied himself with getting some sushi, but I thought I saw the slightest hint of red in his cheeks, and I wondered if my husband felt more than he let on.

29

MATTEO

The dim light in the basement cast shadows on the pathetic man swinging in front of me.

"Where is Arben getting the girls?" I asked. The man sobbed, tears and blood running down his face.

Domenico had found an Albanian spy watching my building.

My. Fucking. Building.

Arben was getting too bold. We should have been able to destroy him in a matter of days, but he was like a ghost. His father had been a pathetic, spineless son of a bitch, but he clearly wanted to make a name for himself. I clenched my jaw as the man let out another shrill scream as Domenico dislocated his shoulders.

The spy was strung up by his wrists, his legs jerking with desperation to touch the floor and alleviate the pressure.

"I don't know, I swear I don't know anything," he choked out. "I was ordered to watch the building, that's it." His underwear darkened as he urinated himself.

"For fuck's sake," Domenico muttered, his face twisted in disgust.

I sliced a long cut in the Albanian's skin, making sure to go through the clan tattoo on his chest. He let out a piercing scream, snot running down his face and mixing with the blood on his chest.

"Arben's forces must be pretty weak if this is who he's sending to spy on you," Domenico said.

"Please, please," the spy begged. "I don't know anything."

"Then what use are you to me?" I sliced another line through the man's chest, but this time I dug my blade deep until blood and intestines spilled out onto the floor.

"Double the surveillance around the building," I said to Domenico. "Cameras, men, everything. If Arben is monitoring movements, I want to know, and I want it stopped."

"Yes, Boss," Domenico responded.

"Good work finding him," I said before leaving the basement. Domenico and his men would oversee the cleanup.

I rode the elevator to my penthouse, the stench of blood in my nose. Angelo had messaged to let me know they were having dinner with Sienna, so I knew the apartment would be empty.

Rage pulsed through me as I stood in the shower, cold water pouring down my body. Usually, I went to the gym to work out my anger, or I would find someone to fuck, but deep down, I knew neither of those options would soothe me tonight. I got dressed, leaving my suit jacket off and rolling up my sleeves, and then headed down to Sienna's floor.

———

"MATTEO!"

Sofiya's cheerful greeting twisted my insides. When was the last time someone had been that excited to see me? Not my sister, who I'd pushed away for years, or my men, who responded to me with respect and an edge of fear, and certainly not my enemies, who called me the Angel of Death.

I sat down beside my wife, drawn like a planet into her orbit. Her cheeks were flushed, eyes bright, and I realized she was tipsy. I cocked an eyebrow at Romeo, who was refilling her glass with sake, and he just grinned.

"You sure you don't want anything else to eat?" Sienna asked Sofiya, who shook her head.

"Trust me, I'm full."

"Sorry for making you eat so much. I was sure there would be at least one you liked," Sienna said with a pout.

Sofiya shrugged. "It's okay. This can count towards my Dream List, so it's worth it."

Angelo raised his eyebrows. "Dream List?"

"About a year ago, Mila and I each made a list of things we want to do before we die. We spent most of our days stuck inside, so we had a lot of time to brainstorm. One of my things on the list is to try something new every week for a year. So this week can be sushi."

There was a lightness to her I hadn't seen before. I found myself wanting to run my fingers along her skin, to tuck a piece of bright blonde hair behind her ear, and to know every item on her list.

"What other new things have you tried?" Romeo asked.

"Getting married," she said, flicking her eyes to me with a blush on her cheeks.

"That's such a fun idea. I want to make a list like that. What else is on yours?" Sienna asked.

"Umm, a bunch of things," Sofiya said, suddenly shy. "Like get a dog, go to Disney World, see the ocean, things like that."

The things on her list were so *innocent*. How had something so sweet and pure come from Rustik?

I grabbed a set of chopsticks and ate a California roll as the others talked about what they would put on their list. Sofiya arranged the remaining sushi pieces on a plate and slid it in front of me. I felt a strange fluttering in my chest. She took care of me like it was the most natural thing in the world.

I finished eating, and we moved to the living room. I ended up next to Sofiya on the couch. She curled up under a blanket, and my skin itched with the urge to pull her against me. I was struck by the feeling that I would taint her by touching her. My life was one where my skin was regularly marked with blood. Hers was one where she dreamed of having a dog and touching the ocean.

Romeo moved a floral cushion off a leather armchair and sat down. "So, how're you finding the Italian Mafia, Sofiya?"

"So far, so good," she responded with a smile. "And last night, I watched *The Godfather* for research."

Angelo snorted a laugh, causing him to choke on his drink. Romeo thumped him on the back.

"Yeah, that was pretty much Matteo's reaction." She glanced over at me with a smile. "But I thought it was educational."

Sienna raised an eyebrow at me. "Sounds like you had a cozy little movie night."

I fixed her with a scowl, but the smile didn't fade from her lips.

"I made caramel popcorn," Sofiya said.

"Sounds like we need to have a movie night at the Rossis'," Romeo said with a shit-eating grin.

"That would be so fun," she said. Then she yawned for the third time.

I stood up. "Time to go."

All of us moved into the hall, and I noticed Sofiya's old wheelchair sitting there.

"What's this doing here?"

"Romeo and I were racing," she said. "I crushed him, of course. Oh! And we practiced some moves. Look what I can do." She wheeled back onto her back tires, a huge smile on her face. But I was on the verge of a fucking heart attack.

Images of her losing balance and crashing to the ground flashed before my eyes. "Stop that," I growled, running to her side and forcing her back on four wheels.

She stared up at me with an adorable pout.

"It's too dangerous. You're going to hurt yourself."

"But I looked good, right?"

I pinched the bridge of my nose. "You always look good, tesoro," I muttered.

Based on everyone's stunned expressions, I'd spoken loud enough for them to hear.

"Let's go," I said, irritation seeping through my voice.

Sienna squeezed Sofiya in a tight hug, and my body vibrated with something that felt strangely like jealousy. I huffed and got in the elevator, tapping my foot impatiently.

Sofiya joined me, giving everyone a sweet wave before the doors closed.

That night, I couldn't sleep. For once, it wasn't my nightmares keeping me up. It was thoughts of Sofiya—wondering what else was on her list and which items I could help her check off.

I might do just about anything to ensure she was always as happy to see me as she'd been this evening.

And the thought scared me shitless.

30

MATTEO

Sofiya and I fell into a rhythm.

Each morning, I woke early and headed to the gym, working out until I heard her move around in the kitchen. Then I hopped in the shower and jacked off—definitely *not* fantasizing about my wife the entire time—until I came against the tile wall. Then I got dressed in one of my identical black suits and braced myself before heading into the kitchen, where she would be in the middle of preparing something for breakfast.

A couple of days ago, it had been cinnamon rolls. Yesterday it was some sort of Russian pancake.

This morning she was already perched on a kitchen stool, a plate of waffles in front of her. I cursed myself for moving too slowly this morning. I'd missed watching her move around the kitchen like she belonged here, in *our* home.

"Morning," she said sweetly.

I grunted and poured myself a cup of coffee.

"Maybe you'd be less cranky in the mornings if you slept in for once," she said, a smile playing on her lips.

I scowled. "There will be a delivery for you this afternoon."

"What do you mean?" she asked, looking up from her breakfast. The kitchen stool she was on had a back to it, but even so, I couldn't get the image of her falling off of it out of my head. I moved to stand behind her, banding my arms around her chest.

"What are you doing?" she asked, amusement clear in her voice.

"Nothing," I said with a scowl.

She just hummed and speared another bite of waffle. But instead of bringing it to her own lips, she twisted around and held the fork to mine. My lips parted of their own volition and I took the waffle, chewing it slowly.

I was so shocked by my own behavior that I almost missed the smile tugging at my wife's lips. She ate a bite before bringing the fork to my lips again. I should refuse. Mafia Dons didn't eat waffles. But again, I found my lips parting and maple syrup exploding on my tongue.

"What's this delivery?"

I blinked, trying to remember what we'd been talking about. I honestly wasn't sure I could remember my own fucking name right now.

"Right," I said, clearing my throat. "You'll have to wait to find out."

"Very mysterious." She leaned back into my chest with a smile and I tightened my hold on her. Just to make sure she didn't fall. Her body was so soft against mine, fitting against my chest like she was made for me.

"What should I bake today? Any requests?"

I ate another bite of waffle off her fork. "I don't eat sweets."

Her lips curled into a smile. "Right. Made Men probably only consume protein powder and steel nails."

I grunted. Her pretty little smile had stolen all my words.

"I have to go." And yet my feet stayed glued to the floor.

Sofiya twisted in my arms. "I hope you have a good day. Do good Mafia work."

My eyes flitted to her lips—pink, pouty, and perfect. I released my hold on her, retreating from the kitchen before I gave in to the temptation to kiss her.

31

SOFIYA

I grinned as the door shut behind Matteo. My husband might pretend to be cold and distant, but I could still feel the ghost of his touch against my skin. It made me crave *more...* more than friendship. I wanted it all, and I was starting to think it might even be possible.

I finished up breakfast and got ready. I wanted to try a new hairstyle—a crown braid. Mila and I used to spend hours doing each other's hair to pass the time. I had to take lots of breaks because my shoulders were hurting, but I thought the braid turned out really cute.

I swapped my wheelchair for my rollator and headed back to the kitchen, flipping through some recipes I'd saved on my phone. I couldn't figure out what I wanted to make, and the silence of the apartment felt too loud. I headed to the front door and peeked out to find Angelo at his post.

"Good morning, bella. Are you okay?"

"I'm fine. I was just—" I hesitated. Was I being needy and stupid?

He raised his eyebrows.

"Do you want to come inside?"

Now it was time for him to look unsure. Was it because he didn't want to, or because he wasn't supposed to? It was bleak if he truly preferred to stand in an empty foyer for hours than spend time with me.

"You can guard me more easily from inside, right?"

He huffed a smile. "I guess that's true. I'll come for a little while, if that's what you want."

I beamed at him, opening the door wider so he could fit his large frame through.

"I was going to bake something. Do you think Matteo would like traditional cannolis the best? Probably, right? I had this idea for cannoli cupcakes that I thought would be super cute," I mused.

Angelo chuckled. "I'm not sure the Boss is much for desserts."

I smiled to myself. It seemed my husband hid his love for sweets from everyone but me. The day after our movie night, I'd woken up to find the popcorn bowl empty. At first I thought Matteo must have thrown out the caramel corn, but it wasn't in the trash. I had a sneaking suspicion that my husband had eaten it all.

"He seems to like the things I make."

"I'm sure he does," Angelo said, giving me a knowing look.

I got started making cannoli filling while Angelo picked out some music, and I eventually drew him into a game of "would you rather."

"Why the fuck would you rather be stuck on some alien planet than meet Bigfoot?" Angelo asked.

"I said I would only choose it if they were sexy aliens."

"*Sexy* aliens?"

"Read a book, Angelo. Alien romance is very big."

He rolled his eyes and stole another finished cannoli from the counter. Just then, the apartment door opened and I heard the sound of pattering feet before a dog popped its head around the corner. It was a beautiful golden retriever with bright eyes and a wagging tail. And he was wearing a service dog vest.

"Oh, hello." I said as the dog walked over to me and laid its head on my lap. "Where did you come from?"

Matteo strode into the kitchen. "I see you've met Noodle."

I gave Matteo a bewildered expression. "Noodle?"

"They said we couldn't change his name," he said, sounding put-out. "But he was the best they had. Passed all his tests."

I looked back down at Noodle's service dog vest. "Are you saying..." I trailed off, not wanting to speak the words out loud in case I was mistaken.

"This is your service dog."

My lips parted. "You got me a service dog."

Matteo crossed his arms. "Yes."

My husband looked as stern as ever, but inside my heart was *melting*. "What? Why?"

"Getting a dog was on your list, and I figured you might as well get one that's useful."

A lump rose in my throat. I'd only known Matteo for a few weeks and he had already shown more of an interest in my needs and making my life easier than anyone in the world, besides my sister.

"Help me up," I said, extending my arms out to him.

"What?"

"Help me get up," I repeated.

"Why?" He grumbled, but did what I asked, lifting me from my wheelchair. My feet barely skimmed the ground and I was firmly plastered against his body.

"Because I wanted to say thank you," I murmured. I ran my fingers through his hair, savoring how soft the strands were. His jaw was clenched tight, and if I hadn't been observing my husband so closely these past few days, I would have thought he was angry with me.

But I knew better now.

I trailed my hands down his face before cupping his jaw and pulling him closer. Before I could second-guess myself, my lips were against his. At first, he was unmoving, a frozen statue as I kissed him. A thread of insecurity wound its way around my chest. He didn't want to kiss me. Didn't want *me*.

I went to pull away, but then he growled and pressed my back against the wall. His lips were soft and firm all at once, his tongue demanding entry into my mouth. I moaned at the taste of him, at the feel of his control and dominance. His knee slipped between my legs, pressing against my sex, and I inhaled sharply.

A cold, wet nose nudged at my leg, and I broke the kiss with a laugh. "I think Noodle is jealous."

Matteo grumbled, but there was a lightness to his eyes. I looked around and realized that Angelo must have slipped out at some point. Matteo carried me to the couch and gently sat me down, but he remained standing. I called Noodle over and patted the cushion beside me. He wasted no time hopping up next to me and cuddling up to my side.

"Is he supposed to be on the couch?" Matteo asked, frowning.

"You're going to say no to this face?" I squished Noodle's cheeks between my hands and we both stared at Matteo with big, sad eyes.

"Fuck," he muttered, running his hand through his hair.

I pressed my grin into Noodle's soft fur. "What is he trained to do?"

"The dog people are coming tomorrow to work with both of you together," he said. "But he can get you things like your medication bag, open doors, help you balance, and get help if you need it. I asked about attack dog training, but they said he had none. We'll have to rectify that."

I gasped. "You are not teaching Noodle to attack people." The dog in question wagged his tail, his tongue lolling out of his mouth as he looked between the two of us.

Matteo ran his hand down his face. "Not with that fucking name I can't."

I grinned. "Noodle is perfect the way he is." I ran my hand down his soft coat and Noodle leaned in to my touch, looking blissful. "Aren't you the best boy? My sweet little baby."

"He's not your baby," Matteo said, crossing his arms. "He's an employee."

I snorted as Noodle lay his head in my lap. "I think someone is jealous," I whispered conspiratorially as I stroked his soft fur.

"I'm not jealous of a dog."

I held my hand out to my husband. His brow furrowed in confusion, but he took it, and I pulled him down beside me. He sat with a huff, unbuttoning his suit jacket. I held my breath as I rested my head against his shoulder, ready for him to pull away at any moment. But he didn't. He just shifted on the couch cushion and put his arm around me.

I closed my eyes and thought I could get used to this—being held and cuddled. After years of only ever feeling Mila's touch, I was starved for it, desperate to soak up any comfort I could get.

32

MATTEO

I was taking the day off.

I couldn't remember the last time I took a day off.

When I told Romeo before leaving the office yesterday, his shocked expression had turned into a shit-eating grin. He had even texted me this morning, wishing me a happy day with my wife.

I hadn't responded. I wasn't here for her. I needed to supervise the service dog trainers. This was the last day they would work with Sofiya and Noodle.

"I was thinking maybe we could go to the park after the service dog people leave? If you don't have other things to do?" My wife's sweet voice cut through my brooding, and I looked up from my breakfast.

"The park?"

"Umm, yeah. Central Park? I haven't been and, I don't know, it looks pretty in the movies. I bet Noodle would like it. I thought we could walk around and get a hot dog."

Her cheeks blushed so prettily as she said it, but my lips turned down in a frown. She wanted to go to Central Park and eat a hot dog? I couldn't remember the last time I'd gone to the park. It wasn't like I had any business there, and it was way too fucking exposed for my liking. The entire city was my territory, so in theory, it should be fine. Safe. But picturing Sofiya there, out in the world where I couldn't control everything, made my chest tight. I rubbed it absent-mindedly.

"It's okay," she said, and I realized I'd been sitting in silence a beat too long. "I'm sure you have more important things to do." Her smile was brittle, and she wasn't quite meeting my gaze. My heart pumped faster, each thump sending a shock of pain through me because *I* caused that, and nothing in the world was right when my tesoro was sad.

"My men will need to sweep the area we're going to before we arrive, and they'll keep eyes on us the whole time," I said gruffly. A smile transformed Sofiya's face, and I wanted to burn it into my mind forever.

"Really? We can go?"

I nodded down at her pancakes. "You need to eat your breakfast. We'll go this afternoon."

Maybe I could convince her to go to a nice restaurant. Somewhere impressive that showed how I could care for her. Her hand slipped into mine, and she leaned against my shoulder. I froze at the unexpected contact, desperately wishing I wasn't wearing this suit jacket. I wanted to feel the heat of her skin against mine.

"Thank you." Her words were soft as she tilted her head to meet my gaze.

I willed myself to say something, but my mouth was so dry my words caught in my throat. So all I did was grunt and pull her chair closer to me. Now our sides were pressed together. A smile teased at her lips as she picked up her fork to resume eating. Keeping her left hand in mine the entire time.

33

SOFIYA

Matteo insisted we bring my wheelchair to Central Park. It was a smart decision since our outing would require a lot of walking, but it was a surprise that he wanted to be seen in public with me and my chair.

A car alarm made me jump, and Matteo tightened his hold on the back of my neck. I glanced up at him, my eyes lingering on the hard lines of his jaw. He was in a suit today but no tie, and the top few buttons were undone, giving me a peek of his golden skin.

We were outside the apartment, which butted against the west side of the park, while we waited for our guards to finish securing the area. I had been sure Matteo would refuse this outing. Why would he want to flaunt his damaged wife? But as we were out in the sunshine by the edge of the park, I wondered if my husband had been hesitant to go out because he was worried about safety. *My* safety.

Matteo shifted even closer to me, his eyes sweeping the street and his hand twitching towards the gun under his jacket as if enemies were about to jump out at us. His concern sent warmth through my belly and helped wash away my impatience as we waited.

Noodle's tail wagged as he took in all the people on the sidewalk. He was sitting by my chair like the good boy he was, showing off his vest. A group of school children screamed and laughed as they passed us, many of them stopping to wave at him. I petted his head, grinning at how proud he looked at the attention. How would he react if I had a baby? Would they be best friends? My heart ached with longing as I imagined a brown-haired baby with dark eyes.

I pushed the fantasy out of my head.

"Are we going to stand here all day?" I grabbed Matteo's hand, feeling addicted to holding it after this morning.

My grumpy husband let out a long-suffering sigh, squeezing my hand tight as he ran his other through his already-messy hair. He glanced at Angelo, who gave him a nod. They must have decided the area was safe enough. "Fine. Let's get... hot dogs."

I snorted a laugh at his clenched jaw. He had tried to convince me to go to any number of highly reviewed restaurants, but I'd refused. I had always wanted to eat a New York City hot dog—it was on my Dream List. I had to let go of his hand to guide my chair towards the nearest hot dog cart, and I wished we could be like a normal couple and hold hands while walking. As if Matteo sensed my sadness, his hand lightly landed on my shoulder and gave it a squeeze. He kept his hand there, glaring at anyone who got in my way as we navigated the sidewalk.

"What do you want?" he asked me with a dark scowl as he took in the vendor's picture menu.

"A hot dog with ketchup and a Coke."

His expression turned incredulous. "You wanted a plain fucking hot dog with ketchup?"

"Yes," I answered primly.

He slowly shook his head. "I'm not sure I can allow that, tesoro. I'm pretty sure it's the law that hot dogs must be served with mustard and relish."

My heart skipped a beat. My husband, the Mafia Don, had just cracked a joke.

"Good thing my husband isn't committed to following the law." I kept my face serious, but I felt like singing, dancing, pumping my fist in the air, especially when the corner of Matteo's mouth twitched.

"Fine," he huffed.

"Oh, we should see if Angelo wants one." I looked around, catching sight of my guard about ten feet away. I waved him over as Matteo growled. I had asked Sienna why Matteo didn't like Angelo, and she had looked so confused. She'd said Angelo saved Matteo's life and that being assigned to me was a huge honor for the young guard. I had to conclude that my husband might feel slightly possessive of me, and the thought made me so happy I could levitate.

"What did you need, principessa?" Angelo asked, bending down so we were eye-level.

"I was just wondering if you wanted a hot dog."

Angelo grinned, ignoring Matteo's continued growling. "I already ate, but thank you." He winked at me before stepping away, leaving me alone with my surly husband, who barked his order at the stand owner. I grabbed his hand, weaving my fingers through his, holding tight until our food was ready. Matteo ordered four hot dogs —three with everything, and one with ketchup. I reached my hand out to grab the two sodas and set them in my lap as my husband balanced our lunch in his hands. I signaled for Noodle to start walking as we headed into the park.

Instantly, some of the noise from the street faded away as we entered a corridor of trees and greenery. Matteo matched his steps to my slow pace, allowing me to take in all the statues and flowers.

"It feels like another world in here," I sighed. Mila and I had always dreamed about the places we wanted to travel. We'd spent the last few years watching *Friends* reruns, so New York had been high on our list. I swallowed the lump in my throat that she wasn't with me to see this.

He guided me to an empty bench. "Where do you want to sit?"

I eyed the bench. It didn't look super comfortable. I decided to maneuver my chair to the end of the bench so we could still be next to each other. Matteo sat beside me and handed me my hot dog.

I let out a happy hum at the first bite.

"Is it all you dreamed?" Matteo asked dryly.

I nodded with enthusiasm. "Best hot dog I've ever eaten."

"Try a bite of mine," he commanded.

I wrinkled my nose as I took in the toppings on the hot dog he was holding out. I wasn't sure what came over me as I leaned in and took a bite right out of his hand, keeping my eyes on his the entire time. His eyes grew dark and heated, and my cheeks flushed. I had meant the move to be teasing, but the air between us felt charged with need. God, was it possible my husband wanted me?

"How was it?" he asked, his voice hoarse.

I leaned back, chewing thoughtfully. "Disgusting." I took a long sip of Coke, and Matteo snorted a laugh. I joined him, and it might have been the best moment of my life.

We ate quietly, and I pretended not to notice as my husband fed small bites of food to Noodle.

We finished our lunch and Matteo threw out our trash. "Did you want to explore more?"

For a minute, my mind imagined what it would be like to peel his clothes off and explore every inch of his body, allowing him to do the same with me. I cleared my throat. "Yes, please."

I signaled for Noodle to get up from his spot by my chair, and he gave a cute little stretch as he came to my side. I had only had him a few days, and I couldn't imagine my life without him. Without both of my guys.

Matteo's hands hovered over my chair handles, but he didn't grab them, didn't take over and push me, and my heart warmed. He was listening to me, even though I knew he wanted to take over.

"Do you think..." I started before trailing off, suddenly nervous.

His hand cupped my cheek, his thumb caressing my jaw. "What is it, tesoro?"

"Could we try holding hands while we walk?" I hadn't had a chance to really test out my motorized assist outside, but I only had to steer with one hand when I used it, leaving my other one free.

Matteo's hold on my face tightened a fraction as some emotion flashed over his eyes so quickly I almost wasn't sure it was real. He leaned down and pressed a tender kiss to my forehead. Then he straightened, took my hand in his, and we made our way through the park.

34

MATTEO

I'd spent all night trying to make up my mind.

My hand had been on her doorknob twice before I turned back.

Even though Sofiya and I had been together all day, it somehow wasn't enough. I wanted to be beside her in bed, our naked bodies pressed together. I wanted the taste of her sweetness on my lips, the feel of her skin against mine. I wanted to push inside her, to feel her pussy squeeze my cock as she moaned in pleasure.

It had been too long since I'd fucked someone. That *had* to be the reason for my current mental state. But even as that thought raced through my head, I knew it wasn't right. The truth was slowly making itself known.

I *liked* Sofiya. She was fun to be around. Her quick sense of humor, sassy mutterings under her breath, and brilliant smile *did* something to me.

It made me feel out of control, and I didn't like it.

So when Romeo called me before sunrise, I was already awake. And now I was staring at a burning truck, courtesy of the Albanians. Each lick of the flames fueled my rage.

"How the fuck did they learn about this transport?" I asked Romeo.

"Bianchi is missing," he said. "The only ones who knew about this were the inner circle, the driver, Bruno, and Bianchi. The driver and Bruno are dead."

"How would they even get to him?" I hissed. It didn't make sense that Bianchi was an informant for the Albanians. He was a young kid, loyal to the Family. When his father died of a heart attack a few years back, I had made sure his mother and sister were provided for. How could I have missed that he was a traitor?

"I don't know," Romeo said, exhaustion heavy in his voice. "But now Arben has half a million in weapons."

The first of the sun's rays broke over the horizon, bathing the world in red.

"They know Bianchi can't continue being an informant after this, which means they either made a misstep in exposing him, or we have a rat infestation," I said.

Romeo nodded. "You want to set up decoy trails?"

"With next week's drug run. And"—My jaw clenched, unwilling to speak the words—"I'll ask Rustik to provide us men as well. We'll have more eyes on the decoy transits that way." The Albanians had proven to be more cunning than I'd anticipated, and I wouldn't make the mistake again. But the idea of asking the Pakhan for help, particularly after knowing how he treated Sofiya, was like ash in my mouth.

The alliance was doing what I needed it to do—keeping us from having to fight a war on two fronts. Now that we had peace with the Russians, we could focus our energy on the Albanians.

But I was still tempted to tell Rustik to go fuck himself. He didn't deserve to breathe air after how he'd treated his daughter.

"I guess you have to get some benefit out of being married," Romeo muttered.

I swung my head towards my second-in-command, who immediately realized his mistake. He raised his hands in front of him in a placating gesture.

"I don't mean anything against your wife, fratello."

"This is not the day to fucking test me," I said. "Get this cleaned up so we can fucking go."

I rubbed at my chest even though I knew the strange tightness wouldn't dissipate until I was back with Sofiya. One of my soldiers had betrayed me. A vital shipment of weapons was gone. Arben was making me look like a fool. But what I was angriest about was that it had pulled me away from my wife. I wouldn't get to see her get up this morning, looking all messy and rumpled. And for that, the Albanians needed to die.

35

SOFIYA

"What do you want, Angelo?" I peered at the pastry case, mouth watering at all the different cakes. This was one of the most popular bakeries in the city, and I wanted to try everything for inspiration.

"I don't need anything, bella."

I glanced up at Angelo. He was crowding my chair, his eyes flitting around the busy shop.

"Of course you do. If I don't spend a lot of money, Matteo will yell at me."

Angelo snorted. "As if the Boss would yell at you." He glanced at the case. "Just get me whatever you think will be best, not that it will be better than your baking."

My cheeks flushed at the compliment. "What if we just get one of everything?" It was excessive, *extravagant*, but I wanted to try it all. And we were supporting a small business.

"Good plan, Mrs. Rossi," Angelo said with a grin. Then his eyes returned to the door where two businessmen were entering. "But maybe we should take them back to the apartment."

"Is something wrong?"

"No," he said quickly.

"Convincing."

Matteo had been gone when I woke this morning. When I asked Angelo where he was, he had just muttered something about the Don needing to check on something upstate, but it was clear he was on edge.

"What's going on?"

Angelo's eyes flitted around the cafe. "Not here. Let's just get the things and go."

The tattooed girl at the counter's eyes grew wide as I asked her for one of everything, but I managed to stop my hand from trembling when I tapped my credit card. It was more than I'd ever spent, and I hoped Matteo had been serious when he said he wanted me to spend his money.

"We might need to make two trips to the car." I eyed the growing tower of pastry boxes.

Angelo grunted, his stance still tense. When the boxes were ready, he helped stack them on my lap and hung a bag from the handle of my chair.

"See, this is the perk of the wheelchair," I said, earning me a small smile from Angelo.

Noodle subtly nosed the boxes, and I gave him a stern look. He quickly sat back, eyes filled with the adorable yet slightly heartbreaking remorse only a dog can manage. His expression quickly changed to a happy pant as I pet him on the head and gave him a treat.

"Let's go," Angelo said gruffly.

The tension radiating from his body set me on edge, and I was ready to be back home in the apartment with Matteo anyway. It was getting harder to be away from him. Our day yesterday had been perfect. He still showed little outward affection, but cracks were appearing in his usually impervious shield. I wanted to see what more I could get from him.

I followed Angelo out of the bakery, calling a "thank you" over my shoulder to the girl at the counter.

Before I could maneuver around everyone on the sidewalk, a curse tore from Angelo's lips. "Fuck!"

My heart leapt to my throat as his hand grabbed the back of my neck.

"Get down, Sofiya!" he yelled, urging me to the ground. I let out a low cry as my knee hit the sidewalk, the pain jolting through my leg like a dagger. The bakery boxes went flying. What was happening? Confusion and frustration flooded me until I heard the gunshots.

Shit shit shit.

My heart rate skyrocketed. I was a total sitting duck—no weapons, barely able to move with the pain in my leg, and completely exposed on the sidewalk. I lurched forward and grabbed Noodle, wrapping my arms around him and pulling him to the ground. He licked my face and gave a low whine, but stayed with me.

People ran around us and screams filled the air. Angelo's body blocked mine, his arms raised as he returned fire at whoever was shooting at us from across the street.

"We need to get to the car," he gritted out as he crouched down. He grabbed my arm and dragged me a few feet until the bulletproof SUV offered us protection. Bullets pinged against the car, and Angelo ducked for cover before taking more shots. I kept my hand on Noodle's harness, making sure he stayed down.

"Call the Boss," Angelo urged, pulling his phone out of his pocket and tossing it to me. "Now, Sofiya."

My hands shook as I called my husband. He answered on the second ring. "Pronto."

"Matteo." My voice broke, and I choked back a sob.

"Sofiya? What's wrong? Where's Angelo?"

"Someone's shooting at us outside the bakery. Please come."

36

MATTEO

"Please come."

The words were like a dagger to my heart. Hearing the panic in Sofiya's voice made sweat prickle on my brow.

"Get to the bakery," I barked at Romeo, who was driving. We'd just gotten back to the city and were only minutes away from the apartment. Romeo sped up and made a turn, heading to the bakery a few blocks away. Angelo had cleared the trip with me this morning, and I said yes because I knew it would make Sofiya happy. And now she was in danger.

"What's happening?" I asked through gritted teeth.

"The shooting stopped," she whispered.

There was a rustling sound and then Angelo was on the phone. "Three men shot at us. I killed two, the third got away. Police are on their way."

We turned onto the block where the bakery was. People were huddled behind cars and the street was uncharacteristically empty for midday Manhattan. Police sirens sounded in the distance, and I cursed. I jumped out of the car before Romeo could bring it to a full stop and ran towards the black SUV I recognized as one of mine.

I rounded the car and my heart almost stopped when I saw Sofiya sprawled on the sidewalk, her arms wrapped around the dog. Angelo was beside her, helping her sit up. A sharp burst of relief and gratitude hit me—he was uninjured and had protected my wife.

I knelt on the ground, supporting Sofiya's back. "Fuck, tesoro mio. Are you hurt?" I couldn't remember the last time I'd sounded so panicked, but as she looked up at me with tears streaking down her cheeks, I couldn't keep my mask in place.

"Boss, we need to go," Romeo said, coming up behind me. "I'll smooth things over with the cops, but it will be easier if you're not here."

We had most of the force in our pocket, but a daytime shooting was still a disaster to cover up.

Sofiya was doing something with her knee, a grimace on her face.

"Are you hurt?" I repeated. "Can you move?"

"I'm okay," she said. "Just had to pop my knee back in."

I blinked, staring down at her jeans-covered knee. When she released it, I gently gathered her in my arms and Romeo opened the back door of the car for us. Angelo got in the driver's seat to take us home while Romeo stayed behind to talk with the cops. We passed the first police vehicle as we turned onto the main road.

"Who was shooting at us?" Sofiya asked, her voice small. I kept my touch as gentle as I could as I held her close to my chest. I pressed my face to her hair, breathing in her scent.

I could have lost her.

"Albanians," I spit out, hating how harsh my voice sounded. Arben had played me like a fool. He'd known I would go upstate, leaving my wife exposed. But how had he known where she would be?

Her eyes were wide. "Why would they do that?"

"I don't know, tesoro." I brushed the hair out of her face. "I'll find out and they'll pay." I didn't want her to be scared, but it was obvious that the Albanians were targeting her to get to me. This is what I'd always feared when considering marriage. Being too exposed, too vulnerable.

I'd done my best to create distance between us these past few weeks, but now I couldn't bear the thought of being apart from her. I thought keeping my distance would protect myself from vulnerability, but maybe it had just caused more problems for both of us. Sofiya reached out a tentative hand, and my eyes fell closed as she brushed it along my jaw.

"Noodle was such a good boy," she said, shifting in my lap so she could pet the dog. "Were you scared, malysh? You were so brave."

Something hot burned in my chest, and it was definitely not jealousy at whatever pet name she just called the dog.

"He looks fine," I said dryly. Noodle's tongue was lolling out of his mouth as he leaned his head into Sofiya's hand.

We pulled into the apartment's underground garage and Sofiya stiffened. "Wait, did someone get my wheelchair?"

I met Angelo's eyes in the rearview mirror, and he shook his head. "Make sure Romeo gets it," I commanded, and he nodded.

"I'll carry you inside." I wasn't sure I'd be able to let her go even if we did have her chair.

I waited to see if she would protest, but she relaxed into my hold. The feel of her head resting on my chest settled something inside me.

"Angelo," Sofiya said, reaching out her hand to the guard as we got out of the car. "Thank you for protecting me." Her voice cracked and she blinked quickly as she took his hand.

The fact that he had saved my wife's life today was the only thing keeping me from chopping off his fucking hand. I wanted to be the only one she touched.

"Of course, bella," he responded.

I just grunted and moved towards the elevator with Sofiya in my arms.

"Call the doctor," I barked out.

"I don't need a doctor," Sofiya protested.

"Don't argue," I said, giving her a stern look. "You won't win this one."

"I'm glad you know I'll win most of our arguments," she said primly.

Fuck. I almost felt tempted to smile as the elevator ascended to our apartment.

37

SOFIYA

Matteo wouldn't stop fussing. I had three blankets layered over me, and he kept bringing me beverages—water, tea, coffee, soda, and a large glass of grappa—a strong Italian liquor. The last one made me cock an eyebrow, but my harried husband hadn't even noticed.

I was learning Matteo's subtle tells. He wore a stony expression, his tone stern and serious, but he couldn't hide how he ran his hand through his hair when stressed, the way his fists clenched with anxiety, and the slight crinkle of his eyes when happy. With every delivered beverage and food, every gruff question asking how I was doing, my chest grew warmer.

I hadn't gotten the elaborate wedding I'd dreamed of or the smiling groom or the quiet, peaceful life in the countryside, but more and more I was thinking I'd ended up with something better.

"Do you need another blanket?" Matteo loomed over me, messy pieces of hair falling across his forehead and a slightly crazed look in his eyes.

The urge to tease him was strong, but instead, I held out my hand.

"What? What is it?" Matteo asked, staring down at me.

I snorted a giggle and grabbed his hand. "I don't need any more blankets. Will you sit down with me?"

His eyes were fixed on our joined hands. For a moment, I thought I might have overstepped, but then Matteo gave me a squeeze. I tugged at him and he sat beside me on the couch. His body was stiff as he kept space between us. When we first met, I would have interpreted his behavior as being irritated with me, but I was growing increasingly suspicious that my husband might like me.

Might care for me.

I shifted on the cushion until our bodies were pressed together. When he didn't move away, I rested my head on his shoulder.

"What are you doing, tesoro?"

Could he hear the way my heart pounded at the term of endearment?

"I'm... leaning."

"Leaning?"

"Yes," I said.

"Okay. You lean all you want." He adjusted his body so his arm was around me and then I was pulled tight to his chest. He was warm and comforting as I melted against him. Then his hand ran down my hair, and I was pretty sure I had actually died and this was heaven.

"I'll take being shot at every day if it leads to this," I said, snuggling deeper into Matteo's embrace.

His hold on me tightened. "Don't fucking joke about that."

I ran my nose down the column of his throat, surprising myself with my boldness. "Who says I was joking?"

He sighed. "How about I promise to hold you every day if you promise not to get shot at?"

"Deal."

"Are you sure you don't need another blanket?" he murmured.

"Not when you're here to keep me warm."

He ran his hand down my arm. "Are you hungry?"

I tilted my head to meet his gaze and raised a tentative hand to cup his face. Matteo leaned into my hand, and my breathing sped up. "There is something I need."

"What? Anything," he said seriously.

I bit my lip, my heart racing. The adrenaline from earlier must have addled my mind because there was no way I was actually going to say it out loud. "A kiss."

Matteo blinked. "What?"

"I want a kiss."

His brow furrowed, and I held my breath, sure he would refuse me. But then his hand cupped my face, his thumb running down my cheek. "If that's what you need, how can I refuse you?" Then he was tilting my face, his lips meeting mine with a softness so in contrast to his typical harshness, and I wondered if this was a side of him saved just for me. I would choose to believe it, even if it wasn't true, because the way he was clutching me close was a feeling I never wanted to forget.

"Fuck, I shouldn't be doing this," he said between hungry kisses.

I whimpered and ran my fingers through his hair, giving it a tug. "Yes, you should."

"You're hurt." He pressed hot kisses down my jaw.

"I'm not." I put my arms around his neck and pulled myself sideways into his lap, feeling his hardness press against my thigh. Dr. Amato had wrapped my knee to stabilize it, but I was completely fine otherwise.

He groaned, his hips giving an involuntary thrust against me. "I should be taking care of you."

"You are taking care of me." I moved my lips back to his and this time, I ran my tongue along the seam of his lips. They parted with a groan and then Matteo let go of his carefully curated facade, gripping my face with one hand and my ass with the other.

He was devouring me—his tongue hot as it pressed against mine, his hand threading through my hair with a stinging grip. I moaned and he swallowed the sound as he ran his hands over my body. I grew wet and needy and suddenly couldn't stop thinking about feeling my husband inside me. His fingers brushed against my nipples, and my kisses grew more desperate.

"Please," I gasped.

"What do you need?"

"You. Everything." I was beyond complete sentences as I ran my hands down his chest. With every move I made, I was braced for rejection, for the moment my husband realized he didn't want this, didn't want me. But the fear and adrenaline from today's life-and-death experience was shifting, transforming—urging me to go after what made me feel alive.

"You want me to touch you?" Matteo's voice was low and gravelly.

Without second-guessing, I shifted so I was straddling him. I arched into him, and felt a jolt of pleasure as I ground my pussy against his hard-on, but the movement also caused an ache in my hips that told me my joints weren't happy being spread around my broad husband.

"What is it?" Matteo asked, his brow furrowed.

"Nothing—"

"Don't lie." His stern tone made me grow wet, even as the pain in my hips increased.

"I maybe can't sit this way," I mumbled.

Matteo moved instantly, rearranging me on his lap so I was sitting sideways again. "You're hurting."

It wasn't a question.

My cheeks burned. Why couldn't my body just cooperate for once?

"I don't want to stop," I said, meeting my husband's gaze head-on, challenging him to argue.

He ran his thumb across my lip. "You think I have much more self control than I do, tesoro, if you think I can stop now."

A smile broke out across my face. I hadn't ruined it with my dysfunctional body. He still wanted me.

He ran his hand up my leg, gently squeezing my thigh. "What else do I need to be careful of?"

My heart felt like it was going to burst at his care for me, and I couldn't stop myself from leaning in for a kiss.

"I'm not sure," I said, a little breathless. "Just don't freak out if I dislocate something."

He frowned. "You will not dislocate anything."

"I'm not sure you can command that." I traced my fingers along his jaw. "But I'll try my best."

He pressed his forehead to mine, and for a moment, we quietly breathed each other in.

"I'm taking you to bed. Our first time isn't going to be on this fucking couch."

He tightened his hold on me, slipping one arm behind my knees, and stood. Nervous butterflies fluttered in my stomach, but I wrapped my arms around his neck and took a deep breath. For the first time in my life, I felt desirable. I didn't want to be a disappointment to my husband.

38

MATTEO

My cock strained against my pants as I carried Sofiya to my bedroom. I loved the weight of her in my arms, loved the way she clutched my neck and pressed tentative kisses against my skin. Why had I resisted this? How had I ever thought I could go without my beautiful wife?

I pulled her into a kiss before lowering her to the bed. I crawled over her, being sure to keep my weight on my forearms so I didn't put pressure on her joints. I wanted to make this good for her. I never wanted to hurt her. I'd thought my heart would stop when I saw her sprawled on the sidewalk, and I was fighting the need to coddle her with the desperate need to claim her.

"You want this?" I asked. It would kill me if she said no, but I would never force her.

"Yes," she said, running her fingers down my jaw. Her touch was so gentle. I couldn't remember being touched like that since my mamma died, and I felt that strange twinge in my chest I now realized was *emotion*.

I kissed her forehead as I ran my fingers through her golden hair. "You are so beautiful it fucking hurts."

She wrapped her arms around my neck and pulled me close. Our lips crashed together—messy and wild and perfect. I groaned as my cock grew impossibly hard. This was already the hottest experience of my life and all we'd done was kiss.

I ran my hand down her body, savoring her curves, until I cupped her pussy. She was so fucking hot, even through her leggings.

"Mmm, wait a second," Sofiya said.

I pulled back, meeting her gaze. My heart lurched when I saw an edge of panic in her eyes.

"I need my wheelchair." She glanced at the door. We'd left her wheelchair in the living room.

I brushed the hair out of her face, still amazed that my hands were capable of doing something so tender. "Why do you need it, tesoro?"

Sofiya blinked quickly and averted her gaze. No, we weren't doing that. I gripped her chin firmly in my grasp. "Don't hide from me," I growled. "Tell me."

"Please," she said, her voice fragile. "Please, can you just bring it here?"

Her breaths were coming faster now, and I was worried she was on the verge of a panic attack.

"Okay. I'll go get it. But then we're going to talk." I kissed her forehead and forced myself to get out of bed. I pushed her chair from the living room back to her. "Is this okay?" I asked, positioning it on her side of the bed.

She nodded, and the tension lining her face eased.

I got back in bed, unable to stop myself from running my hand down her stomach to her covered pussy. I cupped her heat, savoring her soft gasp.

"Now, my beautiful wife, talk to me."

She bit her lip, her bright blue eyes looking so unsure. But I stayed still and silent, forcing myself to be patient for her sake.

"I've had sex once before," she blurted out.

I gritted my teeth against the rage rushing through my veins like molten lava. Only my wife's soft, perfect body underneath mine kept me from leaving to track down the fucker who had touched what belonged to me.

"I'm sorry. I'm so sorry." Her eyes glistened with tears.

I ran my nose down the side of her face, breathing in her sweet scent and forcing myself to be calm. I hated that I wouldn't be the first one inside her, and I was determined to kill this fucking stronzo who had taken her virginity. But I wasn't angry with her.

Never with her.

"I just wanted to feel normal for once," she added.

I pressed a soft kiss to her cheek. "It's alright, tesoro. Just tell me what happened."

She chewed her lip, still looking like she was bracing herself. I ran my thumb over her lip, and she took a deep breath.

"Yuri was someone I'd known since I was young. He was over for a dinner party my parents were throwing—one of the last ones I was ever allowed to attend—and he asked me out on a date. I wasn't really interested in him, but I thought he was nice and I just... I wanted a chance to get out of the house and not feel so trapped. We went to dinner and then he wanted to go to his friend's house because they were having a party." She took a shuddering breath. "The house was packed when we got there and everyone was drinking. I got a little overwhelmed by everything, so Yuri suggested we go upstairs where it was quieter."

I kept my face pressed into her neck as my jaw clenched.

"I wanted to bring my rollator but he said it would be fine to leave it. He carried me upstairs." There was a slight hitch in her voice, and I gathered her closer to my chest.

"When we got up there, he put me on the bed and it was obvious he wanted to have sex. I wasn't sure about it, but I guess I mostly just felt lucky that he found me attractive at all."

I couldn't contain my growl. "What the fuck?" I cupped her face with both hands and looked at her intently. "You are the most gorgeous woman I've ever set my eyes on."

Sofiya blinked. "Really?"

"Tesoro mio, how could you even ask that?" My heart ached as I planted soft kisses down the side of her face. Sofiya had been hidden away for most of her life, so I shouldn't be surprised that she didn't know how breathtaking she was.

Her fingers curled in my hair, holding me close. "You wouldn't prefer someone who wasn't damaged?" Her voice was so soft, so fragile.

The muscles in my jaw clenched. I'd had similar thoughts about her when we first met, but I had been wrong. "Next time you say something negative about yourself like that, I'm going to spank your ass. You are fucking perfect."

"Did you just threaten to spank me?" she breathed. I pulled back to take in her expression, worried I would see fear there, but all I saw was heat and intrigue.

"Oh, baby, does the idea get you hot?" I pressed the heel of my palm firmly against her pussy. "Is your sweet little cunt growing wet at the idea?"

She bit her lip and shook her head.

A wide grin spread across my face. "Liar."

Her cheeks flushed a fiery red.

"Don't worry, tesoro. I'll always give you what you need. Now, finish your story."

My cock was rock hard against her thigh, and I fought the need to push inside her, to mark her with my cum over and over so everyone knew she belonged to me.

"It... umm... well, it was over quickly," she said, shutting her eyes. There was enough light in the room that I could see the delicate red flush on her cheeks. "It hurt, but wasn't particularly memorable."

"Fucker," I grunted.

"And then his friend knocked on the door, needing something. He went to go talk to him and I was left half-naked on the bed. I wasn't sure I could get back down the stairs without falling, so I just had to wait for him."

That motherfucking bastard. He took my girl's virginity and then left her stranded in a house filled with drunk scum. I used all my training as Don to keep my voice even. "How long?"

"What?"

"How long did he leave you there alone?"

Sofiya bit her lip again and I scowled as I freed it, running my thumb over the tender skin.

"Almost an hour," she whispered. A tear escaped down her cheek and it felt like a dagger to the heart. "I must have been really bad in bed to make him run away like that." She tried to smile at her poor attempt at humor, but I wasn't having it.

"No," I said, cupping the sides of her face. "No. You will not take any of the blame for that asshole's behavior. He took advantage of you and left you in a vulnerable position." I swallowed hard. A lifetime of not expressing myself told me to shut up, but she deserved more from me. "I would never do that to you. *Never*."

Her fingers ghosted down my cheek, catching on my stubble. "Have I told you I like when you have a beard?" she murmured.

I grinned and rubbed my cheek against hers. There was a light puff of air against my skin as she giggled.

"I know you're not like him," she said. "I just... it just makes me feel safer to know I can get away if I need to."

I rested my forehead against hers. "I'll give you what you need. But one day, you'll know that the safest place for you to be is in my arms."

"When did you get to be so sweet?"

I chuckled. Even with the enraging story she'd told me, my chest felt lighter than I could remember. I would deal with the bastard who hurt her in the morning, but for now, it was all about her.

My treasure.

My wife.

"I don't fucking know. What have you done to me?" I asked.

Her crystal blue eyes met my dark ones. "Hopefully the same thing you do to me."

"And what is that?"

"You make me *feel*." Her lips brushed against my cheek.

I groaned as I ran my hands down her back until I cupped her plump ass. "Fuck, you're perfect. Will you let me inside you, tesoro? Will you let me show you how deeply you belong to me?"

"Please, Matteo." Nothing could prepare me for the thrill of hearing my name on her lips as she arched against my cock. I tightened my grip on her, wishing I had more hands so I could touch every part of her at once. One time with her would never be enough. A million times with her wouldn't be enough.

I pulled back enough to draw off her shirt and bra, revealing perfect breasts tipped with pretty pink nipples. My cock ached at the perfection of her. I placed kisses on each nipple and then down her stomach. Sofiya sucked in sharply and squirmed. I pulled back, and she covered her stomach with her arms.

"Sorry, I know I'm too big. It's been hard to move a lot and I've gained weight this past year and—"

I bit down lightly on her nipple, causing a shocked gasp to slip from her lips.

"I never want to hear you say shit like that again." I nipped her other breast for good measure. "And stop trying to hide yourself from me. It's unacceptable." I shifted her arms away from her stomach and replaced them with my hands, caressing and squeezing her softness.

"Unacceptable, huh?"

"Yes. And you're to obey me, remember?"

She gave my shoulders a playful shove. "Oh, stop it."

"That's not very obedient, *wife*."

"I don't know that I'm in a very obedient mood, *husband*."

I grinned and pulled down her leggings and underwear in one swift movement. "I can be quite convincing." I worked my way down her body until I was gazing at her cunt. It was the prettiest I'd ever seen, pink and wet with a perfect triangle of blonde curls. Sofiya made a little noise in the back of her throat, and her hand went to cover her pussy. I growled, taking her wrist and gently pressing it to the bed.

"Don't you dare hide from me. *Never*, tesoro. I will look at you whenever I want, for however long I want. Your body belongs to me."

"Well then, you shouldn't get to hide from me," she said with a pout. She tugged at my shirt with the hand that wasn't currently pinned.

I chuckled, kissing away her pout. "Oh, you are going to be a brat." But I obliged her, stripping off my shirt and savoring the way her eyes widened as she raked them down my chest.

"Do you like what you see?"

"Yes," she said with a mischievous smile. "Now these." She tugged on my pants and I smacked her thigh, but I couldn't deny her anything. I took off the rest of my clothes and lay over her, reveling in the heat of her skin against mine. I had fucked a lot of women throughout the years, but I'd never felt this close to anyone.

"You're so beautiful." My lips skimmed across her skin as I moved down her body, pressing hot kisses down her breasts and stomach until I reached her pussy.

She stiffened. "Are you going to... I mean, you don't have to—"

"Sofiya," I said sternly, "I am going to eat your pussy whenever the fuck I want. Understand?"

She blinked up at me as she bit her lip against a smile. "Okay, husband."

I moaned as I breathed in her scent, rubbing my stubble against the sensitive skin of her inner thigh. My mouth watered and I couldn't hold out any longer. I licked a long line from her entrance to her clit, groaning at her sweet and salty taste.

It took her a while to relax, but with each lick, each time my tongue circled her clit, she let go a bit more until she was gripping my hair and practically riding my face.

"That's it, baby. You're doing so well for me."

I shifted so I could cup her ass with one hand, canting her up so she was at a better angle for me to press a finger into her slick, hot entrance. A curse slipped through my lips as I felt how tight she was, my cock jerking at the thought of sliding inside her.

I worked her until she let out a soft moan, taking that as my sign to press a second finger inside her. She instantly tensed around me.

"Shh, tesoro, I've got you. You don't have to be afraid."

"Sorry," she said. "I'm being stupid."

"There's no rush. We'll take all the time you need." My aching cock begged to differ, but I was going to make this good for her, even if it killed me. I would erase the feel of any other man inside her, ruin her for anyone in the future.

She was mine.

She slowly softened around me, and I thrust my fingers in and out. Her wetness grew until my hand and face were drenched with her.

"That's my girl," I murmured. "So fucking good for me. Look at you, absolutely soaking me."

She looked away, as if embarrassed.

"No," I said. "Keep your eyes on me. I want to watch you fall apart."

"Oh, God," she said as she clutched at my hair, my shoulder.

"I am your god," I growled.

I kept working her with my fingers and then sucked her clit into my mouth. She shrieked, her back arching off the bed with the intensity of her orgasm.

"Good girl." I pressed another kiss to her cute clit. "So good for me." I worked my way up her body, feeling smug at her stunned expression. "Such an obedient little wife, coming for me."

"Shut up," she said, rolling her eyes, but a smile played on her lips.

"Naughty girl, talking to your Don like that. What am I to do with you?"

She arched against my hard cock with a gasp. "I'm sure you'll figure it out."

I gripped her thighs, spreading them before pushing the head of my cock inside her slowly. "Yes, it seems like I will." Fuck, she was wet and hot and tight. I rocked in another inch and she inhaled sharply. I cupped her face, gazing into her eyes. "Are you alright? Am I hurting you?"

She closed her eyes and shook her head, taking deep breaths. "It's okay. You just feel really big." Her eyes popped open as if she could sense my smug expression. "Don't even start with some toxic man crap."

I kissed the tip of her nose. "I would never." I rocked in a bit more, even though I thought the restraint would kill me. I reached between us and played with her clit. "There you go," I murmured as her pussy relaxed around me. "Just breathe and let me in. You can take me. You're made for me."

We both moaned as I thrust into her fully. We gazed into each other's eyes, the silence between us broken only by our panting breaths. But the silence didn't feel cold or stilted, especially as Sofiya ran her fingers through my hair. It felt like the world had shrunk down to just us, just this moment.

"Come again for me." My voice was hoarse, desperate. My body craved her pleasure, was fucking feral for her orgasms, knowing I was the cause of her pleasure.

"So bossy," she said, but then her lips parted with a gasp. I continued thrusting into her, moving my thumb against her clit, until she tightened around me. She threw her head back, mouth open in ecstasy.

I couldn't hold back my moan as I spilled inside her.

Sofiya.

My Sofiya.

My breathing was heavy, my heart practically beating out of my chest. "You've done something to me. Bewitched me."

Her lips were parted, eyes wide as she gazed at me. She was perfect. I wanted to stay inside her forever, but I needed to take care of her, make sure she wasn't too sore.

I reluctantly pulled out, my eyes hungrily taking in where my cum was spilling from her perfect pussy.

"That was..." Sofiya trailed off with a dreamy expression.

A wild grin spread across my face as I imagined filling her over and over until she carried my child.

I kissed her softly on the lips, savoring her sweetness, until a realization crashed over me like a spear of ice through my chest. I pushed off of her, my feet hitting the floor.

39

MATTEO

"Shit."

I paced by the bed, needing to do something with the frantic energy gripping me.

Sofiya sat up, drawing the sheet around her so her body was covered. I would have demanded she stop hiding her perfect curves, but it was taking everything in me to keep myself from losing my shit.

"Matteo?" Her voice was hesitant, barely above a whisper.

My throat was too tight to respond.

"Was it... did I do something wrong?"

"What?" I whirled back to face her. "You were perfect." My words came out in an angry growl. How dare she even question herself when that was the best fucking experience of my life?

A soft smile tugged at her lips and it was like the sun breaking through the clouds. The vise grip on my chest eased.

"Then why are you pacing?"

"Are you on birth control?" My question was too abrupt, but I couldn't find it in myself to soften my words the way she deserved.

Her lips parted and she blinked quickly. "No, I'm not. Was I supposed to be? I'm sorry."

I let out a deep breath. "I'm fucking all this up." I sat back down on the bed and pulled her to me.

"You don't want to have a child with me?" Her question was so tender it broke my chest open.

I gripped her jaw tight, forcing her to meet my gaze. "I want nothing more than to pump you full of my cum until you're round with my child. It would be a dream come true. But... can you have kids safely?"

I cursed myself for having my head up my ass that I hadn't thought this through. What if pregnancy was dangerous for her? It wouldn't detract from how I felt about her, although it would be a complication in terms of securing my legacy. For the first time in my life, my loyalty to the Mafia didn't feel like the most important thing.

"Oh," she said, chewing her lip. "I guess I don't actually know."

I freed her lip, running my thumb across the soft skin. "We'll talk to the doctor tomorrow and get an answer." I rolled my shoulders. Good. A plan. That's what I needed to feel in control.

Sofiya said nothing. Her fingers twisted in the blanket. I frowned, taking her hands in mine. I was struck again by how much smaller she was than me. My hands easily engulfed hers.

"What if I can't?" she whispered.

"Then you can't." I ran my fingers through her hair and leaned down to kiss her cheek.

"But you need an heir." She was growing tense under my touch, and I scowled. She'd been perfectly relaxed and flushed with pleasure until I ruined it. I needed to fix this.

I stood from the bed again, but this time I reached down to scoop up my wife. She clutched at my shoulders, as if there was the slightest risk of my dropping her.

"What are you doing?"

"Getting you in the bath," I said, striding into the bathroom. "Can you sit on the counter? Or should I get your chair?"

"Counter is fine," she responded softly.

I placed her down and turned to the bathtub. I wanted a repeat of our time in the tub the other night, but this time would be even better because I could touch her however I wanted. The water should soothe any soreness she felt, which was good because my cock was already growing hard again.

I turned the hot water on before looking under the counter for the bath shit. My eyes landed on a bottle of bath oil. Lavender. That felt like something Sofiya would like.

I straightened and held the bottle out to her. "This okay?"

Her brow was furrowed as she nodded. I ran my thumb up her forehead, smoothing out the skin. "What's wrong?"

"I'm sorry if I'm a disappointment."

My heart stuttered. "What?"

"If I can't have kids. And just all of this," she gestured vaguely at her legs, but her hand movement drew my eyes to her pussy, distracting me for a moment. I blinked, tearing my eyes away.

"You are not a disappointment. You will not even think that. I forbid it." I glared at her and to my surprise, she giggled.

Grown men would fall to their knees and beg for mercy if I looked at them like that. But here she was, *laughing*.

I ran my hands up her legs. "It seems like you're not taking me seriously, tesoro. Laughing at your Don is very naughty."

Heat flared in her eyes.

"What are you going to do about it?"

My cock twitched as it hardened and I groaned, pressing my forehead to her shoulder. I nipped at her skin. "I just might have to punish you."

She wrapped her arms around my neck, her hand cupping the back of my head. "Maybe I would like that."

I cursed and forced myself to push away from her. "Stop distracting me," I bit out, turning to the tub.

The sound of her laughter followed me as I poured in the bath oil.

I settled her in the bath first and then got in behind her.

"Are you comfortable, tesoro?"

"Yes," she said with a sigh, snuggling back into my chest.

I ran my hands down her front, lingering on her breasts before cupping her pussy. She whimpered and I leaned in to kiss her cheek. "How sore are you?"

"Umm..."

"Be honest," I said, tweaking her nipple.

She huffed and pinched my leg. "Fine. I'm very sore because of your big dick. Happy?"

I snorted. "Fuck, you're cute. But no, baby, I'm not happy that you're hurting."

"I guess you'll just have to take care of me, then."

I placed another kiss on her cheek, gently collaring her throat with my hand. "I guess so."

40

MATTEO

Nothing could have pulled me away from Sofiya except for the promise of destroying those responsible for the attack on her. She'd been sleepy after the bath and I'd tucked her into bed with a body pillow between her legs and heating pads wrapped around her. She fell asleep quickly, and I stared at her for too long, hating the thought of leaving her.

But I had a traitor to find and kill.

I texted Romeo to come up to the apartment and he slipped in a few minutes later. I didn't want to leave in case Sofiya woke up and needed me.

"Tell me you've tracked down the bastard that got away," I said.

His grimace told me everything, and the rage I'd suppressed for Sofiya's sake hit me full-force.

"How did they know where she was? Arben has to be behind it, which means he is after my fucking wife." My voice grew louder until I was almost shouting. Romeo's eyes widened at my outburst.

I glanced back toward our bedroom, worried I'd woken her. When I didn't hear anything, I sat down on the couch, weariness seeping into my bones.

"How is she?" Romeo asked.

I swallowed hard. "She's okay." *This time.* But what if it happened again and I couldn't get to her in time?

The dog popped his head up from his bed in the living room and came over to me, nudging my hand. I begrudgingly patted his head. Sofiya had fussed over him all evening, saying he deserved extra treats after his trauma. At her request, I'd made him scrambled eggs.

I sighed. "I can't believe Bianchi was the traitor. Or at least, that he was working alone."

"I agree, but I can't figure out who it would be." Romeo sat beside me. "We could have Franco investigate our own ranks, in addition to setting up the decoy runs."

I nodded. "Do it. Nothing is more important than eliminating the Albanian threat. I'll work on setting up the decoy runs tomorrow and we'll carry them out at the end of the week."

"Are you really going to ask Rustik for reinforcements?"

"Fuck," I muttered. Asking the Pakhan for reinforcements would show that I was vulnerable. Even with our alliance, I didn't trust him. "He's been pushing to come to the city. Says he wants to personally inspect the trade routes."

Romeo got up to pour us drinks from the bar cart. "Sounds like a load of bullshit."

I took the whiskey from him. "I agree. But it could be good timing. If we invite him to come next week, we can see if we still need reinforcements. If so, we can discuss it in person."

Romeo lifted his glass to me in assent.

A wave of exhaustion came over me. I'd been so focused on making sure Sofiya was safe, I hadn't let myself feel the depth of my fear. But now, it all replayed in my head—how scared she'd sounded on the phone, the endless minutes before I got to her.

"I'll head to the office now," I said. "Figure out the decoy plans."

"No, fratello. Take the night off and spend it with your wife." He clasped me on the shoulder, squeezing tight.

"What if I can't protect her?" As soon as the words were out of my mouth, I regretted them. I couldn't allow any cracks in my armor to show, even to Romeo, this man I'd grown up with.

"You can, you will. I know it. Because you always take care of those close to you."

I started shaking my head, but Romeo wrapped his hand around my neck. "You didn't fail them. It wasn't your fault."

I threw back the rest of my drink and got up. "I'll talk to you in the morning."

Romeo sighed and got up. "I'll see myself out."

I put our empty glasses in the kitchen and grabbed a dog treat from the container on the counter, throwing it to Noodle. After years of spending late nights out monitoring my city or hunched over my desk in my office, it felt strange to slip into my bedroom to sleep. Stranger still that my bed wasn't empty.

I stripped my clothes off and got under the sheets.

"Is everything okay?" Sofiya mumbled, eyes closed as she rolled to face me.

I ran my hand down her hair. "Yes, tesoro." She smelled like lavender and I breathed her in, adjusting the heating pad that had slipped off her hip. "But I need you to stay at home until we destroy the Albanians."

"You really think they were after me today?"

I closed my eyes and gathered her close. "Yes. But I'll protect you. I promise."

"You already protect me better than anyone."

My heart twinged at her words. I gathered her to my chest, hoping to God they were true.

41

SOFIYA

Gentle kisses on the side of my face pulled me from sleep, and I made a disgruntled noise.

"Sorry, tesoro. I have to go to the office, but Dr. Amato is here to see you first."

I shook my head. "Want to sleep."

Matteo chuckled, his lips brushing against my neck. "You don't even have to get out of bed. She's going to talk to us about pregnancy before I have to leave."

That woke me up. I pushed to a seated position but must have moved too quickly because a sharp pain shot through my knee like lightning. "Shoot."

"What's wrong?" Matteo's voice was panicked.

"Nothing." I patted his hand. "My knee just wants to pop out of joint. I need to wrap it again today and put some ice on it."

"I'll get it now." He practically ran out of the room, and my heart squeezed at his care.

A few minutes later, Matteo, Dr. Amato, and Noodle entered. I let out a squeak, pulling the sheet up to cover my naked body. Matteo swore and ran to the closet to get one of his t-shirts. He slipped it over my head and then moved the sheet aside to press an ice pack to my knee.

Noodle grabbed my medication bag off the nightstand and placed it in my hand before jumping up on the bed, placing his head on my lap.

"What a good boy." I rubbed his head and swallowed my morning meds. I was getting so much better at actually taking them on time with Noodle's help.

"Sorry for intruding," Dr. Amato said, smiling as she took in both my guys' behavior. "Matteo said you had some questions for me."

"Will it hurt Sofiya to have a baby?" he asked.

I raised my eyebrows. "Jumping straight in, I guess."

Dr. Amato sat down in a chair beside the bed. "This isn't my area of expertise. I've done a bit of research and it looks like people with EDS do have a higher risk of some pregnancy complications, but there's no reason to think it won't be possible for you to carry a baby."

I took Matteo's hand and squeezed tight. He squeezed it back.

"What complications?" he asked.

"Again, I'm not an expert here. But the studies I read suggested a possible increased risk for premature labor, bleeding, and C-section. But the research also suggested that pregnancy is well-tolerated in women with hypermobile EDS. If and when you get pregnant, we'll make sure you have the right specialist care so you and baby are taken care of."

Matteo wrapped his arm around me and I leaned into his side. I let out a small sigh of relief until something else dawned on me. "Would my baby have EDS?"

Dr. Amato gave me a thoughtful look. "From what I read, there's about a fifty percent chance that any child you had would have EDS. Of course, as you know, symptom severity can vary widely. There's no way to know if your baby would have EDS and how it might affect them."

My chest tightened as I tried to process everything she'd told me. There was so much uncertainty, and I didn't know how to cope with it all. I looked at Matteo, but he wore his usual impenetrable expression.

"Thank you, Aria," he said. "We'll reach out if we have more questions."

The doctor gave me a smile and said goodbye before leaving.

Matteo pulled me into his lap. "What are you thinking, tesoro?"

I fidgeted with his tie, trying to gather my thoughts. "I've always wanted to be a mom." I swallowed hard. "But what if... what if our baby is like me?"

He stroked my hair and pressed a kiss to my forehead. "We would be so lucky if the baby was like you." I opened my mouth to clarify what I meant, but he cut me off. "And if our child had EDS, we would make sure they received the best medical care possible."

I blinked as tears filled my eyes. "But does it make me a bad mom to pass my disability on to a baby?" Mila had never been interested in children and she'd never understood why I wanted to be a mom so much. I didn't really understand it either, but I'd always dreamed of having kids and raising them in a loving, happy family—so different from the one we grew up in. And after Matteo's care for me, and the intimacy of last night, I longed to have a baby with *him*. To see him be a dad. I could handle whatever pregnancy complications came my way as long as my baby was okay.

Matteo cupped my face and ran his thumb across my cheek. "You could never be a bad mom."

"What would you think if we had a child who used a wheelchair? Especially if we had a boy?" I pressed.

Matteo shrugged. "Then he would use a wheelchair."

"But what would others think? They wouldn't accept him as Don."

Matteo scowled. "The fuck they wouldn't. It wouldn't make him any less capable, and I would kill anyone who said otherwise."

His words eased the tightness in my chest. Hearing him defend our future child, defend *me* as a wheelchair user, meant everything. I snuggled further into him. "So murderous."

"Anything for you. Or for any babies we're lucky to have." His hand dropped to my stomach and for once, I wasn't anxious about my belly rolls. I imagined my body swelling with new life and wondered if maybe my Dream List could become a reality.

42

MATTEO

I groaned, pushing away from my desk. I'd been in my office all fucking day, making plans for our decoy shipments with Romeo and Domenico. We would tell our soldiers about our plan to drive additional weapons into the city from our northern warehouse to make up for the lost shipment, but each group would be told one of five different routes. We would track which route was intercepted by the Albanians, showing us which men to question.

We were still working to finalize our plans, but it had been hours since I said goodbye to Sofiya this morning. The slow-growing obsession I had with my wife had accelerated like wildfire after being inside her. I needed to touch her, hold her, confirm she was safe.

I'd abruptly announced to Domenico and Romeo that we were done for the day—citing dinner as an excuse—and kicked them out of my office. Excitement strummed through me at the thought of spending the evening with Sofiya as I gathered up the large gift bag and headed upstairs to our apartment. I came to a sudden stop when I saw her in the kitchen with three of my men. Angelo, Enzo, and Romeo were all crowded around the kitchen island while Sofiya sat on the seat of her rollator, a pretty smile on her face.

I. Saw. *Red.*

That smile was only for *me*, and now she was using it up on other men.

Angelo caught sight of me first and immediately straightened up, his eyes widening. "Boss."

Enzo jolted to a standing position, looking guilty as hell, but Romeo stayed leaning over the countertop as he gave me a shit-eating grin. The only one who didn't seem to sense my murderous rage was Sofiya, who moved to get up.

I let out an annoyed huff. I should be the one walking to *her*, especially after her day yesterday. She'd managed to stand by the time I crossed the room, and my arms were immediately around her. I wanted to scold her for not waiting for me, but first I had three men to murder.

I kept Sofiya in my arms as I turned to face them.

"Why are you in my house?" I asked, my voice ice cold.

"The lovely Sofiya invited us," Romeo said, standing up and stretching his arms above his head. I didn't know what the fucker was doing here. He'd left my office just minutes before I did.

"I'm trying out new cookie recipes and I invited them in to be my taste-testers," Sofiya said.

I looked down at my beautiful wife. Her hair was braided in a crown around her head, and her eyes were bright and happy.

Killing three men in our kitchen probably would make her unhappy.

I cast my gaze over the counters, which were perfectly clean, with no baked goods in sight. "And where are these cookies?" I asked, making sure to inject my voice with warmth even as I scowled at my men over the top of her head.

"Oh," she said, her eyes shining with sadness. I cupped her face, ready to eliminate whoever, whatever was upsetting her. "I'm afraid we ate them all."

I closed my eyes and breathed through my rage. These bastards came into *my* home, spent time with *my* wife, and now they ate all of *my* cookies? My hand twitched towards the gun tucked in my waistband.

"Just kidding!" Sofiya said with a giggle. "I wouldn't do that to you."

My eyes popped open. "Do you think that's funny, tesoro?"

"Just a little bit," she said.

My hand moved down her body and I almost cupped her hot little pussy until I remembered my men were still here. "Leave," I barked at them. Enzo and Angelo looked relieved to get out of here, but Romeo grinned as he walked towards us and pressed a kiss to the top of Sofiya's head. I growled, trying to figure out how to kill him without injuring my wife.

"Thanks for sharing your sweetness with us today," he said before sauntering towards the door.

"Thanks for your help," she called out. "Tomorrow we'll have to try some cake recipes."

The door closed, leaving us alone.

I lifted Sofiya onto the kitchen island. "They're here to guard you, not eat cookies." I kept my arms around her. "And if you need a taste-tester, you have me."

"But you're at work," she said, trailing her fingers down the side of my face.

I scowled, hating the reminder that anything could pull me away from her. My hands flexed on her hips. "I'll work from the kitchen when you need a taste-tester."

Sofiya smiled but then it fell, making me feel like the world had gone dark.

"You're sweet." She kissed my jaw, and I decided in that moment I might not mind being called *sweet* by my wife. "But I know you can't always be here."

"Those men are here to protect you, tesoro. They're not supposed to be taking advantage of you."

Her brow furrowed and she met my gaze with her bright blue eyes. "I invited them in." Her voice was soft, hesitant. "They didn't want to come at first, but I said it was okay. Was that wrong?"

I hated the unsure look on her face. She should never feel unsure about anything when she was in my arms.

"No. You didn't do anything wrong." I sighed as I placed another kiss on her forehead.

"But you didn't like them being here." It was a statement, not a question.

I said nothing in response.

"Okay," she said, a tight smile on her lips.

"Okay what?" I asked.

"I won't have them in here anymore. I'm sorry it made you uncomfortable. I just... It's empty here when you're gone. But that's fine."

I hated the way she was forcing a smile onto her face, hated the way she averted her eyes as if she was ashamed.

I wouldn't have it.

I gripped her chin again and forced her to meet my gaze. "You don't apologize," I gritted out. "You should have told me you were lonely."

"But that's not your problem," she said.

When would she realize that everything that had to do with her was my problem? No, my *honor* to fix.

"You'll come to work with me tomorrow," I announced. "Your guards can come inside the apartment, but only if you invite them. And you will tell me if any of them does anything to make you upset or uncomfortable."

I picked her up, supporting her weight with one hand under her ass and the other around her waist. I managed to wrap the gift bag around my hand. I wanted to change out of my suit and I wasn't about to spend another second away from her.

She wrapped her arms tightly around my neck, her lips pressing a soft kiss to my skin.

"But tesoro?" I said as I walked into my bedroom. *Our* bedroom, because she wasn't about to sleep in the fucking guest room ever again. "If they ever eat *my* baked goods, made for me by *my* wife, I can't be held responsible for their murder."

Sofiya giggled as I gently laid her down on the bed. I leaned over her with a scowl. She wasn't taking my threat seriously enough.

"Don't worry. As if I'd let them do that." She pulled me down for a kiss—the second one she had initiated today—and something in my chest softened. "Now, get changed so I can cuddle with you."

My cock twitched at her demand. I cocked an eyebrow. "Is that how you speak to your husband?"

Her cheeks flushed and she ran her hand through my hair. "I think he might like it."

I growled, pressing my face into her neck. Her skin was so soft, and she smelled like sugar and vanilla. She giggled and pushed me off her. "Change first unless you want me to trap you on this bed in your suit." Her fingers trailed down my tie as if she wasn't sure she wanted to let me go.

"I have a better idea." I pulled away from her just enough to strip off my clothes, tossing my tie across the room. Then I peeled off her clothes as if unwrapping a present, savoring every new inch of skin that was revealed.

"You're full of good ideas today," she teased.

"So you'll come to work with me?" I kissed a line down her neck and chest until I reached her soft stomach. I licked and kissed it, paying extra attention to the area after she'd shared her insecurities.

She squirmed a bit, but didn't push me away. "Oh, I have a choice, do I?"

"No," I gritted out.

She just hummed and nudged my head lower. I grinned, loving her unexpected confidence.

"What's in the bag?" she asked, excitement in her voice.

"Something for us to try out." I continued moving down her body until I was level with her pussy, and then I dove in.

I took a long, slow lick, groaning as her scent and taste surrounded me. Her fingers brushed through my hair and it made me want to fucking *purr*. I couldn't get enough. I licked and sucked, noting exactly what made her squirm and whimper. I was determined to learn everything about her body. I needed her as addicted to me as I was to her. She consumed my thoughts, and that was only after one night spent inside her. The reasonable part of me screamed *danger,* warning me to not let my guard down, to not let her get under my skin. But it was hard to care about that with the sweet taste of her pussy on my lips.

"Try out how?"

I ignored her question, too consumed by her sweetness to pull away long enough to answer. I circled her clit with my tongue, keeping a steady rhythm as she writhed against me.

"*Matteo.*" Sofiya's voice was breathy and desperate as her hold on my hair tightened.

"I'll show you once you come." I pressed two fingers inside her, groaning at how warm and slick she was. My cock twitched, desperate to be surrounded by her heat. I needed to find a way to stay inside her all the time.

She let out a moan, which turned into a scream as I sucked her cute little clit into my mouth. She clenched around my fingers, and I couldn't stop myself from grinding my cock against the sheets. Precum wept from the tip like it was just as desperate to be inside her as I was.

Sofiya panted as she came down from her orgasm, her expression soft and relaxed. I licked her clean, savoring her little whimpers and how she twitched under my touch.

I ran my nose up her slit, tempted to start all over again, but then she nudged my head. "I want to see what's in the bag."

I grinned at the little whine in her voice. I was going to enjoy spoiling her.

I set the bag on the bed and she eagerly moved into a seated position. Her arms came to cover her bare breasts and I tugged them away. I refused to let her hide away any part of her body, especially her perfect pink little nipples.

Her brow furrowed as she pulled out a large foam pillow.

"It's a sex pillow," I said at her confused expression. "I've ordered more. They'll be here tomorrow." I planned to fuck her often, and I'd read pillows like this would make things easier on her joints.

Her lips parted. "That's so thoughtful."

I snorted. "Yes, very thoughtful." *No selfish motivation here at all.*

She grinned. "Well, I guess I should try it out." She ran her hand along it. "Umm, how does it work?"

I pressed my face into her hair and chuckled. All the stress from my day had somehow melted away. "Let me help you."

I gently arranged her over the large wedge pillow, my hands refusing to leave her skin. Her plump little ass was high in the air, her chest pressed to the sloping cushion and arms extended in front of her. I gripped her legs, spreading them apart to reveal her pussy lips. She gave her ass a little wiggle, and I had to grip my cock to keep myself from coming.

"I like this," she said. She pushed up to a seated position on her knees, angling her body to face me. "And... I have an idea." She was chewing her lip again, and I scowled as I freed it from her teeth.

"What's your idea, tesoro?"

"We don't have to do it."

I fixed her with a stern expression.

"Okay, fine," she huffed. "Can you sit against the headboard and spread your legs?"

I wanted to demand she tell me every detail of what she wanted to do, but I forced myself to cede control, at least for this moment. I moved against the headboard, spreading my legs wide.

She looked determined as she arranged the wedge between my legs. I furrowed my brow, trying to figure out what she was planning.

Then she draped herself over the pillow, positioning her face *right by my cock.*

Her eyes flickered uncertainly to mine, and then she reached out, her small hand encircling it. I should encourage her, say *something* to put her at ease, but I was too busy focusing all my brain power on not coming embarrassingly quickly.

Then her little pink tongue flitted out and *licked.* I let out a loud curse and my hips twitched without my permission. She giggled.

Fucking *giggled.*

"Are you laughing at me?" I growled.

Her wide eyes met mine. "Never." Before I could respond, her mouth was on me again, except this time she took the head of my cock in her mouth and sucked.

I fisted the sheets and clenched my jaw. I would not come in less than a minute. I *refused*.

I closed my eyes, blocking out the seductive vision of Sofiya hungrily sucking my cock.

My hips jerked again, trying to push deeper into her mouth.

Think of something else. Anything else.

Torture.

Blood.

The pile of invoices on my desk.

It was no use. Her mouth felt too good.

"Fuck. *Fuck*," I groaned.

Sofiya pulled off me and my body screamed to push her back on me. "Am I doing good?"

"Yes," I said tersely. I wrapped her hair around my hand and urged her back down to my cock.

She grinned. "Feeling impatient, husband?"

"Don't toy with me, wife," I growled. She giggled until I added, "Or next time, I'll bring you to the edge over and over, but never let you come, even when you're sobbing and begging."

She blinked and then practically lunged at my cock, taking it to the back of her mouth until she gagged. She pulled back, blinking tears from her eyes. I ran my thumb across her cheeks. "That's my good girl. You can take me." She blinked, her gaze so trusting as I guided her back on my cock. This time, when she sucked me in deep, she only gagged slightly as she took me to the back of her throat.

My grip on her tightened as I felt myself about to come. I tried to hold off, to prove to my innocent little wife that I had more stamina than this, but then her cheeks hollowed, her hand tightened around the base of my cock, and it was over.

I let out a shout as I spilled in her mouth. My head fell back against the headboard and my breaths were ragged. That was the best blowjob of my life.

Sofiya cocked her head. "I wasn't sure how it would taste, but it's not bad."

I slung my arm over my face. She had just destroyed me, sucked my soul out of my dick, and here she was, casually analyzing the experience.

"Is it usually that quick?" she mused.

I removed my arm from my face and stared at my wife. "What did you say?" My voice was low, dark.

She met my gaze with wide eyes, but there was a slight twitch to her lips.

She was...

Fuck. She was teasing me.

A peel of laughter burst from her lips and I growled. "You think that's funny?"

"Maybe just a little."

I shifted forward, cupping her face. "You're going to regret that, tesoro."

"Oh, yeah?"

I shook my head, my mouth twisting with the effort of keeping the smile off my lips. She went to move off the pillow, but I held her down, my touch firm but gentle.

"What are you—"

I cut off her question by bringing my hand down on her ass. She turned to stare at me, lips parted. "Did you just spank me?"

I smirked and my hand came down on her other ass cheek. "Maybe you'll learn not to tease your husband."

She gasped as I spanked her again. "I don't know if this is the right thing to do if you want to discourage me."

My cock grew hard again at the realization that she fucking *liked* this.

I brought my hand down twice more on her ass before rubbing my hands along her pink, heated skin. My fingers dipped between her legs. Her pussy was soaked. "Mmm, my naughty girl likes this."

She shook her head and let out a sound of protest, but it just made me break out in a feral smile.

I moved fully behind her, running my hand down her back. "Are you still comfortable?"

"Yes," she sighed.

"You would tell me if you weren't?"

"Promise."

And with that, I could no longer hold back. I tightened my grip on her hips and thrust inside her. She inhaled sharply at the stretch and I knew she was probably still sore from last night. I slowed my movements and ran another hand down her skin, soothing her. "Good girl, taking whatever I give you."

Her ass jiggled with every thrust and even though I'd come just minutes before, my spine tingled as I held back my orgasm. I angled our position so her clit rubbed against the wedge with every thrust as I tried to fucking burn the sound of her every moan and cry into my brain.

Finally, *finally* she tightened around me, and we both cried out as we came.

I rested my forehead against her spine, breathing her in.

Memorizing everything about this moment.

43

SOFIYA

"We're leaving for the office in ten minutes." Matteo's command was abrupt, but his eyes flitted to my face as if he was nervous I'd say no.

He was standing by the bed—*our* bed—already dressed in his black suit and tie. And looking very sexy.

I stretched my arms above my head, ignoring the way my shoulders clicked with the movement.

"Okay, husband." I hid my smile when his shoulders relaxed.

As if I would deny spending time with him.

As if I would deny him anything.

Fuck, I was in so deep.

Matteo leaned down and pulled the comforter off of me in one swift movement. I squealed at the cold air hitting my bare skin, but he just smirked. He ran his hands up my thighs, his predatory gaze not leaving my face even when his fingers brushed lightly against my pussy. I grew wet, and I wanted more.

His lips met mine in a gentle kiss, but when I wrapped my arms around his neck to bring him closer, he pulled away with a low chuckle. I jutted my lip out in a pout, indignation filling me. I wanted him to tear my underwear off and give me an orgasm with his mouth, fingers, or cock. I wasn't picky. But instead of taking things further, he just gave my hip a gentle pat before straightening up.

"*Matteo*," I whined.

"Get dressed, tesoro. Ten minutes."

"But..." My mind felt hazy with arousal, but I was still too shy to form the words, to demand he give me an orgasm.

He ran his thumb across his lower lip, and I scowled. He knew exactly what he was doing. "Be a good girl for me and you'll get rewarded." His words made a shiver zing across my skin. Then he winked and left the room.

For a second, I was tempted to finish what he started, but I didn't have time. And no matter how torturous his game, I was intrigued enough to play.

I pulled on a blue plaid skirt that stopped a few inches above my knees and a silk cream blouse. I eyed my wheelchair but decided to take my rollator instead. My knees and hips felt solid today, and I was sure I could make it to the elevator and back without any issues.

Matteo was leaning over the kitchen counter, frowning at his phone, and Noodle was curled up at his feet. Both of them looked up when I walked in. I couldn't stop my smile at both of my boys giving me their full attention. Noodle immediately came to my side, standing solidly next to me in case I got dizzy. The service dog people had explained how Noodle was trained to stay close and help me maintain balance.

Matteo joined us, crossing the room to me and brushing my hair out of my face. "Your legs aren't hurting today?"

"I feel good. Ready to do important Mafia work."

His mouth twitched. "Important Mafia work indeed." He gave me a soft kiss on the lips and then surprised me with a smack to my ass. He smiled and handed me Noodle's leash and harness.

"You're in a good mood today," I said.

Matteo just hummed as we got on the elevator and headed down to the tenth floor, keeping a possessive hand on the back of my neck the entire time. His office was the only one on that floor—a massive room with floor-to-ceiling windows. The three floors below housed the rest of his staff.

"Don't you get lonely here by yourself?"

Matteo snorted. "No. Besides, this floor is mainly for Mafia business, as you call it. The lower floors are our legitimate businesses—administrative offices for our various hotels and real estate holdings."

I nodded as I looked around the room, my heart bursting when I saw a dog bed in the corner. "You got a bed for Noodle?"

Matteo said nothing, but I thought I caught the slightest blush on his cheeks. I bit my lip against my smile as I removed Noodle's leash, squeezed his face, and gave him a kiss. "You go take a little snooze while mama works." Noodle walked over to his bed, tail wagging, and immediately curled up on the cushion.

I turned back to my husband and raised my eyebrow. "There's only one chair." A single large leather chair sat behind his imposing desk.

"I removed the other one. People were getting too comfortable in here."

"You want people to be uncomfortable in your presence?" I didn't point out that he apparently wanted *Noodle* to be comfortable.

"I'm the Don, Sofiya." He sat down in his chair. Even seated, he looked imposing, like the king of the city. My cheeks heated as he ran his thumb across his lower lip.

I moved closer. "Does that mean you want me to be uncomfortable?"

Matteo's eyes grew dark as he ran his gaze slowly down my body. "Never. You are my queen." He snagged me around the waist and pulled me onto his lap, my back melting against his chest. "Are you comfortable now, wife?" His lips brushed against the shell of my ear and I shuddered, memories of last night—of his lips pressed against other parts of my body—flooding my mind.

"Yes," I said, my voice breathy.

"Good. You're the perfect decoration for my office as I work."

I shouldn't have grown hot and squirmy at his words, at the way he was treating me like an object, but I couldn't stop from shifting in his lap. His arm banded around my waist, holding me tight.

"But you said I would get a reward," I said.

"Only if you're a good girl and stay still and quiet while I work."

A whimper slipped through my lips and he chuckled, opening his laptop and pulling up his email. I tried to pay attention to what he was typing, to the many spreadsheets he pulled up, but my body only grew more restless and needy. Matteo said nothing, diligently doing his work, but he couldn't hide his hard cock pressed against my back. My panties were absolutely soaked as I squirmed against him. Matteo shifted his hand down my stomach until he was cupping my pussy. I moaned, arching against his hand to get some friction, something to help my burning need.

"You're not being a good girl, tesoro. Your little pussy is so hot and needy. Are you trying to distract me from my work?"

I shook my head.

"Mmm, I don't believe you. I think you need something to keep you in place."

My breathing sped up. What was he going to do?

"Hold on to the desk for me."

He shifted me off his lap, his hands staying on my hips to keep me steady. Then he reached under my skirt and peeled down my underwear. I heard the sound of a zipper and then I was back on his lap. My thoughts were jumbled, and I didn't understand what he was doing until he lifted me by the hips and pressed the head of his cock against my entrance. He lowered me down in one swift motion, and I cried out loudly at the stretch of him. I was soaked, but there was still a delicious sting and feeling of fullness. I waited for him to thrust in me again, but he just banded his arm around my waist and went back to his emails.

"What... aren't you..." I trailed off, too aroused and desperate to form coherent sentences.

"I warned you, tesoro. You need to learn to sit still. Now my cock will keep you in place while I work."

"But—"

"Shh, I need to concentrate, Sofiya."

His stern chastisement made my cheeks burn, but I grew wetter all the same. I did my best to sit still but couldn't stop soft whimpers from slipping through my lips. Time slowed as I watched the minutes tick by on Matteo's computer, each feeling like an eternity until I couldn't stop shifting my hips. I needed to come.

"Matteo, please."

His hand smacked my thigh. "Behave yourself."

The growl in his voice was the only thing indicating he wasn't as unaffected by this as he seemed. I was about to complain again when his phone rang. My mouth parted when he picked up. I leaned my head back on his shoulder, unsure if I wanted to scream or cry. My pussy had never felt this desperate before.

"The delivery has to be at the warehouse tomorrow, Enzo. There's no flexibility." Matteo's voice was hard, but his hand crept up my body until he was cupping my breast. "Tell the supplier he can either fulfill the shipment on the promised timeline, or I'll personally teach him a lesson on timeliness."

I gasped as Matteo pinched my nipple through my shirt. I should have been horrified by his words, that he was threatening someone while playing with me, but I couldn't find it within myself to care as he twisted my other nipple. The pain went straight to my clit, and I couldn't take it any longer. I pressed my hands on the desk, using my grip as leverage to pull myself a few inches off his cock and slam myself back down.

"Handle it, Enzo. I have some punishment to dole out on my end."

Goosebumps covered my skin as my husband hung up the phone. Heavy silence blanketed the room, and I bit my lip.

"That was very naughty, tesoro." His voice was deadly, pure Mafia Don. I shivered, a slight edge of fear to my arousal. "I see you'll need a lot of training to learn to do as you're told. Don't worry, I'll be persistent until you learn discipline."

Oh God oh God.

I should be protesting, should refuse to let him talk to me like that, but my body betrayed me. I let out a needy moan, gripping his arm.

Matteo pressed his face to my neck, breathing in deeply. "But right now, we need to take care of your punishment."

"Punishment?"

"Yes, Sofiya. I wouldn't be a good Don if I let people get away with whatever they wanted." He moved us closer to the desk until my stomach was against the edge. Then he pressed his hand against my back until my chest was flush with the hard wood surface.

"Reach out and grab the edge of the desk."

I did as he commanded. He moved his chair back, causing his cock to slip out of me, leaving me empty and aching. The desk supported my torso, but the way the desk's surface pressed against the top of my thighs made them ache. The pain didn't last long because my husband lifted me enough to slip a cushion under my hips.

His lips pressed against my ear. "Does this feel okay, baby?" I nodded. Apparently my husband had purchased an entire store's worth of sex cushions, and it made me feel so freaking cared for.

"Tell me the second anything starts hurting. Well, anything besides your ass."

His chuckle was dark and taunting as he stepped back, holding me in place with a firm hand on my back. His other hand came down on my ass cheek without warning, and I cried out at the sting. He didn't let me catch my breath, striking the opposite cheek. Each hit of his palm sent a shock of pleasure through me, and wetness coated my inner thighs. He kept going, alternating rapidly until my skin was hot and my clit was burning and desperate. My fingers tightened on the edge of the desk as I fought the temptation to reach back—I wasn't sure if I wanted to cover my ass or pull him closer.

"It's too much," I cried out.

"You can take it." He ran his hand up my back, the touch soothing. I relaxed fully into the surface.

"Good girl. That's it, just surrender to it."

His spanks lightened until they were a gentle caress against my skin. I felt like I was floating as he stripped me of my skirt and blouse. His fingers finally pressed against my clit.

"You're absolutely drenched for me, wife. I love this pretty little cunt."

"Please," I begged.

"Shh, you've been such a good girl for me. I'll give you what you need."

His cock pressed against my opening and I whined as he slipped inside, but this time he didn't torture me. He thrust in and out, his movements matching my own desperation. I clung to the desk as my orgasm exploded over me, tearing a loud moan from my lips.

"Fuck, I want to record that sound," Matteo groaned. He thrust a couple more times before coming inside me. He pressed his body against mine, and I savored the weight of him against my back, the vibrations of his rapid heartbeat, and the ragged sound of his panting breaths.

"You did so well for me, tesoro."

Pleasure had stolen my words from me, but I melted into his praise.

If this was what important Mafia work was, count me in.

He stood and slipped my clothes back on before lifting me into his arms. As much as I loved my husband's body, it was his single-minded care for me that led me to curl into his chest and warm at his murmured praise.

44

MATTEO

"You ready to go into the office in a few minutes?" I kissed the top of Sofiya's head as I passed her in the kitchen on the way to get coffee.

"I already made you a cup," she said, gesturing at the mug in front of her.

My lips quirked. "What is this, tesoro?"

"A caramel latte."

"In a golden retriever mug?" The cup had small golden retrievers around it, all wearing absurd outfits.

She looked down at where the dog was resting by her feet. "We should go shopping for some outfits for Noodle."

I grimaced, knowing I couldn't refuse her but dreading Romeo's face when he saw the dog in a fucking rain jacket or whatever Sofiya had in mind.

"Speaking of shopping—I thought I told you to use your credit card."

"I did!"

I pulled out my phone and read out the credit card transactions —an order for lunch delivery and a clear phone case.

"See, I used it."

"You spent seventy dollars."

She bit her lip, looking unsure, like she really thought I was angry with her. I sighed and rounded the island so I could pull her close to my chest. "Baby, I need you to spend at least fifty thousand a month. Preferably closer to a hundred thousand. If you don't, it looks like I'm not providing for you as your husband, as Don. Do you understand?"

"I think I'll need a few more pastries," she whispered.

I laughed and she pulled away quickly, as if trying to catch the smile on my face. I just arched an eyebrow at her and she cuddled back into my chest.

"It's hard to spend money when I can't leave the apartment."

I pressed a kiss to the top of her head, hating that I was failing her. She wouldn't be safe until I destroyed the Albanian threat. "It's temporary, tesoro. I promise." The only benefit was having an excuse to keep her with me at all times. "We have work to do this morning." I pulled away enough so I could grab my latte, taking a sip even though I hated to ruin the little heart she'd made with the foam.

"Lots of important Mafia business?"

I threaded my hand through her hair, using my tight grip to tilt her head back. "Cheeky. But yes, lots of important Mafia business to do. But even more important, we need to continue your training."

Her lips parted with the slightest whimper. I couldn't stop a wide grin from spreading across my face.

Her lip stuck out in a pout. "I don't need training."

"You definitely do. But don't worry, I'll help you become a good, obedient wife."

Her eyes flashed with fire and arousal. She liked me toying with her, degrading her.

We headed down to the office. My cock was already growing hard. This might be Sofiya's training time, but my cock was so conditioned that I couldn't ride the elevator without getting an erection.

———

"I THINK I'm getting the hang of this Mafia business. Maybe you should make me CEO," Sofiya said, bouncing lightly on my cock.

"CEO of Mafia business?" I asked dryly.

"Yeah." Sofiya clenched around my cock, and an involuntary grunt left my lips. I brought my hand up to collar her throat as my lips skated down the side of her face. "And what will I do if you're CEO?"

"Hmm," she said, drumming her fingers against the desk. "You can be my assistant. That way, you'll have to *obey* me."

My lips quirked at the reminder of her little rebellion at our wedding, followed by a tight feeling in my chest at the reminder of how the day was nothing like she deserved.

"Do you want a honeymoon?" I blurted out.

She twisted around, trying to see my face, but the movement caused both of us to moan at the change of position. Sofiya squirmed against me, trying to get some friction. It took everything in me to hold her hips firm. This was torture for both of us, but the feeling of having her completely at my mercy was too heady to give up so soon.

"Would you want to go on one... with me?"

I huffed. "I certainly don't want to go with someone else."

"Yeah," she said, a soft smile playing on her lips. "I would like that."

She had no idea how wrapped around her finger I was. The feeling was equally exhilarating and terrifying.

I went through more emails, savoring her little whimpers.

"Wait, stop," she said abruptly. "What's that?"

She pointed at the email I was reading, confirming my plan was underway.

"Hmm?" I said, feigning ignorance.

She turned to me, wearing a stern expression. "Why does this email say you've successfully seized Yuri Kozlov's assets?"

I shrugged. "Just part of Mafia business."

"It's part of regular Mafia business to seize the assets of the man who took my virginity?"

My jaw clenched at the reminder that this man had been inside her, and I tightened my hold, trying to press even deeper inside her.

"Yes." I cocked an eyebrow, daring her to protest.

She turned back to the email and read the rest. "You donated the money to a charity that provides mobility aids?"

I nuzzled into her neck, breathing in her sweetness. I'd wanted to do more. I'd toyed with having Kozlov killed, of going to Chicago and doing it myself. But killing him would jeopardize the alliance.

So I settled for anonymously taking his money.

His house.

Sending his wife evidence of his affair.

And if he'd happened to get mugged on the way home last night? Well, things happened in large cities all the time.

Sofiya remained silent and I wondered if I had upset her by my actions. Surely she didn't care about Kozlov? Didn't feel some sense of loyalty to him? Before my anger could build, Sofiya grasped my hand.

"Fuck me."

"What?"

"I need you to fuck me, husband."

I gripped her chin, turning her face toward me. Her pupils were wide, lips parted.

A slow grin spread across my face. My little wife was turned on by my actions.

"Hold on, tesoro. I'm going to make sure you feel me for the rest of the day. And the moment the feel of my cock fades from your pretty little cunt, I'll be back inside you. You will never doubt who you belong to."

"Yes," she gasped as I thrust inside her, hard.

45

MATTEO

"This has gone on too fucking long," I said, tossing back the whiskey Romeo had poured for me. "We need to find the traitor."

Franco *still* hadn't been able to track down Arben. We'd been out all night chasing down leads after a report that he had been spotted in Brooklyn, but had come up empty. And then I'd spent all morning in the office, sorting through encrypted emails.

I breathed through the rage burning under my skin. Someone in the Family was betraying me and making me look like a fool in the process.

"Fuck, I know, fratello," Romeo said, resting his face in his hands.

"Someone has to be helping him hide. There's no way that idiot is doing all of this on his own."

"You still suspect the Irish?"

"Franco's been watching Finnegan, but hasn't found anything. I was thinking about arranging a call with him, or even a meeting. Try to feel him out."

Romeo looked skeptical. "Could be dangerous if they are in an alliance with the Albanians."

I nodded and poured myself another drink. "I won't do it until we're out of other ideas. But it might come to it."

"You know Lombardi is throwing an engagement party for his daughter tomorrow. All the capos will be there."

"Fuck, I forgot about that."

"I think you should go. See if anyone is acting suspiciously. With enough alcohol, someone might slip and give something away. It's also a good chance for you and Sofiya to appear together, to show you have a strong marriage."

I groaned. I'd kept Sofiya hidden from the Family for too long. I wanted to show her off, wanted everyone to know how goddamn lucky I was to have her as my wife, but I also wanted to keep her to myself. It was the only way to protect her, and to keep men from *looking* at her. But Romeo was right.

"Organize it," I said. "I want extra guards."

Noodle padded into the kitchen, tail wagging, and Sofiya rounded the corner behind him in her wheelchair, looking deliciously rumpled. My heart skipped a beat at the sight of her. Her face was free of makeup and her hair was a little messy, but she looked well rested. I'd been forced to leave her yesterday evening to chase down leads all around the city and had only seen her for a minute when I returned this morning. She'd been so exhausted I'd made her stay in bed instead of coming to the office with me. She hadn't been happy about it, and I hadn't either. Being apart from her was painful, but I wouldn't do anything to jeopardize her health.

"Good afternoon, tesoro. How're you feeling?"

She was wearing leggings and a sweater, and I had the urge to buy a sweatshirt for myself just so she could steal it. The possessive beast in my chest wanted her in my clothes.

"Better," she said with a soft smile as she entered the kitchen. "I don't know why I'm so tired lately. Hey Romeo, how're you doing?"

"Good, besides *starving*. Matteo said you hadn't baked anything lately."

A smile played on her lips. "Huh, he must have forgotten the strawberry shortcake I made yesterday. It's in the fridge."

"Oh, really?" Romeo said, turning to me. "You should really

have your memory problems checked out. Probably all those knocks to the head."

"I'll give you a knock to the head," I muttered.

Sofiya rolled towards me and grabbed my hand. "Be nice. You have to learn to share."

I lifted her out of her wheelchair and onto the kitchen island. "I don't *have* to do anything, tesoro. I'm the Don." I wrapped my arms around her and gave her a gentle kiss. She was so soft and warm against me.

"No, you're my *husband*. Which means you have to be nice to me." She ran her hand through my hair. She did it every chance she could.

I chuckled against her skin, kissing a line down her neck. "I can think of plenty of ways I can be nice to you."

"Umm hello, I'm still here," Romeo said, waving a fork at us as he ate a mouthful of strawberry shortcake.

Sofiya slapped her hand over my mouth before I could snap at him. "Be nice," she hissed, scowling. I nipped her hand and she pulled it away, lips fighting a smile.

"Do you like it?" she asked Romeo, nodding at the dessert.

"Fucking delicious. I think the chocolate cake is still my favorite, though. You know I have a birthday coming up soon. You might have to make me another one."

"When's your birthday?"

I snorted. "It's in July. Three months away."

Sofiya grinned. "I'll make you another one before then. As long as you're nice to me."

"I'm *always* nice to you," Romeo said in something that sounded suspiciously like a whine.

I tucked a piece of Sofiya's hair behind her ear and kissed her forehead. "What did you get up to last night, tesoro?"

"I played poker with Angelo and his friends."

My grip on her hips tightened. "You did *what*?"

She cupped my face. "Are you about to be grumpy?"

"I am never *grumpy*."

"Ahh, sorry. I should have said, are you about to get all murderous and threaten to kill Angelo and his friends?"

I crossed my arms and she laughed. "I had fun. Angelo's been teaching me how to play."

Romeo snorted. "I would pay to see that. You have the most expressive face in the world. I'm not sure it's your game."

"No, I'm getting pretty good," she insisted. "I can even remember which cards are best to have now."

Something dawned on me. "What did you play with?"

She cocked her head. "What do you mean? We played with chips."

I met Romeo's gaze over her head, and he covered his mouth to stop himself from laughing. Angelo's poker nights had a two grand buy-in, and the winning pot often reached ten grand. My innocent little wife obviously didn't realize the *chips* represented real money.

I needed to ask Angelo how much she owed after I pummeled him for bringing her to poker night. I wouldn't ruin her fun by telling her about her debt, even if I didn't like the idea of her being around other men without me there. A muscle in my jaw ticked, and I tightened my hold on her.

"They were all gentlemen," she said, reading me like a book.

I just grunted.

"I'm taking the rest of this," Romeo said, holding up the pan of strawberry shortcake.

"I will fucking kill you," I said. Except I would have to remove one of my hands from Sofiya to reach my gun.

"Enjoy it, Romeo," she said, blowing him a kiss.

The bastard caught it and winked at her. "See you tomorrow night." He ran out the door, dessert in hand, and Sofiya turned to me.

"What's tomorrow night?"

I groaned, pressing my forehead to hers. "Just another thing that's going to keep me from tying you up in bed and having my way with you every hour of every day."

She nipped my lip. "Remember when you insisted we were just roommates?"

"I have no memory of that."

She bit my lip harder. "Romeo was right. You really do need to have your memory checked. What's happening tomorrow?"

"One of my capos is throwing an engagement party for his daughter." I hesitated, unsure if I should tell her what I suspected about a traitor. Sofiya was trustworthy, I *knew* that, but something held me back. I'd made the mistake of trusting before, and it had cost me everything.

Her hand tightened on my jacket. "You want me to go with you?" She sounded shocked, a little line appearing between her brows.

"Why wouldn't I?"

"Well... I just wasn't sure if you'd want to be seen in public with me."

Something squeezed my chest. "And why wouldn't I want that?" My voice was low, an edge of warning in it. My wife squirmed and avoided eye contact. I gripped her chin, forcing her to meet my gaze.

"Sofiya."

"My father never wanted to be seen with me after I got my rollator. And now I'm in a wheelchair."

"I'm not your fucking father," I bit out.

She jolted, startled, and blinked quickly. "I know. I'm sorry." Her lower lip started to tremble, and I felt like the biggest asshole in the world.

"Tesoro mio." I wrapped my arms around her, lifting her in my arms and carrying her to the couch. "I hate that you could think for even a second that I would be ashamed of you. You are the most beautiful"—I kissed her forehead—"sweet"—I kissed her nose—"perfect wife." I kissed her lips. "The only reason I wouldn't want you with me is because it means other men will look at what's mine."

Her cheeks flushed a beautiful shade of pink. "You're ridiculous."

I pulled her in for a kiss, licking into her mouth and groaning at her sweetness. She could think me ridiculous all she liked, but I wouldn't hesitate to remove the eyes of any man whose gaze lingered on my wife.

46

SOFIYA

I tugged on my dress as I looked in the mirror, hating how the fabric awkwardly pooled around my stomach and hips, making me look even bigger than I already was. Tonight was important. It was the first time Matteo and I would be going to a Family event, and I didn't want to embarrass him. I was wearing one of the dresses Sienna got me—the sparkly, silver one. It had felt magical and perfect in the dressing room with her, but now reality was setting in.

My father's cruel words kept playing in my mind, telling me what a pathetic waste of space I was. I heard my mother point out my new fat rolls, acquired after so many afternoons baking for Matteo and the guards. Would my husband be ashamed to have me by his side at events? Bratva wives were always perfectly thin and glamorous as they stood by their husbands. I had hoped to feel confident and elegant at this dinner, but instead I just felt a little sad and frumpy.

I patted Noodle's head. "Fetch my bag." He pranced off to get my medication bag from its spot by the bed, placing it in my lap when he returned. I gave him a treat and then fished out my pain meds, dry swallowing two pills.

I jolted when Matteo's reflection appeared behind me in the mirror, meeting my gaze with dark eyes. His expression was serious as always, but I thought I was getting better at picking up little microexpressions in my husband's face. I took in his perfectly tailored black suit, stretching across his muscular chest, and the way his hair fell lazily in his face. I wanted to run my hands through it.

Without a word, he pulled out a black velvet box from his coat pocket and placed it on my lap. His lips skimmed the top of my head as he leaned over my chair.

"For me?" I asked, trying to keep my voice cool, as if my insides weren't melting.

He just gave me a look in the mirror.

I grinned and bounced a little. "It's for me."

I ran my fingers down the smooth velvet and opened the box. Inside was a delicate silver locket with flowers engraved around the edge.

"It's beautiful." I tilted my head back and gripped his tie, pulling him down to meet my lips in an upside-down kiss. "Thank you," I whispered as my lips brushed against his.

My husband stood back up, clearing his throat as he straightened his tie. I held back my smile. I had flustered him.

He took the necklace and clasped it around my neck. His hands lingered even after it was on. "This belonged to my nonna."

My hand fluttered to the locket, holding it tightly. "Thank you," I said again. My throat felt tight. I couldn't believe he thought I was special enough for a gift like this.

"Don't take it off," he said gruffly. His jaw and shoulders were set —tight, unmoving—and I'd learned this was his tell. He was *nervous*.

I cocked my head to the side, still looking at him through the mirror. "Why? Is there a tracker in here or something?" I joked.

His jaw clenched. "Yes." That was all he said as he crossed his arms, meeting my gaze with a hard stare, as if daring me to challenge him.

"Okay," I said, biting the inside of my cheek to keep myself from smiling.

My protective husband.

He blinked. "Yes, okay. That's right." He cleared his throat again. "Are you ready to go?"

"I'm ready," I said, taking one last look in the mirror. With the locket on, I didn't feel as self-conscious about my dress anymore.

I maneuvered my chair so I was facing Matteo. He leaned down once more, but this time his hands ran down my side and hips. His touch was slow, sensual, possessive. His thumb and forefinger gripped my chin. "You look stunning, tesoro," he murmured, leaning forward to kiss my forehead.

This time, I couldn't stop my smile.

47

SOFIYA

My stomach fluttered with anxiety. I squeezed Matteo's hand tight, my eyes fixed on the lights illuminating the tree-lined road we were driving down. The capo's house was about an hour outside of the city.

Matteo put his arm around me and pulled me as close to his side as my seatbelt would allow. "Why are you so nervous, tesoro?" His nose skimmed the side of my face, and he placed the whisper of a kiss against my cheek.

"It's been a long time since I was out in public like this... at a party. Are you sure I belong here?"

Matteo pulled back enough for me to see his disapproving expression. "You belong by my side, wherever I am, and I'll kill anyone who says otherwise."

"I'm not sure murder would help the situation much."

Matteo just grunted as if murder solved everything. I elbowed him in the ribs, exasperated.

"Hitting your Don. That deserves some punishment, Sofiya." His stern tone mixed with his smirk and the way his hand crept up my thigh heated my insides.

I let out an involuntary whimper and Matteo chuckled, his breath ruffling my hair. His lips dipped to my ear, his words just for me. "Are you wet for me, tesoro? Do you want me to pet this needy little pussy?" His hold on my thigh tightened, heightening my arousal.

I eyed Romeo and Angelo, who were sitting up front, and Noodle, who was curled up at my feet, before giving my husband a small nod.

"Mmm." He cupped my pussy through my dress. "Too bad we're already here."

I glanced out the window. We had come to a stop in front of a massive mansion. I whipped my head back to my husband. "But..."

Angelo and Romeo exited the car, leaving us alone.

Matteo grinned and gently kissed me. "I guess you'll just have to be a good girl and wait until we get home."

"No," I whined.

He gripped my chin. "If you're good for me, I'll eat that sweet pussy when we get home. I'll make you come on my tongue, fingers, and cock. But"—He ran his fingers through my hair and then gripped tight, tilting my head back to meet his hot gaze—"if you're a naughty girl, I'll spank you and fuck you, taking my own pleasure from your body without letting you come."

I squirmed in my seat, pressing my thighs together with my soaked underwear tight against my core.

"There, that's the expression I like seeing on my wife. Needy and begging, knowing she has to be a good girl and obey."

I breathed in sharply. "You're mean."

He pulled my hair, causing my lips to part. "That's right, tesoro. Mean and cruel and dangerous. Don't forget it." He gave me a hard, claiming kiss and then he was out of the car, rounding it to open my door.

Romeo had already gotten my wheelchair out, but Matteo was eyeing the steps leading into the mansion as if he was going to destroy them.

"I can walk if you help me," I suggested.

Matteo ran his hand through his hair with a huff. "No, you won't. I will carry you, and then have a discussion with Lombardi."

"Miliy, you can't be upset with your capos for not having wheelchair-accessible homes."

His eyes flickered at the term of endearment. I hadn't meant to say it, but it felt right as it slipped from my lips. It wasn't a term I'd ever heard spoken in real life—my mother certainly wasn't going to call the Pakhan *darling*—but I'd read it in one of the few Russian romance novels I'd had access to. I loved having a name that only I was allowed to use for my husband. It made me feel like he actually belonged to me.

Matteo's arms framed the car door opening, his body caging me in. "You're very free with your demands today, wife."

I shrugged. "It's because I'm brilliant and you should always listen to me."

He ran his hand along his jaw and I knew he was trying not to smile. I took the opportunity to run my eyes down his body. Matteo stood tall and strong in his black suit, pure power radiating off of him.

He caught my wandering gaze and raised a questioning eyebrow.

"Just admiring my husband," I said. "Either that or deciding if I'm going to kill him for leaving me unsatisfied."

"I might be concerned about your threat if you didn't sound like a fierce little kitten."

I rolled my eyes. "I keep telling you I'm a great shot. I could probably destroy all your men easily in a shoot off."

Matteo leaned down, brushing a lock of hair out of my face. "Whatever you say, tesoro. Now, let's get this tedious party over with. We have a busy night ahead of us when we get home."

My cheeks heated when Romeo gave a little cough, clearly having heard my husband's words.

"Come on," Matteo said. He maneuvered me out of the car and into his arms. I handed Noodle's leash to Angelo.

"Maybe you should just stay in my arms all night."

"Your arms will get tired."

He jiggled me in his hold, making me laugh. "As if."

I grinned, pressing my smile to his throat. He smelled so good, like leather and smoke and rain. "Have I mentioned that I like your beard?" I ran my fingers down his sharp, unshaved jaw.

"You might have." Matteo took the steps up to the house with ease.

The heavy front door was flanked by four guards who all bent their heads when they saw Matteo, murmuring "Boss." Matteo gave them a curt nod and then the butler opened the front door for us, revealing a foyer so opulent it hurt my eyes. Every surface was gilded in what seemed to be real gold, with massive framed oil paintings hanging from the walls.

"Umm... They definitely like gold," I said.

Matteo snorted. "Feeling inspired to make over our apartment?"

"I've always said if you can view a room without sunglasses, you're doing it wrong. What do you think, Angelo? There's a distinct lack of gold in your apartment."

Angelo hid his laugh with a choked cough as a short man in a black tux approached us.

"Don Rossi! Welcome to my home. We are honored to have you here. Everyone is gathering in the gardens." The man—who I assumed was Riccardo Lombardi, one of the capos of the Five Families—glanced at how Matteo was holding me and then at my wheelchair in front of Romeo.

"Your house is not accessible by wheelchair," Matteo said, by way of greeting. "Fix it." He strode past Lombardi through the sitting room and out the open French doors leading to the yard. The setup out here was just as opulent as the interior—golden candlesticks on linen-covered tables, flower arrangements that must have cost thousands, and a crowd of elegantly dressed members of the Family.

My cheeks burned as everyone turned to take in our entrance. "Can you put me down?" I whispered. I was plenty embarrassed to be seen in a wheelchair, but being carried in Matteo's arms was so much worse. In his arms, I was prominent and noticeable. In my chair, I became invisible.

Matteo must have heard the distress in my voice because he helped me get into my chair without argument. Still, he wore a disgruntled expression—one that I now understood to mean he was frustrated that he wasn't holding me anymore, not angry with me.

"Come on," he said, gripping my hand firmly. "I have to *talk* to people."

"You sound as if you'd rather be tortured," I said with a grin.

"He probably would," Angelo said.

I snorted and took the dog leash from him. Noodle stayed close by my side as Matteo led me further into the courtyard.

The Made Men almost shoved each other out of the way in an effort to get to Matteo first, looking like peacocks as they puffed up their chests in an effort to be impressive. They all greeted me kindly enough, but their attention immediately returned to their Don.

After thirty minutes of listening to tedious conversations about shipping routes, weapons manufacturing, and drug running, I was overwhelmed and bored in equal measure. I couldn't focus on what anyone was saying with all the noise, the bustle of people, and my fear of being judged. Noodle rested his head on my leg and the weight of it grounded me, but I had still reached my limit.

I tugged on Matteo's hand. He immediately held up his hand to stop the man in front of him mid-sentence and turned his attention to me.

"What do you need, tesoro?" He leaned down and cupped my face.

"I'm going to go with Angelo and get a drink. Do you want anything?"

"Fuck," he muttered. "I should have gotten you something when we got here."

"You have important things to do."

He scowled. "Nothing is more important than taking care of you."

I smiled and ran my thumb up his furrowed brow. "You do take care of me, miliy. Now, do you want a drink?"

"You get one for yourself. I'll join you soon." He kissed me on the forehead before reluctantly turning back to the man in front of him, who was staring at our exchange with bewilderment.

Angelo and I headed to the outdoor bar. "Why did that man look so shocked?" I asked him.

"The Boss has never been seen with a woman all these years," he said. "And they've certainly never seen him treat someone like he does you."

My cheeks heated at how special his words made me feel. I gave Noodle a treat while I waited for Angelo to bring me a drink. A group of Mafia wives stood to the side of the garden with perfectly styled hair, elegant dresses, and expensive jewelry practically dripping off of them. When they caught me looking, they all quickly turned away. A squirming, uncomfortable feeling rose in my chest, but I forced myself to sit tall, trying to take my husband's words to heart. I was a queen and belonged here just as much as they did.

"Where do you want to go?" Angelo asked, my drink in hand.

"How about there?" I pointed to a quiet spot at the edge of the lawn. Twinkle lights were strung above us in this part of the garden, making it feel almost cozy. We headed over there, my new wheelchair handling the terrain easily.

"I wonder if they're worried my condition is contagious," I quipped, nodding at the women who were sneaking looks at me.

"Ignore them, bella. If they were smart, they'd be all over you trying to gain your favor."

I hummed, taking my drink from Angelo. I should be grateful they were keeping their distance. I didn't have the energy for small talk tonight, but the feeling I'd had most of my life of always being unwanted and left out crept up my throat. I blinked and looked away from them.

Noodle moved his head back on my lap, as if sensing I needed some extra support. I stroked his head absentmindedly as I observed the crowd.

There were at least fifty people here. Most of the men were significantly older than Matteo, which filled me with a measure of pride at how young he was when he'd taken over as Don and how successful he'd been all these years. The atmosphere was lively with people drinking and laughing, but there was also an edge of tension I recognized from the Bratva gatherings I'd attended. The feeling that traitors and threats could be lurking in every corner.

"Shit," Angelo said, looking at his watch. "Romeo needs backup inside the house." Tension lined his jaw as he wavered, unsure of what to do.

"I'll be fine here. I have Noodle and Matteo is just over there."

He looked down at his watch again and cursed at whatever message Romeo had sent. "Do not move from this spot, Sofiya. I mean it."

"I won't," I promised.

My guard gave me a curt nod and then strode quickly towards the French doors. Matteo caught his movement and looked over at me, his face like thunder. I gave him an awkward wave and thumbs up. He checked his watch, his expression growing tense.

I hoped everything was okay inside. It had to be something significant if Romeo needed backup.

I turned back to my drink, eyeing the maraschino cherries at the bottom. I was trying to discreetly fish them out when a gorgeous woman sat down beside me. I looked up, shocked that someone had approached me. Noodle wagged his tail, but stayed focused on me.

The woman looked to be in her twenties and had perfectly curled, fiery red hair and a smattering of freckles across the bridge of her nose. She was wearing a tight-fitting green silk dress, and I felt momentarily envious of her thin figure and graceful movements.

"God, these parties are boring, aren't they?" She turned in her chair to face me, a bright smile on her face. "I'm Leona."

"Sofiya," I responded.

"Oh, I know," she said with a wink. "The mysterious Bratva princess who has stolen the Don's heart."

I blushed. "I'm not sure about that."

"Oh, but I am." Leona's voice was sultry as she reached over and wrapped a curl of my hair around her finger. I stared into her dark eyes. Her presence was equally alluring and dangerous. "All these men think they're so powerful, out here posturing with their guns and their cocks. It makes it easy for them to overlook us," she continued.

I raised an eyebrow. "I'm not sure anyone could overlook you."

Leona chuckled as she leaned back in her chair and crossed her legs. "That's because you're smart and observant. I am, too, which is why I know *you* wield the most power in this room. And all of them" —she gestured at the packed lawn of the men posturing in their suits —"are too blind to see it."

"I'm not sure about that. I've spent most of my life feeling weak and invisible." The words were out of my mouth before I could stop them. In mere minutes, Leona had torn down my defenses. Or maybe I'd spent too many years alone that my defenses had grown as pathetic and vulnerable as me.

A feral smile split Leona's face. She leaned in towards me until her face was close to mine. Her eyes flitted to my lips. "How dangerous you'll be when you claim your power. I can't wait to see it."

My heart beat faster. I felt like I was pinned by a predator, and I didn't know if she was about to kiss me or kill me.

"Leona." Matteo's enraged voice rang out, and I whipped my head up to take in my husband storming over in a cloud of rage.

"Don Rossi." She leaned back in her chair, the picture of ease. "Nice to see you."

"Give me one reason I shouldn't kill you right here." Matteo vibrated with cold anger as he angled his body in front of mine.

Leona snorted. "Fuck, that line was *so* predictable." She peered around him to catch my gaze. "It was lovely to meet you, Sofiya. I'm sure our paths are destined to cross in the future." She reached out as if to stroke my face, but Matteo caught her wrist. She let out a bright laugh, did some sort of move to release his hold, and melted away into the shadows at the edge of the yard.

Matteo moved as if to chase her, but I snagged his hand. He looked down at where our fingers were joined.

"You don't need to do anything. She was just being nice."

"Nice?" He ran his hand down his face. "I swear to God, Sofiya. How do you get into so much trouble everywhere you go? Leona Byrne is the top assassin in the Irish Mafia in Boston."

I raised my eyebrows. "Seriously?"

Matteo sat down in the seat Leona had just vacated. "Yes, seriously. What am I going to do with you, tesoro? I should kill Angelo for leaving you alone."

"There was something happening inside. I told him to go, so don't get mad at him."

My husband's heated gaze made me squirm again. "You're just racking up punishments." He brought my hand to his lips and gently kissed it. "What were you two talking about?"

"She was just telling me I'm the most powerful person here," I said with a grin.

"Well, she's right about that," Matteo muttered under his breath. "Come here. I need you close so I don't go inside and murder your bodyguard."

He pulled me out of my chair and into his lap. I snuggled into him, soaking up his scent and his warmth. "Don't you have more people to talk to?"

"They can wait." He kissed my forehead.

A tense hush had fallen over the crowd, everyone trying to catch glimpses of their Don's unusual behavior. "Isn't this going to tarnish your image? Make you seem less intimidating?"

Matteo tightened his hold on me as I tried to sit up. I didn't want to do anything to jeopardize the authority he'd worked so hard for.

"I didn't give you permission to move, Sofiya."

My fingers tightened their hold on his jacket as arousal shot through me.

"I'll be more than happy to show anyone here who thinks I'm less powerful because I adore my queen the error of their ways." The words were delivered as a low threat, and it sent another shiver through me.

Movement caught my eye as Angelo and Romeo strode towards us. I wrapped my hand around the back of Matteo's neck. "You can't kill them."

"I'm the Don. I can do what I like," was his only response. I let out a long sigh, glad I was on his lap so he couldn't easily attack my guards.

"Boss, I—" Angelo started.

Matteo held up his hand, silencing him. "You and me, in the ring tomorrow."

Angelo gave him a curt nod before turning his gaze on me. "Are you alright, Mrs. Rossi?"

"Matteo's the one who's mad at you, not me, so cut it with the Mrs. Rossi crap," I said, rolling my eyes. "I'm perfectly fine. My husband is irritated because I had a perfectly lovely conversation with an Irish assassin."

Angelo's jaw clenched. "Leona Byrne?"

Matteo nodded.

"Shit," Romeo said.

"Leona isn't an Irish name, is it?" I asked.

"It's Italian," Matteo said. "Her mother was the daughter of one of our capos. She ran away to be with the second-in-command in the Boston Mafia—Leona's father. Leona claims her Italian heritage only when convenient. Have Franco look into what she's doing in my city, and ask him why the fuck we didn't know she was here."

Romeo lifted his chin in assent before pulling out his phone.

"What was going on inside?" I asked Angelo.

"Apparently, Lombardi's daughter isn't thrilled with her fiance," he said with a grimace.

"What do you mean?"

"She's in love with one of Riccardo's foot soldiers, or at least that's what I gathered when he showed up to try to claim her," Angelo said.

I turned to Matteo. "Her father can't force her to marry her fiance if she's in love with someone else." I could hear how ridiculous my words sounded as I sat on the lap of the husband I never would have chosen, but now would never give up.

"He's her father, tesoro. It's the way things are."

"It's not fair," I said quietly.

Matteo ran his hand through my hair.

"Can you at least make sure nothing happens to the other guy? The soldier?"

"He insulted his capo," Matteo said.

I cupped his face and stared into his dark eyes. "Please. He doesn't deserve to die because he loves her."

Matteo sighed before turning to Romeo. "See that it's done."

"Yes, Boss," Romeo said before he headed inside.

"Time to go," Matteo said. He kept me in his arms, holding me tight as he strode out of the party, ignoring everyone who tried to get his attention. Angelo followed with Noodle and my wheelchair.

Matteo settled me in the back of the car, pulling me flush to his body once he got in. He ran his thumb across my cheek in a gesture that felt painfully tender.

"Did you find out any useful information?" I asked as we got on the road.

"I certainly found out a lot of useless information," he said.

My heart twisted slightly at his non-answer. He was letting me in more, showing his care for me, but he still didn't trust me fully with Family business. Just then, his lips brushed against my forehead, and I told myself it didn't matter. I would take whatever pieces he was ready to offer because I loved him.

I loved him.

The realization that I had fallen in love with my husband crashed over me in a riot of emotion. I'd fallen in love with Matteo bit by bit, my heart expanding with every kindness he showed me, with every time he let me glimpse the real him.

I wasn't sure if Matteo would ever, *could* ever, love me. He'd locked his heart away after his parents' murder and I had to accept he might never unlock it. But as I curled into his side, feeling content and safe and accepted, I knew I'd been given more than I could ever ask for.

48

SOFIYA

"I need to feed you," Matteo said, trailing his fingers down my arm. The car was dark as we headed home. "Do you want to order something when we get back?"

A sign on the interstate made me gasp as I pointed at it. "Oh my gosh. Can we go to Sonic? Mila and I used to see ads for it on TV."

"What's Sonic?" Romeo asked.

"It's a drive-in. So you eat in your car," I said, bouncing excitedly. "It seems so fun."

Matteo ran his hand over his face. "Tesoro, please, I beg you. Let me spend more than a couple of dollars on a meal for you."

I leaned forward to kiss his prickly cheek. "This will probably cost more than the hot dog."

He grumbled, but didn't stop Romeo from taking the exit. A few minutes later, we pulled into the restaurant and parked by an illuminated menu. Matteo was closer, so I unbuckled and crawled over him to get a better look. His hand rested on my ass, giving it a hard squeeze, and I smacked his shoulder.

"What do you want?" I asked.

"A table to eat at," Matteo said.

I grin. "I will order for you, then. Romeo, Angelo—do you know what you want?"

"Oh, yes," Angelo said. "This is so much better than some pretentious party food."

"That's the spirit."

Romeo rolled down the window for me and I placed our order, making sure to get enough milkshakes for all of us, even though the guys insisted they didn't need dessert. Silly Mafia men. I also got a plain burger for Noodle. He had been such a good boy at the party. Just having him around made me feel more settled.

"You happy?" Matteo asked once we had our food.

"Yes." I leaned into his side as I dropped my voice. "And this means that we won't have anything else we need to do when we get home."

A small smirk tugged at his lips. "You devious, naughty girl."

———

Matteo carried me out of the elevator, his body practically buzzing with energy. Enzo was at his post outside our door, and I gave him a little wave as we charged past him. Angelo had offered to take care of Noodle's evening routine, so my husband and I were free to head straight for our room.

Matteo laid me down on the mattress, bracketing me with his arms as he leaned over me. "I have an idea for something I'd like to try." His voice was low and sultry, sending a shiver through me.

"What's that?"

His lips parted, and then he hesitated for a moment. This caught my attention—it was so rare for my husband to second-guess anything.

"I used to be a member of a club when I was younger. A BDSM club," he clarified.

My heart sped up.

"Have you ever heard of rope?" He pinned me with his heated gaze.

"Like tying someone up?"

He nodded. "It's something I enjoy and would like to share with you. I've done some research on how to modify it so it's safe for you."

"You want to tie me up?" I sounded breathless as I pressed my thighs together, growing wet just at the thought.

"I think you'll enjoy it." He ran his thumb across my lips and I parted them, taking his finger in my mouth and sucking on it. "Good girl," he murmured. "So good for me." He pulled his thumb out, running it along my lower lip.

"What do you like about it?" I asked.

"Mmm, many things. I like seeing my partners fall deeper into submission. Rope is about trust and communication and body language. It's the interplay of pain and pleasure, of dominance and submission. It gives me a feeling of control that I crave."

A spark of arousal shot through my stomach, but I also felt an uncomfortable, jealous feeling tighten my chest.

"What is it?" he asked, brow furrowed as he took in my scowl.

I stalled answering him, not wanting to sound petty and immature. He collared my throat, his hold on me pure dominance as he forced me to meet his gaze.

"I don't like thinking of you with other women." I spit out the words, trying to free myself from his hold. He wasn't having it. He pinned my hands down, allowing no movement. A smile twisted his lips, adding to my outrage.

"Don't laugh at me," I snapped.

"Never," he said, his expression sobering. "I was smiling because I like seeing you possessive over me." His lips skimmed against my skin. "You have nothing to worry about, tesoro. None of those women meant anything to me. I didn't have a connection with them beyond what we did in a scene. Playing with you would be completely different."

"Why is that?" I asked, still a little grouchy.

"Because I care for you. Because watching you fall apart with pleasure is the most beautiful thing I've ever seen. Because I don't want this to be a one-off scene. I want more with you. I *need* everything."

I buried my face in his neck, needing a minute to take in his words. He stroked my hair in a soothing, patient rhythm.

"How would it work?" I finally asked.

"We'd start slow. Explore how your body responds, what you like and don't like."

"And if I don't like it?"

"Then we don't do it."

"Does that mean..." I trailed off, not even wanting to speak the words aloud. He gripped my chin, raising a single eyebrow. I huffed. "If I don't like it, will you go to the club and find other women to tie?"

Matteo's expression darkened like thunder. "No, wife. I will not be finding other women."

Even though his voice held stern censure, it eased the tightness in my chest. I chewed my lip. "What do you mean that you like being with someone submissive? I don't know if I can do that, be that. I don't want to be a doormat."

A sound like a growl rumbled in Matteo's throat. "You will never be a fucking doormat. You are my queen. Your submission is something you give freely, and have already given me. How does it feel when I train you in the office? When I'm controlling during sex?"

My cheeks burned. "It feels good, in a dirty way."

Matteo nodded, no sign of judgement in his expression. "There you are, tesoro. You gift me your submission beautifully already. I crave control. You crave letting go."

"Oh. I guess I thought submission was something different."

"I might push you to your limits. I'm a dominant, commanding asshole. But you always have the power. If anything feels off and we need to pause, just tell me or say yellow. And if you get scared or hurt or want to stop for any reason, say red."

I ran my fingers along his jaw and nodded. He shifted so he was straddling my hips without putting his weight on me.

"I don't know how I got so lucky." His gaze lingered on me, and it made me feel sexy, not self-conscious.

He cupped my cheeks and then slowly ran his hands across my collarbone, my arms, and then back up, tracing a pattern up and down my torso. I breathed in sharply when he cupped my breasts, but he kept his touch frustratingly light. I tried arching into his touch, and the smirk tugging on his lips told me he knew exactly what I was doing.

"Is someone feeling needy?" His lips brushed against my ear and a shiver went through me.

His hands continued their path down my body, squeezing my hips and thighs. He teased the bottom of the dress, pushing it up my legs before taking it off completely. I inhaled sharply. He'd barely done anything yet and my skin was already on fire.

He lifted my leg and pressed his lips to my ankle. The feel of his fingers, lips, and breath against my skin built the heat in my core, especially as he worked his way up my leg. But when he got to my pussy, all he did was press a feather-light kiss to my clit through my lace underwear before kissing his way up my other leg.

"Matteo," I whined when he returned to my sex, this time just breathing on it. "I need more."

He chuckled darkly as he sat up. "You'll take exactly what I give you, tesoro." His skin was all heat against mine as he stripped off my bra and took my nipple into his mouth, leaving me squirming.

When he moved off the bed, I let out an indignant noise and reached for him.

"So needy," he responded with a chuckle.

He disappeared into the closet and emerged with a black bag. He pulled out a length of rope before getting back on the bed and arranging me into a seated position. He sat behind me, his chest pressed tight against my back, supporting me and making me feel cherished and protected. Then the length of rope was in his hands, trailing across my skin.

"How does that feel?" His words vibrated against my neck.

"Good," I said. The rope was firm and textured, but not too rough.

He hummed as he started wrapping the rope around my chest. He lifted my breasts, squeezing each in his large hands before running the rope underneath them. His hand collared my throat, and I shuddered. "You're doing so well for me." When he removed his hand, I looked down at the diamond rope pattern on my chest. Its hold on me was firm, like an extension of Matteo's touch. "How does it feel?"

I turned my head and placed a soft kiss on his lips. "Good."

He returned my kiss with a hard one of his own before moving out from behind me and lowering me to the bed. The movement caused the rope to shift against my skin, the friction of it contrasting with the softness of the mattress. Then he moved my arm out to the side and closed a wide padded cuff around my wrist. I met his gaze, eyes wide.

"I'm not going to bind your arms tight, just enough for you to feel it."

"Feel what?" I whispered.

"Feel my control over you."

He tied a length of rope to the wrist cuff and then attached it to the side of the bed frame before repeating it on the other side. I pulled against the rope, a flicker of panic running through me when I realized I couldn't move, couldn't get up. His hands were heavy on my stomach as he observed me, patient as I adjusted to all the sensations.

His touch grounded me. I took a deep breath and my muscles relaxed.

"So good," he murmured against my skin. "So brave, so beautiful."

His words filled that hurt place inside me that never felt like enough, healing the raw edges of the wound I'd carried for so long. I didn't fully believe that I was brave or beautiful, at least not yet, but I would never tire of hearing him say it.

49

MATTEO

My little wife was rope drunk, her mind going to that sweet space where she could let go completely. Her body was relaxed, yielding perfectly to her bondage.

I leaned forward and pressed gentle kisses to her forehead, nose, and lips. I was rewarded by a little whimper. The sweetest sound I'd ever heard.

My hand ran down her chest, checking that the rope wasn't cutting off circulation before I grabbed another length. "I'm going to tie your legs, baby."

It had been a while since I'd done rope—at least, with an intimate partner. I used my skills frequently to torture my enemies.

But nothing could have prepared me for the intensity of tying Sofiya.

I'd researched how to modify rope for Ehlers-Danlos, even talking to one of the riggers at the club who had experience with EDS. Sofiya's EDS meant that she was extra flexible, but I would need to be careful not to push her body into positions that would put a strain on her muscles or risk dislocation or inflammation of the joints. Her skin might also mark more easily—there had been some bruising when I spanked her—so I used soft leather cuffs for her wrists. The last tie I wanted to do was a mermaid tie on her thighs, which would hold her legs together.

I stayed focused on what I was doing, even though my cock was rock hard and pressing painfully against my pants. Sofiya looked like a fucking goddess in her chest harness, and I kept checking her for any signs of distress. My heart was pounding, both from my excitement and arousal, but also the edge of anxiety I carried—the fear of doing something wrong and hurting her.

I finished tying her legs, the pattern highlighting her creamy thighs.

"You're perfect," I murmured.

I wedged my hands between her glorious legs and cupped her pussy. My cock grew even harder at the feel of her slick heat drenching my hand. "You're soaked for me."

She whimpered again and tried to arch against my touch, but the ropes held her fast. "Please. Please, Matteo. I need..." She moaned as I ground the heel of my hand into her pussy.

"I love hearing you beg. Love hearing you so desperate for me." I pushed one finger inside her, groaning at how she squeezed around me. "I'm going to take you like this. Your sweet legs tied together, trying to keep me out." I ran my nose down the column of her throat, breathing in her sweet scent tinged with salt. "And you'll lie there and take it, because you don't have a choice." I gripped her ass cheeks and squeezed hard. "But you'll fucking love it."

She shuddered and whined and struggled against her bondage until I took mercy on her. I gripped her hips tightly, checking one more time that the rope wasn't pinching or cutting off circulation, before thrusting fully inside her.

Sofiya let out a choked scream.

"That's right, scream for me, tesoro. Scream for the way my cock is forcing its way into your cunt." I could barely form words. This was the tightest she'd ever felt, even tighter than our first time. Sweat dripped down my back as I thrust again, trying to fully seat myself inside her.

"Matteo," she cried out. "More."

I let out a curse and leaned down, our lips meeting with desperation.

"Fuck, baby, I'm going to come embarrassingly quickly. I need you to come with me."

She whined as I pinched her nipples, her cunt squeezing around my cock. I circled her clit with my thumb, silently begging her to come before I made a fool of myself. Just as my spine was tingling and I was seconds away from blowing my load, she came with a cry. I gasped a sigh of release and let go, filling her tight, hot cunt with my cum.

Her eyes locked with mine, wide and glassy with pleasure. We breathed in the same air, our hearts beating in time, and I had never been this connected to another being in my entire life.

We stayed in that trance even as I pulled out, removed the rope, rubbed lotion into her soft skin, and held her close.

"Thank you for making me feel so safe," she said, her lips brushing against the tattooed word "lealtà" on my chest.

I pressed my face to the top of her head, breathing in deeply. I wouldn't, *couldn't*, say it out loud, but she made me feel safe, too.

50

SOFIYA

The morning light streaked through the bathroom window. I leaned back in the bathtub, the warm water washing over me, and sipped my coffee. The coffee *my husband* had made for me, complete with a misshapen blob of foam on top. I smiled to myself thinking of how he'd scowled as he handed it to me, muttering something about "lack of cooperation" from the foam.

I'd been expecting to be sore after our foray into rope last night, but I'd woken feeling strangely relaxed. It was probably due to my husband's fussing over me. He'd looked murderous when he saw the rope had left a few marks on my skin and had insisted on rubbing lotion on them after kissing each one.

But I *liked* being marked by him.

He'd given me a long massage last night, and this morning he'd insisted I get in an Epsom salt bath. I'd tried to convince him to get in with me, but he and Romeo were busy with something and he didn't have time. I tried not to be too upset that we wouldn't get our office training time today... that I wouldn't get to spend the day with him.

Matteo entered the bathroom, dressed in a suit, and crouched down by the tub. I put down my coffee cup and lightly brushed my fingers along his jaw. My lips were still swollen from kissing him late into the night.

"You sure you can't come in with me?"

He slipped his hand under the water and tweaked my nipple. "Seeing you in there, wet and soft and fucking beautiful, is the biggest temptation of my life. But I have to go." He gripped my chin, tilting my head up to give me a kiss. "There's something waiting for you in the closet when you get out."

My heart skipped a beat. Had he gotten me a present? "What is it?"

Matteo chuckled as he stood. "My impatient, greedy girl. You'll have to go see."

I grabbed his hand before he left. "Will you be back tonight?" I bit my lip, unsure if my question was too needy, but I missed him when he was gone. I slept so much better when he was in bed with me.

"Yes, baby. I'll be back tonight. Be a good girl for me." He leaned down and gave me one final kiss before leaving.

I sat back in the tub, trailing my fingers through the water. So much had shifted in the past few days between my husband and me. I wished I could talk to Mila about it all—I could practically hear her excited scream at the recent developments—but she'd gone radio silent again. I was doing my best not to panic over it, but the constant worry was still there.

The suspense finally got to me—I needed to see what Matteo had put in the closet. I called Noodle over and leaned on him while I got out of the tub.

"What do you think the surprise is, malysh?"

I quickly dried off, wrapped my robe around myself, and pushed open the door to the closet.

I stopped in my tracks.

Matteo's walk-in closet was massive—the size of my childhood bedroom—and until now, it had contained a long row of his suits on one side and the clothes Sienna got me on the other. But now the back wall was filled with a large display of jewelry that looked like it was out of a movie. My heart pounded as I moved closer. The wall was lit, highlighting bracelets, necklaces, and earrings arranged in a rainbow of gemstones, and in the center was a diamond tiara.

"Holy shit."

I approached the display slowly, as if an alarm would go off if I got too close. Tucked behind the tiara was a note. I picked it up with trembling fingers.

For my queen

I flipped the card, looking for more writing, for some sort of explanation for my husband's sudden over-the-top lavish gift-giving, but there was nothing.

I sat down on the seat of my rollator and stared at the jewelry. It didn't feel like it was really mine. But then again, nothing in my current life felt real.

I ran my fingers along the edge of the card, taking in all the details of Matteo's handwriting—the unexpected swoop and flourishes of his letters—before pressing it to my chest. Warmth spread within me because no matter what, this card was real. While I wouldn't read into it, wouldn't let my mind believe my husband's gifts meant *love*, they did mean *something*.

I smiled as I ran my fingers over the diamond tiara.

51

SOFIYA

I was on the kitchen stool, using the pasta maker I'd found in the back of the pantry, when the door opened and Sienna skipped in.

"Sofiya! I've missed you! Matteo is keeping you to himself way too much."

I met her hug, keeping my floured hands and wrist braces in the air so I didn't get it all over her cute outfit.

"He's been very protective since the attack," I said.

"Some say protective, some say overbearing monster."

I grinned. I'd loved how intense things had been with Matteo and me the past few days, but I'd missed Sienna.

"Homemade pasta for lunch? Girl, you're making me look bad. You're practically more Italian than I am."

"I'm trying," I said with a little shrug. "Cooking is the one thing I've always been good at." I was wearing my wrist braces today to keep them stable while I used the pasta maker.

"I'm sure you're good at about a million things," Sienna said.

It was sweet of her to say, but it wasn't true. I wasn't very smart and I barely had any skills, but feeding others made me feel like I was bringing some goodness into the world.

She hopped up on the seat beside me. "How was the party last night?"

I passed another sheet of pasta through the machine. "It was... well, I'm not sure. Matteo talked Mafia business with the men. Most of the women were pretty standoffish." I was used to the stares and whispers from the Bratva wives, but I'd hoped things might be different here. "But I met this woman named Leona."

Sienna's eyes widened. "Leona Byrne?"

"Yeah. Do you know her?"

"Holy shit. I didn't know she was back in town." Sienna handed me the next sheet of dough. "We were friends, but I haven't seen her in ages. Her mom, Aurora, was best friends with my mamma. I don't know exactly what happened, but from what I've gathered, I think mamma helped Aurora leave the Family and marry her Irish boyfriend. I think they were happy together until my uncle came into power. He killed Aurora for defecting." She cleared her throat, and my heart squeezed.

"I'm sorry to hear that."

"Yeah, well... Anyway, Leona grew up in Boston, but she wanted to go to NYU for college."

My lips parted in surprise. I had so many questions. "She went to college?"

"Yeah. She had to get special permission from Matteo to be allowed in the city, but I forced him to agree so I would have a friend in my program. We both studied business management and were close in school. But once she graduated, she officially joined the Irish Mob, so she's not supposed to be in New York at all."

"Matteo wasn't happy to see her at the party."

Sienna snorted. "I bet. Did he tell you what she does?"

"Umm, he said she's an assassin?"

Sienna grinned. "Yeah. It's pretty badass. The Irish teach their girls fighting and combat, and Leona always had a talent for it."

It wasn't hard to believe. Leona's entire energy screamed *danger*.

"Were you taught combat and all of that?"

Sienna shook her head. "I can shoot a gun in a pinch, and Angelo's taught me some self-defense, but that's it."

"I could teach you how to shoot, if you wanted," I said, remembering that there were *two* things I was good at: cooking and shooting.

Her eyebrows raised. "Really?"

"Yeah, my brother taught me. I'm still trying to get Matteo to let me go to the shooting range, but I guess we'll have to wait until the Albanian threat is taken care of, anyway."

"The second it is, let's do it! And I bet Angelo would teach you self-defense skills, too."

My lips curled into a smile as I imagined what Matteo would think about that. "I'd love that." I moved on to cutting the pasta into strips. "I didn't know you went to college. Is it normal in the Family for girls to go to school?"

"My papà started allowing it back in the day. Mamma wanted to study Italian Literature, and he could never say no to her." Sienna smiled, but there was an edge of sadness to it. "He permitted Aria to study medicine, and slowly it became more common. I guess it's not like that in the Bratva?"

"Not at all. I don't know any women who went to college. Mila and I didn't even get to go to normal school." My cheeks heated with embarrassment. "We had tutors come to the house, but even that stopped several years ago. I'm sure I'd fail if I ever took a real class."

Sienna squeezed my hand. "I'm sure you would do great. I can help you sign up for classes if you're ever interested."

My mind whirred. Would Matteo really let me take classes? I could read and write pretty well, but other than that, my education was severely lacking. "I'd always thought it would be fun to take some culinary classes," I admitted softly.

"Oh, that would be fun. Maybe I could join you. I don't know a thing about cooking or baking. Matteo and I pretty much survived off of microwave meals after our parents died. Once he became Don again, he hired Giana, and she's cooked for us all these years. I can't wait for you to meet her. She's going to love you."

I was a little nervous to meet this woman who obviously meant so much to Sienna and Matteo, but it would also be nice to have more company.

I got down from the stool and grabbed my rollator. I moved to the lower cabinet, leaning down to grab a pot, and was hit with a wave of dizziness. Noodle was at my side instantly, and I leaned against him, the room spinning.

"Sofiya?" Sienna's voice was hazy, like it was coming to me through water.

I took a deep breath, clinging to Noodle until my vision cleared. He nudged me until I was sitting down on my rollator.

"Are you okay?" Sienna was by my side. "Should I call Matteo or Aria?"

I smiled as I rubbed Noodle's head. "All good. Just got dizzy."

"What can I do?"

"Can you grab a pot from under there?" I pointed at the lower cabinet. "I was going to make cacio e pepe if that's okay with you?"

Sienna grabbed the pot and filled it, throwing concerned glances my way. "You could feed me plain pasta and it would be fine with me, but cacio e pepe sounds perfect. If you're sure you're up to it? If not, you could tell me what to do and I will attempt not to burn the kitchen down."

I snorted. "No, I really think I'm okay now." I grabbed my glass of water off the counter and drank the rest of it down. I needed to stay hydrated.

Sienna moved the pot to the top of the stove. I stood again, this time moving slowly, but my dizziness had passed. I busied myself with the pasta preparations.

"That smells so good," Sienna said, looking over my shoulder at what I was doing. "I think we need to have lunch together every day."

I grinned. "I'm not sure Matteo would be thrilled with that arrangement."

"We can't all bend to his will," she said, rolling her eyes. "By the way, how did he react to seeing Leona?"

"He wasn't particularly thrilled, but he didn't do anything to her."

Sienna smirked. "Don't worry, Leona can hold her own."

I bet she could. But I still wouldn't tell Matteo I'd found a card with her phone number tucked inside my purse.

"How are things going between you two?" Sienna asked.

I blushed. "Matteo and me? Good."

"If he wasn't my brother, I'd be demanding all the dirty details because that blush says it all."

I laughed. "No dirty details, promise." I hesitated before adding, "He did give me a gift this morning."

"Ooh, what is it?"

"Umm... an entire closet full of jewelry," I mumbled, my face heating further. Would Sienna think it was too much? That I didn't deserve it?

Sienna gasped. "Can I see?"

I nodded and she took off for the closet while I finished up lunch. Her eyes were bright when she returned.

"Damn, my brother did good. Well, whoever he hired to pick that stuff out did good. You'll look amazing in all of it."

"You think I should really wear it? It all seems so... *excessive*."

"That is the point," Sienna said with a wink. "You're in the Mafia now. We live for excess."

———

"Did you and Sienna have a good time today?" Matteo asked.

We were curled up on the couch. It was almost midnight, but neither of us wanted to go to bed. He'd only gotten home a few minutes ago, and I wanted as much time with him as possible.

"We did. I made pasta and she invited herself over for lunch every day from now on."

Matteo scoffed, trailing his hand over my hip. He must have turned up the heat when he got home because I was comfortable in a cami and lace boy shorts, and he was shirtless. I trailed my fingers down the tattoos on his chest. I'd looked up what the words across his chest meant in Italian: family, honor, loyalty. I wondered how I fit into that equation.

"Why did you give me a closet full of jewelry?" I whispered.

"I didn't. It's just the back wall."

I pinched his nipple and laughed when he jumped. He gave me a hard smack on my ass but couldn't hide the way his lips twitched.

"Why?" I asked again.

"Because you deserve it."

"It's too much."

"No, it's not. Don't argue with me, tesoro."

I pressed my smile into his chest. "Okay, miliy."

A satisfied little smirk bloomed across Matteo's face at hearing my nickname for him. He played with my hair, his eyes closed and expression as serene as I'd ever seen it. The movie we'd put on played quietly in the background, forgotten. It was moments like this that I wished he wasn't the Mafia Don and I wasn't the Bratva princess. I wished we could just be Matteo and Sofiya.

"How was Mafia business today?"

His lips turned up in an almost-smile. "Fucking terrible. It took me away from you."

"You sweet talker." I cupped his face and kissed his cheek. "Oh, I was doing some reading today and I learned a new word." I'd purchased some self-help books in addition to my growing horde of romance books. Personal growth and all that.

"What word is that?"

"Alexithymia."

Matteo cocked his eyebrow.

"It's when you struggle to feel and name your emotions. A lot of people who experience childhood trauma apparently have it." I kept my voice neutral, like I was just sharing an interesting fact, but I couldn't stop my eyes from flicking to his face and then back down to my hands.

"Is that so?"

"Yeah. I just thought it was interesting."

Matteo moved quickly, angling his body towards me and caging me so his body pinned me against the cushions.

"Are you trying to diagnose me, tesoro?"

I gazed up at him, keeping my eyes wide and innocent, but I couldn't stop the slight twitch of my lips. "I would never do that, miliy."

"Of course not," he said, gripping my chin between his thumb and forefinger.

"Anyway, you're very in touch with your emotions," I deadpanned.

Matteo swore as his lips turned up in an unwilling smile. "Brat."

"Your brat." I pressed my lips to his, running my fingers through his hair and pulling him closer. I nipped his lip and pressed my tongue against his, loving the taste of him. He grasped my neck, but instead of deepening the kiss, he pulled away, leaving me cold. A hint of rejection worked through me.

"Don't look at me like that, tesoro. You are irresistible. But I have to talk to you about something." His serious tone made my stomach drop.

He twirled a piece of my hair around his finger. "We've arranged a dinner tomorrow. With your father. He's coming into town."

I froze, but my heart certainly didn't. It sped up, as if knowing I would be within a few miles of my father soon. I knew it wasn't realistic, but I'd hoped never to see him again.

"I know, tesoro." He pulled me onto his lap, cradling me to his chest. "I don't like it. But we need his support in this war with the Albanians. Arben has formed an alliance with someone, but I can't figure out who. I should have been able to end this weeks ago."

I hated the self-blame I saw in his eyes. "It's not your fault." I rested my head on his chest. I didn't know the extent of what was happening, but if partnering with the Pakhan would help my husband destroy his enemies faster, I wouldn't make it harder for him. "Do you want me to come to the dinner?"

He sighed and pressed a kiss to my forehead. "I won't force you. But the wives will be in attendance."

"My mama?"

"Yes, I believe so."

There was no way for me to avoid it. My absence would be questioned, and Matteo's authority with it. "I'll come, then," I whispered. "Where is it?"

His arms tightened around me. "My cousin's restaurant. We'll be the only ones there."

"Is Mila coming?"

"I don't think so." At my dejected expression, he brushed his fingers across my cheek. "We'll have her visit once this is all settled. Okay, tesoro?"

I nodded. "Yeah. I just miss her. And I'm afraid the Pakhan will do something to hurt her."

Matteo's expression darkened. "What makes you say that?"

Shit. I couldn't have him walk into a meeting with my father ready to murder. "No reason."

"You're a terrible liar." He rearranged me so I was facing him and cupped my face with both hands. "Tell me. Did he hurt you? Raise a hand against you?"

I chewed my lip. "I don't think I should answer that."

Fire blazed in his dark eyes. "I will kill him, Sofiya. I swear it, I will fucking end him."

"No, you will not. You're in an alliance with him. You need his support."

"No one hurts you and gets away with it."

"He hasn't gotten away with it." I smoothed my fingers over the lines in his furrowed brow. "*I'm* the one who got away. To my new, amazing life with you."

He swallowed hard. "I won't kill him... yet. But I swear to God, tesoro, he will pay. You're not coming tomorrow night."

"Yes, I am. I have to, or you'll look weak." If I wasn't there, it would suggest that Matteo didn't have control over his household.

He knew I was right because he let out a displeased sound in the back of his throat before gripping my jaw and pulling me in for a hard kiss. "I'll protect you. I vow it. And one day I will punish him for every bit of pain he's ever caused you."

We stared at each other, the silence holding all the unsaid words between us—my longing, my love for him. I leaned into his chest and we stayed there, wrapped in each other, as the movie continued playing.

52

SOFIYA

My father was late.

It shouldn't come as a surprise—it was yet another way for him to try to assert his power in every situation by subtly disrespecting Matteo, even though he needed this alliance just as much as my husband did. I didn't know much about the Pakhan's business dealings, but I knew he had been coveting New York trade routes for years. Leave it to my father to let his pride interfere with maintaining his own best interest.

Matteo's hand rested on the back of my neck, his hold the only thing keeping me even remotely calm. My father couldn't hurt me anymore. He could try, but I had people in my corner now. Angelo, Romeo, and Domenico were stationed around the restaurant, and even more men were in the back and surrounding the perimeter. The worst the Pakhan could do was humiliate me, but I trusted my husband to not pay attention to whatever vitriol my father spouted about me.

I fidgeted with my new diamond bracelet. Matching earrings swung lightly against my skin. They were beautiful, but my favorite was still the delicate locket Matteo had given me. It was warm as it rested against my neck. The jewels were armor against the Bratva women I knew would be in attendance.

Three black G-Wagons pulled up outside the restaurant, and Matteo tightened his hold on me slightly before letting go. I grabbed his hand as he stood. "Don't do anything to ruin the alliance just for me, okay?"

A flash of fury crossed his face and he leaned down, hands resting on the sides of my wheelchair, caging me in. "*Just* for you, tesoro? I know you're not implying that you wouldn't be worth it, that you aren't my priority. Because if you were, I would have to bend you over my knee right here."

My cheeks heated. "No, I definitely wasn't suggesting that."

He pressed a kiss to my lips with a fierce scowl, straightening up as the front door swung open.

One of the Italian guards held it open, and the Pakhan entered. His sneering gaze raked over me, and I clenched my fists. He was followed by his second-in-command, Bogdan, a cruel man around my father's age. I'd done my best to keep my distance from him my entire childhood. He was a man who loved inflicting pain on others. Following him were two of his guards I recognized as Igor and Arkadi. I could already feel myself shrinking, trying to make myself a smaller target for their ridicule.

The wives entered behind the men. My mama, wearing a pea-green satin dress with a full skirt, Bogdan's wife Yulia, and two younger women who must be married to the guards. I thought the pretty brown-haired one might be named Liliya.

I wished Noodle was by my side. He'd been in my life for such a short time, but now I couldn't imagine being without him. Enzo had taken him for the evening and while I missed him, I would never risk Noodle by having him close to my father. When I was six years old, I'd found a tiny kitten in a ditch by our house. I'd named her Zvezda —Star—and nursed her in my room for weeks. She'd grown strong under my care, delighting Mila and me with her little acts of mischief in our room, until the Pakhan discovered her and drowned her in front of me.

There was no fucking way Noodle was getting anywhere near him.

Matteo's expression was relaxed and impassive as he welcomed our guests. Was I the only one who noticed the white hot rage simmering under the surface?

"Come, let's eat," he said, guiding everyone to the large table in the center of the restaurant. It was set beautifully with lit candlesticks, flowers, and wine.

"Sit at that end," the Pakhan instructed my mother, dismissing her with a wave of his hand.

Matteo had the seat of honor at the head of the table and guided me to the seat at his right hand.

"Bah, let your wife sit at the other end, Don Rossi. That way, us men can have a real conversation."

Your wife? Classic. How quickly he'd removed any reminder of his relationship to me.

"My wife sits beside me," Matteo said, his voice like ice.

"Well, she's certainly not *standing* beside you," Yulia said in Russian, her voice just loud enough to ensure I heard her.

I gave her a sickeningly sweet smile and responded in Russian. "Bold words from a woman whose husband can't get away from her fast enough. You arrived last night? That means he must have found at least three women to fuck already."

It was a low blow and I felt a little guilty, but Yulia's furious expression gave me some pleasure, too.

Matteo met my gaze, and I shook my head slightly. I could hold my own against the Bratva women. He took my hand and helped me into my chair before standing behind me, his hands on my shoulders as he stared my father down, daring him to say something.

The Pakhan burst out laughing. "Young love! How we all remember those days."

None of his men cracked a smile. I doubted they would know what love was if it smacked them in the face.

Everyone took their seats, the Bratva wives relegated to the opposite end of the table. One of the new guards sat beside me, which I was thankful for. It was bad enough to have to look at the Pakhan and Bogdan, I didn't think I could tolerate sitting next to them.

Dinner crawled by, filled with polite, bland conversation. Matteo's hand never left my skin—either resting on my leg under the table or holding my hand on top of it. A few times, I caught my father's gaze flitting to where my husband and I were touching, and I felt a sick sense of satisfaction. He had sold me to the Italians with no concern for my well-being, and it had backfired spectacularly. Angelo caught my eye over my father's shoulder and winked. Warmth curled in my stomach. I finally had a real family who freely gave their care and protection.

My mama stayed silent, but she eyed my plate of food. Her expression was so clear I could practically hear her scolding words about my weight gain. I took another large bite of fettuccine, staring her down the entire time. She looked away, disgust twisting her lips.

As we neared the end of dinner, servings of tiramisu and Sambuca appeared. Angelo rubbed his stomach as he eyed the large trays of dessert from his position by the wall. I needed to make sure he got some later.

My father stood up and announced that the men needed to try the vodka he'd brought. They moved to the side of the restaurant with a fireplace and large leather chairs. This time, I squeezed Matteo's hand and gave him an encouraging look. He needed to go with the rest of the men to appease my father. He leaned over and brushed a kiss on my cheek. "Behave yourself."

I rolled my eyes. "You behave yourself," I hissed back.

His dark expression told me he was imagining spanking me. He jerked his head at Angelo who was immediately at my side, escorting me to where the other women were sitting on couches. But I only had eyes for my mama. Her dress clung to her stick-thin frame and her eyes looked even more blank since the last time I saw her. I reached out and clutched her hand. Her skin was cold to the touch.

"Mama, are you okay?" My feelings about my mother were endlessly complicated. She had failed Mila and me over and over, and there was no kindness in her. But I also knew she was a victim of the Pakhan, and I held onto the desperate hope that she could break out of this fog someday.

She met my concerned gaze with blankness.

"Mama, please," I whispered, wishing the other wives weren't within hearing distance. This would be gossip fodder for the Bratva inner circles, I was sure. "Talk to me."

"What could she possibly have to say when you show up in *that*?" Yulia said, voice scathing as she gestured at my wheelchair.

I dropped my mom's hand and swallowed hard. I refused to be ashamed. Feeling accepted by my new family was slowly helping me accept myself. How dare these women try to make me feel bad for using a wheelchair?

"Isn't it wonderful? My husband got it for me."

"As if that makes it better," she sneered.

Mama sat silently. I wished I knew how to reach her.

"Tell us, Sofiya, how are things with your new husband?" Liliya asked. "He's certainly handsome enough."

I raised an eyebrow. "They're wonderful. And you're newly married?" She was twirling her ring around her finger.

"To Arkadi," she said, gesturing at the black-haired guard currently standing behind the Pakhan, her smile turning tight. "Another handsome man."

I inclined my head.

The other young woman I didn't know spoke up. "Is that your ring?" Her voice was filled with pretend outrage.

I looked down at my gold band, so plain, especially compared to the Bratva wives' ornate diamond rings with their three entwined bands. This was the ring my husband had given me when he didn't want me. I wondered what it would be like to have a ring that was attached to a happier memory.

"I thought the Mafia was engaged in the diamond trade," Yulia said. "I guess this *wonderful* husband of yours didn't think you worthy of one."

I said nothing but shook my wrist, making sure the light caught the diamonds in my bracelet. Yulia rolled her eyes and I smirked.

I looked over my shoulder at Matteo across the room. The men were drinking as smoke from their cigars swirled around them. I knew I'd been the one pushing him to go over there without me, but now I desperately wanted him next to me. Actually, I wanted to be curled up on his lap on the couch in our home, away from all these horrible people.

His gaze snapped to mine, his stare as intense as ever. I broke all rules of etiquette and blew him a kiss. There was the slightest tilt to his lips before he returned to his conversation.

53

MATTEO

I'd tortured a lot of men over the years. Killed a lot, too. I had long since learned to go deep inside myself to that cold, dark place that was devoid of humanity. But nothing about me was unfeeling as I sat across the table from Rustik Ivanov. Sofiya still refused to give me any details about what her father had done to her, and that told me everything I needed to know.

I lifted my glass as Rustik made a toast.

His days were numbered.

"I've heard whispers of some troubles in your city," Rustik said, downing another shot of vodka.

I inclined my head. "The Albanians are growing bold." I didn't want to give too much away, refused to show any sort of weakness in front of these men, but I needed to see how much they already knew.

The Russians glanced at each other. "So we've heard," Rustik said. "Arben is even more reckless than his father."

"Are they interfering with drug routes?" Bogdan asked, his heavily accented voice slurred. His eyes were glassy, and I wondered if he was just drunk or if drugs were also involved.

"No," Romeo answered. "Our trade routes are in hand. Our concern is the trade the Albanians are trying to bring *into* the city."

Rustik lifted his eyebrows. "The skin trade?"

I inclined my head. Everyone knew of my father's and my distaste for it. So far, Rustik hadn't dealt in it, one of the only reasons I'd agreed to this alliance. I wasn't sure why Rustik had avoided it—it certainly wasn't due to any human decency.

"Arben needs to be taught a lesson," I said.

"Another round!" Rustik shouted. The waiter rushed over and filled our shot glasses. Rustik held his up. "To teaching lessons."

I tipped my head towards him and took the shot. The vodka burned going down.

I fucking hated vodka.

"Tomorrow morning, we'll examine the port warehouses," Rustik said. "And then we can turn our eyes to the Albanian problem. Now, enough of business." He smacked his hands against his thighs, suddenly jovial. "Are you satisfied with your wife?"

My jaw clenched hard enough to break a tooth. If this bastard said anything against Sofiya...

Bogdan snorted as he threw back another shot. "I told you it wouldn't be a problem, Pakhan. She is a pretty one, even if she is a cripple."

A red haze fell over my vision, my furious heartbeat sounding in my ears. I didn't even have to look at Rustik to know he would do nothing, say nothing, to defend his daughter.

Bogdan leaned in, lowering his voice, although it was still loud enough for everyone in the room to hear. "I guess a cunt is a cunt. Doesn't matter if she can't use her legs."

My gun was in my hand before I even thought to move, my body acting on pure instinct. I took aim at his kneecap and pulled the trigger.

His scream pierced the air and blood spurted from his wound. I locked eyes with Sofiya across the room. Her eyebrows were raised, lips slightly parted.

Rustik swore as the man fell to the ground. His guards all pulled their guns on me, and my men did the same to them.

I sat back in my chair as if I had no care in the world. "I apologize." I turned to Rustik, ignoring the screaming Bogdan. "I should have allowed you the privilege of taking the shot, as it was your daughter he was insulting."

Rustik clenched his fist, eyes filled with fury, and we both knew my apology was all for show. I was deferring to him while also pointing out his failure in standing up for his own blood. My fingers twitched with the urge to shoot him as well, and with the way his eyes flitted to my weapon, I wondered if he sensed it. But I just smirked and placed the gun back in my chest holster.

He inclined his head towards me. "You saved me a bullet."

I threw back the rest of my drink and stood. "It's getting late. I will meet you at the warehouse tomorrow morning." I turned before he could say anything, effectively dismissing him, and strode over to my wife.

I leaned down and gripped her chin. Her stunned eyes met mine.

"Time to go, tesoro." She nodded and moved towards the door, but stayed silent. I maintained a calm, confident expression, but my insides were twisting. Was she scared of me now?

54

SOFIYA

Matteo was silent the entire car ride home. He kept my hand clenched in his, refusing to let go even as we got out of the car and went up to our apartment.

"I'll go to Enzo's and pick up Noodle for the night," Angelo said as we exited the elevator.

I barely had the chance to say "thank you" before Matteo practically pulled me inside and shut the door.

He dropped my hand and took a few steps away, wearing an unreadable expression.

"So..." I said, breaking the silence. "You shot my father's second-in-command. In a restaurant."

Matteo crossed his arms, his scowl fierce. "I would do it again."

"Is that right?"

"Yes."

I crooked my finger at him. "Come here."

That muscle in his jaw ticked, and he huffed a long sigh. I bit my lip to hide my smile. He lasted a few seconds before he walked towards me. I raised my arms and he leaned down, allowing me to circle his neck. He lifted me in one swift motion, his hands cupping my ass.

I ran my nose down his face, breathing him in. "You seem to be laboring under the delusion, husband, that I am upset about what you did." I smiled at the flash of surprise on his face. "I've had very few people in my life stick up for me, and never like that." I cupped his face, running my thumbs down his cheek before pressing my lips to his. "You've earned yourself a reward."

He pressed my back against the wall, and I whimpered as his cock rocked against my core. "And what will my reward be, wife?"

I ran my fingers through his hair. "Whatever you want. Have your way with me."

"This is quite a dangerous offer."

"Why is that?"

"You've just given me strong motivation to shoot a lot of men, tesoro, just so I can claim my prize."

I laughed against his skin. "Good thing you can claim me anytime—no bullets required—so please don't shoot more people on my account."

"I will do as I see fit." His tone was disgruntled, and I squeezed him tight as he carried me to our room.

He flicked our bedside lamp on, the soft glow illuminating the bed as he laid me down on it.

"Have I told you how beautiful you look?" He kissed down my neck and across my collarbone.

"You might have mentioned it."

"I will never say it enough. No words will ever be sufficient to describe your beauty."

I blinked furiously. I would *not* cry at his sweet words.

He brought his lips back to mine, deepening our kiss, and I wrapped myself around him, needing to do whatever I could to merge our bodies. His taste and scent surrounded me as he ran firm hands down my skin. He pulled away with a curse.

"I need this off of you," he said, tugging at my dress.

I rolled over so he could access the zipper. He pulled it down, his breath skating across my skin as he pressed hot kisses down my spine. He slowly stripped off the dress, groaning when he saw my tiny black thong.

"Fuck." He bit each of my ass cheeks, causing me to squeal, but he kept my panties on. "Roll over, baby."

His hands caressed my skin as I did what he asked, his thumbs circling my beaded nipples. He pulled back just enough to remove his coat jacket and roll up his sleeves, exposing his thick, muscled forearms. I reached for him, needed to touch him, but he caught both wrists in one hand. "I need to be in control tonight."

The vulnerability in his eyes made my chest tighten. "Whatever you need, miliy."

He kissed me on the forehead and helped me sit up, arranging a bolster behind my back to give me support. He crossed the room to pull a length of rope out of his dresser. The tension I'd been carrying since last night when I found out I'd have to see my father lessened as my husband strode towards me, loosening his tie. Maybe I needed to surrender control tonight as much as he needed to take it.

Matteo ran the rope across my skin, the slightly rough edge of the hemp causing a shiver to go through me. He took his time tying a chest harness, kissing me and teasing my clit as he wrapped the rope around my breasts and down my torso in a diamond pattern. The rope's tight hold contrasted with the gentle, tantalizing way his fingers brushed against my skin, leaving me wanting more.

"You're doing so well for me. Letting me tie you up, use you how I want." His words were a whisper against my skin and I swayed, trying to lean closer to him.

He kept a firm hold on me, arranging me so he could take the end of the rope and thread it between my legs. I whimpered as he pulled it tight between my pussy lips. My lace underwear provided a small layer of protection, but the rope rubbed against my clit, setting me on fire. He ran the rope between my ass cheeks, and I gasped as he tugged it tight, tying it to the back of my chest harness.

My lips were parted and I was panting. My clit was swollen and needy, desperate for friction, and the tight harness was a constant reminder that I was completely under Matteo's control.

"Eyes on me," he said, voice low. I found myself slipping deeper into submission as I met his dark gaze.

"Please," I begged.

He arranged me so I was facing him, my legs straddling his thigh. His tie and jacket lay forgotten on the floor, but besides that, he was fully clothed. I was vulnerable and at his mercy, and I felt completely safe.

He held the chest harness and rocked me back and forth, each movement sending a pulse of pleasure through me as I rubbed against the rope and his leg. I tried to move faster, but he was fully in control, drawing out my pleasure until I was whining and moaning in his grasp.

"So beautiful," he murmured.

We breathed in time with each other, our heartbeats synching as I fell deeper under his spell. I was floating—tethered to the earth only by his touch. A few times, my eyelids fluttered closed and he smacked my thigh in punishment.

"I'm going to see you fall apart for me, tesoro. Your body belongs wholly to me. Mine to touch, mine to command, mine to control."

"Yes," I breathed.

"No one else will touch you. No one will ever feel how drenched you get for me."

"Only you." The fog was settling in heavier now, my mind floating to the delicious place only he could bring me to. Absolute surrender, because I knew there wasn't any place in the universe as safe as his arms.

He growled and sped up his movements, pinching my nipple until I cried out. My orgasm broke, washing over me like waves. I clutched his shoulders, digging my fingers in to stop myself from floating away.

"Good girl, you did that so well for me." His lips brushed the shell of my ear as he kept murmuring praise. He lowered me to the bed and untied the rope, placing kisses on every spot of my skin rubbed red before gathering me to his chest. He cupped the back of my head, his fingers gently stroking my hair. "Fuck, Sofiya, *fuck*. It's you and me, forever."

I sucked on his neck, wanting, *needing*, to leave my mark on him, too. The quiet between us was easy, gently wrapping around us.

"I probably left a wet patch on your pants," I whispered.

"Good. I need your scent on every pair I own."

"You're ridiculous."

I trailed my hands down his chest, undoing the buttons of his shirt before moving lower. I squeezed his hard cock through his pants, and he thrust against me with a moan. God, I wanted to hear him make that sound over and over. I unzipped his pants and he lifted his hips, helping me shove them down until my fingers wrapped around his warm, smooth cock.

He breathed in sharply and cupped my ass, squeezing firmly. I let out a little cry as he hitched me up, slipping his cock between my pussy lips. "Are you tired, baby?"

"No," I said with a smile. "Wide awake."

He rolled us so he was hovering over me. His thick thighs pressed between mine, his cock teasing my entrance.

"Don't keep me waiting," I murmured, my lips brushing his throat.

He pressed in, teasing me with just the head of his cock. "I would live inside you if I could." Before I could answer, he thrust all the way in, and I let out a cry at the stretch. His arms bracketed my body, keeping me as still as possible as he rocked in and out.

"Fuck, I'm going to come quickly. Come with me, baby. I need to feel that perfect pussy of yours squeeze my cock."

He paused to ease a pillow under my hips. The change in position took pressure off my joints and made it so every thrust hit that perfect spot inside me. It was like electricity through my core and I whimpered, clutching at Matteo as I came. He followed seconds after, both of us riding our pleasure, our hearts racing where our skin was pressed together.

"Perfect. You're so perfect," he murmured, gently kissing my lips before rolling off of me. I curled up as Matteo went into the bathroom. He emerged a few minutes later with a damp washcloth and cleaned me, making my cheeks heat. I always felt a mix of pleasure and embarrassment when he took care of me in this way.

He lay back down beside me, and I snuggled into his chest.

"Everything feels right when I'm with you." My words came out mumbled, but his grip on me tightened. "I always dreamed of having this, but never thought I would. Thank you."

"You never have to thank me," he murmured. He sounded like he was half-asleep, and I smiled against his bare chest.

Sleep was pulling me under, but just before it did, the words I'd held back for so long spilled out of me. "I love you."

Matteo's chest continued to rise and fall steadily. I planted a gentle kiss on his skin and then closed my eyes.

55

MATTEO

"*I love you.*"

I kept my breathing steady so Sofiya would think I was asleep, but my chest felt like it was about to burst.

She loved me.

Loved *me.*

Everything was the same as it had been a few minutes ago, and yet nothing was the same. The universe had shifted and I had been transformed.

I was a man loved by Sofiya Rossi.

Somehow, against all odds, against my own fucking idiocy and stubbornness, I had won the love of my precious wife.

I tightened my hold on her as her breathing evened out. I would never get enough of this, of her. I craved her every waking moment, my mind even seeking her out in sleep.

And I wondered if that was what love felt like.

56

MATTEO

Domenico entered the office, his jaw clenched and a laptop in his hands.

"Report," I said.

"Yes, Boss." Then he hesitated.

I had to hold back a growl. I should be with Sofiya right now. I hadn't wanted to leave bed this morning, especially with how tired she'd been lately. I wanted to spend all day wrapped up in each other, fucking and touching and listening to her sweet voice as she trailed her fingers along my bare chest. If I hadn't wanted to kill the Albanians before this, I would have simply because they were taking me away from my wife.

Domenico cleared his throat, opening the laptop. "I found the traitor."

I cocked an eyebrow, my expression giving nothing away. But inside, my heart was pounding with the need to *destroy*. Bloodlust rushed through me. Finally, we had them.

"Who is it, then?" Romeo asked.

Domenico set the laptop down on the desk so it was facing me. "I didn't want to believe it," he said. "But it's Mrs. Rossi."

It took me a second to process his words, but once I did, rage engulfed my chest.

No.

He was wrong. Fucking *wrong*.

Domenico shifted as he glanced down to where he knew my gun was hidden under my jacket. He should be nervous that I was going to shoot him after he *accused my wife of being a traitor*.

"You gave me permission to look into everyone in the Family and monitor communications," he continued hurriedly. "I installed spy software on your wife's phone when she got her new one. I did it as a precaution, of course not expecting to find anything, but then I noticed a pattern of strange calls and messages."

He shifted so he could scroll on the screen, revealing a file with text message screenshots. My eyes blurred as I took them in. Sofiya had been texting an unknown number with an upstate area code, sending them insider information about our movements. Information she easily could have gotten sitting with me at this very desk. While my cock was *inside her*, she'd been working to betray me.

Romeo's brow furrowed as he met my gaze, and I knew we were both remembering my parents and the betrayal no one had seen coming.

Domenico scrolled through a seemingly endless series of calls and messages. Most of the recent texts were sent mid-morning—the times she had told me she was too tired to get out of bed. When she was alone in the apartment.

Romeo eyed me carefully, as if waiting for an explosion. But the anger inside me burned dark and cold.

"Why would she do this?" he asked.

"There are messages between Mrs. Rossi and her sister, Mila, that suggest that Mila is in love with…" Domenico trailed off.

"Spit it out," I growled.

"Arben," Domenico said.

The name sent a chill through me.

"Rustik would never allow Mila to marry Arben and destroy our alliance," Romeo said.

"Unless Arben claimed the city." Domenico's words hung in the air.

If the Albanians gained control of New York, Rustik would be much better off breaking our alliance and siding with the Albanians.

Sofiya loved her sister. Said she would do anything for her. Did that include betraying her new family, betraying *me*?

"Are Arben and Rustik working together?" I asked.

"It doesn't look like it," Domenico said. "This is all Mila and Sofiya's plan. Arben promised Sofiya a house anywhere in the world she wants," he continued as he paged over to a text exchange between Mila and my wife.

SOFIYA

I've always been a prisoner. I can't do anything without being watched and I'm so tired of it. Are you sure he can really get me free?

MILA

Arben says it's all set up. A house by the ocean, and I can visit you in secret whenever I want. No one will ever know.

SOFIYA

Ok. Let's do this, then.

I didn't think anything could have the power to destroy my world as much as hearing the shots that killed my parents, but the pain piercing my chest right now proved me wrong. I'd spent years hardening my heart, but somehow Sofiya had wormed her way in. And now my world was falling apart all over again.

"Wait outside, Domenico," Romeo gritted out, gesturing at the door. My enforcer hesitated for a moment before giving me a nod and leaving the room. When the door closed behind him, I turned to my second in command.

"It might not be what it looks like, fratello."

I ran my hand down my face, letting my mask slip a bit in his presence. "She said she loved me." The words felt like ash in my mouth.

"She does," Romeo said.

"How do you explain this?" I shouted, gesturing at the laptop. The messages went back to the first few days after we were married.

The day I'd abandoned her in the apartment. But things had gotten better since then. *I* had gotten better. And still, she chose her sister over me.

Romeo's suffocating silence stretched across the room like a tangible thing, stealing the breath from my lungs.

I was a man of action. Always in control, always with a plan. And yet my head was empty. My entire world was crumbling, and I couldn't see the next step in front of me. Against my better judgement, I had opened myself up to Sofiya, bared my soul to her. And this was how she repaid me?

Romeo opened his mouth to speak but was interrupted by a sharp knock at the door.

"Boss," Domenico called out. "I have Ajello on the phone. It's an emergency."

I raised my chin at Romeo, and he opened the door.

My enforcer entered, eyes wide. "There's an ambush at the northern warehouse. Our men have barricaded themselves inside, but they might not last long. Ajello says Arben is there."

"Fuck!" I roared. This was the moment I'd been waiting for—the opportunity to take Arben down. Why did it have to happen now, when I needed to deal with Sofiya?

Unless that's *why* it was happening now. Was Arben in the city because he was making some sort of move with Sofiya?

"Fuck, Boss, they won't last much longer without backup," Domenico said. Even across the room, I could hear shouts through the phone's speaker.

I pulled my jacket on. I had to move *now*.

"Get Sofiya and put her in a basement room," I told Domenico. Each word was agony, but I couldn't see another path ahead.

"What?" Romeo hissed, eyes wide.

I met his shocked expression with my hard one. He might be my brother in all but blood, but I was the Don and my orders could not be publicly questioned. Romeo recognized his mistake and gave me a nod. His jaw remained clenched.

"You don't want me to come with you?" Domenico asked.

"No, stay with Sofiya." Possessive rage rose in me at the idea of another man being close to my wife. My body certainly hadn't caught up to the fact that she was a traitor. How much of our time together had been a lie? But I had no choice. My priority had to be going after Arben. While Domenico was an asset in a fight, I needed someone I trusted to stay here. He was the one who had helped me identify traitors over a decade ago when I was fighting my uncle to win back what was mine.

"What do you want me to do with her once she's in the basement?" he asked.

"Nothing," I gritted out. "Don't harm her, just put her in the room. Make sure she doesn't have her phone or any other way to communicate. I will get her when we return." I turned to Romeo, unable to ignore the urge to defend my actions. "If she is the traitor, hopefully her time in the room will scare her enough to confess."

Romeo didn't voice his question, but it hung in the air between us as clear as day—*what if she wasn't?*

I couldn't take that risk. My men were in danger, my entire empire threatened. I couldn't leave her unsupervised when I was gone. It was possible that she and Arben already had some sort of plan in place, and if she suspected she was caught, she might try to run.

Never.

Never, tesoro.

You will never run from me.

"Yes, Boss," Domenico said. "I'll see to it."

Romeo and I grabbed additional weapons in the armory before heading to the garage with ten of my best men.

We would go to the warehouse, destroy the Albanians, capture Arben, and then I would return and get the truth from my wife.

57

SOFIYA

Angelo put the heavy cast-iron pot in the oven for me while I supervised nervously.

"It will turn out great, principessa," he said, shutting the door against the high heat.

"I don't know," I said, twisting my hands. "It's my first time baking sourdough. I probably messed it up."

Angelo scoffed. "Don't worry. It's not like the Boss won't eat whatever you put in front of him."

"That's an exaggeration," I muttered, but my guard's expression told me I was full of shit. There was a mischievous glint in his eyes and I blushed, reminded of how Matteo had eaten *me* out on the kitchen counter just yesterday.

Noodle nudged my hand and I scratched his ear. "Do you want to go for a walk, malysh?"

"We have time to go around the block before the bread is done," Angelo said.

"Okay, let's go for a quick walk, then," I told Noodle, who spun around excitedly.

I rolled towards the front door, but it opened before I got there. For a moment, I hoped Matteo was back early, but my heart sank when I saw it was Domenico. Noodle moved in front of me, his body on alert.

"What's going on?" Angelo asked, hurrying to my side.

"Is Matteo okay?" I asked, glancing between the two men.

"The Boss is fine. I'm here for you, Mrs. Rossi." The enforcer's face was impassive, but there was a glint in his eyes that made me shiver.

"What do you mean?"

"The Boss asked me to bring you downstairs. He's waiting for you there."

An uncomfortable feeling rose in my chest. Matteo trusted Domenico, but I didn't want to go anywhere with him.

"I haven't heard anything about this," Angelo said.

Domenico huffed. "The Boss sent me up to get her. He has a surprise for her." His voice was calm, but tension crackled in the air.

"I stay with her," Angelo said.

Domenico shrugged. "Suit yourself."

I went to put Noodle's harness on, but Domenico stopped me. "Leave the dog here."

"He comes with me," I said coolly.

Domenico rolled his eyes. "Fine, fine, do whatever you want."

Angelo was messaging someone on his phone as we got in the elevator, and I knew he must be confirming whatever this was with my husband. I took a steadying breath and ran my hand down Noodle's soft ears. I was overreacting. Matteo just had a surprise for me. There was nothing unusual about that.

The elevator door opened, and Angelo cursed as he moved in front of me, blocking my view.

"Why the fuck are we down here, Domenico?" Angelo seethed.

"I'm just following Boss's orders." Domenico grabbed the handles of my wheelchair and pushed me forward, forcing Angelo to jump back.

A chill washed over me as I saw we were in a basement, not the garage. It was dark and cold, and in front of me there was an open door leading to a small cell.

Angelo roared and pushed Domenico in the chest. "What the fuck is this?"

I breathed in sharply as Domenico drew his gun on my bodyguard. "What are you doing? Don't shoot!" I screamed.

"I'm carrying out the Boss's orders," Domenico said. "And I won't tolerate any treason."

"You're lying." Rage danced in Angelo's eyes, and I was terrified he would attack Domenico and get shot. Just then, his phone rang.

"Romeo," Angelo said, relief washing over his face as he answered. The rest of the conversation was completed in rapid Italian. I only caught a couple of words, but the horror in Angelo's eyes was all too easy to understand.

He hung up.

"Sofiya," he said, his voice gentle.

"No," I croaked, shaking my head. "What's happening? Don't leave me here."

My bodyguard looked anguished. "It's just until the Boss returns. It shouldn't be long."

"Please," I begged. "Please don't do this."

Domenico grabbed my wheelchair, pushing me into the cell. Noodle whined, refusing to leave my side.

"Get out."

Before I could process Domenico's command, he tipped the wheelchair forward, and I cried out. I managed to grab onto Noodle, who steadied me and prevented me from hitting the ground too hard.

The enforcer grabbed Noodle's leash and started to pull. Tears spilled down my cheeks as I shouted at him to let go. But he just sneered and dragged my crying dog out of the cell, slamming the door behind them.

The room was shrouded in darkness.

And I was alone.

I DIDN'T KNOW how much time had passed when the door opened again. Domenico entered, dragging a metal chair in one hand and holding a flashlight in his other. I peered around him, trying to spot Angelo or Noodle, but the door shut with a loud clang, leaving me alone in the small room with the enforcer. I clenched my jaw hard to keep my tears from falling.

"You thought you were being quite clever, didn't you?" Domenico asked, flipping on the flashlight. It cast threatening shadows along the walls.

"I don't know what you mean."

A sinister smile spread across his face as he leaned back in his chair. "I'm going to enjoy watching the Boss get information from you. When I first saw him torture a man, I'd never seen anything like it. That man was a traitor, too. The Boss kept him alive for a full week, slowly carving away his fingernails and then his fingers and then his limbs. Every part of his body was so mangled by the time he finally died, he barely looked human. It was... *inspiring*."

Chills wracked my body, and my armpits grew damp. "I'm not a traitor."

Domenico snorted. "At least you have a couple hours to practice your acting."

Anger flared in my chest. "I'm not acting."

"We've known for weeks that someone was feeding intel to the Albanians. The Boss certainly didn't expect that it was you, but the evidence is overwhelming." His eyes darkened as they raked over my body, and I suddenly felt horribly naked. "I wonder if he'll start with waterboarding. It's incredible what he can do with such a small amount of water. Or maybe taking each of your pretty little toenails. If I'm lucky, I'll get a turn."

My mind rejected his words. Matteo cared about me. He would never hurt me. Domenico must have gone rogue.

But then... Angelo had confirmed the order with Romeo.

Panic flared in my chest. "This is all a misunderstanding," I said, but my words sounded weak.

Domenico just laughed. I moved as far away from him as I could in this tiny, disgusting cell. The concrete floor was cold and dirty, and my position made me even more vulnerable in front of the horrible enforcer.

"Goodbye, Mrs. Rossi. Not that I'll be calling you that for much longer. I hope you enjoy your stay."

―――――

THE ROOM WAS BLANKETED in oppressive darkness, making it impossible to know how much time had passed. I curled my body around my knees, trying to generate heat. But it was futile—the damp cold of the concrete floor and walls felt like ice through my clothes. My chattering teeth broke the silence, but nothing could distract me from the pain in my bladder.

I half-scooted, half crawled to the metal door and banged my hands against it.

"I have to go to the bathroom. Please let me out." My voice was hoarse from the hours I'd spent screaming for help when I was first put in here. I finally slumped against the door as tears streamed down my face.

I was alone.

Completely alone.

My arms gave way under me and I crumpled to the ground, my body too weak and tired to support myself anymore. The hard floor was excruciating under my hips, but there was nothing I could do about it.

I closed my eyes, imagining Matteo storming into the cell and rescuing me. But even my imagination couldn't offer me relief as the image shifted, Matteo's expression turning cruel. He sneered down at me. "Now I can finally be rid of you."

My sobs choked me. "Don't leave me here," I whispered over and over, until my lips were moving in silent agony, my voice stolen.

I was the most pathetic creature in the world as hot urine spread down my legs, pooling on the floor. Sad and pathetic and small. Because I thought I'd finally found it. Love, care...something that felt like family.

But it was never real. Because even now, even as my heart was breaking, I knew no matter what he did, I would never be able to do this to Matteo.

I loved him too goddamn much.

What a fool I had been.

58

MATTEO

I blinked my eyes open, feeling drugged and hazy.

I went to touch my face and my arm felt like it was on fucking fire.

"Not a good move."

I turned my head to the right, following Romeo's voice. His face looked haggard, with dark shadows under his eyes.

"You look like shit," I croaked.

Romeo snorted. "You're lucky there isn't a mirror in here because I look better than you."

I believed him if I looked anything like how I felt. "What happened?"

Romeo handed me a cup of water from the side table by the bed. "Bullet to the arm. One of the Albanian soldiers on the ground wasn't entirely dead, apparently."

"Fuck."

By the time we'd arrived at the warehouse, Arben was nowhere to be found. We'd overpowered the Albanian soldiers without much difficulty, freeing my trapped men. We'd been working to load up the soldiers we caught in vans when I'd gone down.

"What's the damage?"

"You had surgery. They said you should have a full recovery, but you need to be careful for the next six weeks."

I groaned. "I fucking hate being shot."

Romeo snorted. "You do it often enough."

"How long have I been out?"

"Since yesterday afternoon. It's ten a.m. now."

I looked around the room, my vision blurry, to see if Sofiya was here. My heart sank when the memories of the previous day came back to me. Fuck, how had everything gotten so twisted up? I needed to get back home to get to the bottom of things. It was hard to argue with the messages I'd seen, but it still felt impossible that she had betrayed me. She was a damn good actress if it was all true. I scrubbed my hand down my face. Or maybe she'd made me soft.

I was sure she'd be spitting mad when I returned to the apartment. I tried to find the coldness that had been fostered inside me as Mafia Don, but I couldn't erase the guilt I felt that she'd spent any time in the basement.

I pushed myself up to a seated position, cursing the weakness in my arm. "We need to get back home."

———

I LEANED against the elevator as it brought us to the top floor. All I wanted to do was drag Sofiya into the shower, kiss every inch of her body, and pull her against me in bed while I slept.

And then I'd wake up and fuck her a couple of times.

But too much stood between me and that fantasy.

I got off the elevator and found Angelo standing outside the apartment. His face was a mask of rage and he didn't meet my gaze. I clenched my jaw at the insubordination, but he was Sofiya's guard, and I understood why he was pissed at me. I would address him later.

"Do you want me to come in for backup?" Romeo asked.

He probably should, if only to prevent Sofiya from wrapping me around her finger. I needed to question her, to get to the bottom of whatever was going on. I nodded and swept past Angelo into the apartment.

Noodle greeted me at the door, bouncing with energy. I went to pat him on the head, but he ran away into the bedroom.

Fuck, even the dog didn't like me right now.

"Sofiya?" I called out. She must be in our room.

My steps were heavy with exhaustion. Before I could get to the room, Noodle ran back out, throwing Sofiya's medication bag at me. A jolt of panic went through my chest. Was Sofiya hurt?

I rushed into the bedroom, but it was empty. I called out for her again and checked the bathroom. I ran back to the living room.

"She's not here," I said to Romeo, who was pulling something out of the fridge.

He immediately put the container back, springing into action as my second-in-command. He beat me to the front door, throwing it open.

"Angelo, where is Sofiya?" he asked.

Angelo turned, looking at both of us with confusion. "She's where you left her." He looked straight at me as he spoke, his eyes filled with fury.

It took a moment for his words to sink in.

Where *I* left her?

"She's still in the fucking basement?" I roared.

Romeo swore behind me. My hands shook as I pressed my finger to the elevator reader. It opened right away.

"Get in," I said to Angelo. "And fucking explain what's happened."

"You said Mrs. Rossi should stay in the cell and that no one should let her out but you," Angelo said.

I slammed my fist against the elevator wall. "And no one thought to do something when I didn't return *after a few hours*?"

"When you didn't return, I tried to get her out. Domenico said he called Romeo, who confirmed that she needed to stay there until you returned."

I swung my head towards my brother, who held up his hands. "He didn't call me. I never said that. I assumed she was back in the apartment, too."

Domenico was a dead man.

My heart raced and I wanted to scream at how slow the elevator was. The second the doors opened, I sprinted through the basement to the cell Sofiya was in. No one was posted outside it, and the keys were nowhere to be found.

"Get the spare keys from my office," I screamed at Romeo. I turned back to the door. "Sofiya, tesoro, can you hear me?" I knew she couldn't. This was the room we used for torture. It was soundproof.

But that didn't stop me from calling her name through the metal, letting her know I was here and she'd be out in a minute.

Romeo was out of breath when he returned with the keys.

I unlocked the door with shaking hands and then flung it open.

Nothing could have prepared me for what I saw.

Light trickled into the room, highlighting my wife crumpled on the floor and soaked in urine.

I fell to my knees and gently rolled her over onto her back. Her eyes were closed and her skin was cold.

"No, my love, please be okay," I begged as I gathered her in my arms. "Romeo! Get Aria here immediately!"

I ran back to the elevator as fast as I could without jostling Sofiya. "Stay with me," I begged her still-unconscious form.

Angelo tore off his jacket and wrapped it around her as we all piled into the elevator.

"Sofiya, can you hear me? Please, baby, please say something."

She let out a whimper, and the sound was relief and torture at the same time.

The elevator doors opened on the top floor and I ran into the apartment.

"We're going to get you warm." I tried to keep my voice soothing, but it was a lost cause. Nothing could be calm or soothing while my wife lay almost-unconscious in my arms.

Her eyes fluttered open.

"There you are." My voice shook with relief. "Let's get you in the bath. The warm water will help you."

A look of horror contorted her face. "No, please, no water. I promise I'll be good. Please don't do that." She struggled in my embrace, but her movements were weak and lethargic. Still, I held her tighter to keep her from falling or hurting herself further.

"Sofiya, love, what's the matter?" My heart raced as she continued to struggle and cry out, each sound she made another dagger twisted in my chest.

"Please don't. Not the water. Please, I'll be good, I promise." Her words were slurred as her eyes drifted closed again.

Romeo ran into the room. "Aria's on her way. She said we have to warm her core first. Get the wet clothes off and put blankets on her."

Angelo ran into the room, his arms laden with blankets.

Releasing Sofiya onto the bed was one of the hardest things I'd had to do.

The other two left the room while I stripped her clothing. I ran a warm washcloth over her skin, cleaning her, before layering the blankets over her.

I jumped when the bedroom door opened. It was Aria. She moved quickly to Sofiya's side, pulling a warm compress out of her medical bag. I wanted to shout at her to hurry as she silently took Sofiya's vitals, but I held my tongue.

"Her vitals are strong," she finally said. "And her body temperature is rising."

I couldn't stop staring at my wife.

"How did this happen, Matteo?" she asked.

Words weren't sufficient to detail what I'd done. To expose my shame.

Her eyes darkened as Romeo explained everything.

Sofiya stirred on the bed and I moved closer, but Aria stopped me. "You need to leave."

A red haze fell on my vision. "I'm not fucking leaving her. I have to take care of her."

"You're the one who did this," she seethed. "Do you think Sofiya is going to stay calm with you in the room? She is my patient, and I'm saying you need to get out. You can come back in only if she asks for you."

Angelo appeared in front of me, his broad body looming over me.

"Let's go," he said, looking down at me like I was dirt.

For the first time since I was a child, I felt small.

I let him push me out of the room and away from my love.

59

SOFIYA

I was numb as Dr. Amato took my blood. She was on her third attempt to stick me, but I barely felt it.

I was piled under blankets, but the only thing keeping me warm, keeping me somewhat tethered to reality, was Noodle's soft body against mine. He refused to move from my side. His head rested against my chest, the pressure keeping my panic at bay.

"Sofiya? Can you hear me? Sofiya?"

I jerked as I realized Dr. Amato was speaking to me. Time was running too slow and fast. The room spun around me, adding to my disorientation. I turned my head to face her. Her forehead was pinched with concern, her eyes sad, but I felt nothing. It was as if the cold had frozen my emotions.

Fine by me.

I didn't want to feel. Didn't want to *be*. I'd thought I had everything I wanted. Everything I dreamed of. Now it was gone, and the worst part was I didn't understand why. What had I done to make my husband hate me? To make him want to torture me? Had anything we experienced been real?

I flinched as Dr. Amato touched my face.

"I'm sorry," she murmured. "I'd like to take your temperature again and also give you a bag of IV fluids. You're very dehydrated."

I couldn't find any words to speak.

"How about some hot chocolate?" she asked. "It will help get you warm."

I closed my eyes. Maybe I could block out the whole world.

Maybe I could just fade away.

Noodle nudged his cold, wet nose against my neck. I tried to ignore him, but he grew more and more insistent until I painstakingly removed my hand from underneath the weight of all the blankets to pat his head. A surge of emotion went through my chest at his gentle touch, the softness of his fur, but I quickly squashed it down. I wasn't brave enough to face reality.

I curled around Noodle's body, wrapping both arms around him. "I missed you," I murmured. "Did you miss me?"

Noodle let out a long sigh, as if saying *yes*.

"Do I have your permission to give you IV fluids?" Dr. Amato asked.

I stayed pressed against Noodle, but nodded. It wasn't like I cared about what happened anymore. The doctor could do whatever she wanted.

A metallic taste in my mouth told me she'd started the fluids. I kept my eyes closed.

"I'm going to bring your blood work to the lab, and I'll be back this evening to check on you again." She hesitated before asking, "Do you want anyone to sit with you while I'm gone?"

"No," I said, my voice hoarse and broken.

I didn't want anyone to see me.

No one was safe.

Dr. Amato opened the door, and I caught a brief glimpse of Matteo before it shut again. He looked ruined, with dark marks under red-rimmed eyes.

What did he have to be upset about?

I pressed my face into Noodle's fur and closed my eyes, letting sleep take me away.

———

"Sofiya?"

Dr. Amato's words floated their way to me, as if they had to cross a great chasm of space to reach me.

Noodle's tail wagged, thumping against the mattress, but he didn't move from his spot. Anxiety seized me when I realized he probably needed food and to go outside. Had anyone fed him while I was imprisoned?

I pushed myself to a seated position. "Has Noodle been fed?" I asked, an edge of panic in my voice.

"Oh," Dr. Amato said, brow furrowed. "I'm not sure. I could ask someone?"

I chewed my lip, my fear of seeing anyone warring with my need to ensure Noodle was taken care of. "Angelo," I finally said. "Can you bring him in here?"

A few minutes later, my bodyguard entered the room. The expression on his face was one of agony. He fell to his knees by my bed.

"I won't ask for your forgiveness, because I don't deserve it. I should have killed Domenico, should have done whatever was necessary to stop him from putting you in there."

I swallowed hard against the lump of emotion in my throat.

"All I can say is that going forward, my loyalty is to you and only you. I am yours to command."

I knew what happened wasn't Angelo's fault. The blame rested on the Don. But all I'd been able to think about while trapped in that cell was how I had given my trust away too easily to everyone around me.

"Has Noodle been fed?" I asked, my voice hoarse.

At the sound of his name, Noodle perked up. He turned to Angelo and licked his face.

"Yes, I've been feeding him and taking him out," Angelo said.

"Okay," I said. My lower lip started trembling, and I curled back on the bed, wrapping my arms around my dog. "You can go now."

Angelo breathed in sharply, like he wanted to say more, but then he stood. "I'll bring him dinner in about an hour."

Dr. Amato returned to the side of the bed. "Sofiya, I have your lab results back."

I stared blankly at the wall. I didn't care about my lab results. What could she tell me that I didn't already know? That my body was broken. *I* was broken.

"The results were mostly within normal range, but they also revealed—" She trailed off before clearing her throat. "Sofiya, you're pregnant."

Her words jerked me out of my fog. "What did you say?"

Aria eyed me carefully. "You're pregnant."

A flood of emotions cracked the numbness I'd surrounded myself with, nearly taking my breath away. I sat up, my hand going to my stomach under the blanket pile.

Noodle moved to my lap, pressing his nose against my belly as if he already knew that a life was growing there.

I shut my eyes tight, but tears still streaked down my cheeks. This had been my dream, all I'd ever wanted, but now it felt like I was trapped in a nightmare.

"I know this is a lot to take in, especially since you're still in shock," Dr. Amato said, her voice gentle.

A horrible thought gripped me and I reached out to grab the doctor's hand, squeezing it tight. "Did you tell the Don?"

"No, I wanted to tell you—"

"You can't tell him," I said, tightening my hold on her hand. "He *can't* know." My thoughts were muddled and I was tripping over my words, but my body was screaming *not safe, not safe.*

Her eyes shifted to the door and then back to me. "He's going to find out eventually."

I dug my nails into her hand, her arm, pulling her body close to mine. "You have to promise me not to tell him. Promise me." I knew what I was asking, what it could cost her to betray the Don. But I needed her to understand, needed her to protect me and my baby.

She took a slow breath, staring deep into my eyes. "Okay, Sofiya," she said slowly. "I'll keep quiet. For now."

For now.

At least her silence should buy me some time to figure things out. I released her arm. I'd left crescent-shaped indentations in her skin.

"Is the baby okay?" I whispered.

"I'm not sure. Your body has gone through a lot of stress." At my panicked expression, she put a gentle hand on my shoulder. "That doesn't mean the baby isn't okay. Do you know how far along you might be?"

I tried to remember how long it had been since Matteo and I first had sex, but my mind was racing too quickly to think clearly. "It can't be more than a couple of weeks."

Dr. Amato nodded. "It's been just over two weeks since you asked me about pregnancy."

God, it felt like a lifetime ago. Our first time having sex had been so magical, so perfect.

It was all a lie.

"Blood tests can show pregnancy more quickly than urine tests," she continued. "Do you remember when your last period was?"

"I haven't had one since before the wedding," I said, running my hand down my face. "I should have suspected something. But my periods can be unpredictable."

Dr. Amato clasped my hand between hers and gave me a gentle squeeze. "You've been through a lot lately. It doesn't surprise me you didn't notice."

Noodle nudged my stomach again. My entire world had shifted in the last few minutes.

"Can't you do an ultrasound to see if the baby's okay?"

Dr. Amato shook her head. "It's really too early to see anything on an ultrasound. Generally, you have to wait until at least six weeks to see anything."

My heart sank. I wanted to see my baby *now*, wanted to know that I hadn't already failed them. How could my body be a safe home to my baby when *I* wasn't safe?

Tears filled my eyes and I let them come. I had been ready to give up, to let myself fade away from this life filled only with pain and suffering. But now I had a reason to keep going. I would give this baby all the love I'd dreamed of and never gotten, no matter what it cost.

60

SOFIYA

Dr. Amato brought me dinner on a tray along with a large mug of hot chocolate. Before she left for the night, I asked her to send Angelo in.

I'd spent the last hour thinking things through and had come up with a plan. It was crazy, risky, and would require me to trust at least one person.

Angelo stood at the foot of my bed, his shoulders set, hands clasped in front of him.

"Did you mean what you said?" I asked. I was proud that my voice had regained some strength. I needed to be strong for my baby. "That you'll do anything to protect me?"

"Yes," Angelo said without hesitation.

"You'll help me? Not Matteo?" It physically hurt to speak his name.

"My loyalty is to you, Sofiya. I swear it."

"Okay." I fidgeted with the blanket, wishing I had the strength to stand. It was hard to exude power and confidence while bundled up in bed.

I took a deep breath and squared my shoulders. "Then you will help me escape."

His eyes widened. "What do you mean?"

"We need to leave. I'm not safe here. And..." I looked at him closely, desperately hoping I wasn't making a mistake. I wanted to trust Angelo. I *needed* to believe I still had someone on my side. "And I need to protect my baby."

Angelo grew pale, and his eyes flitted between me and the door. He took a hesitant step towards me, waiting to see if I would protest or if Noodle would growl. When we were both quiet, he sat down gently beside me.

"You're pregnant, bella?" He placed his hand gently on top of mine.

I quickly wiped a rogue tear as I nodded.

"Does he know?"

"No. I just found out. Dr. Amato said she wouldn't tell him yet. But we can't wait. He'll find out soon, and I need to protect this baby from him."

"Sofiya, he would never hurt your baby. The Boss was shown evidence that you had betrayed him by making a deal with Arben, and he felt he had no choice but to act. He didn't mean for you to be in that cell so long."

Anger flashed in my chest, and I pushed away Angelo's hand. "Oh, so I should be grateful he only wanted me there for a short time? Just long enough for *Il Diavolo* to tell me all the ways my husband would torture the information out of me?" I spit the words out, my hands shaking. Noodle whined and laid across my lap.

Angelo's eyes were wide. "The Boss would never torture you."

"He already did," I said, seething. "Are you on my side or not?"

Angelo swallowed and glanced at the door again. A pit of dread formed in my stomach as I waited for his answer. Had I miscalculated *again*?

"I'm on your side," he finally said. "Always."

I let out a shudder of relief. "I need a phone that isn't traceable."

He pulled out a flip phone from his pocket. "What's your plan? You can't go back to Chicago."

"No," I said, taking the cell phone. "Not Chicago."

I grabbed my purse off the nightstand and slipped Leona's card out from the hidden pocket with shaky hands. If her mother had escaped the Italian Mafia, maybe Leona would be willing to help me. I hated to trust yet another person, but what else could I do? I wouldn't involve Mila, the Pakhan would never be on my side, and I couldn't trust anyone else in the Family.

She picked up on the third ring. "Hello?"

"Leona?"

There was a long pause. "Well, this is a surprise. I didn't expect to hear from you, Mrs. Rossi. To what do I owe the pleasure?"

"Who are you loyal to?" I asked, trying to sound fierce.

She snorted. "What is this, a Gallup poll? I'm afraid I don't have the—"

"I need to know," I snapped. "Who are you loyal to? The Italians or the Irish?"

I was half expecting her to hang up on me. She had no reason to talk to me, but maybe she heard something in my tone, because after a few torturous moments, she responded.

"Your husband's uncle murdered my mom. What do you think?"

"Good," I said. "Because I need your help."

61

MATTEO

Sofiya was on the other side of the bedroom door. We were separated by mere inches of wood, but it might as well have been an ocean.

Dr. Amato had come and gone throughout the day, refusing to give me any information except that Sofiya was stable. She'd left for the night, telling me she'd be back in the morning.

And now Angelo was in my bedroom with my wife. He'd gone in there a couple of hours ago. She'd asked for *him*, wanted *him*, not me. Because he hadn't been the one to lock her away in a cell. He wasn't the one who'd betrayed her.

My men were stationed outside the front door. Romeo was the only one I'd allowed to stay with me. No one else could witness my shame, witness their Don fall apart over a woman.

Romeo rounded the hallway, his jaw tense and tie askew. He had a drink in one hand and his phone in the other. He extended the phone to me. "It's Franco."

I put the cell to my ear.

"Boss, Domenico has a secret apartment in Brooklyn."

My heart pounded in my chest. "What?"

"I found him on surveillance cameras. He's been going to this apartment at least once a week for the past three months."

I swore and turned to Romeo. "Franco's sending you an address. You need to get there now! Take men with you. Be prepared for a fight."

"Yes, Boss," he said, clasping me on the shoulder before running out of the apartment.

I wanted to go with him but that would mean leaving Sofiya. And I was done putting anyone else above her.

I hung up, and an oppressive silence fell over the apartment. All the vibrancy Sofiya had brought into this space was shattered.

I paced the hall as I waited for Romeo's report. I fantasized about all the ways I would torture Domenico, how I would peel the flesh from his skin. Slowly, so he stayed alive for days. Weeks.

He would beg for death, and I would not grant his wish until he was utterly destroyed.

My phone was at my ear the moment it rang.

"He's dead," Romeo said. "The bastard's mutilated body greeted us as we walked into his apartment. Looks like they poured gasoline on him and set him on fire."

I seethed as rage boiled my insides. "Who?"

"The Irish."

It took me a moment to process what Romeo said. "The fucking Irish?"

"I know. There's a shit ton of evidence that *Il Diavolo* was coordinating between the Irish and the Albanians to kill you and take your territory."

"Motherfucking bastard!" I turned and punched a hole in the wall. I deserved to feel the pain in my knuckles. I deserved to suffer every day for the rest of my life for what I'd put Sofiya through. "I trusted him!"

This meant all the evidence he'd showed me about Sofiya's betrayal was false. I waited for the sense of relief to come, but none did. Because I'd already known. She wouldn't betray me.

She loved me.

Used to love me.

Because I was sure all those feelings were gone now. And it was all my fault.

"The apartment is trashed and the laptop screen was broken, but the hard drive was intact. There's a shit ton of emails here between Domenico and Ronan Finnegan. Finnegan ordered Domenico to turn Sofiya against you so he could marry her. Then there would be an alliance between the Russians, Albanians, and Irish. Domenico arranged the attack on the warehouse. You were meant to die there."

Ronan Finnegan had risen to power in the Irish Mob around the same time I ascended as Don, and we'd had an informal truce all these years to stick to our own territories and stay out of each other's way.

What a fucking fool I'd been. Everything I'd built was falling apart. I'd sacrificed everything for the Family, for my empire, and look at where it'd gotten me.

"Why would the Irish kill Domenico now?" I gritted out. Anger burned in my chest that I hadn't been the one to kill him, this traitor who had tortured my wife.

"Maybe they realized that you would never let him live after what he did, so they got to him before we could. You were right about the Irish involvement in the skin trade. There are spreadsheets here detailing how the Irish are selling girls to the Albanians."

I closed my eyes as fire burned in my chest. Ronan Finnegan was a dead man, and this time I would ensure I had the pleasure of killing him. "Gather whatever evidence you can get from the traitor's apartment and then come back here," I commanded Romeo.

My fingers clenched around my phone after I hung up. I would need Rustik's support in this war. The Irish Mob wasn't as hierarchical or organized as the Five Families or Bratva, but I wouldn't underestimate their strength. Not again.

I stared at the bedroom door, wondering if I should force Sofiya to listen to me, to explain what had happened. But what use would it be for my wife to know I had been taken in by a traitor in my own ranks? How would that repair what I had broken?

Still, my hand hovered over the doorknob. It physically hurt to be away from her.

I clenched the handle, the metal cold against my skin. Before I could turn it, an explosion shook the building.

I threw the bedroom door open. "Angelo! Guard Sofiya!" My wife was bundled up on the bed, Noodle beside her, a shocked expression on her face.

"Yes, Boss," Angelo responded.

I tore out of the apartment. Who was attacking us—the Albanians? The Irish? I would not let them get my wife. I would protect her until my dying breath.

I ordered two guards to stay by the apartment door while the rest ran to the stairwell. The explosion had been on the east side of the building.

Fuck. *Sienna.*

I'd ordered her to stay in her apartment.

I tore down the stairs to her floor, relieved when I saw it was intact. I ordered one of my men to check on her while I continued down the stairwell. Acrid smoke filled the air as I neared my office. I went ahead of my men, barging through the door with my gun drawn.

My office was destroyed. The window was shattered from where an explosive had obviously flown in. But the room was empty besides fluttering paper and splintered furniture.

Warning bells sounded in my mind, but it was cloudy with exhaustion and pain. My shoulder was on fire, and when I glanced down, I saw blood seeping through my shirt. I must have torn my stitches.

My heart pounded, my gut telling me I needed to get back to Sofiya *now.* I called my men to me and ran back up the stairs. My watch vibrated and I glanced down at the alert—the fire escape alarm had gone off.

Fear like I'd never felt before flooded me as I threw the apartment door open and found it empty.

62

SOFIYA

We waited until the front door slammed shut behind Matteo before jumping into action. Angelo helped me out of bed and into my wheelchair before he slipped on the backpack we'd packed with essentials. Noodle's harness was already on, and Angelo grabbed his leash as we hurried to the opposite side of the apartment to the fire escape.

Angelo threw the window open. "That will have set off the alarm. We need to move quickly."

I stood from my chair, locking my knees to keep from falling. The room spun around me, and I leaned on Noodle to keep myself steady. Angelo squeezed his massive frame through the window and then reached for me, dragging me into the cool night air.

"Come on, Noodle." I tugged on his leash. Noodle gave me an expression that told me he was very unsure about this plan. Angelo leaned forward and grabbed hold of Noodle's harness, pulling him through.

"Maybe you should carry Noodle instead of me," I said, eyeing the treacherous metal stairs.

"You first. I'll come back for him if needed," Angelo grunted.

The loud sound of an approaching helicopter made speaking

impossible as Angelo quickly climbed the stairs, holding me to his broad chest. We reached the roof just as the helicopter was landing on the pad. I bounced in Angelo's arms as he ran towards it. His hand covered my head when we neared the helicopter door where Leona was standing, a feral smile on her face.

Angelo lifted me up and Leona grabbed my arm, pulling me inside. I cried out when a sharp pain burst from my shoulder—she had dislocated it.

"Shit, Sofiya, are you okay?" Angelo asked.

"Go get Noodle," I shouted. Angelo turned back to the fire escape just as a gunshot sounded from the other side of the roof.

Matteo was running towards us, fury in his face. His guards weren't far behind them, and all had guns drawn, pointing at the helicopter propellers.

"We have to go," Leona shouted.

I looked back at the fire escape just in time to see Noodle's head pop over the roof's edge as he struggled to pull himself over. Angelo cursed and jumped into the helicopter. Before the door was even shut, we were in the air. I screamed, trying to get to my dog, my best friend, but the ground disappeared from under us.

Angelo pulled me into a seat and buckled me in, careful to avoid my shoulder. He grabbed my face with both hands. My tears soaked his skin.

"I'm sorry."

I couldn't hear over the sound of the helicopter, but I read the words on his lips.

I held my hand over my chest, my heart shattering. My sweet Noodle. I had abandoned him.

Angelo sat down in the seat beside me, and Leona was across from us. She handed us each a headset. Angelo put mine on for me. Instantly, the noise around me dulled and I could hear Leona's staticky voice.

"Well, that was exciting. I had a *feeling* I should stay in New York, like something exciting was about to happen."

My world had just been ripped apart and here Leona was, acting like we were on some sort of fun field trip. "Sit back and relax," she continued. "We'll be in Boston in no time. Ronan is going to be *so* excited to meet you."

63

MATTEO

Watching the helicopter fade into the distance joined with the memory of hearing the gunshots that took my parents and finding Sofiya lying still on the floor of that cell.

All my worst moments were my own fault.

Romeo put a tentative hand on my shoulder. "Let's go back downstairs. Figure out a plan." When I failed to move, he tightened his hold on me. "Come on, fratello. Sofiya needs you focused."

"I'm the last thing she needs." My voice was as flat and cold as my heart felt. My wife had taken all the warmth and light in the world away.

"That's not—"

"She ran from me, Romeo. She couldn't stand to be around me because of what I'd done, so now she's run into the arms of *fucking sex traffickers!*" I clutched my hair and spun around, needing something to destroy, when my eyes caught on Noodle struggling to pull himself onto the roof. I sprinted over to him and grabbed him by his harness, pulling him into my arms. He was breathing heavily and rested his head against my chest. I clutched him close, pressing my face to his soft fur. "How could everything go so wrong, huh?"

He whined softly.

"I will get her back. I promise you."

He lifted his head and licked my face, and I realized there were tears falling down my cheeks. I wiped them away and cleared my throat. "Alright, we've got to pull ourselves together and get our girl back."

I took a deep breath and moved Noodle off my lap. He sat, meeting my gaze with a solemn expression, and I nodded. I pushed myself off the ground and buttoned my suit jacket, standing tall as Don.

I returned to where Romeo stood with the rest of my men. "We need to track where the helicopter is landing and contact Rustik for backup. The Irish have taken my wife. We are at war."

———

ROMEO AND ENZO dragged a large table and chairs into my office, and everyone gathered around. Franco had emerged from whatever dark lair he usually worked in and was currently tracking the helicopter's flight path.

"They're landing in western Massachusetts, not Boston," he said.

"Romeo, get the jet ready to follow them," I commanded.

Franco pushed his long, messy hair out of his face as he bent over his laptop. "Once they land, we should be able to track their exact location with Sofiya's necklace, if she still has it on."

I froze. In my panic, I'd forgotten the tracker. For the love of God, I hoped she still had it on. I opened the tracking app on my phone and held my breath as it loaded. And there it was, the tiny dot representing the love of my life flying over Connecticut.

"We've got her," I said. "Everyone needs to be armed and ready. We can't know how many of the Irish and Albanians will be there, but they'll likely be ready for us." I nodded at Romeo to take over prepping our soldiers while I stepped out to call the Pakhan.

My heart pounded when he answered. I cleared my throat. "Ivanov. The Irish have taken Sofiya."

My father-in-law, the Pakhan, this man I despised, let out what I assumed was a curse in Russian. "How could you let this happen?" he roared.

I clutched the phone, my desire to shout and curse tempered only by my own self-blame. "I'm calling upon our alliance to rescue her and take down the Irish. They're allied with the Albanians to bring the skin trade to New York."

Rustik cursed again. "Send me the location. My men and I will be there."

This man had no love for Sofiya, but in our world, image was power, and the kidnapping of his daughter made him look weak.

I hung up, sent him the coordinates of the Massachusetts airport, and returned to the office. My men were ready, and more soldiers would meet us at the airport.

"Fuck, does Sienna know what's happened?" I asked Romeo in a low voice as we exited the office.

"She's been kept in her apartment. She knows something has happened, but not what."

"I'll stop by her apartment right now and meet you in the garage."

Romeo nodded, and I called Noodle to my side. He kept pace with me as I flew up the stairs to Sienna's floor.

I nodded at the guard who was positioned outside her door and let myself in. She jumped up off the couch and ran towards me.

"Matteo, what the fuck is going on? They said you'd been shot?" Her eyes roamed down my arm. "And I just heard something on the roof."

"Sofiya's been taken by the Irish," I bit out. "We're going after her now. You need to watch Noodle."

Her eyes widened. "Oh, Matteo." She pulled me in for a hug I didn't deserve. "What happened?"

"I don't have time—"

"I swear to God, Matteo, you are not walking out of this room until you tell me what is going on."

How was it that everyone feared me except for the women in my life? "I got evidence that Sofiya was a traitor—that she was feeding information to the Albanians."

Sienna's jaw dropped. Then she shook her head slightly. "There's no way that's true."

Her immediate dismissal of Sofiya's betrayal made me feel even worse. How could I have believed it even for a second, even when faced with a shit-ton of evidence? "Yeah, well, right after I got the news, I was told Arben was attacking one of our warehouses." Now it was so obvious that Domenico had orchestrated the whole thing. "So... I had her put in the basement until I returned."

Sienna took a step back, her eyes transforming into judgemental slits. "Are you fucking serious?"

"She was only meant to be in there for a couple of hours to scare her, but then I got shot. When I woke up in the hospital, I assumed she would be waiting for me in our apartment, but she was still in the basement." I turned away from Sienna's horrified expression. "I never meant for this to happen. It was all a setup by Domenico. He was working with the Albanians, but he's dead now."

"And the helicopter? The roof?" Sienna's voice was ice cold.

"Sofiya and Angelo left with the Irish. And—" Fuck, I didn't want to speak the words. "The Irish have an alliance with the Albanians to expand the sex trafficking trade into the city."

Sienna's expression turned horrified. "What? Are you sure?"

"Yes. Now I have to go." I gestured at Noodle. "His stuff is in the apartment."

"Are you kidding me? You're just going to leave me with that and walk out? How could you put your wife in a fucking cell for what, hours? Days? No wonder she left!" Her hands landed on my arms and she shook me, sending shocks of lightning through my injured arm. "What is wrong with you?"

"Everything, apparently!" I screamed. "I'm not cut out to be a husband, or a brother, for that matter. I know all I am to you is a disappointment! I'm the reason you don't have parents, the reason we spent two years in hiding and poverty. I have failed every single person in my life, so why bother with relationships?"

Sienna took a step back, blinking. "Is that what you think, Matteo? You're the reason I'm still alive! How can you be this stupid? Our uncle would have killed you! And that means I would also be dead, or worse. How long are you going to punish yourself for something that wasn't your fault? You don't allow yourself to be human, and now it's lost you the love of your life."

My jaw clenched. "I'm not capable of love."

She threw up her hands. "You wouldn't recognize love if it shot you in the face. Which is why you don't understand that *I* love you. Romeo loves you. Sofiya...well, at least she did love you."

My limbs felt weak and my chest, hollow. "And I ruined it."

"Yeah, well, fix it."

"How?" My voice was a hoarse whisper.

"Figure it the fuck out. But start by bringing her back here."

I nodded curtly as I spun on my heel and strode to the door. I paused with my hand on her doorknob. "You know I love you. It's not enough, but I love you."

And then I walked out.

64

SOFIYA

P ain swam through my arm and shoulder, and I gritted my teeth against it. "Can you put my arm back in place once we land?" I asked Angelo.

He looked at me with panic. "Shouldn't a doctor do that?"

I shook my head. "I'll tell you how to do it. It's not hard."

A wave of nausea washed over me and I didn't know if it was caused by anxiety, morning sickness, or pain. The helicopter hit a patch of turbulence and my stomach lurched.

"Was riding a helicopter on that list of yours?" Angelo asked. He was trying to distract me, and I appreciated him for it.

"No, it was not." And for good reason, apparently, as we hit another bump. "I think I'll be sticking to airplanes. Or better yet, cars."

Leona smiled broadly. "Where's your sense of adventure?"

"Must have left it back in New York," I muttered.

I placed my hand on my belly and willed my baby to be okay. I hated that I couldn't do more to protect them almost as much as I hated myself for missing Matteo. I kept getting assaulted by memories—of him being tender with me, of the feel of his arms and the brush of his lips. I'd felt protected and safe with him.

Until I hadn't.

I faced the window and wiped tears from my face.

The helicopter flew lower as we neared an empty airstrip surrounded by fields.

"Once we land, our pilot, Finn, will drive us to see Ronan. We've been doing some work out here in western Mass, which is why we're not landing in Boston."

"What kind of work?" Angelo asked, voice hard.

"That's for me to know and you to find out," she said with a wink.

Angelo met my gaze, looking as unimpressed as I felt, but there wasn't time to say anything further as we were landing. I gritted my teeth as I was jostled around, every movement aggravating my shoulder.

I let out a pained cry once we touched down, and Angelo was instantly in front of me, his knees pressing against mine.

"Tell me what to do."

"You need to help get the shoulder back in place, but you don't have to force it. Just put your hand on my elbow and let the weight of your hand pull it down." I bent my right arm, and he moved his hand to the crook of my arm. "Now, take your other hand and massage my shoulder and bicep."

He did what I asked, looking serious and focused as he held me firmly. The pilot—Finn—and another man who'd been sitting up front watched us curiously as Angelo continued his massage. After a few minutes, my shoulder shifted. "I think it's back in." My muscles were still sore and I knew I needed to be extra careful for the next few days, but I was able to move my arm around more easily.

"Wow, I expected that process to be more dramatic," Leona said.

"Oh, I try to keep my life low-drama," I deadpanned.

She snorted. "That's exactly how I would describe—"

"Leona," Finn bit out. "Approaching."

All of them, including Angelo, pulled out their guns. I cursed internally that I still didn't have a weapon. I should have pushed harder to get one. At least then I wouldn't be a complete sitting duck, stuck in a helicopter I couldn't even get out of on my own.

"It's not our men," Leona said, all traces of humor gone from her voice.

I leaned forward enough to see a line of black cars approaching.

"Shit," Finn said. "Can we make it to our car in time? Or should we try to get off the ground and land somewhere else?"

Furtive glances came my way, and my cheeks burned. I was obviously the weak link here.

"Start the engines, Finn," the other man said. "We should have enough fuel to get to Westover Airport."

The two men moved to the cockpit while Leona and Angelo stayed by the open door, guns drawn. The engine started up, and it felt like my heart was beating in time with the vibrations.

"Take cover!" Angelo shouted, leaning out of the helicopter to close the door as bullets started pinging off the metal frame.

"They're trying to take down the tail and blades!" Finn shouted.

The helicopter lifted off the ground and then lurched, slamming back down. Angelo threw himself over me, and I curled my body over my stomach. The sound of breaking glass was followed by rapid gunshots, but I had no idea where they were coming from.

"There's too many of them," Leona shouted. "I messaged Ronan, but he's twenty minutes away."

Angelo shifted off me, twisting around to take shots out of the shattered door window until his gun clicked. "Fuck."

"Surrender now and save your lives," someone shouted from outside the helicopter.

Finn crawled to us from the cockpit. "Their cars are bulletproof and I'm out of ammo. Leona—"

"No," she said. I couldn't see her from my cramped position, but she sounded furious. "We can't give up."

"We can get out of this," the other Irish man said. "But we have to surrender first. Ronan will come for us."

I clutched Angelo's arm, sharp terror stabbing my chest.

"They'll just kill us, Aidan," Leona said. "We don't even know who they are. They have no reason to keep us alive."

Suddenly, the helicopter door swung open. Four masked men stood there, rifles pointed at us. "Drop your weapons," one of the masked men shouted as he waved his gun. He had an accent, but I couldn't place it.

One by one, Leona, Finn, Aidan, and Angelo dropped their guns. Another man walked up behind the armed guards, but he wasn't masked. He looked to be in his late thirties with buzzed hair and a stocky build.

Angelo inhaled sharply and shifted in front of me, blocking my view. "Arben."

My blood ran cold.

"Angelo Conti," a sneering voice responded.

Then a loud shot rang out, and Angelo crumpled in front of me.

Everything faded, my entire world narrowing to my unconscious bodyguard, my *friend*. An agonized scream left my lips as I lunged at him. "Angelo!" I pressed my hands over the gunshot wound on his chest. Hot blood gushed against my palms and tears fell against the back of my hand. "I swear to God, I will kill you if you die on me."

Loud shouts and the sound of metal filled the air and then cold hands grabbed me from behind, ripping me away from Angelo and pulling me backwards out of the helicopter. I screamed and thrashed, but whoever was holding me had an iron grip and my shoulder was weak and aching, leaving me helpless.

A rough bag covered my face and I was shoved into a car. Before the door closed, I thought I heard someone speak in Russian.

65

SOFIYA

Rough arms threw me to the ground. I caught myself before my face hit the floor, sending a sharp pain through my shoulders and wrists. The door slammed and I was left alone, the cold already seeping into my skin.

I ripped off my tear-soaked hood and peered around the dim cell. It was similar to the one in Matteo's basement, except there was a tiny window high on the wall with bars over it. Apparently all the Mafia heads followed the same interior design plan.

Tears dripped down my cheeks and I clutched my chest, feeling like my heart was being ripped out. I refused to believe Angelo was dead, but my hands were still drenched in his blood. My stomach lurched and I breathed slowly through my nose to keep myself from throwing up. My mind was sluggish and exhaustion pulled at me. I was tempted to curl up on the filthy floor and close my eyes, but I needed to stay alert. Was it the Albanians who got us? But then... why had I heard someone speaking in Russian? I couldn't make sense of any of it.

My shoulders curled inward as the truth settled in my bones. It was my fault Angelo was shot. My fault the Irish were captured. My plan had been reckless and stupid.

My lower lip trembled and I sucked it into my mouth. I had to get a grip. I didn't deserve to wallow in self-pity. I needed to fix this.

I looked around the room to see if there was anything I could use to escape, but there was nothing. At least they hadn't tied me up, not that my arms and legs would do much against an enemy.

They would have to be sufficient. My body was all I had.

I used the wall to stand so I could test my legs. My hips were hurting and my ankles felt unstable, but this was life or death, so I would deal with the consequences to my body later. I gently rotated my shoulder and massaged my arm, willing everything to stay in place.

I stood on my tiptoes to peer out the window. All I could see was a sliver of gray sky. The minutes ticked by and I finally sat down again. I needed to conserve energy.

A crash outside the room jolted me from a haze of sleep. I pushed myself up to a standing position just in time for the door to swing open. The light from the hallway stung my eyes, but when they adjusted, I saw the Pakhan standing in the doorway. It was the first time in my life I'd been glad to see my father. Relief washed through me as I realized Matteo must have called him for backup against the Albanians.

But then he turned to me with the same dark, twisted expression I'd seen on his face too many times.

My heart sank. He wasn't here to rescue me. *Of fucking course* he wasn't.

"Sofiya."

"You're working with the Albanians?"

He pulled out a cigarette and lit it, blowing the smoke in my direction. "At least you're not a complete idiot, unlike your husband."

"Why?"

"Like I would explain my decisions to a girl like *you*," he spit out, derision heavy in his voice like I was scum on the bottom of his shoe.

"Please let me go." It killed me to beg him, but I was out of options.

His expression twisted into a sneer. "Don't worry. I have plans for you." And with that, he shut the door, locking me back in.

I let out a scream. How was this my life? What had I done to deserve such a shitty father? I slumped back down to the floor. There was a lump in my throat, but I was too angry to cry.

I jolted when the door opened again, but this time, three men stood in the doorway. One of them looked vaguely familiar—he was one of the Pakhan's soldiers—but the other two were strangers.

My heart raced. The look in their eyes could only be described as sinister, but I forced down my terror. I needed to stay sharp—this could be my only chance to escape.

I stayed on the floor, trying to figure out a plan.

"She's prettier than I imagined," the first man said. He was bald and wearing a black military-style uniform.

The Bratva soldier smiled a disgusting, yellow smile. "It's her legs that don't work. Her face, tits, and ass aren't affected. Besides, I kind of like when they just lie there while you fuck them."

"What about her cunt?" the third man said. He was blond and only looked a few years older than me.

"I guess we'll just sample it and see," the bald man said.

The Bratva soldier looked nervous for the first time. "The Pakhan said she wasn't to be touched. She's to be married."

"She's already married," the blond man said.

The bald soldier took another step towards me, and my eyes flitted to the gun at his waist. I tensed my muscles to stop myself from moving. I needed to time everything carefully. "That won't matter once her husband is dead. Widows can get re-married."

Oh God. No matter how tangled my feelings were about Matteo, I didn't want him dead.

And I would rather die than be sold to another man of my father's choosing.

The Bratva soldier shut the cell door behind him, leaving us all in darkness. The putrid scent of sweat soaked the room. "What does it matter if we fuck her? She's already used up, anyway. And it's not like Arben is buying her for her cunt."

Bile rose in my throat, but I swallowed it down. This alliance had been a sham from the beginning. The Pakhan had played us all, using me as a chess piece in his twisted game.

The men moved closer, discussing who was going to "take my cunt first." I blinked, willing my eyes to adjust to the darkness.

One of them crouched over me, and I moved. With my right hand, I grabbed his crotch and squeezed hard. The man's shocked scream filled the room and he shoved me aside, but I'd already managed to grab his gun.

"You fucking bitch!" he screamed.

The sound of three gunshots echoed around the tiny room, followed by the thud of three bodies.

Adrenaline rushed through me, allowing me to stand without pain. I carefully stepped around the bodies and carefully opened the door. I was sure someone must have heard the gunshots, but no one came running. The light from the hallway spilled in the room enough for me to see that all three of the guards were dead. I'd hit each of them in the forehead. I was rather impressed with myself. They'd been standing so close it wasn't like it had been a difficult shot, but to hit them all with dead accuracy in the dark was still pretty good. Dimi would be proud.

I grabbed the other guards' guns off them, tucking them into my waistband. Blood pooled on the floor, soaking into the knees of my jeans. My hands shook as I searched their pockets to find a phone. When I fished one out, my heart sank to see there wasn't any service. I would need to get to a better spot and call Matteo.

66

MATTEO

I stared at Sofiya's unmoving dot on the tracker app. She'd been inside the warehouse for forty-five minutes. Every second of the wait had been agony, but we didn't know how many of the Irish were inside, and we had to be strategic.

At least, that's what Romeo kept telling me.

The warehouse was in the middle of nowhere. A long gravel driveway cut through open fields to reach the entrance of a gray building. There was an abandoned outbuilding within sight of the warehouse, and that was where we waited for Rustik. He had landed at the same small airport we used and was on his way.

A call came up on my phone. My finger hovered over the answer button, but it was an unknown number so I sent it to voicemail.

"Rustik is three minutes out," Romeo said.

"Let's get into position." We'd planned with Rustik while he was on the plane. My men and I would take the east side of the warehouse and he would take the west. We would work our way to the middle to free Sofiya and destroy the Irish and Albanians.

The warehouse was quiet as we approached. I met Romeo's equally confused gaze at the lack of guards. Hopefully, that meant they weren't expecting us and we wouldn't face much opposition.

"Rustik is in position," Romeo whispered.

I nodded at my men. Twenty of them had come with us and I looked each of them in the eye now. These were men who had been loyal to me and, for the older ones, loyal to my father. The Mafia, these men, were Family, but my family would never be complete without Sofiya.

"Thank you for standing with me," I said. A few expressions of shock flashed across the faces before me. "There's no one else I would trust with my wife's safety." Their faces turned serious and their chests puffed up with pride. I turned back to Romeo. "Let's go."

The inside of the warehouse was dark. Shadows from the small, barred windows played across the concrete walls. I led the way through a small, quiet room until we came to another door. Romeo tested it and it creaked open, and we all moved into a pitch black windowless space. There was a soft thud as the door shut behind us. Before I could reach for my phone to turn on the flashlight, the room flooded with lights—blinding, bright lights that illuminated a massive room with endless pallets of stacked boxes.

And a line of uniformed, armed men facing us.

At the front of the line stood Domenico.

A very *alive*, sneering Domenico.

A moment of confusion was followed by a lightning bolt of rage. I raised my gun. "Give me one reason I shouldn't kill you."

Domenico's smile was something sick and twisted. "My very good friend is with your wife right now. Anything that happens to me will happen to her."

The puzzle pieces fell into place, each one highlighting what an absolute fool I'd been. I'd been trying to figure out who the Albanians had allied with, and all along it was *Rustik* fucking *Ivanov*. Who had worked with my enforcer. And framed the Irish to distract me.

"I see you've finally figured it out." Domenico stretched his arms, looking completely at ease, knowing that I couldn't do anything to him and risk Sofiya. "It's been exhausting having to bow and scrape to you all this time. I supported you all those years ago, but you've grown weak. You're nothing compared to Arben and Rustik."

Romeo snarled beside me, and I pressed my hand to his chest.

My heart was pounding. I had no idea how we were going to get out of this.

"Now, time to use your pitiful brain cells and surrender. You, of course, will have to die, but I promise to be gentle," Domenico said.

I clenched my jaw, resisting the temptation to shoot him in the mouth.

"But if your men surrender, I'm sure we can find them a place in Arben's new empire."

"If you think we would ever serve you—" one of my men growled.

"Fuck, the idiocy runs deep in the Family," Domenico said. The man next to him snorted.

I flicked my eyes to Romeo, trying to weigh the odds.

We could shoot at them. There was no way they would allow any of us to live, so we might as well take as many of them down with us.

But then, what would happen to Sofiya? I wasn't convinced Rustik would kill his daughter, but I wasn't willing to take that risk, especially knowing he had no reservations when it came to hurting her. Or selling her off to be married.

Motherfucker.

Another piece of the puzzle fell into place. He was going to marry her to *Arben*.

"How do I know you actually have Sofiya?" I needed to buy us time.

Domenico shrugged. "That's just a risk you'll have to—"

A gunshot rang out from across the room. Blood trickled from Domenico's mouth before he fell forward.

Mayhem broke out. "Open-fire!" I screamed. My men fired on the line of Bratva and Albanian soldiers, who continued to be struck from behind by some unknown shooter. Bullets pinged past me as I crouched down and shot at the swiftly falling men. The concrete floor and walls kicked up dust, and then the lights went off, drenching us in darkness as shouts and bullets filled the air.

And then an eerie silence fell. The flashlight on my phone highlighted Domenico's body, surrounded by dead soldiers. I turned the light on my men, who looked mostly unharmed thanks to whoever had shot at the enemy soldiers from behind. The shooter must still be in this room, but it was impossible to spot him with stacks of crates creating a perfect hiding place.

"Francesco's been shot," Romeo said. "Seems like a flesh wound, but Ajello is going to bring him back to the car to check on him."

"Good." I addressed the rest of the men. "Spread out across the warehouse and find Sofiya."

I turned to Romeo and lowered my voice. "I'm going to see if there's another door this way." I jerked my head at the other side of the large warehouse space.

Romeo lifted his chin and the rest of my men spread out to check the rest of the rooms in the building.

I felt along the wall for a light switch but couldn't find it.

I made my way through the room, my eyes skimming across the walls and moving around the pallets, my gun raised in my arms in case I ran into the shooter. Whoever they were, they didn't seem to be my enemy, but I didn't trust anyone who hid in the shadows.

A loud scraping noise and shouts sounded from outside. My heart pounded faster as I made my way along the wall to the other side of the room, feeling for a door. My fingers hit a bump, and I realized it was a light switch.

I flipped it. My eyes raked across the room, and then I saw her.

Sofiya. My love.

Her eyes were wild and she was crawling towards a door not far from where I stood.

Relief like I'd never experienced before stole my breath away.

She was here.

She was *alive*.

I called out her name and ran toward her. She turned, the expression on her face was one of confusion and relief. Her lips moved, forming my name.

Then an explosion hit the side of the room and I was thrown back.

67

MATTEO

A strangled sound left me as the breath was knocked from my lungs and something hard landed on my legs. I blinked through the dust filling the room and saw a large chunk of concrete from the blown-apart wall pinning me to the ground. I could wiggle my toes so I didn't think anything was broken, but I couldn't move from underneath it.

I turned my head, desperate to catch a glimpse of Sofiya. I shuddered in relief when I saw her about ten feet away, covered in dust but seemingly unharmed.

"Sofiya, love, are you alright?"

She coughed and wiped her face with her sleeve. "I'm okay. Are you?"

"Yes, just stuck here."

She nodded and tried to push herself up to a standing position, but fell back to the floor.

I winced as her knees hit the ground. "Be careful," I growled.

She rolled her eyes. "Still bossy as ever." She chewed her lip as she looked at the large hole in the wall. "Who set off the explosion?"

Before I could answer, there was a loud shout. At first, all I could see through the gaping hole was a flash of green and blue from the outside. But then Rustik appeared, surrounded by his men.

I locked eyes with Sofiya. "Run!" I mouthed.

I tried to move the concrete off my legs but couldn't shift it. I grew more frantic as my wife moved *closer* to where I was instead of across the room to the exit. She positioned herself behind a twisted metal beam that must have fallen from the ceiling. There was a gun in her hands, and I realized she meant to stay and fight.

"Tesoro, no, you can't do this. Get out of here," I hissed.

She ignored me and peered around the chunk of rubble, the gun held tightly in her hand. Fuck, why hadn't I taught her to shoot? I felt around for my gun, but all I could feel were bits of rock and glass. It had flown from my hands in the explosion, so now I was minutes away from death, and so was my wife.

Rustik's men shouted as they navigated the piles of rubble. The rattle of gunshots filled the room as one of his guards took aim at me. The cement blocks around me deflected most of the bullets, but then a line of fire burst through my thigh and I knew I'd been hit.

I gazed back at Sofiya. She would be the last thing I saw before I died. I drank her in greedily, memorizing the way she brushed her tangled hair out of her face, the determined set of her jaw, the steady way her hands wrapped around the gun. Her determination was contagious, and it filled my chest. I refused to believe my tesoro would die today. As the life bled out of my body, I would trust that she would make it. Reinforcements would arrive in time for her if only she would *run*.

"Sofiya, please, run, hide. Don't do this, *please*." I was the Bratva's intended target, not her. Rustik would gain nothing by killing his daughter, but if she stayed, she could become collateral damage.

Sofiya ignored me and aimed her gun before pressing the trigger and firing off shot after shot. Bullets pinged off the metal beam she was hiding behind, but she didn't flinch. Her shots looked effortless, and while I didn't turn my head to see if any of them landed, my breath caught at how magnificent she looked.

Screams joined the smell of gunpowder and blood in the air. With each beat of my heart, I prayed to a God I didn't believe in that Sofiya would be spared.

My ears rang as all grew silent. A look of pure rage transformed

Sofiya's face. She tried to push to her feet, but her strength failed her. "Rustik!" she screamed. "Come back and face me, you coward! Coward!" She screamed something in Russian and then let out a string of curses.

My heart was beating so fast I thought it would explode with terror. Any moment now, I would see the light leaving my wife's eyes, knowing it was all my fault.

There was a thud of fading footsteps, the sound of crunching rubble, and then silence. Confusion filled me. Where were the other men? I broke my promise to not look away from Sofiya and painfully turned my head towards the opening in the wall. Bodies littered the ground, blood soaking the ruined floor.

They were all dead.

"I told you I could shoot." Sofiya met my gaze with a cocky tilt to her head before slowly pointing her gun at me. "You're the one who doubted me."

My lips parted. Had she really taken all of them out? A dozen men on her own? She was a better shot than me, than any of my men.

"God, tesoro, you've never looked so beautiful." I smiled as I eyed the barrel of the gun. "Are you going to kill me now? I deserve it."

"I haven't decided yet," she said. Then her eyes flitted to the blood pooling under my leg, and her lip started trembling. "No," she gasped.

"It's okay." My body was growing cold and numb, and I knew I didn't have long before the blood loss forced me unconscious. "I can go now, knowing you'll be okay."

"No," she repeated, shaking her head as her voice hitched. She lowered the gun to the floor and started crawling towards me.

"Tesoro, no," I begged. I tried to move, tried to do *anything* to stop her, but my limbs weren't responding. "Sofiya, please, stop."

Shattered bits of glass littered the ground and my perfect, precious wife was dragging herself through it to get to me.

"I thought you were just stuck," she said as she reached me. "I didn't see..." A tear escaped her eye and it broke my heart. I had enough strength to brush my fingers against her arm and it was like heaven, just to feel her again for the last time.

"I'm so sorry," I said. "I'm so sorry for hurting you and for failing to protect you. You are so precious. I love you so much." My words came out slurred.

Her hands landed on my thigh, keeping pressure on the wound, but I could barely feel them.

"I swear to God, Matteo, you will not die on me." Tears dripped down her cheeks and I wanted to kiss them away. I hadn't truly recognized what a treasure she was until it was too late.

"After all the shit of these past few days, I will never forgive you if you leave us alone," she snarled. She stripped off her shirt and used it to keep pressure on my wound. "You have to be here for me." Her voice broke as she added, "And the baby."

Her words floated to me through the air, landing softly on my mind as I faded from the world.

68

SOFIYA

There was a man sitting beside my bed. My vision swam as I squinted at him.

He looked to be in his late thirties or early forties, with brown hair, a smattering of freckles across his nose, and black glasses framing his bright green eyes, which were now fixed on my face.

Something tugged at the back of my mind. How did I know this man?

I turned my head, taking in the room. I was in what looked like a high-end hospital room with a strange man wearing a suit.

"You're awake," he said in a heavy Irish accent.

At the sound of his voice, it all came back to me. I'd been trying to staunch the bleeding of Matteo's leg when this man had run into the warehouse through the massive hole in the wall with a group of soldiers. They had gotten Matteo out from underneath the slab of concrete and taken both of us to the hospital. I must have passed out on the drive.

"Who are you?" I croaked.

"I'm Ronan, head of the Irish Mob."

"Oh." I should be panicking, but I felt strangely numb. "Should I be screaming for help right about now?"

He smirked. "Not sure it would get you anywhere, but you can always try."

"I'll save my voice," I said dryly.

My mind whirled as I slowly emerged from the heavy mental fog. And then the panic hit. I opened my mouth to try and form words—what happened after I passed out? Was Matteo...

He must have read the fear in my eyes. "Matteo is okay. So is Angelo."

Relief washed over me so intensely I thought I might pass out. I fell back against the pillows. "You're sure? They're really okay?" I sniffed.

"Aww shit, lass, I can't handle tears." He patted my hand somewhat awkwardly. "Yes, they're both okay. The Don is out of surgery. He's still unconscious, but they saved his leg and he's going to be fine. Your bodyguard, Angelo, is also out of surgery. The Albanians left him on the airfield, and we were able to get him to the hospital. He had to have a blood transfusion, but the doctors are confident he'll make it. They're both recovering in rooms on this hallway. This is my private hospital."

I tried to stop my tears, but they dripped down my cheeks onto my gown. "Thank you so much," I blubbered. "How are Leona and Finn and Aidan?"

Ronan sat back in his chair with a smile. "Leona said you were a sweet girl. She was on the other side of the wall when the Russians threw the grenade and had to have surgery to remove shrapnel from her side, but she's already trying to get out of bed." He rolled his eyes, but there was affection in his voice. "Finn and Aidan are both a bit bruised, but okay. We had to sedate you after pulling you off the Don because you were so distraught. You slept for twelve hours. The doctors dressed the cuts on your hands, arms, and knees. You also had a dislocated shoulder and a couple of ribs."

"What about—" My voice was so hoarse I could barely get my words out. Ronan took a glass of water from the side table and held it out to me. I gulped down the entire cup gratefully, and he poured me another. "Did the doctor say anything about the baby?"

Ronan froze as he returned the water pitcher to the table. "You're pregnant?"

My tears kept falling because I didn't know what the answer to that was anymore, so I just nodded.

"Right. Let me get someone." Ronan hit the call button by the bed and looked over at me with an air of panic.

A nurse quickly entered the room. "You're awake," she said with a broad smile.

"Mrs. Rossi has just informed me that she's pregnant," Ronan said. "Get someone to check her over immediately."

The nurse blinked and then rushed out of the room.

"How much pregnant are you? I mean... how many months?"

I raised an eyebrow. Apparently pregnancy was how you ruffled Mafia men. "Just a few weeks. If I'm still pregnant."

His expression softened, and he took my hand. I squeezed it in gratitude.

The nurse returned and another woman walked in behind her.

"Mrs. Rossi, it's so nice to meet you. I'm Dr. Aisling Sullivan. I'm an OBGYN."

"Nice to meet you," I mumbled.

She smiled. "I hear you're pregnant?"

"I just found out a few days ago from a blood test. But the past few days have been... a lot." I didn't know how much I could say.

"This is Mr. Finnegan's private hospital," she said, glancing at Ronan. "So we understand his line of work."

Well, that made things a bit easier to explain. "I don't know if all the stress and everything hurt the baby." My voice cracked.

Dr. Sullivan gave me a sympathetic look. "Well, your blood work does indicate pregnancy, but it takes hCG levels a while to return to normal after miscarriage." She continued quickly when she saw my panicked expression. "I'm not saying you did have a miscarriage, just that blood work might not be an accurate indicator of pregnancy. Let's do an ultrasound and see what we can see. We won't be able to see much at this stage, but that doesn't mean Baby isn't perfectly healthy."

"How can the baby possibly be healthy?" I sobbed. "I've done nothing to protect them."

"Oh, honey, no," Dr. Sullivan said.

Ronan squeezed my hand harder. "Sofiya, from what I saw, you were absolutely incredible. You saved yourself and so many others in there."

Dr. Sullivan passed me a box of tissues, and I took them gratefully.

"Just take a deep breath for me and we'll take a look. We'll do a transvaginal ultrasound. Have you had one before?"

I shook my head.

"It might be a little uncomfortable, but it shouldn't be painful."

Ronan excused himself, letting me know he would stay right outside the door, and Dr. Sullivan and the nurses got the equipment ready. The doctor arranged my legs into stirrups and pressed the ultrasound wand inside me. I breathed through the discomfort, keeping my gaze on the computer screen, desperate to make sense out of the staticky black and gray shapes. The doctor was quiet, and I felt like screaming.

Then she smiled. "There," she said, pointing at a little blurry dot in the middle of a black oval. "That's the yolk sac and embryo."

The world stopped as I stared at the screen. It was barely anything, just a little blur, but it was proof that I was still pregnant. "Is there a heartbeat?" I choked out.

"Not yet, but that's to be expected. Based on this scan and from what you told me, you're about five weeks along."

I frowned. "That's not possible. We only started having sex a few weeks ago."

She smiled. "Gestational age is actually based on your last period, not the actual conception date. You should have another ultrasound in about three weeks. I can do it if you're still in the area, or we'll get you set up with another OBGYN. But you'll be able to see more then, and possibly hear a heartbeat."

She removed the ultrasound wand and helped me sit up.

"I just really want this baby to make it," I whispered.

She patted my hand. "I want that, too."

The nurse took my vitals, and the doctor checked my shoulder and ribs. As she was heading out, she asked if I wanted Ronan back in the room, and I nodded. I didn't want to be alone right now.

Ronan walked back in and took his seat by my bed. "Is everything okay with the baby?"

"Yeah, seems like it."

He patted my hand again. "I'm glad to hear it."

I pressed my hand against my stomach, willing the little life in there to make it. "Can I see Matteo and Angelo?"

"Neither of them are awake right now, and you need to rest."

"*Please.*"

"Fuck. Fine. But you have to use this wheelchair." He pointed at a chair in the corner of the room, and I nodded. I wasn't sure if he knew I used one normally, or if he was just being protective.

Before either of us could move, the door flew open. Ronan whirled around and pointed his gun at... Leona.

69

SOFIYA

"What are you doing in here?" Ronan snarled. "You're supposed to be in bed."

"Please, it was barely a flesh wound." Leona looked amazingly put together, her hair flawless. The only thing that hinted at her injury was a bandage around her bicep.

"You just had surgery on your fucking arm!"

Leona ignored Ronan and walked to my side. "Sofiya, I just spoke to Mila's bodyguard."

I frowned. "Nikolai? What do you mean?"

"He called Sienna because he couldn't get ahold of you, and Sienna called me. Rustik is back in Chicago with Arben, who is going to marry Mila *tonight*."

Nausea churned in my stomach. "What? No." I threw my legs over the side of my bed. "I have to get to her. What exactly did Nikolai say?"

"He said he needs backup. Mila is being watched too closely for him to get her away."

"I have to get to Chicago."

"I already called the jet," she responded.

Ronan swore. "Leona, what the hell?"

She fixed him with an ice-cold glare. "Ronan, this wedding

would cement the alliance between Arben and Rustik, who, in case you forgot, are your enemies. So you can either sit here, twiddling your thumbs while you wait for the Albanians and Bratva to attack your city, or come with us."

"I swear to fucking God. Why did I allow you to come back to Boston? I should have made you stay in New York."

"Because you know I could kill you one hundred different ways if I wanted to."

"Oh yeah, that," he responded wryly. He met my imploring gaze, and he scrubbed his hand down his face in a move that made my heart ache with how much it reminded me of Matteo. "You can't come with us. You're *pregnant*."

Leona raised her eyebrows.

"Mila is more important." I was unflinching as I met his gaze. I desperately wanted my baby to survive. I didn't understand how I could love something I'd only known about for a day this much, but it paled to the love I had for my sister. She was my best friend, my forever partner in life. I would go to the ends of the earth for her. Risk everything for her.

Ronan's jaw clenched, but he grabbed the hospital wheelchair from the corner of the room and put it by the bed, allowing me to transfer into it.

"Fucking fine." He moved to the door, muttering something about exhausting, strong-willed women.

Leona put her hand on my shoulder as I moved to the door. "We'll stop them," she said, full of confidence. "And I need the chance to see which of us is a better shot. The answer is me, of course, but I'd like to lay any rumors of your prowess to rest."

I rolled my eyes, but I was beyond grateful to have her on my side.

70

MATTEO

M y eyelids weighed a thousand pounds as I fought to pry them open.

I squinted as I took in the white room. No windows. Antiseptic smell. Some sort of medical equipment beeping softly in the background.

I turned my head, my muscles screaming at the movement, until my eyes landed on Romeo. "Am I in hell?" I croaked.

Romeo had dark circles under his eyes and he hadn't shaved. "You should be. Not sure how you got out of that one, fratello."

"What happened?"

"The Bratva set off the explosion. It blocked us from being able to get to you. We had to fight through the rubble." His expression was grim, his jaw clenched. "We finally made our way through and found Ronan Finnegan."

"What?" I tried to sit up.

"Lie the fuck down," Romeo snarled. "He was there with Sofiya, stopping the bleeding on your leg." His eyes flicked down to where the hospital blanket covered my legs. I tore it off and groaned when I saw the thickly bandaged gunshot wound and the mass of bruising on my thighs.

"Ronan's men got you free and transported all of us here to his private hospital. You would have died if not for him. Angelo, too."

"Angelo?"

"Arben's men shot him at the airstrip. He had surgery, but he'll be okay."

I didn't know how to feel about Angelo. He had been one of my most loyal men, but his loyalty had obviously shifted to my wife. His actions had put her in danger. "Where is she?"

"Sofiya is in a room down the hall. She's okay," he added quickly at my panicked expression. "She has some cuts and bruises, but she's fine."

Rage burned in my chest that she had any marks on her body. "I need to see her."

Romeo sighed. "You lost a lot of blood and had to have surgery on your leg. You need time to recover."

"Fuck that." I pushed myself into a seated position and swung my legs over the bed.

Romeo put his hand on my chest. "I can go get her."

"No," I snarled. "I will go to her." It was the least I could do after all the pain I had caused her.

Romeo grumbled, but got up and grabbed a wheelchair from the side of the room. "You're going in this. Non-negotiable."

"I am your Don," I said in a low voice.

"Yes, yes, you're very fierce and scary. Now get in the fucking wheelchair."

I broke out in a sweat at the effort of moving off the bed. My breathing was ragged and I felt dizzy. Romeo gave me a disapproving look but didn't say a word as he pushed me into the empty hallway. I hated being stuck in the wheelchair, and I realized I was experiencing just a sliver of what Sofiya did every day.

"What happened with Rustik? Arben?"

"They both got away with some of their men. The rest of their soldiers were either killed or captured. Ronan is holding them."

"Fuck. I owe him now, don't I?" Something dawned on me— was he the one who'd shot Domenico and the rest of his men?

"I'm afraid you do. At least we know they're not involved in the skin trade."

We turned a corner. "That's Sofiya's room." Romeo pointed at a door down the hall.

"Why isn't there a guard outside the room?" I snarled.

"Ronan is inside with her."

"What?" I whipped my head to glare at my second in command. "Give me one reason why I shouldn't kill you right now for letting a man I don't know, a rival Mafia head, in a room with *my wife?*"

"I would be shaking in terror if you were currently strong enough to wipe your own ass," Romeo deadpanned. Before I could say anything else, he added, "Finnegan is the reason we're not all dead. We didn't have enough uninjured men to stand as guards, so he offered to stay with her."

"*You* should have stayed with her."

"I'm your second. I stay with you."

I clenched my jaw but didn't respond because we were finally in front of Sofiya's room. I pushed the door open. My heart pounded in anticipation at seeing my wife. Would she scream at me? Kick me out of the room? I deserved it. I deserved all her anger, her judgement. I would withstand it all just to be close to her, to satisfy the desperate craving in my body to be with her always.

I was prepared for anything she threw at me, but what I wasn't ready for was finding an empty bed. Romeo ran ahead and checked the bathroom. He shook his head when he turned back around.

"My phone," I choked out.

Romeo pulled it out of his pocket and I opened the tracking app, sending out a prayer to the universe that she hadn't taken her necklace off.

Her dot was at the airport, and my heart thudded against my chest. My hands shook as I called her. No answer.

"I'm calling Ronan," Romeo said. He held the phone to his ear and then cursed, hanging up and shaking his head.

Just then, my phone rang, but it was Sienna, not Sofiya. I almost didn't answer—I had to stay focused on my wife right now—but then I realized my sister would likely have Leona's phone number.

"Matteo, Sofiya is going to Chicago," Sienna said immediately when I answered.

"What?" I put the call on speakerphone so Romeo could hear.

"Nikolai called me. Rustik is forcing Mila to marry Arben. Sofiya, Ronan, and Leona are going to stop the wedding."

"Get the plane ready," I told Romeo.

Sienna inhaled sharply. "Matteo, you can't go. Romeo said you'd been shot, which makes that the *second time* this week."

"If you think for one moment I'm going to let my wife face Rustik and Arben alone, you don't fucking know me!" I roared.

"Fuck, Matteo," Sienna said with a sigh. "Just be careful, okay? I need you both to come back."

"I will," I promised. Romeo moved me to the door, and I took the call off speaker. "How's Noodle?"

Sienna paused for a moment before answering. "He seems sad. He just lies by the door crying. I think he misses Sofiya."

That made two of us.

"I'll bring her back home," I vowed. "For all of us."

There was no life for me without her. I may have been too foolish to see it at first, but now that I knew, I would never let her go.

71

SOFIYA

Car horns blared at us as Leona wove in and out of the Chicago traffic, each one raising my blood pressure.

"It's rather inconvenient of them to hold the ceremony during rush-hour," she said as she cut off another car.

"I'm not sure convenience was on their mind," I bit out.

"Do you know the church?" Ronan asked. He was clutching the door and his seat as Leona took another turn too quickly.

"Not well. It's the one I got married in, but I was just there briefly for the ceremony."

"Ahh, wonderful. Filled with good memories, I'm sure," Leona deadpanned.

If my chest wasn't so tight I could barely form words, I might have laughed.

"The ceremony has already started," she continued. "So we're going to make quite an entrance."

Ronan ran his hand down his face with an exasperated sigh. "Aren't you supposed to be good at stealth? Any ideas for ways we can rescue Mila *without* all of us dying in the process?"

Leona shrugged. "I always have time to plan and gather intel before my missions. It's kind of exciting to fly by the seat of our pants. Maybe I should try it more often."

"Leona," Ronan growled.

"So touchy," Leona said, her voice tinkling with laughter.

Ronan locked eyes with me over his shoulder, and I knew we were both mentally preparing for our imminent deaths.

Leona took another turn, and I saw the church ahead of us. She parked right in front. "I have a good feeling about today. Things are going to work out."

Just then, three black G-wagons pulled up beside us, blocking us in.

"So glad you had a fucking good feeling," Ronan said, reaching for his gun.

The passenger door of the first car flew open and someone familiar got out. I threw my door open, uncaring that the man was pointing his gun at me.

"Dimi!" I shouted, tears streaking down my cheeks.

My brother swore, holstering his weapon and ordering his men to stand down. He ran to me, pulling me into a firm hug. "What are you doing here, Sofiya?"

"Same thing as you, I'm assuming. Rescuing Mila."

He swore. "You two will be the fucking death of me. Stay in the car while we take care of this."

He released me and motioned to his men, who had all exited the cars. They ran up the church stairs and disappeared through the front door.

"What are the odds we're going to stay here?" Ronan asked.

"Negative ten," Leona responded. She reached into the glove compartment and handed me a pistol. I checked to see it was loaded and then tucked it in the back of my jeans.

"I thought so," Ronan said. "Fucking Mafia women." He got out of the car and offered me his arm, half carrying me up the stairs to the church. He insisted on going through the door first, which made Leona roll her eyes, and then the three of us crept through the empty lobby to the sanctuary.

What I saw when I peered through the window into the sanctuary made my blood run cold, and I didn't hesitate to throw the door open.

The Pakhan was at the front of the church. My mother stood beside him wearing a lurid neon-yellow satin dress. But she barely registered in my mind because my father's arm was around Mila as he pressed a knife to her throat, while his other hand held a gun.

Dimitri stood in the church aisle, staring down our father. "You've lost," he said. "Your men are loyal to me." I glanced around the room to see all the Bratva soldiers, men I'd known all my life, facing my father with guns drawn.

"Traitors!" the Pakhan screamed. His eyes were wild, and it terrified me. He was a man with nothing to lose.

I continued my walk up the aisle, willing my knees and hips to stay strong. There was no way to get a clear shot when he was holding Mila in front of him. But maybe I could distract him, do *something, anything,* to save my sister.

My father's eyes locked on me, filled with cruelty, and the barrel of his gun drifted to point at my chest. "My other useless daughter," he sneered.

Each furious pounding of my heart urged me on. *Do something. Do something. Do something.*

"Are you really going to murder both your daughters? And your unborn grandchild?" My voice was steady and filled with contempt.

My mama inhaled sharply, and Mila's eyes widened as they flicked down to my stomach.

The Pakhan let out a harsh burst of laughter. "My defective daughter and the weak Mafia Don are having a baby. What a perfect match." He waved the knife around as he spoke, and my palms grew slick with sweat.

"Is this"—I waved my hand—"really how you want to be remembered?"

He let out a harsh bark of a laugh. "*Remembered*? You seem to be under the delusion that I won't be leaving here alive."

A barrage of gunshots sounded from outside, and all of us froze. My mind whirred as I tried to figure out who was shooting. Dimi's eyes met mine, and he subtly shook his head. His men weren't responsible for those gunshots.

My armpits were soaked with sweat, and I breathed through a

wave of dizziness. I kept my eyes fixed on the Pakhan, ignoring the neon flash of movement behind him.

"It's over, Rustik," Dimi said, raising his voice over the cacophony outside. "You've lost."

"The fuck I have!" he screamed. His arms flailed in agitation, momentarily loosening his hold on Mila.

Everything happened at once in a blur of sound and color. My mother's hands closed around the heavy candelabra on the altar. She lifted it and struck her husband hard across the back of his head. He let out a pained roar and turned towards my mama, gun raised. I didn't hesitate. I pulled my pistol out from behind my back, the movement fluid, automatic.

I took aim and pulled the trigger.

The bullet went straight into the side of the Pakhan's head. Blood bloomed from the wound like a flower, and then he crumpled to the ground.

This man who had caused so much pain—in his own family, in countless lives unknown—was dead.

I glanced around the room, heart pounding in fear that the Bratva men would turn on me, but none moved. A few raised their chins at me in a sign of respect.

The heavy candelabra slipped from my mother's grasp, hitting the marble floor with a loud *clang*.

"Spasibo, mama," I said.

She met my gaze, and there was the briefest flash of *something* in her eyes—fire, determination—and then it was gone, replaced by the familiar blankness that pervaded my childhood.

And then the back door to the church crashed open.

72

MATTEO

Romeo drove us through the crowded streets of Chicago as we chased down my wife. The last time I was in this city, I thought I'd married a helpless, timid girl.

How fucking wrong I'd been.

"We should enter through the back entrance. It might give us an edge of surprise," Romeo said as we turned onto the familiar street of the church I was married in. "And maybe you should stay in the car until we—"

"Don't think about finishing that sentence," I growled.

Romeo sighed as he turned into the alleyway by the church, driving until we met the small gravel pad by the dumpsters at the back.

Enzo and Ajello were with us. I wished I could have brought more men, but I'd chosen speed over force.

Only time would tell if I would regret that decision.

Romeo threw the car in park and reached for the door handle. "Don't die, fratello."

"Right back at you."

The four of us exited the car—Enzo and Ajello flanking me while Romeo took the lead. Just as we neared the metal slab of the back door, it burst open. We dove behind the dumpsters for cover as a group of men ran out, speaking Albanian. With Arben right in the middle of the group.

"Arben stays alive. Kill the others," I hissed before leaning far enough past the dumpsters to take my first shot. An Albanian soldier went down, causing absolute chaos. The other men took wild shots as they ran, and we were able to pick them off in mere seconds, leaving Arben standing in the middle of a pile of bodies. He took aim at the dumpster that concealed us, his hands shaking and skin pale as he emptied his magazine. His shots all went wide and then his gun clicked, signaling that he was out of bullets.

I lunged from behind the dumpster as Arben tried to reload his gun with shaky hands, and shot him in the calf. He went down screaming, and Romeo, Enzo, and Ajello ran forward to disarm him and push him to the ground.

I hated that we needed to keep him alive. I wanted nothing more than to gut Arben, to carve the organs out of his pathetic flesh. But he had information we needed—the locations of the trafficked girls, the list of any other allies. The only sense of satisfaction I got as Enzo and Romeo tied and gagged him was the knowledge that I would be able to torture him for as long as I wanted.

Days. Weeks. Months.

Nothing was too much for this bastard.

My guys shoved him in the trunk of the car. I signaled for Ajello to stay with him while Romeo and Enzo turned toward the church door.

The muffled sound of a gunshot from inside rent the air, and my heart fucking stopped. I lurched towards the back door, any thoughts of my safety forgotten. My wife was in there and I would stop at nothing to get to her.

Romeo caught my arm before my leg fully gave out. Sweat prickled my forehead, but I kept pushing up the steps and through the door.

73

SOFIYA

The back door slammed open and a dozen guns raised to point at... *my husband*.

My heart skipped a beat.

He's here. He's here.

The last time I'd seen him, he'd been unconscious and drenched in blood. Seeing him now, standing tall even though his skin was ashy with pain, filled me with relief.

I hadn't forgiven him yet—I couldn't even be sure he was here to help me—but my heart didn't care. The part of my soul that belonged to him longed to run into his arms.

He looked between the Pakhan's prone, bleeding body and the gun in my hand. He cocked his head, and I knew he was asking if I had shot my father. I nodded, and softness filled his eyes. "Proud of you," he mouthed, and that's what did it.

I stumbled towards him. The moment I was close enough, he pulled me into his arms. I clung to him and I swore our hearts were beating in sync, as if to declare how much they had missed each other.

"The Albanians are dead," he said, his voice loud and clear. "We've captured Arben."

"Rustik Ivanov is dead." Dimitri's voice rang out, strong and authoritative. He stepped over our father's body onto the church altar.

"Sofiya, Mila, come." Dimitri's command echoed around the hall.

Matteo's arms tightened around me, but I gently pushed them away until he reluctantly released me. I moved towards Mila, my sister, my heart. Blood dripped from a shallow cut on her throat, but she was *alive*. We threw our arms around each other, trembling with relief.

"Are you hurt?" I asked.

"No," she said, voice breaking. "I'm okay."

I pulled back and cupped her face with my hands. My vision darkened when I saw the shadow of a bruise on her cheek, peeking through her makeup.

"He hurt you, too, didn't he?" she whispered. "I didn't know."

I swallowed hard. "It doesn't matter now."

"It will *always* matter to me."

My face crumpled, and I took a slow breath in and out.

She tightened her arms around my waist. "Can you manage?" Her chin jutted at the three stairs leading up to the altar where Dimi waited for us.

I nodded. There was so much adrenaline running through my body I didn't feel any pain.

She took as much of my weight as she could as we made our way to the new Pakhan. Dimi's second-in-command, Maxim, joined us. Facing the sanctuary, he shouted, "Everyone kneel for the new Pakhan, Dimitri Ivanov."

The Bratva soldiers knelt down, followed by my mother and Maxim. Mila and I locked eyes, unsure if we should kneel. In the end, I stayed standing, as did Matteo and his men, and Ronan and Leona, while my sister bent the knee. Mila was still part of the Bratva, but I was now a Mafia queen.

The room filled with shouts of the men my brother had somehow won over. "To the Brotherhood! To the Pakhan!"

"I vow to be worthy of the loyalty you have shown me," Dimitri shouted in Russian. "To the Brotherhood!"

The men stood and cheered, and I was sure the vodka would flow tonight.

Dimi pulled Mila and me into his arms, holding us tight. "I'm sorry I wasn't here earlier. So fucking sorry."

I choked back a sob. Now wasn't the time to fall apart. "What have you been doing? How did you do all of this?" I asked.

He pulled away from us and shook his head. "I can't talk about it yet."

I let out a sound of frustration. I was so fucking exhausted with the secrets and being kept in the dark. But maybe that was just the inevitability of life in organized crime.

Out of the corner of my eyes, I saw my mama sway as she went to stand. I jolted towards her, but a Bratva soldier named Anatoly, an older man with silver hair, grabbed her arm before she passed out and guided her into a pew. I shot Dimi a look, and he nodded. There was no love between him and my mother, but I knew he would make sure she was taken care of.

"You can both stay here with me," he said. "I'll keep you safe."

I felt a presence behind me and turned to see Matteo at the bottom of the altar steps with Romeo at his side. "If you ever try to convince my wife to leave me, I will end you," he said, ice in his voice.

Dimi inclined his head. "And if you ever do anything to hurt my sister, I will end you."

They faced off, expressions blank, eyes locked, until a slow smile spread across my brother's face. "I look forward to forming a new alliance with you, Don Rossi. A real one."

Matteo's expression remained stoic, and then he nodded.

"And with you," Dimi said, inclining his head at Ronan, who was standing halfway down the aisle with Leona.

"Oh, wonderful. Someone finally realized I was here," he muttered.

Mila and I both snorted a laugh. Now that the male posturing was over, there were more important things to tend to.

I made my way back down the steps and took Matteo's hand. His face was gray with the strain of standing. "You need to sit down. Ronan, can you get the chair out of the car?"

Matteo didn't move, and I gave him a little shove towards a pew. "Sit down." He gave me an incredulous look, but I stood my ground. "Or stay there and pass out. Not sure it's very suitable for a big scary Mafia Don to faint, but I guess it's your choice."

He growled and then sat.

Mila joined me, leaning her head on my shoulder. I wrapped my arms around her. "You don't have to stay here." I couldn't imagine Mila would ever want to set foot in the Pakhan's home again. "Come home with me."

She shook her head and pulled away. "I love you, Sofiya. More than anything. But I need a break from all of this... from the violence and politics and control."

I opened my mouth to argue, but she shook her head. "If I lived with you, all my movements would be controlled. I need space to breathe, to experience freedom."

I wanted to argue with her, tell her it wouldn't be like that, but we both knew better. I had come to terms with the restrictions of my new life as Mafia queen, but Mila had always been a free spirit. I refused to be the one to cage her, even though I wasn't sure my heart could withstand the pain of saying goodbye.

She blinked like she was chasing away tears and pulled me back into her arms. "It's not like it's forever."

"It better not be," I whispered in her ear. "My baby needs their aunt."

She sniffed. "You couldn't keep me away if you tried. I just need some time to complete the items on my list first."

I groaned. Mila's items were a lot more *adventurous* than mine.

I caught Nikolai's dark stare over her shoulder. But he wasn't looking at me—he only had eyes for my sister. "And Nikolai will let you go alone?" I asked, eyebrows arching as we separated.

For the first time in my life, I saw Mila blush. "He's coming with me."

Okaaay.

"You will tell me more," I said, my tone reminiscent of my husband.

A smile curled her lips. "I will."

"You need to check in every day."

"And wear a tracker," Matteo said.

Mila frowned. "I don't—"

"Already done," Nikolai said, coming to Mila's side. She looked up at him with outrage.

"What the fuck are you talking about, Kolya?"

Nikolai smirked. "Don't worry about it."

Mila faced him, arms crossed, but before she could cuss him out, which was what I was sure she was on the verge of doing, Dimi interrupted.

"We need to get out of here and allow my crew to clean up."

Pain gripped my heart. Dimi, Mila, and I had spent years having only each other as allies. Now, Dimitri stood strong as Pakhan with hundreds of men loyal to him, and as Nikolai put his arm around Mila, I realized she wasn't alone anymore, either.

"Come on, tesoro," Matteo murmured, brushing his hand down my arm. He looked as unsure as I'd ever seen him. There were so many words unspoken between us, so much hurt and fear. But he had come for me. I ran my finger down the locket he'd gifted me. I'd chosen to keep it on, knowing he would be able to track me, because deep down, I had hoped he would come. I'd hoped he would care enough about me to chase me.

I rested my hand on his shoulder, taller than him for the first time. "Let's go home."

His eyes softened, and I thought I caught a glimpse of a tear.

Ronan returned with the wheelchair we'd stolen from the hospital, and he and Romeo helped Matteo get in.

My husband grabbed my hand, and we headed back down the aisle for the second time.

Together.

74

MATTEO

We were leaving Chicago. This time, I wouldn't allow any distance between my wife and me on the plane. We were in the bedroom at the back of the jet, curled up on the bed. Sofiya sat between my legs, bundled up in a blanket, and my arms were tight around her. Too tight, but I was scared of letting go. Terrified that at any moment, she would realize who was holding her and push me away.

Neither of us had said anything since getting on the plane, and our unspoken words weighed heavy between us.

"To be fair," Sofiya said, finally breaking the silence, "at least our wedding was better than that one."

It took me a beat to process her words, and then I broke out into a laugh that was fuller and brighter than I'd experienced in *years*. My entire body shook, and so did hers until tears streamed down her face.

"Fuck, tesoro. You are the best thing in the entire universe."

The past few days had been the worst of my life, and the days ahead were filled with uncertainty, but nothing could destroy the rightness of having my wife in my arms. I stroked my hand down her hair. "Sofiya, I am so, so sorry. For not trusting you, for putting you in that cell, for scaring you, not protecting you. I don't expect your forgiveness because I'm not worthy of it, but I need you to know I will work every single day to give you the life you deserve."

My words weren't good enough—*I* wasn't good enough for her —but they were what I had to offer.

She let out a deep breath, and I forced myself to wait patiently for her to speak. "How do I know you won't turn on me again? It was nothing to you to throw me in there." Her voice was broken and painfully vulnerable.

I squeezed her closer, running my hand down her arms, her back, her hips. "I know it doesn't make it any better, but it was *torture* to put you in there. I regretted it the moment we left. But I was raised to believe that being Don means never backing down. I thought that changing my mind, changing my order, would have made me weak."

"And a Don can't be weak."

I swallowed hard. "You know my parents were murdered?"

Her eyes flicked to mine, brow furrowing slightly, and she nodded.

"The night they were killed, Sienna had roped me into watching a movie with her. We were in the den and the house phone rang. I picked it up. It was the guard at the gate asking if he could let my uncle in." My breaths grew shallow as my chest tightened. It had been years since I'd spoken of this, since I'd let myself even think about it, at least in my waking hours.

Sofiya ran her fingers across my chest until she gripped the back of my neck. Her touch loosened the lump in my throat enough to keep going.

"There had been tension between my uncle and my parents, but I said he could come in. *I* let him into the fucking house. It wasn't long before we heard a gunshot, followed by a scream. My mother's scream."

It was Sofiya's turn to hold me tight. She didn't interrupt, didn't pressure me to keep going. She was just here, with me.

"I had to make a decision—run to the study to save my parents or escape with Sienna. She was so little, so scared. She grabbed my hand, and I knew I had to save her. We ran to a secret passageway that led out of the house, but before we slipped away, I heard the second gunshot."

My eyes burned and, against my will, a tear ran down my face. Sofiya brushed it away.

"It wasn't your fault."

I shook my head. "I should have done more. If I hadn't let my uncle in, if I had run to the study—"

"Then you would have died."

I knew she was right, even though I couldn't quite make my heart believe it. It was the same thing Sienna had said to me. Romeo, too. "I see their blood in my dreams. Hear the gunshots and the screaming. It haunts me every night... at least every night you're not by my side."

"You make my nightmares go away, too," she murmured.

I wiped away another tear and kissed her forehead.

"I want to forgive you," she said softly.

I froze.

My heart skipped a beat before it started racing in double-time.

She twisted her fingers in my shirt. "You broke my trust, and it's going to take a while to rebuild that."

"But you think I can rebuild it?"

She tilted her head up. Her eyes were so fucking beautiful. "You'll have to do a lot of groveling. I hope you're prepared."

My lips twitched. "And what will this groveling entail?"

She pressed her face into the crook of my neck and breathed in deeply. "That's for you to figure out. But it involves a lot of New York City hot dogs."

"I will buy you your own hot dog cart. *All* the carts in the city." An idea flashed into my mind and my chest tightened, but this time with a thread of hopefulness and excitement. "In fact, I will help you check off every item on your list."

"Oh yeah?"

"Yes." I would do whatever it took to fulfill every single item.

"Maybe we should make a new list together."

I swallowed past the lump in my throat. "I would love that, tesoro. Just as I love you."

She breathed in sharply. "You love me?"

I had a vague memory of saying it after I was shot, but this was the first time I spoke the words with full clarity. They left my lips like it was the easiest thing in the world. I thought I'd been protecting myself from pain by closing myself off from my wife. But the greatest suffering I could ever endure was being separated from her.

"Of course I do. More than anything."

"I love you, too," she whispered. She held my gaze, her eyes swimming with tears, and then our lips crashed together. I gripped her chin, pulling her close as I devoured her. She shifted on my lap until she was straddling me, and I groaned at the change of position. I got lost in the taste of her, in her sweet scent, in the feel of her body pressed against mine.

I kissed my way down her jaw and sucked a spot on her neck. I needed to mark her, to shout at the entire world that she was mine.

The plane lurched with turbulence, pulling us apart. Sofiya grinned at my scowl, running her fingers across the lines on my forehead. "Wait, am I hurting your leg?" She tried to move off my lap, and I tightened my hold on her waist.

"I thought you'd learned to stay where I put you." I arched my eyebrows. The bullet wound in my thigh burned, but I needed the pain. It was my way of repenting, for suffering a fraction of what I'd inflicted on her.

"Sorry for being concerned for you," she said, rolling her eyes.

"Naughty girl."

She made a little disgruntled sound but curled into my chest.

I ran my hand up and down her back. "My memories from after I was shot are hazy, but"—Anxiety choked me, but I forced myself to continue speaking—"I keep hearing these words repeat in my mind, like through a fog. *Your* words. But I'm not sure if they're real or not."

She stilled in my arms.

"You said something... something about a baby."

Sofiya kept her head against my chest, and I was sure she could hear my frantic heartbeats. She unbuttoned the top few buttons of my shirt and traced her fingers along the words emblazoned on my chest. "I would have done something cute to tell you, but I was a little busy saving your life."

My heart stuttered.

"You're pregnant, tesoro?" I tried to pull back to look her in the eyes, but she pressed her face into my neck and refused to move.

"It's super early, so I could still lose it."

Panic gripped me. "Is something wrong with the baby?" What if everything she'd gone through had hurt the baby? It would be my fault. I'd never thought about what it meant to be a father. Children had always been just an abstract concept of "heirs," but now it was real—a combination of Sofiya and me. And I wanted it, longed for it.

She shifted and I loosened my arms enough for her to pull something out of her pocket. "It's a little crumpled, but there it is."

She handed me a small printout of an ultrasound. I had no idea what I was looking at until she pointed at a tiny white oval. "That's the embryo. The doctor said I'll need another ultrasound in a few weeks. We might be able to hear the baby's heartbeat then."

I ran my fingers down the picture. We'd created that. It was part of us.

"It's a cute blob, right?" she asked.

"The very cutest."

We lay back on the bed, holding the ultrasound, staring at it in contented silence. I brushed my hand across her stomach, willing our little blob to grow strong.

Sofiya started fidgeting with the collar of my shirt.

"What is it?" I asked.

"Shouldn't I feel *something* right now about Rustik? Like sad or guilty about killing my own father? But I don't, and that makes me feel like something is wrong with me."

I hated the uncertainty in her voice. I cupped the back of her head. "No, tesoro. You don't have to feel anything about it. When I killed my uncle, all I felt was relief. I admired him when I was younger, even saw him as a second father figure. But in the end, he was nothing to me, and neither was your father." I stroked her hair and kissed her temple. "I know all I feel is pride. Pride at how strong you are, how protective."

"Thanks, miliy."

Hearing the term of endearment on her tongue made my heart ache.

When it was time for our descent, we moved to the front of the plane. A smile twisted Sofiya's lips when I buckled her seatbelt for her. She would just have to get used to me taking care of her.

I played with her hair as we approached the airport, pausing when I realized I still had an unanswered question. "Did you see who shot Domenico and the other men with him?" I asked. "They must have run away afterwards." The explosion and everything that happened after had wiped it from my mind, but it didn't sit right that I didn't know who had saved me. "For that matter, how did you get away from Rustik?"

Sofiya snorted. "Are you serious?"

"What?"

She fixed me with an exasperated expression. "Maybe Domenico was right about your lack of brain cells."

I furrowed my brow, and she just rolled her eyes.

"I killed three guards who came into my cell to—" She swallowed, and my hands flexed around hers. She had just told me they were dead, but the urge to return to the warehouse to kill them again overtook me.

"Did they touch you?" My voice was low, dangerous.

"No, I stopped them before they... Well, anyway, I took their guns and was looking for the exit when I saw Domenico. I realized he must have been the traitor and I followed him. After that, it was easy to take them out."

My mouth gaped.

She rolled her eyes and then patted my cheek. "Don't worry. I won't think less of you, even though you're a way worse shot than I am."

I shook my head. "You're magnificent, tesoro."

She settled back into my chest. "I know."

75

SOFIYA

I felt a million pounds lighter as Romeo carried me off the plane, a grumbling Matteo following behind with Enzo's help.

It would take time to heal the pain between us, but I felt hopeful that we could both be stitched back together.

Matteo loved me.

He loved me.

His love was precious, especially now that I understood fully what it cost him to give it.

We got to the bottom of the steps, and I let out a cry of joy when I saw Sienna waiting for us with Noodle on one side of her and my wheelchair on the other. Tears filled my eyes as Noodle started doing a happy dance. His entire body wiggled furiously, and he cried with excitement.

Romeo set me down in my wheelchair, and I held out my arms to Noodle. "Hi, baby. I missed you so much." He gave me kisses, and I pressed my face into his fur. "I'm so sorry I left," I murmured, my voice low and just for him. "It wasn't because of you. You're the bestest boy always."

I pulled back, and he gave me a big kiss on the face. I hoped that meant I was forgiven. Noodle rested his head in my lap, tail wagging, and I looked up at Sienna. There were tears in her eyes as she threw her arms around me. "Fuck, are you okay?"

"Yeah." I held her tight. "I am."

"Do you want me to kill him? Because I will. I brought a gun."

"I can hear you," Matteo said dryly.

She pulled away enough to give her brother a dirty look.

"Hold off on the killing. For now, at least." I patted Sienna's hand. She was still scowling. "If you kill him, I won't get the pleasure of seeing him grovel. And... my child won't have a father."

Her jaw dropped and she let out a scream as she jumped up and down. "You're pregnant? Oh my God!" She pulled me into another hug and then hugged her brother, her anger momentarily forgotten. "I can't believe it. I'm going to be an aunt." Tears streamed down her face.

Her excitement warmed my heart, but I also experienced a flash of discomfort—that familiar feeling that said I shouldn't get too happy, shouldn't look forward to the future because it would bring only disappointment. "It's still really early, so there's no real guarantee that Baby will..." I trailed off, unwilling to speak the words.

"This baby will be absolutely perfect." Her voice was so fierce I almost believed her.

Matteo gripped my shoulder, leaning heavily on Enzo for support as he kissed the top of my head. "Let's go home, tesoro."

I smiled and pressed my hand on top of his. "Yeah. Home."

THREE MONTHS
LATER

76

MATTEO

"So we're not staying in Los Angeles?"

I gave Sofiya a look. "No, we are not having our honeymoon in Los Angeles."

She looked out the plane window. We were refueling at LAX before the next leg of our trip. "How am I supposed to know? I'm sure L.A. is cool."

I pulled her from her seat and into my lap. She gave me a knowing smile as she ran her fingers down my jaw. I could only go a few minutes without touching her before I got a tight, itchy feeling in my chest.

"You will love our destination."

Sofiya nipped my lip. "You say that like a threat."

"Hush." I cupped her face, running my thumb across her soft cheek before pulling her into a kiss.

It had taken a while to convince her to show me her complete Dream List. Everything about it was pure innocence, and I'd made it my life's mission to help her do everything on it. I'd planned our honeymoon specifically so she could cross off some items. Once we completed it, I would have her write another. And another. Until the only memories she had were happy ones.

I begrudgingly relinquished my hold on her for take-off. She stayed glued to the window as we left the ground, but I couldn't take my eyes off her. I curled a lock of her hair around my finger.

Once we were in the air, I unbuckled her and drew her back into my arms. Sofiya snuggled into my chest, her eyes falling closed.

"Do you think Noodle will be okay with Sienna? I still think we should have brought him."

"He'll be so spoiled. This is a vacation for him, too."

She hummed. We'd decided not to take Noodle since it was a long flight and I would be with her our entire trip, helping her with whatever she needed. It had been hard to convince Sofiya to leave him, but Sienna had promised to send at least daily pictures and updates.

I ran my hand through her hair. "You tired, pretty girl?"

"Mmm, maybe a little sleepy."

I picked her up, loving the way she clung to me, and walked to the back bedroom. Angelo and Enzo lifted their chins as I passed them. They were here as our bodyguards while Romeo was in charge at home.

I settled Sofiya on the bed. She made a disgruntled noise when I pulled away.

"I'm not leaving," I reassured her. "Just going to tell the crew not to disturb us and grab some water. Do you need anything?"

"Just you."

Fuck, I would never get used to that. Sofiya had shown me more kindness than I ever deserved after how I'd treated her. The first few weeks had been hard. I'd had to destroy the remaining pockets of Albanian and Bratva threats and reestablish my control over my city, all while healing from my injuries and trying to repair my marriage. I'd tried grand gestures, extravagant gifts, fancy dinners, but I slowly realized that what Sofiya really needed was me showing up consistently. Keeping my promises. Sharing my *feelings*.

It was all worth it when she said sweet shit like that.

When I returned to the room, she was curled up on her side, eyes closed. I stripped down to my underwear and got in behind her, making sure the blanket was settled around her.

"I want you inside me," she murmured.

I ran my hand down her swollen belly. "You need to sleep, tesoro." Her pregnancy was going well, but she was tired lately. I'd asked Sofiya's doctor about a hundred times if it was safe for her to go on a long flight, and she had reassured me it was fine. Sofiya didn't know I'd hired an OBGYN to stay at our resort, just in case something happened.

"But I still want you inside me."

My hand froze on its path down her hip. "While you're asleep?"

She nodded and scooted further back against me, grinding her sweet little ass against my rock-hard cock. I slipped off her sweatpants and underwear before running my finger through her pussy. "You're soaked. Does the idea of me using your sweet little pussy while you're asleep make you wet for me?"

She whined and I thrust two fingers inside her. "Answer me."

"Yes, yes, it does. Please, I need you."

I pressed a kiss to the top of her head. "That's my good girl. You know I'll always give you what you need."

I took off my boxers, the tension in my chest easing even more at the feel of her warm skin against mine. Maybe I would start insisting she stay naked all the time. At least when we were home. Her changing body made me feral. I wanted her filled with my cum every moment of every day.

I placed a cushion between her legs to give her the support she needed before slipping inside her. I groaned into her hair, breathing in her sweet scent. "I'll never get enough of this. I want to live inside you."

She moaned and pushed her hips back, taking more of my cock.

"You like that idea, tesoro? Do you ache when I'm not inside you?"

"Yes. It's too empty."

"Mmm, maybe I need to get you a pussy plug to keep you full whenever I can't. Remind you who this cunt belongs to."

She breathed in sharply, and I grinned. "Oh, my little wife likes that idea."

I fucked her slowly as she shuddered, each thrust a reminder of my ownership, my *love*. Our breathing synced and I pressed my hand to her breast, feeling her heartbeat against the palm of my hand.

When she came, her orgasm was soft, washing over her like a wave. I followed, groaning as I spilled inside her. But instead of pulling out, I kept my cock firmly inside her, making sure none of my seed leaked out.

I dozed off and when I woke, Sofiya was still asleep and I was still inside her. I shifted my hips, keeping my thrusts as gentle as possible so I didn't wake her. It wasn't long before I grew hard again and she let out a little whimper.

"Shh, that's a good girl. Don't wake up. Just let me fuck you back asleep." I pressed my hand to the front of her throat, lightly collaring it as I kept thrusting. I dragged out my orgasm, never wanting this moment to end.

———

"Fiji? We're in Fiji?" Sofiya's eyes were bright as the car drove us to our villa. "There's the ocean!"

"Fuck, you're cute."

She threw her arms around me, holding tight. "I can't believe we're in Fiji. I would have been happy with Los Angeles."

"You have things to cross off your list."

She pulled back. "Yes, I'm sure all of this is in service of my Dream List." She shook her head and laced her fingers through mine.

Angelo and Enzo stayed with her as I checked us in at the resort lobby. When I headed back out, I saw her sitting in a golf cart. On the driver's side.

"Tesoro?"

"Can you believe we get two golf carts for our stay?" Her eyes were bright and filled with mischief. She was so much trouble.

"Thrilling. Now, why are you sitting there?"

"Oh, I thought it was obvious. I'm driving us to our villa."

I looked over at Angelo and Enzo, who were in the second golf cart wearing shit-eating grins.

I shook my head.

I was the Don. I would take control of this situation.

"Hop on, miliy." She patted the seat next to her.

Somehow, I found myself sliding into the passenger side. Sofiya gave a little whoop and pressed the gas pedal to the floor, following a staff member who was guiding us to our villa with our luggage piled on the back of their golf cart.

"Slow down!" I shouted. "Have you ever driven before?"

"I drive my wheelchair all the time. There's no one with as much motorized vehicle driving expertise as me!" She took a sharp turn towards the water, and I threw my arm across her body as visions of us ending up in the ocean flashed before my eyes.

"Relax, husband. I've got this."

My heart did not stop pounding.

We rounded another bend and our villa came into view. It was a large wooden house with a thatched roof and wrap-around porch.

"It's over the water! Oh my God!" Sofiya shrieked. "I'm definitely going to get to touch the ocean." She let out a gasp and then faced me. I made a terrified noise in the back of my throat and grabbed the steering wheel. She snorted and rolled her eyes.

"Do they have snorkeling here? That's another thing on my list."

"Slow down," I growled.

She released a put-out huff and then came to a jerking stop beside the other golf cart.

"So, snorkeling?" Her eyes were sparkling, and I kissed her nose.

"Yes, baby, they have snorkeling here."

She leaned into me, and then her smiling expression morphed into something sad as tears filled her eyes.

"Tesoro mio, what is wrong?" I looked around, ready to burn the entire villa to the ground if something about it was upsetting her.

"I just can't believe we're actually here. I can't believe this is my life." She wiped a tear. "Thank you for giving it to me."

I pressed my forehead to hers. "Don't thank me. *Ever.* You deserve *everything.*"

"And that's what you've given me."

77

SOFIYA

Matteo was glued to my side in the water as manta rays swam below us. I stretched out my hand, giddy with excitement. The water was perfectly warm and gentle on my joints. I could stay in here forever.

An entire world existed beneath us, and I was mesmerized. I jolted as a sea turtle swam towards us, grabbing Matteo's hand in excitement. His fingers skimmed down my back as the turtle lazily cut through the water. A tiny thrill of excitement and nervousness went through me as it got closer, and I clutched Matteo's hand harder.

Eventually, it was time for us to return to the boat. My lip jutted out in a pout as Matteo tugged us back.

"Don't give me that face, tesoro. We have to get back and get ready for dinner. But we can snorkel again before we leave." He helped me onto the boat and wrapped me in a towel before I sat down on a cushioned bench.

"I'd like that. And now I can cross snorkeling off my list. Maybe I should add scuba diving to the next one."

He pulled me tight to his side. "No."

"What? Why?"

"It's dangerous."

"I'm pretty sure it's perfectly safe."

His jaw clenched again. "Don't test me, tesoro."

"Or what?"

His growl vibrated against my throat as he nipped my skin, and I smiled. I loved pushing him because it usually just led to him tying me up in bed or spanking my ass.

"What plans do we have for the rest of the day?" A few days ago, we'd kayaked around the island. Well, I'd sat in the front of the kayak while Matteo paddled, refusing to allow me to lift a finger. Then we'd taken a cooking class and learned to make classic Fijian, Thai, and Malay dishes. I'd forced Matteo to wear the supplied apron and Angelo had taken pictures for me while standing off to the side. He and Enzo had faded into the background during our trip, allowing Matteo and me to have time together. We'd had such little time alone the past few months, so I was soaking up every minute.

"Just dinner," my husband murmured, leaning in to kiss my cheek.

The captain came up to us as the crew prepared to set sail. "You must be our good luck charm, beautiful," he said to me. "We don't always see the manta rays, and that was a Hawksbill sea turtle. We don't see them often because they're endangered."

Matteo held me closer to his side and gave the captain a murderous look. The man's face grew white and he quickly backed away.

I rolled my eyes and shoved my husband's side. "No eye gouging," I whispered in his ear.

"No promises, tesoro."

We cuddled close for the boat ride back. The warm wind tangled in my hair, and I thought I'd never felt quite this happy.

78

MATTEO

Sofiya was stretched out on the large cream couch in the villa's living room, resting after our day on the water. Her feet were in my lap and I was massaging them, loving the little noises of pleasure she made. She was wearing tiny lace shorts and a cream crop top that forced my eyes to flit between the curve of her breasts and the strip of bare stomach.

She flipped through the activity book provided by the resort. "They have golfing here." She looked at me over the top of the book. "I think I'd have to divorce you if you took up golfing."

I growled and crawled over her body, bracketing her head with my forearms and meeting her with a furious expression. "You are never fucking divorcing me."

She giggled and arched, rubbing her sweet little pussy against me. The book dropped to the floor, forgotten. "Maybe I need a reminder of who owns me."

I groaned and pressed my face to the crook of her neck, sucking on her soft skin. "Fuck, we have to get ready for dinner."

Her hand slid between our bodies, cupping my quickly hardening cock. "We could just order in."

If it were any other night, if I didn't have something planned, I would have stripped off her clothes and taken her here in a heartbeat. I clenched my jaw and forced myself off of her. "No. Dinner."

She pouted. "Fine, then, if you're going to be all *romantic.*" She huffed as if she was completely put-out by my desire to romance her, but I knew better. She was getting better at letting me spoil her and even though she put up a fight, I knew she loved it.

Just like I loved spoiling her.

Loved *her.*

I pulled her up off the couch and into my arms, walking us into the bedroom.

"You know I can walk. My legs are feeling good today. Probably better than *yours.*" I ignored her. I wasn't going to let my still-healing gunshot wound stop me from carrying my wife. It was mostly healed now, thanks to copious physical therapy, but I still had to use a cane when the pain acted up.

I set her down on the bed, moving her rollator in front of her. "Get ready, baby." I pressed a soft kiss to her lips. When I pulled back, I noticed a pink tinge to her nose and cheeks. I scowled as I ran my finger down the bridge of her nose. "You're sunburned."

"Just a tiny bit."

"I don't like it."

She joined her fingers with mine, a smile playing on her lips. "I'm sorry, but I don't think you can shoot the sun in punishment."

Maybe not, although it deserved it after hurting my tesoro. But until I could punish the sun, I would just have to be more diligent about having her wear sunscreen and a hat.

I kissed her pink nose and then forced myself to leave the room before I got completely sucked into her orbit.

————

SOFIYA USED her rollator to make her way to the restaurant's outside patio, and I kept my hand on her back the entire time. She was wearing a silver sequined dress that hit her mid-thigh, leaving her lush legs on display. Legs that two male restaurant staff members were currently looking at. My hand twitched towards my gun, but Sofiya wouldn't like it if I shot them. I settled for turning my furious, burning gaze at them. Maybe they had some common sense because both of them stepped back, eyes wide, before running back inside the restaurant.

"This view is amazing," Sofiya said with awe in her voice. The patio looked out over the ocean, the smell of salt lingering in the air. My wife took every opportunity she could to be outside, so I'd arranged for us to sit out here where we could watch the sunset as a string quartet played softly in the background. Tonight had to be perfect. She deserved nothing less.

My heart pounded throughout the entire dinner. I barely tasted my food. Why the fuck was I so nervous? I was the Don, and Sofiya was already *mine*.

I took a sip of my drink and focused on her to distract myself from the angry buzz of hornets in my chest. She was glowing. The candlelight sparkled off her eyes as she talked about all her favorite parts of our trip so far. She was so full of life as she bounced in her chair, chatted with the waiter, and made appreciative little noises at every bite of food, making my cock grow embarrassingly hard.

She held her hand out to me and I took it. She ran her fingers across my knuckles. "You seem distracted. Is everything okay?"

We had just finished dessert.

"Everything is perfect, tesoro." I lifted her hand to my lips and kissed it. "Except for one thing."

She cocked her head to the side, but as I moved out of my chair and got down on one knee, her lips parted and eyes widened. I pulled out a small velvet ring box and opened it. "This is the ring you deserved from the beginning."

"Oh my God." Sofiya's eyes shone as they flitted between my face and the ring.

My heart pounded as I slid it on her finger. It was so different from the last time I'd put a ring on her. During our ceremony, my focus had been on the alliance and what our marriage could do for the Family. Now, I was kneeling before the center of my universe, knowing there was nothing I wouldn't do for her. I caressed her hand, possessiveness filling my chest at seeing further proof that she belonged to me.

She ran her fingers through my hair, and I leaned into her touch. "Aren't you supposed to ask me to marry you?"

"We're already married."

"Well, yeah, but you know, it's tradition to ask."

I fixed her with a stern expression. "You will marry me, tesoro."

She snorted. "Close enough." She grasped both sides of my face and pulled me in for a kiss. When we pulled apart, her eyes were sparkling. "I can't believe I'm engaged. I hope my husband doesn't find out."

I growled and gripped her chin. "Are you trying to rile me up?"

"Always."

I narrowed my eyes, but my lips twitched as I pulled her into another kiss.

79

SOFIYA

I laughed as my husband carried me into our villa, unable to take my eyes off my ring. It was perfect. There was a large marquise-cut diamond surrounded by circular diamonds, making it look almost like a flower.

"You like it?"

"I love it. You did such a good job."

"I had help."

"Sienna?"

"Mila."

"Really?" That made a lump rise in my throat. We had spent so many hours as girls talking about rings and weddings, and this made it feel like she was part of my new life. "How did she sound?"

Matteo laid me down on the bed. The large French doors were open to the outside, the warm ocean breeze washing over us. "Good. She had strong opinions on the ring."

"I bet she did." I ran the tip of my finger over it. "It's so pretty."

"I'll buy you a million of them."

I grinned. "Not sure how I'd wear that many."

"Hope you're up for the challenge."

We lay facing each other, gazing into each other's eyes, and then we both broke, our lips crashing together. Matteo gripped the back of my neck, tilting my head back so he had perfect access to my lips, but I wanted more. I wanted to make him lose control the same way he did me.

I tugged against his hold and he released me, confusion in his eyes. It didn't last long as I unbuttoned his shirt and pants, kissing my way down his body.

"Fuck, baby, fuck." He breathed in sharply. "Are you going to suck my cock into that pretty little mouth?"

"Yes," I said, letting out a little moan as his hard cock sprang out of the confines of his boxers. A bead of precum spurted from the tip, and I knelt between his legs and licked it, but the position strained my knees and hips. I tried to rearrange myself, but I was an uncoordinated mess of limbs.

"Sorry, sorry," I said as my knee knocked into his leg.

"Shh, don't apologize."

"I just want to be sexy and not mess this up." I felt strangely emotional, waves of embarrassment washing through me. Matteo had been taking such good care of me. Between the rest he forced on me, my wheelchair, new medication, and starting physical therapy, I'd been in a lot less pain. But pregnancy was also increasing the number of subluxations, and I needed to be careful. "I could try going on my knees on the floor."

Matteo let out a sound that could only be described as a growl before he pulled me into his arms.

"Or we can do this in our bed, where my queen will be comfortable." He scowled as I opened my mouth. "Nothing is more important than your comfort, tesoro. But don't worry, we'll find a position that lets you suck my cock."

I snorted a little giggle, feeling much better. We would figure this out together. I hadn't ruined anything.

He gently stripped me of my clothes before removing his own and lying down beside me. He pulled me into his arms. "There's never any pressure for you to give me a blowjob. And I forbid you from doing anything if it causes you pain."

"I know," I murmured. "But I really want to. I want you to take control. I just wish my body would cooperate more."

"Well, if I'm in charge, your body will be forced to obey me and cooperate."

"So arrogant."

He smirked and wrapped my hair around his hand, tugging my head back so I was forced to meet his gaze. "You have work to do." He raised a cocky eyebrow.

A thrill went through me at his dominance as he guided me down his body until I was lying on my side, my lips level with his cock. He placed a pillow between my legs and one behind my back, giving me the support I needed. I ran my hand down his hip and squeezed his butt.

"Stop teasing," he growled. "Take me into your mouth. I want to hear you gag."

Oh fuck. That shouldn't be so hot.

I did what he commanded, not that I had much choice with the firm way he gripped my hair. I opened wide, my tongue sliding over his slit before he thrust into my mouth. My eyes immediately started to water, and I panicked for a moment as I felt a lack of oxygen.

"That's it, that's my girl. You're taking me so well." There was a softness to his voice, even as he maintained a grip of iron on my hair and neck. His words felt like a warm bath, comforting and perfect as I relaxed my throat and took him deeper. We had practiced deep throating, and I struggled with it but loved making him lose his mind.

He maintained our rapid rhythm, keeping me completely at his mercy. My pussy grew wet at his control, causing me to move my fingers down to touch my clit. But then his fingers surrounded my wrist.

"Mine," he said. "No one touches this cunt besides me. Do you understand?"

He thrust inside my mouth again, cutting off any possibility of answering.

"Look at you, getting turned on sucking my cock like the slutty little girl you are. So perfect for me. Such a perfect little mess."

Drool dripped down my chin and I moaned around him. He cursed, thrusting further into my throat. I choked, but he kept going, forcing me to take him deeper. He thrust inside me twice more before coming with a roar. I did my best to swallow him down, but some cum leaked down my chin.

I tried to move my head back, but his hold tightened.

"No. Tap my leg twice if you need to stop, but I'm not ready to leave the warm heat of your mouth."

I whimpered, loving his complete control over me as I continued sucking on his cock. I was a mess—drool dripping down my chin, tears streaming down my cheeks, throat and jaw sore, but I also felt a strange contentment down in my very soul. Matteo's grip on my hair turned gentle, his fingers lightly running through my strands, massaging my scalp. My eyes felt heavy, drooping until they closed completely, and I was left in the quiet darkness, gently sucking his cock.

I was in a foggy trance and had no idea how much time had passed. Eventually, he hardened again. He cupped the back of my head and thrust lightly into my mouth. I gagged as he hit the back of my throat, and he stroked my hair in apology, but kept going. I'd never felt so used or cherished. This was what I wanted—my dominant, controlling husband who still somehow put me first, even as he fucked my face. He came down my throat again, and this time I stayed calm and breathed through it.

"Fuck, fuck, baby." He gently pulled me up so our faces were level. He grabbed tissues off the nightstand and cleaned my face. Then he propped me up so I could drink from a water bottle.

"Are you okay? Was that too much?" The slight edge of panic in his gaze made me feel like my chest would burst from happiness.

"No, it was perfect." I snuggled into his chest. My jaw was sore enough that I knew I wouldn't be able to repeat that experience for a while, but it had been worth it.

His hands skated down my skin, and he kissed my forehead. "You did so well for me." His fingers continued down my skin until they reached the juncture of my thighs. "You're soaked. Did you like being used as my personal fucktoy?"

I bit my lip as he thrust two fingers deep inside me.

"Answer me." His stern voice was back, demanding my submission.

"Yes, I liked it." My voice came out in a hoarse whisper and my cheeks burned.

"That's right, you did. Because you're perfect for me."

And with that, he moved his way down my body to repay the favor.

80

SOFIYA

I sat on the private dock by our villa, my feet skimming the water. It was the last night of our honeymoon, and I was trying to record every part of this trip in my memory.

Footsteps sounded behind me, and I looked over my shoulder to see my husband approaching. I ran my eyes down his body—taking in the way his dark brown hair curled into his forehead with the humidity, the glow of his golden-brown muscled chest, and the bulge pressing against his black swim trunks.

He sat down beside me and handed me a drink. It was bright red with a fresh strawberry speared on a colorful little umbrella.

"Virgin strawberry daiquiri." His lips brushed against my ear. "Almost as sweet as you."

I blushed as memories of him waking me with his tongue on my pussy flooded my mind... and other parts of me. He ran his fingers across my heated cheeks. "My pretty girl."

I leaned into his side and took a sip. "This is good. Thank you, miliy."

"Anything for you."

I breathed in the sweet scent of flowers and salt in the air and let out a sigh. "I love it here." The sun was setting, sending pinks and oranges streaking across the sky and water.

"We'll come back whenever you want. Just say the word."

"Dangerous offer."

"Did you not hear me say *anything for you*?"

I pressed my grin into his shoulder. I was embracing being a spoiled Mafia girl and loving every minute.

"I rather like this bathing suit," Matteo said. I squirmed under his heated gaze. He'd finally convinced me into a bikini. It was absolutely tiny—black with thin straps that framed my belly. He ran his hand over my growing bump. "We'll come back with Baby."

I snuggled deeper into his side and he put his arm around me, holding me close. Matteo had lightened over the past few months. He was letting me in, surprising me with his smiles and sense of humor. The excitement he had for our baby was almost enough to make me forgive how ridiculously overprotective he'd become.

He kissed the top of my head before removing his arm from around me and setting down his drink. I cocked an eyebrow, but he just winked and slipped into the water. His wet hands grasped my thighs and squeezed tightly.

"Are you going to join me, wife?"

"Hmm," I said, pretending to think about it. He growled and spread my legs, running his tongue up my inner thigh. I set my drink down as he undid the ties of my bikini bottoms.

I glanced over my shoulder. "Someone will see us."

"I forbid it."

"Matteo," I said, exasperated.

"Sofiya," he responded, matching my tone.

Whatever I was going to say died on my lips as he nuzzled the sensitive skin of my thighs and ran his tongue up my already-wet pussy.

"Oh, tesoro, you should have told me how desperate you were for me. You're so fucking drenched, so needy."

I inhaled sharply, my legs widening.

"The prettiest pussy." He placed gentle kisses up my mound, each one of them torture as I begged him to touch my clit. He finally did, circling it with his tongue, but his movements were too light. "Please," I begged. "Please, please."

He chuckled, his laugh vibrating against my sensitive core as he dove back in. This time, his tongue was firm against me and then he finally, *finally* sucked my clit into his mouth. My orgasm crashed over me, rough and fast, tearing a cry from my lips. Matteo pulled away with a self-satisfied grin, but I wasn't close to being done.

Something wet landed next to me. My breathing sped up when I saw it was his swim trunks.

"Are you going to join me, Mrs. Rossi?"

I threw myself off the dock into his surprised arms.

"Fuck, be more careful," he said as he gathered me close to his chest.

"I don't need to be careful when you're here to catch me."

His expression softened, and I pressed my smile to his lips. "You think you have me wrapped around your little finger, don't you?"

"I only think it because it's true."

His hand landed softly on my ass, and I raised my eyebrows at his disgruntled expression. "I can't even spank you in the water."

I snorted. "Rain check. Give me a smack when we get out."

He skimmed his lips down the side of my face. "I'll give you whatever I want." His voice was low, and I held back my whimper.

I turned on my back and floated, loving how weightless the water made me feel. I ran my hand over the bump on my stomach. "Do you think we're having a boy or a girl?" We had an ultrasound scheduled in a few days to find out the sex.

Matteo's hand joined mine, caressing my stomach. "A boy."

I scowled. "Why, because the big bad Don needs a male heir?"

He scoffed and pulled me into his arms, my back pressed tight against his chest as his legs treaded water to keep us afloat. "My naughty girl is feeling very sassy." He nipped at my ear. "No, because if we have a girl, she'll be just as pretty as you, and then I'll have to gouge out all the eyes in New York City... the entire state."

"You're ridiculous." But I couldn't stop my smile. All our scans had been good so far—and we'd had a lot of them since anytime I was anxious, Matteo demanded the doctor come over and do another one. He'd finally just purchased an ultrasound machine for our apartment to make it easier.

I was slowly allowing myself to be hopeful that this baby would be okay.

Matteo tightened his grip on me and towed me through the water.

"Where are we going?"

"I need better leverage."

"Leverage?"

We drew closer to our private beach until Matteo could stand in the water. He arranged me so I was facing him, my arms and legs wrapped around him.

"Ahh, leverage," I said with a smile.

He hummed and wrapped my damp hair around his fingers, tipping my head back. "My perfect, gorgeous wife. The perfect little slut for me."

I shivered in his tight hold, and then he slipped inside me. We both moaned as his cock filled me, stretched me. His hand palmed my ass, squeezing hard as he murmured praise against my skin. He kept rocking against my body and I tipped my head back, taking in the candy-colored sky. Something about this moment—the warm water streaked with pink, his possessive hold, the rough way he thrust inside me and the gentle look in his eyes—healed the little raw edges of my heart. The relief of it was physical, a breath of springtime air after a dark winter bringing the promise that Matteo was *for* me, on my side always, and I was the same for him.

I pulled him in for a salty kiss. "This is everything."

"*You* are everything," he responded.

I pressed my cheek against his and closed my eyes, content to just *feel*. Feel my husband making love to me in paradise, feel my heart mending itself, feel the hope for a bright future.

It was here.

And it was ours.

EPILOGUE
MATTEO

I woke as the bed shifted. The early morning light was barely peeking through the curtains, and Sofiya was going to the bathroom again.

I forced myself to stay in bed. She'd already yelled at me twice this week when I tried to follow her into the bathroom. But what if she got dizzy and fell? My chest tightened, and I bolted upright in bed just as Sofiya walked back into the bedroom.

"Don't worry, husband, I survived the toilet." She rolled her eyes as she said it, but there was a smile tugging at her lips. She looked so gorgeous. Her hand supported her round belly, which was covered in a soft, lacy nightgown. Her cheeks were rosy and the morning light made her messy hair glow, just like it had on our wedding day.

She was perfection.

I guided her into bed with her back to my chest, arranged her pregnancy pillow between her legs, and wrapped my arms around her.

"Merry Christmas, tesoro," I murmured, pressing a kiss to her cheek. "You're the greatest gift of my life." I ran my hand down her stomach, holding her close. She was just a few weeks away from giving birth, and I couldn't wait to meet our baby.

My *daughter*.

We were having a girl, and I couldn't have been more thrilled and terrified. I hoped she looked exactly like my beautiful wife.

"Merry Christmas," she said, covering my hand with hers and giving it a squeeze.

I breathed in her sweet floral scent, enjoying these last moments of it just being the two of us.

I dozed off, content to have this slow morning before chaos descended on our home. I was woken by my little wife grinding her ass on my rapidly hardening cock.

I pressed my smile into her hair. She'd been especially horny these past few months.

"Matteo." My name on her lips was *everything*.

"Yes, tesoro." I ran my hand down her belly until I was cupping her pussy. "I'm here."

"I'm so glad you're with me," she said. "No one else I'd rather live life with."

My heart squeezed as I raised her nightgown and lowered my boxers, gently slipping into her wet cunt. She'd had more dislocations during the pregnancy, so I made my movements torturously slow as I thrust in and out. My hand wandered across her soft skin, soaking in her warmth as I gave her sensitive nipple a soft squeeze. She moaned, reaching back to clutch at whatever part of me she could grab.

"That's my good girl." She tightened around me as little whimpers slipped through her lips. "I love you, tesoro. So fucking much."

She shook as her orgasm washed over her. "I love you," she said, repeating the words over and over.

I wrapped myself around her as I came. I never tired of filling her with my cum or of holding her close like this. She was the most important person in my life, the center of my universe.

———

"I HAVE something for you to open before we have breakfast," Sofiya said as she rolled over to the tree and grabbed a red and gold striped package.

"I have a *pile* of gifts you can open before breakfast," I responded. I had wanted her to open all her presents last night. Actually, I'd been pestering her to open presents since December first, but she said that wasn't how it was done.

As if I cared. I shouldn't have to wait for a certain day to spoil my wife.

She fixed me with a stern look and Noodle did the same as he swung his head toward me. I sighed, unable to argue with them, and walked over to grab my present. I tore the wrapping and found a bright red sweater with a deformed *something* on the front.

I furrowed my brow trying to figure out what the fuck I was holding.

"Do you like it? Sienna and I have been learning how to crochet and I made that for you."

Years of training as Don allowed me to keep my face blank. Sofiya looked so happy I didn't have the heart to tell her the sweater was the most hideous thing I'd ever seen.

"Well, what do you think?" she asked, her eyes shining with hopefulness.

I leaned down and gripped her chin. "I'm honored you would make this for me, tesoro."

She smiled into my kiss. "Well, try it on! I used one of your shirts to get the size right, so hopefully I measured correctly."

I gritted my jaw before pulling it over my head. At least the material was soft, and she had gotten the fit mostly correct.

"Okay, it might be a little bit too cropped," she said, tugging at the bottom of the sweater. "But you look great."

I eyed her Christmas sweater. It was pale blue with snowflakes on it and looked decidedly store-bought. "You didn't make one for yourself?"

"I didn't have time." She brushed her hand down the front of her sweater. "Sienna got this one for me."

"Well, you look stunning, as always."

"Such a flatterer. I need to get started on breakfast."

Sofiya had insisted we have cinnamon rolls on Christmas morning just because they were my favorite.

My sister, Romeo, and I usually got Chinese takeout on Christmas Day and got drunk while watching whatever shitty holiday movie Sienna forced on us. Sofiya had never had a real Christmas and said she wanted to create new traditions for our new family. It wasn't like I could refuse her anything, so we'd gone all out —a real tree, a shit-ton of presents, and Christmas music playing through the speakers.

Sofiya took the cinnamon rolls she'd started last night out of the fridge. "Will you get me the powdered sugar, miliy?"

I grabbed the canister out of one of the upper cabinets and set it on the counter, giving her a kiss on the top of her head. She leaned back against my chest.

"Are you feeling alright?" I asked. "I can finish this if you tell me what to do."

I wouldn't mind if she just stayed in my arms until she had this baby. And then for several months after.

"I'm feeling good, promise."

There was a knock on the door and Sienna poked her head in. "Are you two done with your morning lovemaking?"

"I swear to fucking God," I said, running my hand down my face. "Why did we invite them?"

"Come in!" Sofiya shouted before fixing me with her fierce gaze. "Because they're family and we're all going to have a cozy Christmas morning together."

Sienna came into the living room, her arms filled with Christmas packages. "Romeo is bringing the rest." She set them all down under the tree—the tall, magnificent tree that rivaled the one at Rockefeller Center with ugly homemade decorations Sofiya had insisted we all make over the past weeks. The endless hot glue and glitter had all been worth it when I heard she'd turned Angelo's poker night into a Christmas crafting evening. It was impossible to say *no* to my wife. They'd never stood a chance.

At least craft night had prevented her from adding more to her considerable poker debt. I kept forgetting to ask Angelo how much Sofiya owed. She still didn't realize the chips represented actual money, and I didn't want to ask Angelo in front of her and upset her. I would give everything I owned to make her happy, and if poker night was it, I would pay whatever it took.

Romeo and Angelo walked in, arms laden with presents. They dropped them by the tree, and Sienna told them off for their "lack of finesse and style." The two of them rolled their eyes and joined us in the kitchen while Sienna rearranged the gifts.

Angelo rubbed his hands together as he peered at the cinnamon rolls in the oven. He'd put on at least ten pounds since I married Sofiya. Not that I had a leg to stand on—I'd been forced to add an extra workout to my week with all the sweets my wife made.

"What are you wearing?" Romeo asked me, a glint of laughter in his eyes.

"A beautiful sweater made by my wife," I said before he could say another word. No one would insult my Sofiya.

"Oh, don't be jealous, Romeo," Sofiya said. "Miliy, can you get those three packages from the top of the pile?"

I did what she asked, grinning as I handed Romeo and Angelo packages that felt suspiciously like sweaters. The third package had a tag on it that said "To Noodle, from Mama."

Fuck, she was cute.

"Come here, Noodle," I called out. The dog looked at Sofiya as if asking permission before leaving her side and trotting over to me. I gave him the present and he took it gently in his mouth, looking at me with a confused expression. "You're supposed to tear it open," I told him. He just wagged his tail. I took the gift back with a huff and then unwrapped it. "What the fuck?" I stared at the sweater Sofiya had crocheted for the dog.

"What's wrong?" Sofiya asked.

I took the dog sweater and headed into the kitchen. "Why does the dog's sweater look absolutely perfect?" It was dark green with white trim and even rows of pom-poms sewed onto it.

Sofiya gave me a mischievous smile. "I made his last, so I'd had a lot of practice. But... are you saying you think your sweater is *bad*?"

"Don't even start with me," I said, prowling towards her. She was sitting next to the oven on her rollator, her cheeks rosy, the smell of cinnamon heavy in the air. "I think you did this on purpose because you know I'll never refuse to wear something you made for me."

"I would never be so diabolical, husband." There was a little glint in her eye.

I shook my head. "Of course not, wife."

She pulled me down for a kiss and nipped my lower lip. "Now that you're here, want to pull these out of the oven for me?"

She took Noodle's sweater out of my hands and moved out of the way. I pulled the cinnamon rolls out of the oven and then turned around to see Romeo, Angelo, and Noodle all standing in a row, wearing their Christmas sweaters. Sienna was off to the side, covering her mouth and looking suspiciously like she was holding in laughter.

Sofiya clapped. "I need a picture of all my boys together."

"They're not *all* your boys," I growled.

"We're men, not boys," Romeo added. He crossed his arms, which only highlighted the mess of green tinsel on his sweater.

"Well, whoever you are, stand by the tree so I can take a picture," she demanded before starting towards the living room with her rollator. I let out a frustrated sound and grabbed her wheelchair.

"You're only supposed to use the rollator when you're baking."

I had plans to renovate the entire kitchen so it was wheelchair-friendly, but Sofiya had said we were not doing construction while she was in "nesting mode," whatever that meant. I thought it was absolutely absurd. Sienna had already chosen the contractor and designed the renovation, so we were all set once Sofiya gave us the green light. She was in too much pain these days to use her rollator for more than brief periods, and she'd been getting dizzy more frequently.

Once she was in her wheelchair, I gripped her chin and mouthed "naughty girl." Her cheeks flushed beautifully.

We all moved in front of the Christmas tree and Sofiya took photos of "her boys." Then she and Sienna instructed us into all sorts of formations and combinations. I didn't mind, as long as I got to be next to my wife.

I found I minded nothing as long as she was by my side.

EPILOGUE

SOFIYA

"I'm not sure poker is a very traditional Christmas activity," I said, chewing my lip.

We'd finished our Christmas dinner and were all too full to immediately eat dessert. Matteo had grumbled when he found out I had made everyone's favorites—tiramisu for Angelo, cannolis for Romeo, funfetti cake for Sienna, and chocolate chip cookies for my husband. He wanted me to stay reclined in bed with people waiting on me hand and foot for the last weeks of my pregnancy, but I was feeling good. The exhaustion I'd felt in my first and second trimesters had finally dissipated, and I was filled with the urge to take care of everyone and nest.

"It's not," Sienna said. "But I've heard all about your skills and need to see it for myself."

"It's festive if we drink mulled wine while we play," Romeo said.

"Or hot chocolate," Angelo added, raising his eyebrows at me.

I grinned. "If you all are so desperate to lose, I guess I can't refuse." I squeezed Matteo's hand. "Are you going to play, husband? Please?"

"If it will force you to stay fucking seated, fine."

I grinned, leaning over to give him a kiss on his cheek. It was prickly with stubble. "So cranky."

"Yeah, Matteo, stop being so cranky," Romeo said.

Matteo rolled his eyes. "Let's do this."

———

"How are you doing this?" Matteo looked at me across the table, absolutely bewildered.

I bit my lip to hide my smile. "I'm rather good, aren't I?"

"Have you been *winning* games all this time? I thought you didn't know they were playing with *actual* money. I was getting ready to pay off your debts before the poker club came after you."

I snorted a laugh. "Your lack of faith in me is astounding. How much have I won now, Angelo? I think it's around thirty thousand."

"Sounds about right, bella."

Matteo ran his hand down his face. "Well, shit."

"It's enough to start my new non-profit."

My husband got up with a huff and rounded the table.

"Hey, what are you doing?" I cried out. He ignored me and lifted me off my chair, sat down himself, and arranged me on his lap. "This is cheating," I protested, trying to shield my cards from him.

"I fold, tesoro. I can't lose *all* of my money to you."

I rolled my eyes, but snuggled into his chest as the rest of us continued the game.

"What non-profit are you starting?" he asked, lips skimming the shell of my ear.

"I want to convert some apartments into housing for women who have been sex trafficked. So people like Katya and Stasya can have a home." I'd worked with Dr. Amato to set up housing and jobs for the two girls, as well as a monthly allowance so they never had to worry about money, but I wanted to expand to help more women. I'd been working with Matteo to dismantle the remaining sex rings Arben and my father had run. It made me sick to think that someone I was related to had caused such suffering.

"That's a wonderful idea," Matteo said. Then a scowl overtook his face. "As long as you don't push yourself too hard. You need to rest, and the baby is almost here."

"Don't worry, I'll have plenty of help."

"In that case, I'll donate an apartment building to the charity."

I raised my eyebrows. "What apartment building?"

Matteo shrugged. "There are plenty in the city. Take your pick."

I rolled my eyes, but my chest filled with warmth. His easy acceptance and support of my plan meant everything. I pressed my lips to his ear. "You are so getting a blow job tonight."

He grunted and tightened his hold on my hips.

When it was time for the remaining players to show our cards, I laid mine down with a smile. "Royal flush."

Angelo swore and pushed back from the table. "You're counting cards, aren't you? That has to be it."

Sienna snorted as she looked between the disgruntled men. "Pretty sure that's blackjack, not poker."

Matteo's chest shook with laughter. "Didn't know you were such a sore loser, Angelo." He kissed my cheek. "Now you have another ten grand to add to your charity."

"Yes, thank you all for your donations," I said.

Romeo's usually bright countenance was cranky. "I'm getting my fucking cannoli," he said, heading into the kitchen.

Sienna looked at the two men with delight. "Seeing them like that is worth losing." She got up from the table. "Let's bring all the dessert in here."

"I should help them," I said, trying to get out of Matteo's lap.

"You should not," was the only thing he said in response.

I let out a little noise as Baby kicked especially hard. She was destined to be a dancer or runner with how strong her legs were.

Matteo pressed his hand to my stomach, his face softening as he felt her move.

"Next Christmas we'll have an almost-one-year-old," I murmured.

"I can't wait."

I teared up at the sincerity in his voice. All those years of being so alone and unloved had brought me here—to my new family.

Everyone returned to the room and arranged the desserts on the table. Matteo made my plate first, putting one of every dessert on it.

Our gifts to each other were strewn across the room, including ones from Mila, Nikolai, Leona, and Ronan. Noodle nudged my hand, begging for pets.

I couldn't have dreamed up a better Christmas. But that was my life now—living days that were even better than my dreams.

The end.

Sofiya's Dream List

- Fly on a plane
- Touch the ocean
- Get a tattoo
- Try something new every week for a year
- Learn how to make pottery
- Go to Disney World
- Eat a NYC hot dog
- Ride in a hot-air balloon
- Go snorkeling
- Grow a garden
- Make s'mores with a real bonfire
- Get a dog
- Perfect my chocolate chip cookie recipe
- Learn to cook different cultural cuisines
- Ride on a train
- Go stargazing
- Have super hot sex *Mila, stop it!*
- Skinny dip *Live a little, Sofiya*
- Raise children in a happy family
- Be loved

BONUS SCENE

Need more Sofiya and Matteo? I wrote this bonus scene for them and it's one of my favorite I've ever written! Don't miss out!

ALSO BY EMILIA ROSSI

PREORDER the next book in the **Empire of Royals** universe, *His Juliet!* Until then, I have books out under my other pen name, Emilia Emerson. If you liked *His Tesoro*, you might like these!

A Pack for Autumn

A why choose omegaverse set in a charming small town. Olive moves to Starlight Grove to be their new lighthouse keeper. All she wants is a quiet life alone...but three contractor alphas have their eye on her! Featuring hurt/comfort, fast burn spice, quirky side characters, and meddlesome cat, and PMDD/PCOS rep!

The Forbidden Duet

Forbidden: Part One & *Forbidden: Part Two*

A why choose omegaverse duet set in a dark world with three guys who are absolutely obsessed with their girl! Featuring a traumatized FMC, hurt/comfort, fated mates, three protective alphas, and all the spice.

Cherished

A why choose omegaverse set in the Luna & Sol universe. This comes after *Forbidden* but can be read as a standalone. Fall in love with adventurous Westin and her four guys. *Cherished* also has chronic illness rep!

ACKNOWLEDGMENTS

Writing this book has been so much fun! Last year, an idea for a single scene popped into my head—one where a woman in a wheelchair shocks her Mafia husband with her shooting prowess in the middle of a fight. In my book *Cherished* (written under my other pen name, Emilia Emerson), I explored the challenges of invisible disability and chronic illness. For this story, I was curious to see what would happen if I took a heroine with a visible disability and put her in an image-obsessed Mafia culture. Matteo and Sofiya were born, and these two ran with the story from there! I have loved getting to know them. They completely have my heart, and I'm excited to catch glimpses of them in future books.

Now, for the thank yous:

My first thank you goes to *you,* my wonderful readers, for taking a chance on my Mafia debut. It means the world to me!

To the incredible people who shared their stories with me to ensure Sofiya's experience with EDS and mobility aids was the best it could be: Aimee, Christine, Quartz, Melissa, Domina, Elina, and Mae. It's been a joy and honor to get to know you. Thank you for giving me a glimpse into your lives.

To Charlie, the original Noodle and my best teammate. No one has seen me at my worst like you. Thanks for being my buddy and the best employee I could ask for (even though you keep being crowned employee of the month when *I'm* the one writing the books).

To RE May, aka Rachel, the best Mafia partner I could imagine. Are we the Mafia dream team? I think so. Thank you for your excitement, encouragement, and feedback. There's no one else I'd want to furiously draft Mafia books with!

To Eliana, for your encouragement, beta reading, and help with naming this book. Oh, and for being responsible for *two* additional blow job scenes. Matteo thanks you. I'm so thankful for finding new friends across the world!

To my beta readers: Katherine, Robyn, Brit, and Jenny (even though you hate Matteo). Thank you for your wonderful insights that helped shaped this story.

And last but not least, thank you to my Street Team, ARC readers, and anyone who has shared my books! Being a full-time author is a dream come true, and I couldn't do this without you.

ABOUT THE AUTHOR

Emilia Rossi writes spicy Mafia romance with jealous/possessive men and the incredible women who have them wrapped around their fingers. She also writes omegaverse books under the pen name Emilia Emerson.

Emilia loves to travel, enjoy amazing food, and spend quiet days writing with her dog, Charlie.

Stay up to date on news & announcements:
  Facebook Group: Emilia's Romance Universe
  Newsletter Signup: www.emiliarossiauthor.com
  Instagram: @authoremiliarossi

Printed in Great Britain
by Amazon

58118996R00223